PRAISE FOR ERIC STONE'S
THE LIVING ROOM OF THE DEAD

"*The Living Room of the Dead* is a well-written, suspenseful, enthralling, and very uncomfortable book to read … Not a cheerful book, but a compelling book. Gritty and violent, difficult to put down even in the ugly parts. A fine first novel inspired by a true story."
—PJ Coldren, *Crimespree*

"The author gives the readers descriptions of Hong Kong, Macau and Vladivostok on a par with Paul Theroux's travel pieces … a successful debut."
—Bernard Trink, *Bangkok Post*

"It's enjoyable, all the more so for plotting that is a bit close to the edge sometimes. It's all very "noir", filled with introspection, editorial asides, snide commentary and swearing (impressively in at least three languages.) [Stone] can actually write: the pages turn very quickly."
—Peter Gordon, *Asian Review of Books*

"I was taken for a ride through a slime pit of horrors that had me turning the pages. A very interesting debut. Not for the faint of heart."
—Sally Owen, *Bookaholic*

"Chandler and Hammett come to life in contemporary Macau. Exotic, dangerous, deadly, fun. The first book of a Ray Sharp series. Let's hope there will be many more."
—Allan Folsom, *New York Times* bestselling author of *The Exile*

MORE PRAISE FOR
THE LIVING ROOM OF THE DEAD

"*The Living Room of the Dead* is a stylish, fresh take on classic noir themes. You won't soon forget Eric Stone's vivid depictions of Macau and Vladivostok—or the sad, doomed characters who think they're simply passing through."

—Laura Lippman, Edgar Award-winning author of
By a Spider's Thread

"Auspicious debut thriller by a former journalist who knows the exotic locales whereof he writes: the story is original and compelling, a page-turner with the spare, relentless style of Dennis Lehane or Michael Connelly."

—John Farris, bestselling author of *The Fury*

"Realism that is in turn exciting and unsettling. *The Living Room of the Dead* will keep you reading. Stone runs his plot through enough twists to keep his story complex without making the plot too complicated, no mean feat. His empathy for the prostitution situation in this part of the world is clear and compelling ..."

—Dana King, *New Mystery Reader*

"What a first novel - exotic in setting, expert in the telling, and exciting from first page to last. A unique and compelling novel in every respect."

—Ed Gorman, author of *Everybody's Somebody's Fool*

THE
LIVING ROOM
OF THE DEAD

To Ansho
Watch out for
Russian gangsters.

Eric S

THE
| |LIVING ROOM| |
OF THE DEAD

THE FIRST RAY SHARP NOVEL
BY ERIC STONE

BLEAK HOUSE BOOKS
MADISON | WISCONSIN

Published by Bleak House Books,
an imprint of Big Earth Publishing
923 Williamson St.
Madison, WI 53703

This is a work of fiction. Any similarities to people or places, living or dead, is purely coincidental.

Set in Times New Roman

First Bleak House Books paperback printing: August 2007
First Forge hardcover printing: June 2005

ISBN 13: 978-1-932557-48-0

Printed in the United States of America

11 10 09 08 07   1 2 3 4 5

Cover and Book Design by
Von Bliss Design — "Book Design By Bookish People"
http://www.vonbliss.com

This book is for Eva Eilenberg, my closest companion, a great source of inspiration in the adventures of mind, body and spirit, and one hell of a fine reader.

| |CHAPTER **ONE**| |

My ferry's at noon and I barely make it on board.

It's a lot more impressive than just any old ferry. But you wouldn't know it when it's not moving. Dirty red chipping paint covers a pockmarked hull. The lower deck is hardly visible down by the water line. It has plenty of large windows, but they're grimy, salt-encrusted and you can't see into them. The upper deck looks much the same. There isn't any visible outside deck, other than a short, flat triangle at the prow where there's an anchor and some ropes. It's a flimsy-looking thing and it bobs violently in the chop that beats against the pier. I've hardly crossed over the rolling gangplank before they shut the door and cast off.

I wobble to the only remaining seat, the middle of a row of eight in second class, the lower deck. The first class upper deck has been sold out for a month or more. It usually is on Friday. I squeeze my way past Hong Kong Chinese gamblers rubbing their sweaty palms together in anticipation of hitting the tables in Macau.

The two squared and hard looking middle-aged women on either side of the seat I'm headed for would move away if there were anywhere to go. As I step over one of their feet on my way to sit, they both turn away, to the meek-looking men sitting next to them. They mutter, but it's hard to speak softly in Cantonese. It's a loud language, and doesn't lend itself to quiet conversation. I hear the word *gwailo* a few times. When you're a foreigner in Hong Kong you hear it all the time. It means, "ghost person." At the moment it means me, which strikes me as funny because I'm feeling plenty alive.

I take my seat and I'm laughing. It's hard to stop. Everyone in the row turns to look at me, then they look away. I'm just another crazy ghost person, a *chee-seen gwailo*, and there's no accounting for us.

The ferry rocks and rolls slowly away from the dock, out into the frothy water of the world's most crowded harbor. It taxis onto its right of way and around me everyone is looking a little sick from the motion. But no one is too concerned. We all know what's going to happen next.

A few hundred yards out from the dock the jet engine roars to life. The ferry rises ten or more feet up on its foils and takes off with the same sort of scream and whine and acceleration that the other Boeing products do, the ones that fly through the air rather than over the water. I'm shoved into my seat by it and I close my eyes to enjoy the sensation. Once we're at speed it's a smooth ride, well above the waves, the thin metal foils cutting straight through the waves too fast to rock the boat. I close my eyes. I don't feel like reading.

As always, I'm looking forward to a weekend in Macau. I go there at least once a month, sometimes twice. It's one of my favorite places. I'd live there if it wasn't for the hour and a half commute each way to work and back. I might be the only person on the boat who isn't going there to gamble.

I'd learned my lesson about a month after I moved to Hong Kong. I'd decided to sit down at a blackjack table at the casino at the Ferry Terminal. I found a seat, ordered a drink and within a couple of hours of leisurely play I was up nearly four thousand Hong Kong dollars, about five hundred U.S.

We were a surprisingly congenial group at the table. Most Hong Kong Chinese gamblers don't look relaxed. They don't look like they're having fun. They take it very seriously, like playing the stock market. But this group was different. I was the only *gwailo* at the table, but everyone was friendly and chatty, attempting to speak in English and encouraging when I trotted out my few polite phrases in Cantonese.

But then the fat lady showed up and stood behind me. She was of a type. Loud, verbally and physically aggressive, probably in her mid-40s, squeezed into brightly colored expensive but not chic clothing that was too young for her, with her wrists, neck and the tight bun at the back of her head dripping gaudy, over-sized gold jewelry. She said something nasty about the *gwailo* at the table that made everyone else flinch and the person sitting to the right of me whisper "sorry" in my ear.

The table was full and she wanted my seat. She decided to take advantage of a local rule to get it. At blackjack tables in Macau, if someone walks up and plunks down double your money on your betting circle, they can control your cards. So the fat lady decided to take over my cards and lose until she'd driven me out of my chair.

She leaned hard against the back of my seat, shoving me forward against the table, making sure that her cigarette smoke drifted into my face. I pressed back against her but her leverage and weight were winning that battle. The minimum bet was fifty dollars a hand, about six dollars and fifty cents U.S. I figured the least I could do was make it expensive for her. I was willing to lose all my gains.

I put down fifty dollars. She put down a hundred. The dealer dealt me a nineteen. I would have stood pat. She hit, asking for another card. It was a seven and we went bust. She cackled and announced something nasty to the other people at the table. They just bowed their heads and that time the person on my left whispered "sorry" in my ear.

Over the course of the next hour I only won one hand, a blackjack that she couldn't do anything about. I'd lost about half my winnings, but I was smug in the knowledge that she'd lost twice as much. One of the other people at the table had bought me a drink. Several of them had started making rude remarks back at the fat lady on my behalf.

When I got another blackjack she finally gave up. She shoved me hard against the table, knocking over everyone's neatly piled stacks of chips, blew a large cloud of smoke into my face and leaned in to practically shout *doo lay loh moh*, "motherfucker," in my ear. I smiled and shrugged at my tablemates. The ones on either side clapped me on the back and we settled back into congenial play.

An hour later I had lost the rest of my winnings anyhow. I haven't gambled in Macau since.

What's great about Macau is its atmosphere. Hong Kong's been rich long enough to have torn down almost all the old city and rebuilt it several times over. Macau's only recently put together the money to do that, so much of the city still looks like it did a hundred years ago. There's even a few buildings left from three or four hundred years ago.

It's the last remaining Portuguese colony. It was founded nearly three hundred years before Hong Kong and for the first half of its history was the richest, most prosperous port on this part of

China's coast. Then the harbor, at the mouth of the Pearl River, silted up and the ships became larger at the same time so they needed a deeper port. By the late 1800s Hong Kong had taken over as the thriving city around here and Macau was a sleepy backwater with a reputation for vice.

I have plenty of vices other than gambling for Macau to indulge. I spend aimless happy weekends strolling its neighborhoods with my camera. I'll stop for an espresso here, a cup of tea there, a Chinese snack or a long wine-soaked Portuguese lunch. I'll walk along the beach, the waterfront, through gardens and ancient temple grounds. I'll nap in the late afternoon, walk around some more, have a massage. There are great restaurants for dinner. After that the nightlife runs from silly to sordid and I like it all.

Just before we dock my row drains out quickly. It seems like everyone on the ferry other than me is battling for position at the exit doors. The ferry lists far to the right and I can both feel and hear it smacking against the huge, old tar-soaked wooden pylons. Everyone wants to be first down the gangway, first through the immigration booths and first into taxis to the casinos. As the crowd jostles and heaves against the still closed doors, people've already begun to make bets, shouting out odds and wagers on who's going to win, who's going to lose, how much and anything else where there's an element of chance.

I stay put. I'm in no rush. Not enough of one to risk being trampled underfoot anyway.

Finally the ferry rolls upright and I get out without being pushed or shoved even once. I head toward the overpass that leads to the casino and entertainment mall across from the terminal, when someone calls my name.

"Ray, Ray Sharp."

I look around and see a colleague striding up to me fast. He's in a crisply cut, dark suit. He looks out of place in Macau and I'm not happy to see him.

"Fred." He hates it when I call him Fred. I wouldn't dare call him Freddie or he'd probably hit me and he's a lot bigger than I am. Frederick Lyons IV is the finance editor of *Asian Industry* and the eldest son of an old and esteemed banking family back in England. I don't know how he got the job. When I signed on as deputy editor he was already firmly entrenched. The guy I replaced warned me about him; he's not very bright and he's accustomed to having other people do all his dirty work for him.

But he dresses well, better than most bankers. I doubt he even owns any socks that haven't been handmade by the finest shop on Saville Row back in London. His hair is perfect - black with just the right dignified amount of gray and coifed by a barber who takes a small suite in the Mandarin Hotel once a month to service his exclusive clientele. He's a perfect example of the acronym FILTH. It means "Failed In London, Try Hong Kong."

He irritates the hell out of me and since I'm his boss, I'm also a thorn in his side. Sometimes I get a rather unfortunate kick out of, as he might say, taking the piss out of him. At least he's been well trained since birth to remain civil.

He winces and puts the hand he's offered away when I don't shake it. "What're you doing here?"

"Do you have a minute? Can we go somewhere and talk?"

He looks upset about something. I actually feel a twinge of sympathy for him. There's an Italian restaurant across the street. It's got great little sandwiches and coffee. It's noon, early for lunch in Macau, so it won't be busy.

I order two single espressos. For some reason I don't understand that's better than one double. Fred doesn't seem like the sort of guy who'd drink during the day, but that's what he wants.

"Gin and tonic if you please. Boodles, no ice, no lime." The waitress raises an eyebrow. I doubt she's shocked he's ordering booze, maybe it's the posh accent, the suit. She doesn't think he looks the type either. But she takes the order and is back with it quick.

"You know Fred, you really ought to lay in a stock of white linen suits. You're the most colonial guy I know. That's the official drink of the Empire, isn't it?"

He winces again, but it's just reflex. He knows how I mean it, but he probably doesn't even regard it as a slight. The Empire is not something he thinks his people need to be ashamed of. To the contrary, the world would be a better, more civilized place if only…blah blah blah. I've heard it. I have a lot less patience for it than he seems to have for me. Then again, he's not my boss.

I throw back one of the small cups of strong, bitter brew. "Sorry, I didn't mean anything by it, you know me."

He waves it off but my saying "sorry" probably needles him more than anything else I've said. The Brits say it to each other all the time, to the point where it's completely meaningless. But it seems to bother them when someone else uses it, like I ought to fork over a royalty payment with each utterance.

"Raymond." He knows I hate being called Raymond, even more than Mr. Sharp. It brings a smile to my face that he says it. 'Thatta boy,' I think to myself.

"What do you know about Macau?"

"Why Fred, you thinking of doing a story on it? Could be pretty interesting although the really juicy stuff is all underground and you'd probably end up dead just from asking too many questions before you get the story."

Macau makes most of its money from legalized gambling, prostitution, not zealously enforcing drug laws and sticking "Made in Macau" labels on everything from toys to vibrators to t-shirts that are really made in China but need to get into the U.S. on some other country's import quota. The people making all that money need somewhere legit to park their gains. So lately there's been a rash of building. New housing and office blocks, ugly concrete and glass edifices, most with high vacancy rates, are springing up like weeds after a hard spring rain. It would be an interesting story for a finance writer. Fred isn't the right guy to do it.

"No, no story. What do you know about prostitution here?"

"I didn't think you were into that. I can recommend a few places."

"I'm certain that you can. It's not that. It's my younger brother Edward. He seems to have gone potty over some Russian harlot who works in one of the nightclubs."

"Potty? That means something else in American. Lucky I speak some British."

"It is not funny. He has been spending most of his time here and has been lavishing gifts upon her. He even gave her our grandmother's engagement ring. Our father is concerned. His colleagues are disturbed. This is not simply a small fling. It is most inappropriate. She is, after all, a prostitute. He has been speaking of an attempt to buy her out from under her contract. That does not sound good, whatever it means."

"Okay, it's not funny. Ed's a lawyer isn't he?"

"A barrister, yes. A criminal defense attorney. He had a perfectly good job with the government as a prosecutor but he seems to have gone soft. All he desires now is to defend the dregs of society."

"By that I take it you mean indigent Chinese who're dragged into English-speaking courts and raked over the coals by men from the right schools in Britain wearing dirty, silly wigs."

"Without us there would be anarchy here, no order, no courts, no economy. There might even be communism. I don't see how you can…"

"Okay, okay, let's argue the benefits of empire some other time. Your brother's in love with a prostitute, what do you want me to do about it?"

"I understand that you know Macau. You come here a lot. I hear you speaking about it. Perhaps you know someone I can talk to, or which of the authorities would be most amenable to my entreaties."

"I was wondering what you were doing here. When did you get here? You haven't done anything yet, haven't talked to anyone have you?"

"No, I came last night. I tried speaking with Edward but he wouldn't listen to me. This morning I didn't know who to speak to. I was preparing to take the jetfoil back to Hong Kong when I saw you just now."

"That's good, really, whatever you do, you don't want to speak to any authorities. Your brother won't mean much of anything to them, not even to the honest ones. Russian prostitutes though are very big business. At best you'll just get laughed out of someone's office. At worst, it could be dangerous."

"Well I must do something. What is it that I can?"

"Maybe it isn't such a bad thing. Prostitutes, even Russian ones, are people too. They can fall in love with other people just like the rest of us. Maybe she really does love your brother. Maybe she's a great girl in a lousy job."

"The woman is a whore. It is an embarrassment to my family and to his firm. I also do not know what this business is of him buying her out of her contract. Are people really still bought and sold? What sort of people are they?"

He disgusts me, so it hurts even more to know he's right. At least partially right. There's reason for worry. The Russian mafia, working with Chinese triad groups and some of the more venal higher ups in China's People's Liberation Army, control the flow of Russian women in and out of brothels in China and Macau. They make a lot of money at it and they're notoriously brutal about maintaining their market share and protecting their assets. If Ed starts sticking his nose into their business, or Fred starts asking the wrong questions of the wrong people, things will get really ugly, really fast.

"Okay, Fred, don't do anything about it now. I've got a girl-friend in Jakarta who used to work in a nightclub in Macau."

He raises his verdant, expansive but neatly trimmed eyebrows high onto his patrician forehead and begins to open his mouth. I put up a hand to stop him speaking.

"I'll call her when I get to my hotel. Maybe she can give me a name or two of people to talk to. She was involved with these people. She might know if there's any way to deal with them. Let me see if there's anything I can do, anyone worth talking to. I can't promise anything."

"I suppose that is a good idea. Thank you. Will you call me when you find out anything?"

"I'm not getting back until late Sunday night. I'll see you in the office Monday." He tells me as much as he can about his brother's girlfriend. It isn't much other than the name of the nightclub she works in and her name, Marta.

I was in a good mood before this. The whole thing pisses me off for a lot of reasons, a lot of which come down to Irina. I'm in love with her, dammit. And she lives in Indonesia so I don't get to see her as much as I'd like. And she makes a good living fucking guys for money and I'm not in any position to consider that anything other than her own damn business. At least she's independent, no pimp, no mafia, she's her own boss, she works when she wants. Part of me even kind of likes it. It keeps things at arms length, keeps me independent too. I've never been any good at relationships. I've screwed up almost all of them. This one seems to be working out okay so far.

But I'd like to see her more often than I do. I wish she felt she had some other way to make good money. Sometimes the whole thing makes me mad. This is one of those times.

Ed sounds like a good guy. Why the hell shouldn't he be happy? For that matter why shouldn't Marta? Why shouldn't I? It's assholes like Fred and the mafia that get in the way of that.

Fred starts to say something more and I don't want to hear it. I tell him to go catch his ferry.

| |CHAPTER **TWO** | |

It's just a couple of miles through town to my hotel. Walking in Macau almost always makes me feel good, so I decide to take the long way. I've just got a small backpack and my camera. It's hot and humid, like it usually is, but not so bad as it can get. The first five minutes is the worst, breathing terrible exhaust fumes through the tunnel that leads to the old city. I emerge into the open on a tree-lined, comfortingly decrepit street fronted with yellow, brown, dark green and red painted buildings from the early 1920s.

I stop for fresh lemonade in a little Thai café in the bustling neighborhood nearby where most of the imported Thai prostitutes live. There's a table with four cute girls next to mine. They must work in one of the massage parlors, sitting, numbered behind a glass wall waiting for a customer to pick them. They titter and bend their heads together when I walk in. They get up to leave before I do and one of them with long, straight, dyed yellow-blonde hair comes up to me, smiles, puts her hand on mine and hands me a business card for the Darling Sauna. She's written her name, Nuoy, and number, 24, on the back of it. I smile up at her. "See you later, mister?"

"Maybe."

I finish my lemonade and walk for fifteen minutes down into one of the old Portuguese neighborhoods. I stop at a small European café, sit at an outside table on a cobblestone pedestrian street and eat a ham and cheese sandwich on a hot fresh roll. I wash it down with a potent double espresso.

The café is filled with the Portuguese who live nearby. They have strong jaws, prominent noses and bright eyes. Their complexions aren't swarthy, but they aren't pasty like the Brits in Hong Kong either. They recline in their chairs, slowly smoking cigarettes, letting the ashes grow long and lazily stirring sugar cubes into their cups of coffee. They look at ease, not in a hurry, not anxious, unconcerned.

Any passerby with even the slightest power of observation, would know that I'm a stranger. My clothes, my posture, the haste with which I wolf down my sandwich, no empty sugar wrappings next to my demitasse; all give me away. I'm always looking around, noticing things, waiting for something to happen, wanting something to happen. It's hard to relax sometimes when you're like that. Maybe if I lived here it would be different. But I guess it would take many years before it would be much different.

I give up my table to a group of teenagers who need to practice their afternoon lounging. They're neatly dressed and polite and assure me several times that there is no need for me to move for their sake.

Whitewashed, colonnaded buildings from the eighteenth century surround the main square of old Macau with a fountain in the middle and an op-art array of paving stones underfoot. A group of workmen are setting up a stage where tonight there'll be a concert featuring a Portuguese *fado* singer, selections from a Cantonese opera, a jazz band and finally a cloyingly cute and sweet Canto-Pop singer who has just returned to her hometown after a tour of Hong Kong and southern China.

I walk past it all, wanting nothing more now than to get to my hotel room and call Irina.

It's nearly mid-afternoon but it sounds like I've woken her up.

"Who is this? Is morning. What you want?"

Her voice is especially resonant when she wakes up, like a Russian FM disk jockey with big, lazy bubbles in her vowels. It gives me the shivers to hear her speak. Unconsciously, I stick a hand down my pants while talking with her.

"It's a guy who wants you in Hong Kong."

"Oh, it is Russian girl who wants you too."

We exchange longings for a couple of minutes until I can't take it anymore.

"Irina, stop, this is making me crazy. I'll try and come to Jakarta soon. I'm in Macau."

"Why, you look for new Russian girl?"

"You're all the Russian girl I can handle."

"So, maybe Thai girl then, or from Vietnam."

She loves teasing me about this. We each have our ways of keeping each other at arms length, of pretending things aren't as serious between us as they could be if we let them. I'm an easy target. She's a whore. I'm a john. That's how we met. We're both a lot more than that to each other now. Life is just too damn complicated, confusing and in the end too short to allow any one small set of specifics to get in the way of living it.

"Not this trip. I'm trying to help a guy I work with."

"He need girl?"

"Well, yeah, he probably does, but his brother's already got one and that seems to be the problem."

"What problem?"

"His brother's girlfriend is Russian. She works in the Starlight nightclub. He wants to buy her out."

"So, what problem? No problem to take her out."

"No, not for just a night, I mean he wants to pay off her contract, get her away from the mafia guys and marry her."

"Not good idea. Maybe he wait she finish contract, go back Russia. Wait more, he send her money so she not go again. Maybe year later he go to Russia and marry her. No problem if do that way. Mafia happy, she happy, he happy."

"Yeah, I know, but I think it's gone beyond that already. Do you still know anyone I can talk to who might have some ideas about how to help this guy do what he wants, or even just to see if he's really getting into any trouble? He's a good guy. I told his brother I'd see if I could find out what's going on."

"I have friend from Moscow, from medical university. She is working in nightclub at Lisboa, maybe she help. She is very smart girl, very funny girl, more smart and funny than me. When you fucking her you think about me sometime, okay?"

"Okay, but I wish you were here. I'll pay for your ticket."

"Maybe soon. Now cannot."

Her friend's name is Sasha and she lives in a small apartment near the Chinese border with three other Russian women. I can call her, but not before four. She goes to work at eight.

I take a nap. It's good to have a Friday off. *Asian Industry*'s a monthly and while some weeks I need to work six or seven late days, sometimes there isn't much to do.

I wake up a little after four and when I call Sasha's already gone out. She's left her portable phone at home and one of her roommates groggily answers it. I can barely understand her through the heavy accent.

I'm not surprised she's gone out. I've been in one of the apartments that the Russians put their working women in and no one in their right mind would want to spend any longer awake in one than necessary. They're tiny, hot, cramped, dirty and usually smell terrible. A lot of them are above Chinese restaurants, most likely because no one else wants to rent them, and the walls are covered with grease that seems to ooze up from below. The air is choking with a noxious blend of cooking odors, makeup, perfume and cigarettes.

The woman doesn't know where Sasha's gone or when she'll be back. She starts work at the nightclub at eight; I can find her there then.

I can picture the roommate who answered the phone; barely awake, disheveled bleached blonde hair, her makeup smeared, her head clanging with last night's booze and the memory of whoever it was she ended up in bed with. When we hang up she'll look around for her first cigarette of the day. Drink a glass of water. Rummage through her handbag to count the money she'd made. She may turn on a small cassette player and lugubrious Russian ballads or romantic classical music will seep out of it. She may make some instant coffee or strong tea with the plug-in kettle. There may be a bag of chips or some candy bars to eat. If not, she can go downstairs for some fried noodles or rice.

I hate the picture I've got in my head. It's too easy to see Irina painted into it. She used to work in Macau. She'd done the same thing, lived in the same sort of places. She's out of it now. Her own boss. She's come a long way from it in a lot of ways, but not far enough in others.

So, if I don't like it, why the hell do I support it? Why have I been a customer and probably will be again? I argue with myself about it while I take a shower, thinking about a conversation I'd had with a friend just a week ago.

I'd helped Susan get a job when she first came to Hong Kong, fresh out of college in Texas. That was a few months ago. Her boyfriend Mike, I'd introduced her to him also, was out of town on assignment. It was late Sunday night and we were the last two propping up the bar at the Foreign Correspondents Club.

We were both at least half in the bag. I'd been telling her about me and Irina. She got a serious look on her face and covered one of my hands with one of hers. "We don't know each other all that well, but can I ask you something serious Ray?"

"This about Mike?"

"No. I don't know, maybe."

"Go ahead. I can always lie or clam up."

"What is it with you guys and all these prostitutes? Was it like that back home? What's the deal?"

"Us guys? You mean me and Mike?"

"I guess, yeah."

"I can only speak for myself. You want to know something about Mike, you'll have to ask him."

"Okay."

"As for me, it's easy. I'm a foreigner. I travel a lot. Even though there's hookers all over the place, most Asian countries are actually pretty conservative. Unless I'm a local almost the only way to meet local women is to go to bars. Most of the women in bars here are whores. These aren't the kinds of cultures where single women go to bars. Occasionally, in the richer places like here and Singapore and Tokyo they do, but they're always with friends and aren't looking to meet horny foreigners in their forties."

"Okay so it's easy, but so what? You're not an asshole. You're a nice guy, smart, funny, fairly good looking. If I wasn't going out with Mike and you asked me I'd say yes. Don't you want a more equal relationship? Doesn't it get a little, I don't know, boring or something?"

I tucked that thought away in case she ever does break up with Mike. "What's to say some of these relationships aren't equal? I mean sure, you meet under odd circumstances, but then after that you're just two people and all the usual stuff about whether you like someone or not can come into play.

"Also, like I said, these are conservative countries, it's very hard for a young woman to be independent. It's almost impossible for her to get a decent paying job. She's under a lot of family pressure to get married and start having babies, and no matter what sort of hormonal hell is breaking loose inside her she has to act demure and proper and hide it away. If she doesn't, if she wants to be what you or I would consider liberated, especially sexually liberated, what we take for granted growing up in the U.S., she's making herself an outcast in her society anyhow.

"Other than a few successful businesswomen, most of the independent, liberated women I get a chance to meet in the poorer countries of Asia, and I guess you can include Russia in that now too, are prostitutes, or ex-prostitutes. And I like independent women."

"How independent can they be? You're paying them, some of them've got pimps. What about sex slavery? I've read there's plenty of that."

"Yeah there is, and it's horrible and needs to be stopped. It's obviously lousy that some women feel they have no choice other than prostitution to make a decent, independent living and it's a lot worse that some women aren't even given the choice. But there's plenty of shades of gray, like a lot of things."

"I wish your friend Irina was here. I wouldn't mind hearing what she has to say about all this."

"Yeah, we don't talk about it a lot. She says she doesn't think about it too much. I think when she does she gets depressed."

"I don't blame her."

"Me neither, but I wish she was here too."

Actually I do know what Irina would say. There's a practicality hard-wired into a lot of poor societies that takes the idea of someone being "poor but lovable" and makes it the fodder for jokes. Women can be attractive and poor, and men will savor the thought of swooping in and taking them away from all that. If a man is poor and wants to get the girls, he'd better do something quick to change his economic status. That's the way it's been as far back as anyone knows. Even in modern, sexually liberated America that's the way it is in the movies and on TV and in most places.

That's the line Irina feeds herself. She says that if she was still in Russia she'd be hunting for a rich boyfriend or husband and that she'd be stupid to do anything else. But if that's really the case, why does she insist that I don't pay her and that I don't always bring her gifts? Why does she demand to pay for dinner and drinks sometimes when we go out? Why does she buy me gifts?

I sure as hell don't have any of the answers. I try not to think too much about it. When I do, drinking helps. I can accept things the way they are when I have a little bit of a buzz on. Most of the other expats I know are the same way. But it's a high wire act. You try to drink enough, and often enough, to hold back your conscience, but not so much that the drinking itself becomes a problem. Not everyone gets it right. I do okay, most of the time.

I get out of the shower and take one of those little bottles of vodka out of the minibar, chip some ice from the frosted freezer compartment of the room refrigerator, and then throw it back fast enough that the ice doesn't make any difference. It's just enough booze. The burn is good going down, the warmth in my stomach and the little blur to the edges inside my brain are even better.

| |CHAPTER **THREE**| |

I take the elevator to the immaculately clean, cool, dry, cheaply furnished lobby and then walk outside into the heat and damp. I cross the street to get to the waterfront. It's nearly dusk and I can see the fishing boats going home. Wooden Chinese junks, bobbing through the channel, heading north to the harbor at Zhuhai, the Chinese city that's just a continuation of Macau across the border.

Within an hour the boats will unload their catch and the fish will be on their way back across the border to Macau, at least the dead ones. Having been caught this day, some of them are still fresh enough for Chinese dinner tables. The live ones take their time. They'll be brought over still swimming in tanks tomorrow.

I stroll along the Praia Grande. It used to be one of the most beautiful waterfronts in Asia. It's a long, curving road, lined on the bay side with old Chinese elms and on the shore side with the mansions of the enclave's wealthiest merchants. But now the greedy bastards are filling it in.

A development company is reclaiming the land in the bay and building a road out another three hundred feet or so from the current waterfront. The road will ring around new, tall office buildings and apartments that will look just like the ugly ones already built near the ferry terminal. In a rare nod to esthetics they're not filling in all the land. They're leaving two small lakes. I figure those'll make it all the sadder when they're finished.

A lot of the construction in Macau is the result of dirty money that's desperate for somewhere relatively clean to go. Most of the development seems like a lousy investment and none of it gives a damn about architecture, culture, tradition or even beautiful views. I get sad walking along it so I turn inland.

I walk up the steps, up the hill alongside the Bela Vista. It's an imposing 1880s colonial building that commands one of the best views in the city. It's terraced and fountained garden is almost overrun with a wide variety of flowers and bright, multi-hued bougainvillea. The colonnaded terrace that overlooks the garden and the view is busy with late afternoon drunks. I can hear a small jazz combo playing somewhere inside.

The first time I came to Macau the Bela Vista was a beautiful, thoroughly run down hotel, full of seedy charm. The best bay view suite in the place cost thirty-five dollars U.S. Even though I'd spent more than one night sleeping on the floor rather than on the ancient, lumpy and thin mattress, it was one of my favorite hotels in the world.

Now I can't afford it. I suppose it's a good thing that it was taken over by a ritzy hotel group. It might have crumbled into ruin without them. They put a lot of money into restoring it, rebuilding parts of it, refurbishing and refurnishing it. It went from offering twenty-four or so very cheap rooms, to providing only eight astronomically expensive ones. I miss the old Bela Vista, but I'll begrudgingly admit that its new caretakers have done a great job of fixing it up. I only wish I could stay there.

I could have a drink there. But the terrace looks too crowded and I'd still have to look out over a lost love.

Instead I walk past it and into the maze of narrow streets on top of the hill. It could be almost any working class residential neighborhood in Portugal, except that most of the people and shops I pass are Chinese.

Across the street there's a corner shop that sells both Portuguese pastries and bowls of Chinese noodle soup. An old woman is chopping a huge mound of garlic next to a wok filled with bubbling broth. The smell stings my eyes at the same time as the sweet, yeasty odor of baking custard tarts soothes my nose. I cross the cobblestones to get closer, enjoying the sensual contrast.

In the middle of the next block there's a crumbling stone ruin of a shrine to Kwun Yam, the goddess of mercy. She heals the sick, but apparently not herself. Her statue is broken, missing an arm and both its legs. A garland of orchids, its blooms going brown at the edges, is draped in a circle around it. A couple of oranges are littered in front of her and Coke cans, filled with sand and bristling with burnt out incense sticks are on either side.

Just beyond the shrine, also in ruins, sprouting weeds and even whole bushes from cracks in the pavement, are steps leading down into the old city by the inner harbor. Oddly, in a city that is ninety-five percent Chinese anyhow, the area is known as Chinatown. It's full of narrow streets presenting rows of low, dark houses and shops with bars on the doors and windows. The occasional wider avenue, gaudy with red and yellow neon signs, slashes through the area as well. The smells are of dried, salted seafood, cooking oil, roasting flesh, very ripe fruit and incense. The sounds that spill out of the buildings are of Cantonese opera or Canto-Pop from radios and cassette players, the shrill, staccato cackling voices of game shows and variety shows on televisions and the constant high-pitched clack of mahjong tiles slamming down on tabletops.

At the waterfront on that side of the small peninsula that makes up the mainland part of Macau, the shops along the street across from the docks and warehouses are all set back and down, underneath an old and precarious looking overhang. It's dark back in there and until your eyes adjust you can only guess at what's going on from the smells and sounds that drift out to the sidewalk.

There are a lot of nautical supply stores that smell of camphor and engine oil and tar and hemp rope and emit clangs and thumps. The dried fish and dried shellfish stores have their own distinctive odors. The fish is dusty with salt and stings the eyes; the shellfish is ever so slightly sweet. Barrels and burlap sacks of dried mushrooms and fungus send out an earthy scent, as if someone in the dark interior is working in a bed of freshly turned soil. Sellers of chilies and herbs advertise with a waft of acrid citrus and round, complex notes of coriander and spice blends. There's a shop where they make dumplings and from it comes an incessant thwop of dough on a cracked marble surface.

In the evening food vendors open up *dai pai dongs*, small streetside kitchens, set out folding tables and chairs and fire up their woks. With no more than a huge, sharp cleaver, a large spatula and a ladle they prepare their menus on thick, well-oiled rounds of old hardwood, toss the ingredients through some oil and spices with a huge flame underneath, and dish it up. I've seen a chicken go from live and squawking to perfectly cooked bites at the end of a diner's chopsticks in as little as five minutes.

They are setting up when I get to the waterfront. I walk along in the street so as to avoid getting in the way. It's beginning to get dark and I need another shower before going to the nightclub to find Sasha. I head up past the Floating Casino, a gaudy Chinese wedding cake of a building on a barge moored at one of the fouler smelling docks of the inner harbor, and turn right up Avenida de Almeida Ribeiro that bisects the peninsula.

As I stroll up the slight slope from the inner harbor, the sidewalk is buzzing with streetwalkers, in town for the night from

China. They come in all ages, shapes and sizes; many dressed in jeans and t-shirts, but some wearing tight and very high slit *cheongsams*, the distinctive Chinese sheath dress. Most of them shy away when they see me, trying to blend back into the shadows under the covered walkway. A few approach, whispering soft enticements in Mandarin that do sound much more enticing than Cantonese, and some very few in English.

Before I get back to the hotel I stop at a store and buy a bottle of vodka for my hotel room. Like everything else, it's cheaper here than in Hong Kong. When I get back I make myself a small drink. I prop myself up with pillows to sip it while watching a few minutes of fuzzy CNN on the television. I'm reassured that the world is still as screwed up as usual. Nothing's got any better or much worse since I last checked. Another shower, another small drink, a change of clothes and I'm back out the door.

| |CHAPTER **FOUR**| |

The Lisboa Hotel and Casino is across a busy traffic circle from my hotel. It's the flagship of the man who owns Macau, or at least an awful lot of it. Stanley Ho is rich, powerful and suave. Once he was a professional, now a renowned amateur ball-room dancer. No one is exactly sure where his money originally came from. Speculation points to gunrunning, for the Japanese during the Second World War and then for the communists during the end stages of China's civil war.

These days it's obvious where his money comes from. He owns the ferries and helicopters that take people to and from Macau. He has a monopoly on gambling in the enclave. He owns, or his company operates most of the major hotels in the city and more than just a few of the minor ones. His company has its fingers in the entertainment pie, ranging from the glitziest nightclubs to some of the sleaziest saunas.

The Lisboa looks like the world's largest, ugliest, gilded birdcage. That's intentional. In Cantonese superstition, birds are lucky. The cage keeps the luck in. I imagine it's also supposed to keep Mr. Ho's money from escaping. You'd think that might discourage some of the gamblers.

The façade strobes with neon and blinking bulbs. Every surface is polished and reflective, most of it the color of gold. Behind the birdcage rises a tall, ugly hotel tower, not quite as illuminated but still covered with the same fake opulent materials. It's the ugliest building I've ever seen; probably the ugliest on the planet.

Entering the cage I'm almost tossed back out by the shockwave of noise and light and commotion that explodes in front of me. The air itself feels solid, a dense frozen block of ferociously air-conditioned cigarette smoke and something less tangible like fear or greed. I stop just inside to let my senses adjust, if they can. I shiver where I stand. Just walking through the door lowers the temperature by about thirty-five degrees.

I've been here plenty of times before, but the first few moments always stop me in my tracks. I'm brought around by a shove from behind. Impatient gamblers are trying to get inside and there's some dumb *gwailo* standing smack in the middle of things.

I move out of the way, to the side where I edge along the first row of chirping and clanging slot machines. It's a circular building and I make my way around it counter-clockwise to an escalator that takes me up through the madness to another level of madness.

The coffee shop is on the second floor and it's an oasis of relative calm. I sit down facing the window to the hallway and order a bowl of noodle soup for my stomach and a vodka for my nerves.

On the other side of the glass, passersby weave their way through a gauntlet of brightly plumed whores. They're mostly from China, but better dressed and made up than the ones on the street. There are a few Russians as well. They must be in between jobs at nightclubs, or maybe they've finished their contracts and still have a few days remaining on their visas. When they snag a john, they take him up to one of the rooms they share in the hotel tower. They're rarely up there more than fifteen minutes.

I'm sitting in a birdcage, and the prostitutes are the exotic, tropical birds flapping around. Almost everyone else is in black or brown or gray or some somber shade of blue. They advertise themselves more subtly, with expensive watches, designer handbags or flashy rings. In the avian world it's usually the male of the species that sports flamboyant plumage to attract its mate. Not here. Humans are different, and here they're even more different than usual.

I'm enjoying the show and am not in the mood to go to the nightclub. I'm not enthusiastic about doing a favor for that jerk Fred either. But I resist the strong urge to simply order another drink, bum a cigarette from one of the prematurely cool kids at the next table and stay put.

The Lisboa's nightclub is two floors up. I came into the round building at about six on the clock face, the coffee shop is somewhere around four and the escalator I'm looking for is around one. I thread my way through the girls in the hall, dodging their whispers and light touches. I'm a man on a mission and distraction will have to wait.

A long narrow escalator lifts me through a mirrored tunnel lit with hundreds, maybe thousands of flickering yellow light bulbs. I think they're supposed to look golden and classy but it reminds me of the disorienting entrance to a bad time machine ride at an amusement park. Halfway up I can see the hostess and she can see me. She's wearing a tuxedo that's been tailored so as to make it obvious she isn't a man, or trying to look like one. We smile at each other in anticipation. I don't bother to hurry up the moving stairs but I do wave in greeting.

When I get to the top she comes out from behind her desk and offers me her hand, flat, fingers curved downward. It doesn't look like I'm supposed to shake it, so I just take it in one of mine and gently hold on.

"Welcome to the Lisboa nightclub. Is this your first time here?" Her voice is soft and refined; the inflection perfect, but with enough of an accent to make me think her good English is limited to a few well-rehearsed lines.

I tell her it is, although I know the score already. I've been to plenty of other places just like it. She asks if I'm alone. I say that I am. Still holding my hand, she raises a walkie-talkie to her bright red mouth, punches the button with her thumb and emits a short, sharp blast of Cantonese that includes the word *gwailo*. I just smile and don't take offense. Why bother? The hand unit crackles back at her and she tells me to please wait a moment, someone will be out to help me. She doesn't drop my hand and we stand there waiting, not talking.

In less than a minute a woman about my age, a *mamasan* in her mid-forties, wearing a Dior suit or a very good fake, comes out of the darkness of the club and takes over possession of my hand. Her voice is strong, clear, her English is precise and nearly without accent.

"Hello, welcome. I'm June. What can we do for you tonight? Would you like to meet a beautiful girl?"

"I'm Ray. A friend suggested I might like Sasha."

"Ah, the Russian girls are very popular. But it is early so you will have your pick. You are our first guest tonight. I will be happy to introduce you. If you do not like her do not be embarrassed to tell me. We have many beautiful girls for you to choose from."

June leads me to a semi-circular booth next to the dance floor. A small combo is setting up on the stage. I sit down and she sits close, resting our still joined hands on my leg.

"Ray, are you visiting Macau? Where do you come from?"

"I live in Hong Kong. I'm from the U.S., from California."

"It is beautiful there. I was once in San Francisco, back when I was young and beautiful."

"You're still young and beautiful."

She pecks me on the cheek. "You lie so nicely Ray. That is a good talent."

I laugh and tell her I mean it, which I do. But it's the right thing to say no matter what. It only took my first visit to an Asian nightclub to realize it's a good idea to butter up the *mamasans*.

She asks if I want anything to drink while she goes to fetch Sasha. I ask for a vodka rocks. She pushes a button that's discreetly placed under the table to summon a waitress. A wisp thin Chinese girl with hair to the back of her knees, wearing a gold lame *cheongsam*, materializes almost immediately at my side. She takes my order, scribbles something on a card that's placed in a holder on the table and is gone so fast that I'm surprised I don't see a whiff of vapor.

June returns my hand to my control and pats me on the leg. She makes sure that I understand that just to have Sasha sit with me is going to cost a hundred and twenty Hong Kong dollars an hour, fifteen dollars and thirty-eight cents U.S. to be precise, toted up in six minute increments, plus drinks and tips. If I want to take her out of the club that'll cost more. Anything outside the club is between me and her. I assure her I know how it works. She says she'll be back soon.

That's a little less than half what it would cost in Hong Kong. Sasha's lucky if she keeps a third of it. Her job is to get me to buy her expensive drinks, of which she gets half the price. Once my bar bill gets high enough she'll want me to pay the club to take her out for an hour or two or all night. Then I'll pay her for whatever we do when we leave. I'm not making any plans, but I'm keeping my options open.

My drink, a bowl of mixed nuts, a fruit plate and two damp hand towels, one hot and one cold, get to the table before Sasha does. The waitress guesses right and snaps open the hot towel for me. It feels good in my hands and against my face. It's as chilled in here as in the rest of the building, maybe more so. I figure that the Arctic air-conditioning is their version of salty snacks in a bar. The air is so cold that you practically need a hostess to snuggle with, maybe two, one on each side for warmth.

June comes back leading Sasha by the hand. I stand and shake hands with the Russian girl and then we sit. June sits across from us and makes a formal introduction. She asks if Sasha meets with my approval. When I say "yes" the *mamasan* gets up and takes her leave.

Sasha is shorter than most of the other Russian women I've seen working in Asia. And rounder too, not plump but not sylph-like, athletic or va-va-voom like the others I've met. Her hair, which is tied back in a simple ponytail, is milk chocolate brown, not the real or dyed blonde that's more common. She has non-descript eyes a lighter shade of brown than her hair, Mick Jagger-sized dark red lips and is curvy in a way that leans just a hair to the side of over-stated.

There's something about her that looks cuddly. She looks like someone it'll be easy to get comfortable with. She flashes me a smile that's friendly but neutral. She doesn't seem wary, hesitant, predatory or any of the other things that bar hostesses often are. She puts a hand on my thigh and I turn to face her on the sofa.

The only thing I don't like about her so far is that she's wearing something that looks disconcertingly like a wedding dress.

"You getting married tonight or something?"

She laughs, just a little, and it's a soothing, tinkly, water bur-bling over rocks sort of a sound. It flows from her, taking out with it what little stiffness was in her posture when she first sat down.

"I don't think so. Is it the dress?" She has a nice soft accent and the English flows as effortlessly as the laugh.

"Well, yeah."

"You don't like it?"

"It's okay, just a little funny is all. Do any of your customers find it sexy?"

"I borrowed it from one of the Chinese girls. Some men like to pretend. If you want me to stay I can change."

"No problem. Would you like something to drink?"

"What are you drinking?"

"Vodka."

"I would like a vodka also please."

I reach under the table and ring for the longhaired apparition.

"Vodka? It's too obvious. Are you a nationalist?"

"No, but I also like Chekov and Dostoevsky."

"What about Tchaikovsky?"

"No, not him. Not Korsakov either."

"That's a relief."

The waitress glides in, tidies up although there isn't really anything to tidy, takes our order and vanishes.

"How does she do that?"

"Don't you know? It's magic. This nightclub, they say it is magic. I think maybe it is just a dark nightclub. What do you think?"

"I try not to think. Why do you think I asked for you?"

"Okay, so how do you know to ask for me? I do not know you."

I tell her about Irina. She gets bubbly with excitement and bursts with questions. I can answer most of them, even the ones about Irina's family back in Moscow. It takes a few more drinks to tell everything I know and then for us to swap life stories.

I've heard hers before, with only slight variations. So far as I can make out, the difference between Sasha and nearly all the other Russian prostitutes in Macau is that she managed to scrape together enough money to buy her own ticket. She got here owing the mafia for helping her with the work permit and getting her the job, but she paid that off in the first two months. She still pays them a percentage of what she makes and she pays them more than the market rate for her shared apartment. She won't tell me what it is, but says it isn't too bad. She's been working at the Lisboa for almost ten months.

The first few months Gary, who sounds like her pimp, tried to get her under control. The mafia doesn't like its employees to be independent. He wanted to loan her money for clothes, a TV, a stereo, drugs, anything he thought she might want that would allow him to get his hooks into her. She wouldn't go for it. He offered to give her heroin. She didn't want it. She'd tried it once back in Moscow and it made her throw up. Finally he gave up. Just so long as she cuts him in on her action and the demand for Russian girls in Macau continues to exceed the supply, he leaves her alone.

By the time we've finished our stories, we're knotted together in each other's arms and legs. It's almost warm. We've kissed, chastely, a few times. But then there's a lull after I'm caught up on her life story. Finally our tongues find each other's and enjoy a light tussle in our smooshed together mouths. We come up for air.

"Irina is your girlfriend? Do you love her?"

"Yes, but," and I tell her about it. Finishing off with Irina's telling me to think of her when I'm fucking Sasha.

"Do not think of her too much please. Maybe I am jealous."

"Am I taking you out?"

"If you want."

"Only if you take off the wedding dress."

"What, you don't want to marry me?" She pouts then laughs, louder than before. "Always the bridesmaid, never the bride. Isn't that what you Americans say?"

"I've never said it but I might have to start. Where'd you learn your English anyhow?"

"I'm a good student, better than Irina. In university she was the beautiful one and I was the smart one."

"Irina's pretty smart and you're not so bad looking yourself."

I ring the bell and ask the wraith to bring June to the table. While Sasha goes to change I make the arrangements. It's still early in the evening, but I want to take her out for the night. The price is based on what they expect to make out of her between now and closing time. It's a weekend night and that adds to it. The final bill, complete with drinks and the uneaten fruit plate, comes to nearly two hundred and fifty U.S.

Sasha comes back in black jeans, a white silk cowgirl shirt with red roses stitched onto it and a pair of beat up Nikes. I look at her shoes and raise my eyebrows. I'd been expecting, I don't know what, high heels or something.

She takes my arm in hers. "I know, it is the wrong fashion, but I like walking. I hope you like walking."

I tip June. Sasha and I walk out the door to the escalator.

| | CHAPTER **FIVE** | |

We head outside where it's hot, humid and the exhaust fumes from the taxis lined up by the curb slither around us. My whole body feels like it's fogging up from the climate change. Under an overpass and across the road is the old *Club Militar*, a restored, formal, colonnaded colonial building from the turn of the century. It used to be a military officers club, now it's still private but members of Hong Kong's Foreign Correspondents Club, the F.C.C., can use its facilities. Sasha and I sink deep into the cushions of a soft, plush sofa in one of the sitting rooms and order drinks.

I order a double espresso and a shot of *aguardiente*, a particularly potent Portuguese brandy. Sasha sticks to vodka. We lightly hold hands and move our fingers around in each other's.

We talk about a lot of things. It feels like I'm on a date, one that's going really well. It's comfortable, easy, interesting, sexy. I know I'm paying for her company but the illusion is working. I feel less lonely than I have since the last time I was with Irina. She tells me about Russian politics, how life has changed since the Soviet Union fell apart. She asks me about Asian business and politics and wants to know a lot about Indonesia.

She's getting comfortable with me too. She tells me I'm the only man she's had a regular, interesting conversation with since she got here. Finally she gets back around to Irina.

"Ray, why did you ask for me? Do you miss Irina? Do you want to be with me because I remind you of her?"

"I do miss Irina but that's not it. Irina gave me your name for something else."

She takes her hand out of mine. "She doesn't want us to make love? If that is so, then I am sorry. I will give you your money back."

"No, no, really, I told you the truth about what she said. We can go back to my hotel and you can call her if you want. I don't really know how she feels about it. It might be interesting to find out."

"You are a strange man. If Irina is angry with me then I will be more angry with you."

"Fine, okay, we can go back to my hotel and you can have the bed, I'll sleep on the floor. Whatever, but I need to ask you about something else."

"*Shto?* What?"

"Do you know a woman named Marta who works in the Starlight Club?"

"Why? You want two girls. Irina likes that, I do not."

"No, it's not that."

I tell her all about it and she looks increasingly worried as I do.

"That is not a good idea. The mafia does not like to lose its girls, not even for money. Irina is right, your friend should just tell her go home, then wait and send her money, then maybe in one year it will be okay. Now, it is dangerous."

"That's what I've heard. But Ed's a good guy. I know things aren't easy for Russian girls here. I'd like to help if I can, see if there's anything I can do. Can we talk to her?"

"I do not know. I do not know her. I have seen her; she is very beautiful, very popular. I have a friend who works at Starlight. I will call her and ask; maybe we can meet tomorrow. Tonight it is not possible."

Club Militar is one of the too few civilized places that doesn't allow people to use their wireless phones inside. Sasha goes out to the front porch to make a call and comes back soon. "I spoke with my friend. She will talk with Marta. We can meet for lunch tomorrow."

That's good enough for me. I have other things on my mind tonight anyhow.

It's still early by Friday night in Macau standards and Sasha wants to walk some more. We hold hands and stroll up the hill through the small park next to the club and curve our way around through a neighborhood of ugly low-rise apartment buildings from the 1950s. We're not talking much, but our sides bump into and rub up against each other a lot.

I'm out of breath and trying not to wheeze by the time we get into the gardens that surround the Monte Fortress that overlooks the city. There's a large old cannon pointing straight at the new Bank of China building. I climb up to straddle it and hold out a hand to help Sasha up in front of me. She clambers aboard, turns to kiss me quickly on the lips, then turns around again and nestles into my lap and chest, looking out over the view. I tussle her hair and wrap my arms around her. She lets out a low sigh and pulls them more tightly to her, placing one of my hands on her left breast.

I feel a stirring, but I fight it back sensing this is a quiet, peaceful moment. There'll be time for other stuff later. I love this place, this view, this moment; its sounds and smells and evening breezes. I don't know Sasha well, but I want her to love it too.

The city below is built onto a peninsula. The Pearl River rolls down from China on the east side. The Inner Harbor clogged with small freighters, fishing boats and old wooden Chinese junks cuts up and into the Chinese city of Zhuhai on the west. The channel between the city and Taipa, the first of the two islands to the south, gets narrower every year as more land is reclaimed on both sides.

The fort commands the waterways. In 1622 a Dutch fleet was attempting to take Macau from the Portuguese. The city's defenders were almost out of ammunition when a Jesuit priest who had studied mathematics made careful calculations. One of the few remaining cannonballs was fired, possibly from the very cannon we're sitting on, and blew up the Dutch munitions ship.

To our right, in the middle of the peninsula, just below the fortress, is the façade of the cathedral of St. Paul. It was once the largest cathedral in Asia until all but its ornate front wall was leveled in a fire. It's covered with stone carvings of ships at sea, dragons, skeletons and assorted saints. Below it the old city spreads out in narrow cobblestone lanes, hundreds of year old Chinese shophouses tilting up against Portuguese colonial buildings.

At night it's a quiet city. The occasional car or boat horn, the bark of a dog, the clacking clamor of mahjongg tiles are the only sounds that drift up to our perch. The running lights of boats slide through the blackness beyond the city's lights on three sides of us. It seems peaceful, lovely.

Sasha wiggles a little in my lap and sighs again. I stroke her hair. "I wish I could like this place. It is pretty. You are lucky."

I am lucky. I know it. "I wish you could like it too. Is it always so bad?"

"Yes and no. It is better than being poor in Moscow."

"Is there anything else you can do?"

"Not now. I do not think so. Maybe when I save money. But now, my country is free but I am not."

"What about your family?"

"They're dead. I'm alone. I want to be independent. This is the easiest way."

"I'm sorry."

"Why? I choose this. I have more luck than many other girls."

I don't know what to say about any of this. If anything I could possibly say would sound anything less than stupid. I can't solve Sasha's problems, but I don't want to be part of them either. "We don't have to spend the night together. I can give you some money and you can go home if you want."

She tilts her head back up at me, smiles, kisses me on the cheek. "We can decide later. Now I'm hungry."

Sasha knows a small, all-night Thai noodle shop not too far away. Most Russians don't like spicy food, but she does. We stop at a liquor shop on the way to pick up a bottle of vodka. She likes mixing it into glasses of fresh Thai lime juice. I know throwing more vodka on top of what I've already drunk is probably a bad idea, but I do it anyway. By the time we finish our noodles, we're both plenty drunk.

Sasha's affectionate and silly, laughing a lot, slurring a chatty mix of English, Russian and bits of Chinese. Both of our moods have changed, for the better.

"Ray, darling, I now so *p'yaniy*, so *djoi-yu*, so drunk. It is good, no? Now I am happy. Sometime sad *p'yaniy*, but tonight happy. Are you happy Ray?"

I am happy and I don't care if it's booze-fuelled or not. I don't care if I'm paying for her company or not. We pour ourselves into a cab and go back to my hotel. We get up to my room and sit on the bed together, just managing to take our shoes off and splash a little more to drink into glasses. We toast, to something, anything, toss back the vodka then fall into a tangle on the bed. We kiss for a while and rummage around in each other's clothes.

It's fun and sexy, comfortable. There's no great urgency, no real passion, just two people getting to like each other, getting to know each other, playing with each other. Sasha bites and pokes me and I bite and poke her back. She says she isn't ticklish but I find some places where she is. We wrestle for a while, roll off the bed and claw back onto it laughing, out of breath.

I guess we fell asleep after that because I don't remember anything else until I wake up six or so hours later with coal miners chipping away at the inside of my head. I'm still dressed. So's Sasha, who's curled up and softly snoring in my arms.

Luckily the curtains are thick and the room is dark. My eyes aren't ready for daylight. Having learned from previous mistakes, I'd brought a bottle of aspirin from home. I grope my way through the dark into the bathroom and find it. I chase four down with three glasses of water. I shake three more tablets into my hand, fill the glass with water and take it back to bed.

Sasha's stretched out and groaning lightly. My eyes have adjusted enough to the dark that I can see she's rubbing her temples with her fists. I prop her head up and hold the aspirin and water out to her. She swallows them, mumbles "thanks" then settles back onto the pillow. I curl up around her and throw an arm over her and it's at least another hour or so before I'm awake again.

It's about ten in the morning when we wake up the second time. My head doesn't hurt but the energy vampires have been at me all night. Sasha seems fine, but not quite sure what to make of our having slept together platonically. She's apologetic.

"I'm sorry. I drink too much vodka. It's no good; you pay too much money to take me out of the club. I will give you back the money they give me, but my part is not so much."

I feel like I've been slapped alert. Is that what she thinks? I had a great time last night. "What? I don't care about that. We had a good time didn't we?"

"You are just saying that. You are nice to say that."

"No, I'm not. I like you. We had fun. I hope we can have more fun."

It takes me a while to convince her but I think I do. She cries a little, I don't know if it's from happiness, relief or if in some way it makes her more depressed about her life. Finally she smiles, wipes her eyes on my shirt and punches me lightly on the shoulder before kissing me.

"I like you too Ray. Sometimes I am just a stupid Russian girl."

I hug her, kiss her on the forehead and smile back. "Don't worry about it. I'm going to take a shower and change. Let's go have coffee and then hopefully we can go to lunch with Marta and your friend."

"Okay, but I must go to my apartment first and change clothing."

I think it might be nice for Irina and Sasha to talk to each other, so before I go into the bathroom I call Jakarta and hand the phone over. As I leave the room I hear Sasha talking excitedly in Russian.

I'm just about to get out of the shower when the door opens and Sasha steps in with me.

"That was a short call."

"Too expensive. Irina says hello."

"It's okay, I just thought it would be nice for you two to talk."

"It was good." She reaches for the soap and starts lathering parts of me that I've already washed. I am more than happy to let her clean them again.

"Irina says it is no problem with her if I have sex with you, but you have to pay me."

"So, she's your pimp now is she?"

"No, only my friend. Maybe you are also my friend, but sex is different. It is my job."

It is different. It's slippery and wet. When we begin to lose our footing in the shower we move to the rug on the floor. She wants to pleasure me, but I want to make sure she enjoys it too. I don't want to be just another customer. I move my head to go down on her. She resists for a little, trying to pull my face away from her. Then I feel her relax, the tension leaves her body, then her hands are on my head pressing it deeper into her. Then she tenses again, but differently. I can feel her thighs flexing, squeezing. Then they go rigid for a moment, then quivering, shaking and finally thrumming against my ears before she goes limp and gently pushes my head away, moaning a soft "oh, oh, oh."

She rests for a little, then pulls my face up to hers and kisses me deeply, her tongue searching my mouth. She rolls me over, rolls on top of me, pulls me into her and stares straight into my eyes, not moving any part of her other than an incredible clenching and unclenching of the muscles gripping me inside of her. It doesn't take long. I takes me longer to recover, to catch my breath enough to talk.

"You're good at that."

"Thank you. Not so much good with everyone I think."

I do pay her and it's worth every penny of the five hundred Hong Kong, sixty-five U.S., dollars she wants for "short time." By the time we get out of the room we're in a hurry to swing by her place and then meet Marta and her friend.

Sasha doesn't want me to come up; the place is a mess, her roommates might be asleep, whatever. So I wait downstairs in a tiny Chinese bakery where they serve coffee. Or rather, something like coffee. It's actually a mix of strong red tea from Yunnan province in China, and coffee that's been in a rolling boil for several hours, with sweetened condensed milk and a sprinkling of cinnamon. It comes in a large, thick, chipped glass that's too hot to pick up for the first few minutes. When I do manage to take a sip it tastes pretty good. I must be desperate for caffeine.

I've finished the first glass and am contemplating a second when Sasha returns to save me from myself. I'm relieved to see that she's dressed simply, casually. The only other time I'd ever gone to lunch with one of the Russian nightclub hostesses I met in Macau she dressed in a provocative way that got us dirty looks from the mostly Portuguese customers at one of my favorite restaurants. The waitress, who was usually very friendly, barely managed to restrain herself from "accidentally" spilling drinks all over us.

Sasha greets the elderly woman who runs the bakery in Cantonese. In my experience that's usually a bad idea. A lot of older southern Chinese people seem to hate it when foreigners butcher their language, or even when they don't. The very rare non-native speaker, who can speak the language well, is often regarded with suspicion.

Cantonese is one of the hardest languages on the planet. Depending on who you ask, it has seven, eight, nine or as many as twelve different tonal inflections for each sound. There's a famous joke that I don't understand. I do know the punch line. To me it sounds like: "*gwai, gwai, gwai, gwai, gwai, gwai.*" To a native speaker with more finely tuned ears, it sounds like six different words. It has something to do with old, white prostitutes eating chicken soup at a street stall; either that or strange, elderly turtles crossing the road; or something else that's a mystery to me.

But Sasha doesn't massacre the language. It comes out fluidly, natural sounding. Not quite fluent but good enough that the old woman smiles and greets her back. They chat for a couple of minutes before we leave to walk the few blocks to her friend's apartment.

"You are full of surprises. Where'd you learn Cantonese?"

"I like to study languages. It is not so difficult. The sound is simple, the grammar is simple, the tones, if you listen carefully they are like music."

"Yeah, like heavy metal. It's gotta be the harshest sounding language I've ever heard."

"No, it is not romantic. Not like Russian. More like English." She smiles at me and I go a little gushy inside, like something in there is starting to melt.

| |CHAPTER SIX| |

Sasha's friend Yana, and Marta are waiting on the street in front of their building. They're impossible to miss, I can spot them from a couple of blocks away. Sunrays glint off them in all directions as if they're dressed in mirrored disco balls. As we approach I'm thankful for my sunglasses.

Yana's the shorter one but I don't know it until I look down and see that a good six inches of her is accounted for by the thigh-high patent leather platform boots she's got on. Above those are a couple of inches of fishnet stockings that disappear into a tiny and tattered, sun-bleached pair of cut-off blue jean short shorts. Draped over those is a rhinestone-studded belt. Her belly button is a good six inches or so above that and a ways above that is a thin strip of blinding Mylar that scarcely covers her nipples and low-rise breasts. She's got a big, crooked mouth full of tobacco-stained cattywampus teeth, makeup in colors I associate with baboons in heat and a tangled nest of hair the color and consistency of uncooked thin rice noodles.

It's not that she's ugly or anything, she isn't. Scrub her down, dress her up, clean her teeth or shut her mouth and she'd be a nice, if ordinary looking girl. About a block before we come up to them, Sasha leans over to me and says, "Yana looks like a whore, but she is a very nice girl." If I squint and use my imagination I can sort of see it.

Sasha doesn't have any idea if Marta's a nice girl or not, but she does look like a supermodel, easily one of the most beautiful women I've ever set my eyes on. She's a good two or three perfectly proportioned inches over six feet tall and wearing stylish flats. She's slim with just the right amount of modest curves. There's something about her posture; it's not aggressive, it's not shy, it's just natural, at ease. She looks like someone who fits flawlessly into the world around her. I think she'd look that way anywhere.

Her face is gently rounded with cheekbones just high enough to showcase extraordinary, deep royal blue eyes that sparkle with invitation and charm and intelligence. She's swaddled in something flowing, glistening and white with thin metallic threads. It almost looks like a religious getup and with her looks she could command a following. She's an optical illusion; a woman who looks like everything anyone could want her to be. Somehow the whole package isn't intimidating, which is the biggest surprise of all. When I get to within a few feet of her it's almost as if a tranquilizing perfume is putting me at ease.

Sasha hugs Yana hello, then the two of them turn to us and make introductions. Yana doesn't shake hands so much as stroke my palm while leaning up against me. She might be a nice girl underneath it all but her greeting is pure salesmanship. Marta has a firm, warm handshake and a bright smile. I suggest we pile into a taxi and go to Fernando's.

The driver is pleased. Fernando's is on Hac Sa beach at the far end of Coloane, the second of the two islands that park just off the Macau peninsula. It the biggest possible fare, complete with a chance to charge a premium for crossing the bridge, even though there isn't a toll.

Macau's a small place but it takes nearly a half hour to get where we're going. The taxi dodges through the narrow lanes of the old city, down past the colonnaded shops that line the old main square, around the traffic circle in front of the Lisboa casino and across the bridge to Taipa, the first island.

On the island the road curves past the Hyatt resort and smacks into a blight of construction. High-rise apartments with dubious occupancy prospects are being banged together in the midst of the vegetable fields, duck and shrimp ponds and pig wallows of the small, very old village of Taipa. Parts of the once charming village remain, but they're covered in bamboo scaffolding and spattered with mud and debris.

The road shoots past the ruins of The Duck Pond, once one of the most charming, yet sleazy, nightclubs in Asia; past an always crowded roadside stand that's famous for barbecued duck, and then through what could be the remnants of an ancient city gate, except that it's made of a twelve foot tall, crumbling plaster-of-Paris Coca Cola bottle on the left and a similarly antique orange Fanta bottle on the right.

On the south shore of the island an uninhabited row of colonial houses from 1921, painted in faded yellow, brown and red are lined up behind a grove of undisturbed, large acacia trees. It used to be Taipa's waterfront until the causeway was built to Coloane and the passage between the two islands silted up. It's now just a muddy marsh, sprouting reeds.

On the Coloane side the causeway ends at a small traffic circle that surrounds a smaller park with statues of the stations of the cross. Occasionally there's a pilgrim circling it on kneepads. There's almost always a small offering of fruit, cans of beer or soda pop and burning incense in front of the crucifix, as if to assert that Jesus is just another incarnation, a thinner one, of the Buddha; or perhaps even of *Tin Hau*, the southern Chinese goddess of the sea.

We skid counterclockwise around the shrine and veer off to the left, up a long slope. The road rises gently through thickening woods then curves around and down along the east coast of the island. We finally take a sharp left, into another looming, ugly housing development that seems unlikely to attract many residents, then into a large parking lot set along the edge of a narrow black sand beach on the southern arc of a broad bay.

Fernando's is at the far end of the parking lot. It's a small restaurant with a huge reputation among people who have traveled or lived in Asia. When it first opened it was just one tin-walled room not much bigger than a two-car garage. Fernando himself, a square-jawed Portuguese man from the Azores, runs it.

Back in the 1970s he bought a Volkswagen van and left home. It was still possible to drive from Europe through Africa, the Middle East, Afghanistan, Pakistan, India, Burma and into Southeast Asia without being suicidal or bent on making a political statement. He stopped and got jobs as a cook along the way, mostly in former Portuguese colonies - Mozambique in Africa, Goa in India, Malacca in Malaysia and finally Macau. When he opened his own place it was a Portuguese restaurant, but with quirks that he'd picked up in his travels.

The restaurant is always crowded, so a few years ago he and his brother built a large, airy, brick back room with an outdoor bar alongside it. Most of the year the big windows and doors stay open and overhead fans aid the cross-breezes in cooling the place. In the few cold months the fireplace is lit, but most people at the tables are bundled in sweaters.

The late long lunch crowd hasn't all arrived so we get a table in the back. Sasha's excited about the place, she's heard of it but the few times that men have taken her out it's been to the fancy hotel restaurants. Marta looks as comfortable as I suppose she looks everywhere, even with all eyes in the restaurant on her. Yana looks a little put out. I think she'd rather be in one of the fancy hotels.

I don't care what any of them think. I'm hungry and looking forward to the spicy clams and the barbecued chicken and the roast fish with garlic and even the simple salad. I order two pitchers of sangria. I know we'll need them.

Sasha and Yana have their heads nodded together so I turn to Marta once we're seated.

"Have you been here before?"

"Yes, my friend from England, he take me here."

"You mean Ed? Ed Lyons?"

"Yes, how you know Edward?"

"I work with his brother."

For the first time she looks a little uncomfortable, wary, like she's not sure what's coming next.

"Don't worry, I don't like him either. I think he's a creep."

She smiles. "Creep?"

"A jerk, obnoxious, a fool. I don't know how to explain it."

"I am sorry, my English is no so good."

She turns and taps Sasha on the shoulder and asks her something in Russian. The answer makes her smile again. She turns back to me.

"Yes, I think you are right. Brother Edward is creep."

"Glad we got that straight."

We make small talk for a while, swapping stories. Marta's twenty-three and comes from Vladivostok, Russia's farthest east seaport. It was a closed city until 1992 but the family lived there because her father was a naval engineer. The city is now wide open for business and visitors but tightly controlled by the Russian mafia. This is her first time in Macau and she's been here six months on a one year contract.

I don't want to scare her off so I don't ask too many questions right off the bat. We all make small talk, too much of which consists of Yana babbling about all the fancy restaurants people have taken her to. When the food comes it is, as usual, so good that even Yana cheers up and goes silent with eating.

At some point one of the girls orders two more pitchers of sangrilla. It's plain that there's going to be a nap in my future. I figure I'd better find out what I want from Marta before I hit the point of no return.

She's sucking the tiniest morsels of perfectly cooked meat from some chicken bones, she looks very happy about it and I hate to interrupt.

"Ed's a good guy. How long've you known him?"

She puts down her bones and finishes chewing before she answers. "Five month, he want help me. Ask me marry him."

"Yeah, I heard that. But how can you get out of your contract? I don't think the mafia likes that."

"Manager only want money. We give money, no problem."

"Your manager here, or in Vladivostok?"

"Manager here little money, manager Russia maybe much money. *Nyeh znah-yu*, I no know. Maybe Edward talk manager soon."

"Who's your manager here? Maybe I can find out something."

She's about to tell me when Yana, looking almost panicked, leans across the table and loudly whispers, "*spukkoyny.*"

I guess that means "shut up" because Marta does and the three of them rubber their necks around the room trying to see who might've heard what. Sasha kicks me under the table and mouths the word "later."

After that the three of them speak quietly among themselves in Russian while we polish off the sangrilla then strong espressos that don't really do much to combat the food and booze stupor I'm falling into. I fall asleep in the taxi back to town, waking up only when we pull up in front of my hotel. Sasha wants to come up to my room, the other two head back to their apartment.

| |CHAPTER **SEVEN** | |

Once again we tumble drunkenly onto the bed. We're just awake enough, happy and lethargic, to have quiet, groggy, bellies-full, slow, friendly side-by-side sex since neither of us has enough energy to be on top. It's sweet and cozy, a dessert too good to turn away that we contentedly nibble at with small spoons. We fall asleep immediately after.

When we wake up it's dark and Sasha's in a hurry to get to work. While she dresses I ask her about the Russian "managers" in Macau.

"They are very bad men. Maybe it is not so good of an idea for you to ask questions about them. Too many questions might be dangerous."

"Does Marta work for Gary, your guy?"

"No, Marta's manager is from Vladivostok, he is a crazy man, bad crazy, a murderer. There could be a lot of trouble if you find him and try to talk with him."

"What's his name?"

"No one knows. Everyone calls him 'The Roman'."

"Huh?"

"He has a tattoo, I don't know the word in English, a fighting man with a sword from Rome, ancient Rome."

"A gladiator?"

"Yes. It means he is a very violent man. He enjoys hurting people."

What the hell am I doing? Doing a favor for Fred can't possibly be worth the risk. Who the hell knows what he wants me to do anyhow? I'm not going to try and talk Ed out of being in love with Marta. If he really is, I couldn't do it anyway. But I don't want to see him get hurt and I get the feeling he doesn't know what he's getting into. And Marta, she seems so pure, so perfect, I'm an idiot I know, nothing new in that, but I already feel sort of protective of her.

As I hear Sasha talk, watch her get ready to go, wishing she'd stay and we could enjoy the evening together, a nagging voice is telling me I need to protect her too, and Irina. I'm no fucking knight in shining armor, but there's something churning inside me, egging me on. I'd like to think it's just a bad clam, but I've had food poisoning before and this isn't that.

"Okay, so I don't want to talk with this Roman guy. Do you think Gary'll talk to me? Maybe he'll have some ideas."

"That will be better. I will ask him tonight. Are you coming to the club tonight?"

"I don't know, maybe. You're an expensive friend to have."

"No, I am an expensive lover. I am a friend for free."

"I wish I'd met you some other way."

She touches my face lightly. "I too wish that. But then, probably we never would have met each other at all."

Maybe it's my imagination, but her eyes seem to lose a little life, to harden just a bit when she says that. I sigh and fish five hundred Hong Kong out of my wallet and hand it to her.

"Maybe we can work out a whole weekend discount or something. I can't keep doing this in pieces."

"Tomorrow is Sunday. I do not work on Sunday. If you want, we can go to lunch again tomorrow. Tomorrow we will only be friends. Maybe we will be friends who also have sex, maybe not. I do not know how I will feel."

That makes me smile and shake my head like I need to clear it of something. If this continues I'll have to keep a calendar to track when I need to pay her or not. "If you want, call me when you finish work if I don't see you at the club. You can wake me up, no problem. I'll meet you, or you can come here."

I kiss her on her way out the door.

I'm still full from lunch and a little hazy from the nap so I get up to take a walk and find coffee. Macau is a strange place. Anything that doesn't come to it by truck from China gets to it by boat past Hong Kong, thirty miles to the east. Yet there are some important differences. One is that while it's nearly impossible to get a great cup of coffee in the British colony, it's almost impossible to find a bad one in Macau.

I walk over to *Club Militar* where I park on a sofa and order the usual double espresso and shot of *aguardiente*. I've singed my lips on the coffee and am soothing them in a bath of the brandy when a couple of Portuguese bankers I once tried to interview come into the room. I wave them over and they sit down. They don't bother ordering. The Filipino waiter scurries over with a bottle of expensive cognac and two glasses, all of which he leaves on the table.

The bankers are practically a matched set, although Francisco is blonde and somewhat Nordic looking and Tomas is slightly swarthy and Mediterranean. They are the same size, dressed in immaculate tropical weight linen suits, one in a dark brown the other in a lighter shade. They have pocket hankies poking up in small triangles from their breast pockets that look as if they've been cut from swatches of each other's suits. They have identical gold wristwatches; maybe the bank issues them. They're wearing the same necktie, what the Brits would call a "club tie." I don't know what that means, but it usually seems to involve two or three primary colors in a dull pattern.

I've seen them several times over the past year and they always look as if they are either at, or coming from work. Which is odd as when I first met them I got the distinct impression that they seldom do any work. When I showed up at their office at eleven in the morning for the interview I'd arranged with them, they insisted we immediately leave to "take coffee." We drank espresso and ate small pastries for an hour and a half during which time they told me almost nothing about their business. At twelve-thirty Tomas looked at his watch, grinned and said, "Ah, it is time for lunch."

Lunch was in a private dining room in the fancy Portuguese restaurant at the Lisboa hotel and casino. After we sat down and the attractive Filipina waitress in a low-cut showbiz version of Portuguese native costume had tucked our napkins onto our laps, a tuxedoed wine steward poured us overly large snifters of something pungent from a crystal decanter.

While we drank, Francisco discussed wine with the sommelier. When the wine steward left I thought I could sneak in some interview questions. The bankers deflected them as easily as a casual backhand by a tennis pro toying with a novice.

"Really Mr. Sharp, work? It is so dull. We are bankers. People give us their money and then we give it back to them, trying to keep as much of it as we can for ourselves. Sometimes we give them our money and they pay us for it. What else is there to say?"

I can't recall which of them said that, but it was as good an explanation of banking as any I could come up with. At that point I gave in to the colonial Portuguese way of work. We had two bottles of wine before our food came and three more with lunch. Then, well-stuffed and thoroughly sloshed, we adjourned to another private room where we sat in three plush supple leather chairs.

Three pretty Filipinas in some kind of ethnic déshabillé paraded in carrying three highly polished silver trays, each with a glass of blood red port and a large cigar. They kneeled in front of us to present our drinks, then once we'd taken our glasses they put down the trays to prepare our smokes.

Keeping her eyes on mine the whole time, the woman in front of me delicately, like she was peeling the finest of silk stockings off smooth long legs, removed the wrapper. When the rich brown cylinder was naked, she caressed it lightly with her fingertips, then progressed to gently rolling it between her palms while holding it up to her bright red lips and softly blowing on it.

I snuck a look at my hosts. They were slumped in their seats, their legs spread out on either side of the women between their knees. I returned my attention to the spectacle in front of me.

The young woman smiled up at me and flicked just a little at her lower lip with her tongue. She reached to bring my hand holding the glass of port up to her lips. She took a tiny sip and I could see that she was swishing it around. She opened her mouth wide and slowly slid the cigar deep into it, never taking her eyes off mine and being careful to leave out the end I would put my lips on. She breathed port fumes onto the rich roll of tobacco, then just barely closed her lips around it and glided it back out. It glistened, ever so slightly.

She held the cigar up in front of her and breathed a little more on it. Then she reached into a small bag at her side and brought out a shiny silver snipper that fit snugly over the closed end of the tube. She rocked up onto her haunches to hold it closer for my inspection. Then with a quick, violent snap of her fingers she sliced the end neatly off.

She must've put it into my mouth and lit it, but I was in too much of a daze to notice. I don't even like the things. But sometimes a cigar really is more than just a cigar.

I've never bothered trying to interview them since, but sometimes we meet up for drinks or a meal.

The bankers and I greet each other. Tomas takes out a fat, almost black cigar. "Do you mind if I smoke?"

"No, go ahead, just so long as you don't have oral sex with it."

He laughs. "Ah yes, we must have lunch again someday soon."

"So how's the banking business?"

"It is still good for now. But in four years, who knows?"

Macau will go back to Chinese rule in 1999. "Yeah, what are you guys gonna do then?"

They both shrug their shoulders. Tomas lights up. Francisco looks into his glass, then up at me. "How is the magazine business? Are you here for work or pleasure?"

"Pleasure of course, it's always pleasure here. You two taught me that. Maybe there's something you can help me with though."

They look at each other as if trying to decide which of them is going to say "no." Francisco gets the honor.

"Mr. Sharp, Ray, please, you know we were so happy that you decided not to write the article about our bank. We have our business, but we are a private firm. Let us simply enjoy some drinks."

"No, don't worry, it's got nothing to do with that. I'm just trying to find out some stuff for a guy I work with and it's got nothing to do with your bank. What do you know about the Russian girls in Macau?"

They exchange broad grins. Tomas leans toward me and waves his cigar in the air. "Ah, they have improved the situation very much in Macau. Some of them are truly beautiful and they are very loving. Greedy, yes, but not so experienced that it takes very much to satisfy them. We can take you to a very good club and introduce you."

"It's a kind offer, thanks, but I already have a Russian girlfriend and know some others. What I meant was, what do you know about the business end of it? How do they get here? What are the contracts like? Who's in charge? That sort of thing."

Tomas leans back into his chair. "Oh, that, always the journalist. We do not know much. We do not care to know much. Why would we want to question our good fortune?"

Francisco wants to know why I want to know and I tell him. He considers it for a long minute before speaking.

"My brother-in-law is a policeman. He has told me a little about this. I will tell you what I know, but Ray, you must be careful, these are serious, very serious, men.

"There are three Russians in Macau who control all the women. This man Gary you mention is the best of them. He has women from Moscow, but also from the Baltic states and some of the other eastern European countries. He is a businessman and will listen to reason. He wants his girls to be happy, because then they work better and everybody makes more money. Of course he is mafia and is sometimes violent, but he is from what you might call the new school. He is often at the nightclub in the Lisboa.

"I have never seen the man Gaspar. I have heard that he is from Uzbekistan, or perhaps Turkmenistan. He has some girls but not many. He is mostly interested in drugs and guns.

"The Roman is the most dangerous of all. He is from Vladivostok. People say that he is crazy. His women are slaves. They work until he tells them they can stop and they give him all their money. There are rumors that he has killed several women as a warning to the others to do what he tells them. He has many tattoos. They all mean different things but I don't know what. He spends most of his time at the Starlight nightclub. His girls work there, but when he gets angry with them he sends them to work in a massage parlor near the border, one of those ones with the big window and the girls with numbers behind it."

"Sounds like I picked the wrong guy's girlfriend to try and help out."

"Some of The Roman's girls are very very beautiful, the most beautiful girls in Macau, but we don't go with them. They are desperate. He is crazy. There are other girls who are not so much trouble."

I order us another round of drinks and we talk about less scary things. When they get up to go they invite me along with them to the Darling Sauna. It's the best of the Thai massage parlors in town and it's tempting, but I don't like going to those sorts of places in groups, so I decline.

| |CHAPTER **EIGHT** | |

The Starlight nightclub is in the same building as the Darling, so I catch a ride with Francisco and Tomas. They both warn me again to steer clear of The Roman and that it might be smart to avoid his girls as well. I assure them I just want a look.

The elevator lets me off at the fourth floor entrance. It's tacky and down market compared with the Lisboa nightclub. The red carpet needs cleaning, the mirrors need polishing and instead of little, twinkling golden lights, a string of ugly, flickering large-bulbed red and green lights droops from nails pounded in around the door. I ring a bell and stand in front of the peephole.

After a minute I'm thinking nobody's home so I ring again. Another minute passes before the door opens just enough for me to pass through. I do and it closes behind me. I can't see a thing in the dark. Then I can't see a thing because of the bright light that points first into my eyes and then takes a quick trip around my body. I sense someone big behind it.

"I am apology. We have problem with light in entrance. Please to come with me." It's a deep, guttural, but female voice. A large hand takes rough hold of my left shoulder and guides me forward to an arched doorway that is dimly lit around the edges. We move through it into a large room and I can just make out booths with tables along the sides. Candles in thick, pocked red glass domes flicker in the alcoves. I think there is some sort of small dance floor and stage at the far end; more red and green bulbs are draped in a pattern that hints at it.

The hand prods me into one of the booths. I sit and can just make out the outline of the large person looming over me in the dark.

The whole thing makes me nervous. Sometimes I get talky at times like this. "I don't know, maybe I oughta come back when the lights are on, or at least a few more of them are working. I can't see what's going on. If I get a hostess I won't even be able to see how she looks. I don't do well in caves."

There's a rumbling chuckle from somewhere up near the low ceiling. "Please to wait one minute. I bring light."

I sense more than see my large guide move away and I sit in the dark wondering what in the hell I've gotten myself into. I could use a drink, a stiff one, and a miner's helmet with a fresh battery. I've just about figured that I might be able to find my way out by keeping my right hand on the wall when the big person comes back with the flashlight and two small people with candles.

The small ones are Chinese and I can make out enough of them to see that they're women and dressed in matching red satin *cheongsams*. The big one, who I still can't see any more than the outline of, towers over them by at least a foot and a half. The flashlight fires briefly at me again and while I flinch from it the two Chinese girls put their candles down on the table then move in on me with hot, moist face and hand towels, a small bowl of those dried, horseradish hot Japanese green peas and a drink menu. I ask for a double vodka on the rocks and they slip away. The big one's still there, in the dark somewhere.

"Can I borrow your flashlight for a moment please?"

It feels like a club in my hand and I have to grope around to make sure I'm pointing the business end of it away from me. I snap it on and the beam of light shoots straight out into a highly-polished, broad stainless steel stud that pierces the flesh at the top of a belly button. It shines brightly back at me. The navel is set on a rock hard, rippled stomach. Just above the stud is a tattooed semicircle with something radiating out along its edges, an animal that looks like a reindeer inside it and the Russian alphabet initials "СЕВЕР." I move the beam up and it takes in two large, conical, rock solid breasts defying gravity underneath a loose, narrow stretch of shiny black silk.

I figure at this point I may as well take inventory so I move the light slowly left and right as it heads upward. She has incredibly muscular arms and on her right bicep is another tattoo. This one is of a voluptuous woman with wild red hair, wearing knee-high boots with stockings and a garter belt, holding a sword stabbed through three hearts that are dripping blood.

On her left bicep is a young woman with long black hair cascading over her naked breasts, a finger held up to her lips. I move the light up and over a pair of burly wrestler's shoulders. She's got a spiked, leather dog collar around a thick heavily muscled neck.

Finally I look far up and into a pair of narrowed, light-gray lupine eyes above a large crooked nose that's been knocked around the block more than just a few times in fights. She's smiling with thin, firm set lips painted glossy black, from behind which glint a couple of broad teeth as bright as the reflection off her navel.

I might as well take in the hairdo. It's platinum blonde, about two inches long and spiking straight up and hard enough to impale your hand if you were to pat her on the head. Then again, you'd need a stepladder to get high enough to touch her head. At least I would; and I'm average height.

She stretches out a hand that's a whole lot bigger than one of mine and snatches away the flashlight. "*Ebi tvoyu mat'!*" she spits at me. I don't know what it means but I'm sure it's no more polite than the tour I just took of her body. So I guess we're even. I've moved the two candles to the edge of the table and am beginning to see some details.

I stick out my hand to shake. "Sorry. Ray. What's yours?"

"*Boorya.*" Her name drops like a big hunk of broken marble from her mouth. I've never seen anyone like her. She's at least six-foot three or four and carved from two hundred-plus pounds of stone. Having seen her stomach, arms and shoulders, I can almost believe the breasts are real. She's like the Bride of Frankenstein after hitting the gym five or six hours a day for a couple of years. She'd be kind of sexy if I was into that sort of thing.

I'm trying to figure out what to say next when one of the Chinese girls comes back with my whisky. I motion for her to stick around a moment. I lift my drink at Boorya, throw it back quick and slam the glass on the table. I look up at the giantess. "Uh, can I buy you a drink?"

"*Nyet.* You talking *mamasan.*" I expect to hear thunder when she turns and leaves but she just melts into the dark. I order another drink, another double.

The faint outline of a *mamasan* shows up just after my drink does. She's a lot wider than she ought to be and when I wave one of the candles in front of her I can see it's because she's attached to a hostess on each arm.

"Mister, you want Russian girl or Chinese girl?"

I pick the Russian girl. The *mamasan* and the other girl turn and leave. I feel sharp fingernails poking me in the side. "Please to move seat. I want sit down."

The voice sounds familiar so once she's settled and the nails are raking high on my inner thigh I hold a candle up to her face. It's Yana; Sasha's friend. She looks stoned. Stoned enough not to recognize me even though it's no more than seven or so hours since we had lunch.

"Yana, hi, it's so dark I didn't recognize you at first. It's Ray. How are you?"

She picks up the other candle and holds it to my face. "Oh, yes. Where Sasha? You no boyfriend Sasha?" Her hand has insinuated itself onto my lap. I guess she isn't really all that concerned about my relationship with Sasha.

I remove her hand and hold onto it on the cushion between us. "I just wanted to see this place. Let's talk for a little while. What do you want to drink?"

She wants some sort of champagne cocktail. I hold a candle up to the menu to make sure that it won't be ruinously expensive. It's not too much more than the light dinner I haven't had so I order two. I know she'll drink them fast.

"Who's that gigantic Russian woman at the front door?"

"Oh, you meet Storm?"

"I thought her name was Boorya, or something like that."

"Yes, B*oorya*, same Storm, like rain, like electric and bomb in sky."

"What's she do around here? She isn't a hostess or a *mamasan* or anything."

"No, she guard, do work for boss, Roman."

"Is he here? Not that I could see him if he is, but what's he look like?"

"*Nyeh znah-yu.* I don't know. Maybe in V.I.P. room. You no talk him."

"No, yes I know. I'm just curious is all."

"No curious. No good. You want fucking?"

I do, but not with Yana. "No. I'm sorry, I can't. I have to meet Sasha later."

She isn't happy about that. "Why you come here you no want fucking? You boyfriend Sasha. You buy me drink, no take me hotel. Now, you give me small money, go away, go hotel wait Sasha."

I can see her point. If I'm not going to take her out and pay her for sex I ought to get out of the way. I want to get the hell out of here anyway, the place gives me the creeps. I give her a hundred bucks, about twelve-fifty U.S., for her time. It's less than she wants, but at least she's polite enough to just say "thanks."

| |CHAPTER **NINE** | |

Storm isn't on the door as I leave. I'm hoping to get a look at her in the light but I guess that will have to wait for another time. In the hallway with the flickering bulbs I pause to consider what's next. I could go to the Darling. A bath, a massage and sex from an attractive Thai woman wouldn't be the worst thing that could happen to me. But I'm kind of tired and there's a chance Sasha will come to the hotel later. So that's where I go.

It's a nice enough night for a walk so long as I don't become an innocent bystander. There's been a turf war underway in Macau for the past year. More than a dozen people have been shot, stabbed or blown up. A couple of different Chinese Triad gangs are vying with the biggest gang of all – the Chinese People's Liberation Army – for control of drugs, non-Russian prostitution, product counterfeiting, loan-sharking and pole position if new gambling licenses ever become available.

Macau has long had a hard-earned reputation for vice and sleaze. For some of us that's part of its charm. Violence is something new and unwelcome. I'm more cautious than I used to be when I'm on the street. I pick up my pace toward alcoves or corners when I see or hear a small swarm of buzzing motorbikes headed my way. I try to be more aware of my surroundings. But I am not going to keep off the streets. I like walking around Macau. I won't let the bad guys take that away from me.

I get to the Lisboa and consider going up to the nightclub to see if Sasha's there, but I don't want to spend the extra money. I do go in and wander around in the pandemonium for a little while, soaking up the atmosphere.

I take the escalator to the V.I.P. gambling room on the third floor and watch the action at a blackjack table. A young Thai man in an Armani suit is betting ten thousand dollar chips. That's one thousand two hundred and eighty U.S. dollars for each small disk of black and gold shellac. He casually pushes forward a stack of at least ten at a time to play on each hand. He's flanked by twins; Thai women surgically enhanced to Playboy magazine specifications and dressed to show it off. Behind him are two bodyguards, also in Armani and wearing mirrored sunglasses. They each hold a briefcase and a suitcase and slowly, almost mechanically swivel their heads back and forth.

While I watch I keep track as best I can. In about a half hour the young Thai man loses around two hundred and fifty thousand U.S. dollars. He doesn't lose his smile. The twins look bored. He twists his head around and says something softly to one of the bodyguards.

The bodyguard walks to the cashier's cage, opens his suitcase and hands over several paper-strapped bricks of crisp American notes for which he receives a large tray of more black and gold chips. It takes a bit of a balancing act for him to get back to the table without spilling the chips or letting go of the suitcase or brief-case. The other guard keeps his eyes glued to him the whole way.

There's only so much of this I can stomach. You could feed a whole Thai village for a year and have money left to wire it for electricity with the money this guy's throwing away on one hand of blackjack. Where are the communists when you need them?

They sure aren't across the border. At the next table over, a group of three party functionaries from China have heavily made-up Russian girls by their sides and their own stacks of chips in front of them. They're easily recognizable from their identical, ill-fitting dark suits and bad haircuts. They have an arrogant, pos-sessive look to them. I know it's my imagination. Even if I could read their minds I don't understand Mandarin. But I imagine that I can see them thinking, 'in four years this is all gonna be ours.'

I head downstairs to settle my digestion with a large, hot bowl of wonton noodle soup with barbecued pork in the coffee shop.

I sit at the counter and amuse myself trying to make the same slurping sounds the locals do when they cool their noodles on the way past their lips. I'm bad at it and my lips and tongue are getting burnt. A narrow man with a long face and large round glasses sits down a couple of stools away and orders a cup of coffee. He takes in the sight and sound of my efforts with a bemused expression, and then slowly shakes his head.

"You'll never get the hang of it, I know. I tried. I couldn't either."

He's American, with an easy manner. He sticks out a hand for me to shake. "Bill Warner."

I hand him mine. "Ray Sharp."

"You a tourist?"

"Isn't everybody here? I live in Hong Kong."

"You do look a little familiar. You resting up between the tables or the girls?"

"I just came down from watching the action in the V.I.P. room. It bothered my stomach. Thought some noodles might settle it."

"I know the feeling. I like it here, but there's plenty about the place I don't."

"You got that straight. Whaddaya do in Hong Kong?"

"I'm with the consulate, the ag department."

Now that, I think, is interesting. Hong Kong doesn't have a whole lot of agriculture. Across the border in Guangdong Province they do, but they have their own U.S. agricultural department in the consulate in Guangzhou.

"I hear you've got nearly twenty people in your department in Hong Kong. What's with that?"

"That's where I recognize you from. I've seen you at the F.C.C. You're a journalist."

"Guilty as charged. Deputy editor of *Asian Industry*, I guess that passes for journalism in these parts."

"Well then, you tell me. I take it you've heard all the rumors."

"I know better than to expect you to tell me if you guys are spooks or not, so I'm not gonna ask."

"I just got back from Pakistan. We've got a food promotion there."

What sort?"

"Eggs."

"Pakistani hens don't lay?"

"Ours are better."

"You've got a weird job."

"Yeah, I guess you could say that. So what're you doing here?"

"Mostly the usual. Walking around, lunch at Fernando's, a little *cau-loi*, 'chasing girls' as the locals would call it."

"Ah, the expat life. Ain't it grand?"

"I like it. How long you been in Hong Kong?"

"A little over a year. Before this I was in Moscow. This is a lot better."

"Oh yeah? I'm also here doing a favor for a colleague. What do you know about Russian gangsters?"

"Some. Why?"

I tell him.

"Sounds like you ought to be careful. I'd keep my nose out of it if I were you. One of the things I do know is that these guys play rough. Really rough."

"I keep hearing that."

"For good reason." He looks genuinely concerned but it might just be that he doesn't want the consulate to have to deal with any sort of mess I might make or get into.

"You know anything about tattoos?"

"Why?"

I'd read somewhere that Russian gangsters' tattoos have specific meanings. I describe Storm to him.

"She sounds like a sweetheart. Think I'll stay away from the Starlight."

"Any idea what they mean?"

"Okay, maybe this'll help scare you off. The one with the letters "CEBEP" means that she was in prison in the north, Siberia. That means she's tough, tougher than anyone you've probably ever met. The one with the sword and the hearts means that she's killed three men, one for each heart. She'll get more put on when she kills more. The other one means she can keep a secret. You don't want to mess with her or anyone she hangs out with."

"She works for someone called The Roman."

"Oh fuck. You really don't want to mess with him. Just keep away from there. No one can help you if you get those people mad at you."

We chat about other things for a little while longer, and then swap business cards. "Call me if you want to do any stories about American agriculture and Asia."

"Yeah, like eggs in Pakistan, or maybe Afghanistan."

"Don't knock it, eggs are good food and we've got the best in the world."

"I'll keep that in mind."

I'm tired and a little woozy. I walk back to my hotel, crawl into bed and go to sleep.

| | CHAPTER **TEN** | |

But it's a crummy night for sleep. I'm restless, tossing and turning. I look out across the room at one point and there's this guy I see sometimes. He looks a little like me. I don't know who the hell he is, or if I'm dreaming when I see him or hallucinating from a malaria recurrence, or if I'm going nuts or what. He's just there sometimes and we talk. It doesn't really matter how or why he's there. He seems real enough at the time.

"What was all that stuff about eggs?"

"You mean Bill at the coffee shop. I think he's a spy, C.I.A. We weren't really talking about eggs."

"So what the hell were you talking about?"

"I'm not sure. It's probably better that I don't know. Maybe weapons, something like that."

"What about that Amazon in the nightclub? I didn't know they made women that way. Must be something new; diet or chemicals or breeding or something."

"Yeah, she's pretty scary. You heard what Bill said about her didn't you?"

"They can be ugly customers those Russians."

"What makes you say that?"

"You've heard the stories. That's where your family came from. Why d'ya think they left?"

"There isn't a pogrom going on or anything, these are just a bunch of gangsters protecting their territory. There's people like that everywhere."

"Maybe, but I've never seen anyone who scared me as much as that Storm babe. You oughta listen to what everybody's been telling you and stay out of it. You don't even like Fred, you can't be doing this for him."

"I'm not."

"What're you doing then?"

"Not much so far, just trying to find out if Ed's in any trouble or if I can help keep him out of trouble. You know, I'm also kind of curious, I wanna know what's going on. This stuff's interesting to me."

"Your funeral."

"I hope not."

There's a knock at the door. I shake my head to clear it and the guy's gone. I wrap the blanket around me and get up to answer. It's Sasha, standing unevenly in the doorway.

"It is late. I worry you are asleep. But no, I hear you talking. Who are you talking to?"

I stand aside to let her in. "No one, myself, just thinking out loud."

She moves up close to me, pushing the door shut with one hand and pulling the blanket off me with the other. She reaches down and strokes me between the legs. "You been thinking about me?"

She's slurring her words slightly and I'm still a little out of it from just waking up. I resist for a little, consider pushing her away, but she's persistent with her hands, mumbling low in Russian, her lips are hungry on mine and it does feel really good, and before long I shift gears.

"I am now."

I wake up fast. It doesn't take long for either of us. It's only a few minutes before we're lying on the bed catching our breath, side by side. It would be time for a smoke. If we smoked.

"How was your night at work?"

She gives me a look that says she wants to make sure I'm joking before she answers. "All Chinese men. They do nothing but drink too much cognac and play a stupid finger counting and shouting game. I don't know why they want me to sit with them. Me and two other girls. We sit, talk, drink, nothing more. When they go they give me a tip, not too small, not too big. It's okay."

I don't get it. If she just sits around with strange guys all night, it's gotta be boring. But I guess it's better than having to fuck them. But then the money's not so good. I think I'd probably hate men if I were her. Luckily I'm not.

It seemed like she really wanted to fuck me when she got here tonight. I'm pretty sure she wasn't faking that. I like her. I like her more, the more time I spend with her. I want her to like me too. Maybe it's the hour, my head's spinning a little, I'm not sure what's got into me but I'm feeling insecure. It's stupid. I don't like it.

"Can I ask you something serious?"

"Okay, if I don't want, I won't answer."

"I'm glad you're here. I'm really happy that I met you. But why are you here now? I don't think it's just the money? I hope not. What else? I won't be insulted, really, I just want to know."

Sasha gets a serious look on her face and moves up to prop herself, sitting against a pillow at the head of the bed. I roll onto my stomach and look up at her.

"I also am happy to meet you. Is that strange? I do not know. Maybe. Of course, I want to be honest, I also want money. It is a little confusing maybe. In Macau I am lonely. I have no family, my friends here are only because we are all prostitutes. When I am home, they probably would not be my friends. They only talk about the clubs, the money, shopping, one man is handsome, one man is ugly. It is boring.

"I think maybe you are also sometimes lonely. You are a nice man, you talk to me with respect. We talk about things I do not talk with other people about for all the time I am here. You ask me about my life. And you are a friend of Irina. I do not see her for more than two years, but she is like a sister for me. So strange maybe, you and I making love. In Russia this would be very strange, not possible maybe. But here, now, when I am with you I am not lonely. I feel a little more close to Irina."

It's simpler just paying someone for sex. That's because that's not really what you're paying for. You're paying them to go away afterwards and to not talk too much when you're with them. But that's a whole lot less interesting than what's going on here, between Sasha and me. I don't know what to say. I scoot up a little and kiss my way from her left knee to her thigh to her crotch where I nestle in and gently work on her with my lips and my tongue until she shudders, squeezes me hard around the ears, then relaxes.

Later, I tell her about my night and Storm and her mood goes dark. She listens, nodding.

"She is a very bad woman. It is not good that you talked to her. Already she has killed three men, maybe more. She kills women too. Maybe Yana will have trouble because you go there."

"It should be fine. I was like any customer. I didn't ask questions about Marta or anything. I didn't ask to see Yana; they brought her to me. They just thought I was a regular customer."

"Maybe Yana will tell The Roman or Storm about lunch, about you, about Marta. I don't know, but maybe this is very bad, maybe it is very dangerous."

"Why would Yana do that?"

"She is maybe frightened. These are very bad people, very nervous people. If they think maybe Yana lies to them or does not tell them something, they will be very angry."

"What can I do now?"

"Nothing, do nothing. Maybe it will be no problem. But now there is nothing you can do."

"Did you talk to Gary?"

"Yes. He will take coffee with you in the afternoon."

"Good, but what'll we do until then?"

"I go to sleep. You do what you want. Wake me up at eleven, okay?"

Sasha wiggles out of the clothes she still has on, slithers under the sheet and is softly snoring within no more than a minute or two. It's still not light out so I close the curtains and snuggle in next to her.

| |CHAPTER **ELEVEN** | |

The phone blasts us awake at eleven. It takes another half hour or so to get out of bed and into the shower. While we're getting dressed I ask if there's anything I should know about Gary before I meet him. Is there anything I should be careful about saying, or not saying?

"Remember, he is not a good man. He loves only money. If he thinks you can help him, maybe he can make more money, he will help you. If not, he is not interested. If he thinks you will cause trouble for him, if maybe you will cost him money, he can be dangerous. Not so dangerous as The Roman, but still dangerous."

She also doesn't want me to let on that I met her through a mutual friend. If he asks, I'm supposed to say we just met at the Lisboa.

As we're about to leave the room I get out my wallet. I don't know if I owe Sasha for both last night when she showed up and again this morning. I figure I'll just fork over what I can and see what she says. I'm still uncertain about the whole thing.

She puts her hand on mine and stops me from taking out any money. "It is Sunday, remember? Today I am not working."

I'm not about to argue. We kiss instead. That's a lot better.

Sasha's ravenous and asks if we can go to one of the big, silly buffet brunches that are one of the specialties of hotels in Asia. The Mandarin, which isn't too far from where we are going to meet Gary, has one of the biggest.

We get a table overlooking an inlet off the main channel. It's thick with construction debris and river silt. Luckily the windows are good, thick glass and we can't smell the water. I'm not hungry and the hotel makes a tidy profit off me when all I have is a roll, a couple Chinese dumplings, a piece of pineapple and coffee. Sasha's appetite evens things out. She eats slowly but steadily, making several trips to and from the food stations, coming back each time with two fully loaded plates.

She sees me raise my eyebrows when she returns from her second foray. "I did not eat last night. This morning I am very hungry."

"You're going to add some more curves."

She smiles. "I think you like my curves."

"I do. Enjoy yourself." I snatch a strip of bacon from one of her plates and she sticks her tongue out at me. She puts down her fork and looks at me.

"Do you like me?" It sounds insecure. I smile. I'm glad I'm not the only one.

"Yes." And I do. She's funny, smart, and comfortable to be with. There isn't the sort of explosive chemistry I have with Irina, but Sasha is someone I want to be friends with, maybe more than just friends with.

It's Sunday and whatever it is we've got is good enough for me, for now.

"What about Irina?"

"I explained about Irina. We love each other, but we are also free."

She smiles and takes my hand. "Today we are friends. Next time we meet, we will see. Friends, yes. Maybe something different too, I don't know. What will you tell Irina?"

"I guess I'll tell her everything. She'll ask."

"Yes, she always wants to know everything. Are you sure it is no problem?"

"I don't think so. I'll find out. I'll let you know."

She applies herself back to her plate. By the time she's done we have ten minutes to get to our meeting with Gary. Sasha's told me that he's sometimes late, but it isn't okay with him if whoever's he's meeting is late.

It's a short taxi ride to the Italian café that's across from the ferry pier. We've just settled into our seats, I've ordered my usual two single espressos and Sasha's ordered a cappuccino and a canoli, when Marcello Mastroianni comes up the stairs and walks into the place. Or maybe it's his twin brother. The woman who owns the café comes out from behind the deli counter to fawn all over him.

Sasha leans over to me. "It is Gary."

On closer inspection, he might be the Italian actor's twin, but they were separated at birth and he was raised in Russia. He's wearing a tailor-made suit, but the cut and fit is just slightly imperfect, the cloth just a notch below top. His shoes are good leather, expensive, well shined, but just a bit too bulky, with soles a touch too thick. His watch is a little too sparkly and large. There is a faint, high-starch diet puffiness to his face and not enough tan. His hair's in a buzz cut, but just a shade uneven.

He's also younger than Marcello Mastroianni is these days. I didn't really think he's him, but if he ever moves to Hollywood he can get work with one of those agencies that hires out movie star doubles.

Gary glides over to our table and we get up to greet him. He doesn't look at Sasha but stops to look me over before extending a hand to shake. I hand him mine.

"I'm Ray. Thanks very much for agreeing to talk with me."

He doesn't smile or speak, just grips my hand to the edge of pain, releases it, sits down and shouts to the waitress to bring him an espresso. He pushes his jacket sleeves up above his elbows and on his right forearm there's a tattoo of a naked woman holding an apple with a snake wrapped around her. I know it means something, something no doubt to do with Adam and Eve. I like to think it means he's been corrupted. But then, according to the story, haven't we all?

Gary looks at me with a slight scowl, turns to Sasha and says something fast in Russian to which she replies "*Nyet.*"

Gary turns to me again. "Speak what you want, slowly. But not so slowly I think you think I am stupid. Is very big mistake to think I am stupid."

I can't figure out why he would think I'd take him for stupid. Maybe he's used to people thinking that, in which case maybe he really is stupid. I've never heard of an insecure pimp or gangster before, but I guess they're human too.

"Did Sasha tell you what I wanted to talk to you about?"

"You tell me."

"The brother of a man I work with is in love with one of The Roman's girls. She works at the Starlight. He wants to marry her. He wants to buy her out of her contract. I've told him I don't think it's a good idea but he insists that I find out if it's possible, how to do it and I guess about how much it would cost."

"You meet this girl?"

"Yes, her name is Marta."

"I know her. She is most beautiful girl of The Roman. He will no want let her go."

"Is there any way? How much money do you think he'd want?"

"Too much money. Maybe no money. She very valuable. Try to take her, maybe The Roman kill her, maybe only sell her to Arab or Chinese if in good mood. Maybe kill your friend too. Tell friend, fall love with other girl."

"What kind of money are we talking about?"

"For this girl, a lot money, maybe one, maybe two hundred thousand U.S."

"What if she goes back to Russia when her contract is finished, my friend sends her money, then a year later they get together."

"Maybe that way, maybe no. The Roman very cruel man. Once girl work for him, she belong to him, maybe always. Your friend try take her away, he *pizdepropashchinsk*, fucking disappear."

It all sounds clear to me. Too clear. I'll do what I can to scare off Edward but I can't think of anything else to do. Gary looks me over while I'm digesting what he's had to say.

"Why you ask Sasha at Lisboa?"

It figures that he'd know everything. The *mamasan* must've told him. I need to come up with something.

"A friend told me I might like her. He'd met her before."

"What friend?"

"Just a guy from Hong Kong. He comes here a lot. I don't think he took her out, just saw her when she was with some other guy." I have no idea if he believes me or not. For Sasha's sake I hope he does. He might be the nicest Russian mobster in town, but he still makes me nervous.

Sasha starts to say something and he glares at her. "*Zatkneesb blyad.*" He spits out at her and I know it's insulting from the way she flinches. I don't know if there's anything I can or should do about it.

"*Nichivo.*" She turns to me. "Nothing, nothing important."

Gary stands up and moves over to grab me by the shoulder, hard. He grips me on the chin with his other hand and yanks my face up to look at him. "*Ebi tvoyu mat'!* You be quiet, careful, no more questions. You no say nothing to The Roman, *ni khuya.* You make him be angry and he *poshol v pizdu*, then you make big *upastpizdanut'sya.*"

He pats me hard on the cheek then lets my head go. He leans toward Sasha. "You tell him what I say. Tell him true, no change bad words." He rocks back on his heels and looks at her to see if she'll do what he says.

I have an idea of what he said; at least I've got the gist of it. "I understand. I don't need Sasha to translate."

He doesn't even turn to look at me. "You shut mouth, she tell you."

Sasha looks straight ahead, not at me, at somewhere in between us. "He said, 'fuck your mother.' Do not talk to The Roman, 'say no fucking thing to him.' If you make The Roman mad he will kill you, he will send you back into your mother and you will be dead. The way he said it was, 'you will fall back into your mother's pussy.' It is a very bad way to say this, sometimes Russian language can be very dirty. When he talks like this it is because he is being very serious."

Gary smiles, turns back to me, pats me hard on the cheek again and walks quickly out. Sasha slumps in her chair, maybe it's with relief, maybe something else. I move over to sit closer. I reach out and massage her shoulder. She looks up.

"He's the nicest bad guy in town? Now I really don't want to meet The Roman. What'd he say to you?"

"When? You heard it already."

"No, earlier. You started to say something and he said something nasty, I could tell from the way you looked."

"He told me to shut up. He called me a whore."

I keep quiet and squeeze harder on her shoulder.

"I know I am a whore. Maybe you are not really my friend. I am only a whore. Maybe I have no friends, only customers, only men who want sex."

I can't squeeze her shoulders any harder so I put my arms around her. I like Sasha. I'd like her even if I couldn't have sex with her. I don't know what the hell to do other than hold onto her. There are things about her, things between us that I'll never be able to figure out.

Sasha looks up at me, sniffling. "You like me?"

"Yes, you know I do. I told you, we don't have to have sex, we can just be friends if you want."

"I don't know. You go back to Hong Kong today?"

"Yeah, I've got to go back to work tomorrow. I can come back next weekend."

"Will you call me?"

"Yeah, I'll call during the week and I'll give you my number."

I still have time before my ferry so I take Sasha home in a taxi. I'm going to just drop her off but she insists that I come up to her apartment for a few minutes. Her roommates aren't home. By now she's laughing and teasing, worn out and punchy from the weekend and her upset over Gary having called her a "whore."

"It is still Sunday and I am not working." She takes off her clothes, gets up on her bed on all fours and smiles at me over her shoulder. "Take off your clothes, hurry, I want to make love fast. Then you go to the ferry."

Once again I'm the last one on board.

| |CHAPTER **TWELVE** | |

Fred's trying hard to seem casual as he stops by my desk. I'm no more than half a cup of coffee into Monday morning and having trouble paying attention to the politics of agricultural subsidies in Taiwan. I've got to get it edited in the next hour or so. I wave him off and suggest we go out for a cup of coffee when I'm done. He looks miffed but there's nothing he can do about it.

There's not a lot I can do to help his brother either. I'll try to scare him off, but love makes people stupid. It's happened to me. Why should Ed be any different?

I finally give up trying to make the article anything more than merely competent. We've got something over one hundred thousand readers and my best guess is that maybe a dozen of them are going to bother reading about Taiwanese farmers anyway. I get up and go to Fred's cubicle.

"Hey, ready for that coffee?"

"Yes, certainly."

We head downstairs and across the street to a small hotel coffee shop. I order something weak, bitter and gray that they call espresso. It makes me wish I was back in Macau. Fred wants tea and grimaces but bears it when he discovers they only have Chinese tea. He gets right to the point.

"What did you discover?"

"Ed's in love with the wrong girl, that's for sure."

"Yes, we know that already. What can be done about it?"

"If you want, I'll talk to him. I doubt he understands how bad, how dangerous the people she's involved with really are."

"What does he expect, she's a common prostitute."

"Her pimp, more her owner really, is a guy called The Roman. Everyone's afraid of him. He's known for being violent. He's probably killed a few people, some of his own girls and some others. Marta's his most beautiful girl, his most valuable, he won't just let her go."

"This is all very distasteful."

"'Distasteful' is way too mild a word for what this is. The Roman makes a lot of money off his girls and part of it is that they're afraid to leave him. A few people told me that if he gets mad at one of them he might kill her, or if she's lucky he'll just sell her to a Chinese or Arab man or a brothel and she'll disappear."

"But slavery is illegal. This is outrageous."

"So're drugs. You work for a business magazine; you know how it goes. If there's a market, someone's gonna pander to it. Doesn't matter what it is."

"It is stupid and embarrassing that Edward thinks he is in love with one of these girls. But why should he be in any danger? If this

Roman person is a businessman, surely he will be satisfied with a large amount of money. There must be many of these degenerate women who can replace her."

"He might, it depends on his mood. The guy's a monster though and you might say that clouds his thinking. It's one thing if he's mad at one of his girls and decides for himself to sell her, it's another if someone wants her for himself and wants to buy her. He might decide to make a point and your brother and his girlfriend could end up dead."

"Edward must be dissuaded. He won't listen to me. We don't really talk. Perhaps he will listen to you, could you please try to speak with him?"

"Look, Fred, I doubt I'll be able to talk him out of anything. I'll let him know what I found out, and I won't pull any punches about how ugly and dangerous it could get, but that's the best I can do. He'll make up his own mind."

"My brother can be very stubborn. If he cannot be persuaded to let this matter drop, what can we do? He is making a terrible mistake, but he is my brother and I do not want to see him killed, or hurt because of it."

"We can't do anything. I can just tell him what I know. I'll suggest to him that they should be patient. Marta has another six months on her contract, she should finish it up, go back to Russia. He can send her money there, maybe help her move to Moscow. In a year or two maybe it'll be safe for Ed to marry her and take her out of the country. Then they can live happily ever after."

"What if he won't listen? What if he insists on this folly of buying her out of her contract?"

"Then he's a fool. But it won't be the first time a guy in love's been a fool. He's an adult Fred, he'll do what he wants. All we can do is try to let him know what he's getting into."

"Did you meet this gangster, this Roman?"

"No, but I met his bodyguard. She's scary enough."

"She?"

"You wouldn't believe me if I told you about her. I met another Russian gangster. He confirmed what everyone else was telling me. People say the guy I met's the nicest gangster in town. If that's true, none of us wants to meet The Roman."

"I will speak with Edward. He must drop his obsession for this woman. She cannot possibly be worth it."

"Well, she is beautiful. I can see where a guy might get stupid over her."

"We cannot permit Edward to make this terrible mistake."

"Yep, I agree. Problem is, he's a big boy, like it or not he's gonna make his own mistakes."

"Thank you Ray. Thank you for finding all this out. If you speak with Edward I will be greatly appreciative."

I knew this was going to happen. I really don't want Fred's gratitude, friendship, appreciation or anything else. The problem with these aristocratic types is that they're either at your throat or at your feet and if you let them get close it's always going to be one or the other.

I tell hiim to think it all over and try and talk with Edward himself. If after that he still wants me to talk to his brother, I will.

That's the last I hear of it for the week. The work days creep by slowly. I'm having a hard time concentrating. I call Sasha a couple of times but just get her answering machine. At least Fred isn't pestering me any more about his brother, and that's a relief. We've fallen back into no more than the usual collegial civility.

I deliver the magazine to the printer on Thursday and head home early to change before heading to the F.C.C. to wash the week out of my system.

When I leave my apartment it's crappy out, but there's nothing unusual about that. It's drizzling the hot sour soup that squeezes out of the filthy tureen that a lot of the year passes for the sky over Hong Kong. The streetlights are a jaundiced yellow and cast a mostly useless dim glow over the steps.

And so what if it is. I'm taking the day off tomorrow, heading back to Macau for three days. Sasha finally called back and said she'd show up at my hotel around four in the afternoon. I'm busting with energy, feeling lighthearted, almost skipping down the slippery stairs to the street.

I had a drink at home, watching the city lights come on and the lights on the boats below cruise past and the weather roll in across the harbor. My apartment building was lighting up with people coming home from work, greeting each other, talking about their day, kids playing, moms cooking dinner, some of us getting ready to go out for the night. This whole city is as swollen with life as the clouds are with water. You never know what's going to happen next. That's what I like about it.

Out the door, around back and along the walkway to the road where I can catch a cab into Central. I like the wisps of fog that slink through these dense woods that fill the gaps between the crowded buildings on the steep slopes of The Peak. I like the sounds drifting through the trees, the glimpses of my neighbors through their windows, the burble of water over rocks in the small stream along the path, the soft squishing of my feet on the wet pavement.

I even like the slight thrill of menace I get from a rustling in the brush. It freezes me. It's one of the smaller packs of feral dogs; mangy snarling brutes with poisonous drool, running sores and eyes like fertilized egg yolks. They were cute when they were puppies, which is why someone brought them home for the kids, but then they got too big to share a twenty-by-twenty foot box of an apartment with five or six or seven people. I hold still while they sniff past me, five of them, hungry, but I don't smell like food.

Unfortunately for two young Filipina housemaids, they do smell like dinner. They're eating fried chicken takeaway on a bench along the steps. They must be new to the city or they'd know better. Early evening is when the dogs get hungry. They're quickly surrounded.

One of the girls extends a hand palm up. One of the younger dogs sidles up cautiously to take a whiff. It must like what it smells because it nuzzles its head up against her leg. She scratches it behind the ears, a moment of affection that's probably all too rare for both of them. The other girl is afraid though and the pack senses it. She reaches to protect her meal and gets snapped at by three of the beasts. The biggest one growls at her until she shrinks away. It sticks its snout into the open box and backs slowly off with a prized drumstick.

I'd help if I could, but to what end? I'd only get bitten and then I'd have to get rabies shots and the Filipinas would still go hungry. But the girls don't seem to mind anyhow. The one petting the dog laughs, good naturedly punches her companion on the arm and offers up her box of food to her friend. The dogs strut off into the bushes. I continue down the steps.

The cab driver claims he doesn't know where the F.C.C. is but I know that he does. There's a law, even in Hong Kong, about these sorts of things and I force him to take me there. It can't be more than ten minutes out of his way. It's late summer 1995, just a bit under two years before the place gets handed back to the Chinese. Maybe after that the communists will let him blow off fares. Probably not.

He doesn't think I can understand all the nasty things he's muttering about me in Cantonese. I don't let him know that I can until I pay him, stiff him on the tip and tell him to go fuck himself in one of the few flawless phrases I can spit out in the local lingo. I watch him drive off down the hill, his curses echoing off the plate glass windows of the surrounding buildings, then turn to go into the club.

There's a small break in the throng at the bar. I wedge into it next to a friend of mine to order a drink.

"Hey Greg, crowded for a Thursday."

"Ray. It's the usual suspects, only more so."

"Yeah, there's Saunders in his regular spot. Does he ever change his safari suit? I think he's been wearing it since the early seventies."

"I figure he's got a closet full of them. At least as many as he's got bullshit stories about Saigon and Vientiane. He told me once it's what keeps the young girly reporters flocking around."

"Pathetic, hope I never get that deluded. It's just the free drinks, what else's he got going for him?"

"Don't forget the freebie trips and swank cocktail parties. Being the right kind of P.R. guy can get you laid you know."

"Don't you mean fucked?"

"Semantics, just semantics."

My pint of Carlsberg arrives. I balance a bowl of peanuts on top of it and look around to find a table.

"You see any tables? I'm meeting Susan and Mike and she seems to prefer avoiding the frottage at the bar."

"Can't imagine why. I think there's still an empty up front."

The table's near the front door, mostly hidden behind a standing group, a small Gordian knot of the beautiful people. I can tell by their hairstyles, their casual but expensive clothes, their manicures and leather and metal cigarette cases that they aren't journalists. At least not like any I've ever seen. I nudge Greg and point him at them.

"They're new. They look out of place."

"Probably biding their time until it's late enough they don't look uncool showing up at Lan Kwai Fong."

That's the trendy, heavily expatriate, nightlife and restaurant area just a couple of blocks away.

"They look like they think this place smells bad."

"Doesn't it?"

"Not to me. It's my home away from home."

"Mine too. Why do you think that is?"

"Guilt by association I guess, or at least I hope so. I mean really, look around. Clare's in her usual seat, she danced in the caves at Yenan with Chairman Mao and Chou En Lai at the end of the Long March. Hugh's down there near her, he took that picture of the last American helicopter lifting off from the roof of the embassy in Saigon. John's visiting from Indonesia, I haven't heard the whole story yet but he got that bandage on his head covering the insurgency in Aceh. Even Allen, that old reprobate, has stories, real ones, that make you feel like you're part of history just listening to them."

"Don't go getting soft on me now. You're more believable when you're cynical."

"Don't worry. See that crowd of young pups in the corner surrounding May Ling?"

"The dragon lady of Hong Kong corporate communications? Yeah, what's she up to?"

"I hear she's flogging a freebie to a new Club Med in Malaysia but you have to sign a contract guaranteeing at least five pages of pleasantries before the company'll cough it up."

"Whatever happened to ethics?"

"What's those?"

Greg turns to his drink on the bar and I go to grab the table before anyone else does. Sitting, nursing my beer, I admire the environment.

The F.C.C. is in one of the older buildings still standing on Hong Kong Island. That isn't saying much. For a people who are overly fond of telling outsiders about the glories of their past, the Hong Kong Chinese show almost no sentimentality for their relics. The most glorious historic structures are cheerfully pulled down to make way for the new. Maybe it's because there isn't all that much land and the city needs to make the most of what it's got. Or maybe it's because other than a few ancient temples and clan meeting halls, the British built most of the old structures. Colonialism is not regarded by most residents as one of the highlights of their history.

Susan walks in. She's female basketball player tall and lean and strong. She sports a short bob of jet-black hair and bright blue eyes that perfectly match the businesslike, but ever so slightly sexy silk blouse she's wearing over very tight blue jeans. She's from Texas and some, but not a lot, of her height is in the heels of a pair of well-worn, nicely tooled black cowboy boots. We met a few months ago when she moved to Hong Kong and a mutual friend had given her my name. I set her up with the editor of a travel magazine that was looking for an associate editor.

A couple of weeks ago I introduced her to my friend Mike, here at the F.C.C. He was thrusting out his chest, practically snorting and pawing at the ground with his feet when I did. It all seemed much too obvious to me. She's smart and could pick and choose from most of the guys around the bar, but still she fell for it. They got together. Susan and I have become pretty good pals.

I don't want to risk losing the table so I stay put and throw a hand and a smile at her. She catches them and comes over.

"Hey Ray."

"Hey, where's your worser half?"

"He'll be along soon. Had some sort of big story to file. Hear anything lately from your girlfriend?"

"Yeah, actually, there's a lot to report but I think I'll wait 'til Mike gets here so I don't have to repeat it. We make small talk for a half hour or so until Mike comes up and sits down.

"Hey Mike, been to any good wars lately?"

It's a standing joke between us. He first came to Asia from New York thinking he was going to be a glamorous war correspondent. Within a week he was hunkered down, scared out of his wits, in a muddy hole in an exposed field in Cambodia. He was sure he was going to die and he was a little relieved by that because it meant he wouldn't have to suffer the embarrassment when someone noticed that he'd pissed his pants. That was six years ago.

He survived. He was embarrassed but he survived that too. He did clean himself up and take the next flight back to Hong Kong. He talked his way into a job covering "Greater China" capital markets for the *Financial Reporter*. That seemed a lot safer. At least until today.

"There was a hell of a donnybrook in the Shenzhen exchange this morning. Some P.L.A. captain took offence at his portfolio going into the crapper. He waltzed in with his AK, shot up the place and took a couple brokers hostage."

Susan looks puzzled. She's still relatively new in town, so I explain. "Shenzhen's what the Chinese call a 'Special Economic Zone.' What that means is that anything goes. It's a bastion of totally crazed capitalism run by the world's largest so-called communist country. P.L.A. is the People's Liberation Army, the national army of China. It may sound wacky but it's also the biggest business, and some people say criminal, enterprise in the country. Oh yeah, and an 'AK' is an AK-47; it's an automatic rifle, a machine gun."

Now she looks even more puzzled, and worried. She puts an arm around Mike. "What'd you do? Are you okay?"

"Yeah, I'm fine. Bunch of us turned over some desks and dove behind 'em. The guy was all hopped up on something. He didn't see us or he didn't care. The police came in pretty quick and he shot himself, splattered brains all over their nice, shiny new electronic ticker."

"Jesus Mike, I hear things've calmed down some in Cambodia. Maybe you'd be safer back there."

"Yeah, I hear that too. Just wait 'til they get their stock exchange up and running though."

That deserves another round of drinks so I wave my finger in the air over our heads and Roland, the head bartender, brings them right over.

Mike asks what I'm up to and I tell them about my weekend in Macau. Susan looks shocked. "What is it with you guys? I thought you were just business reporters."

We both laugh. "So Mike, you wanna tell her or should I?" He's got a mouthful of peanuts and he gestures at me.

"It's like this; this is Asia, these are developing countries, you just don't get the neat boundaries between business and politics and crime and everything else that you do in the U.S. Business stories are political stories, war is economics. Crime is everything and anything. Hell, most of the time sex is economics."

"Hell, while you're at it, sex is war a lot of the time back home too Ray." Susan punches her boyfriend when he says it, but she's laughing.

"Anyway, you'll find it out soon enough even with your travel magazine, nothing here makes sense by itself, it's all tangled up together."

"Sounds complicated."

"That's the fun of it, but it can be frustrating. Dangerous too, if you have a knack for getting in the thick of things like Mike seems to."

"It's not just me buddy. Least I'm not hanging around Russian gangsters and Queen Kong. A nice clean bullet in the brain'll be the least of your worries if you make those fuckers mad."

"I'm done with it. I just hope Ed's done with it too. He's a good guy. I don't know how he escaped out of that gene pool. Maybe the milk man got to his mom or something."

| |CHAPTER **THIRTEEN** | |

Susan and Mike want to go to Wanchai. It's where the sailors go to get fleeced by bargirls and to pick up Filipina house-maids when the fleet's in town. It's where a lot of expats go to do the same thing.

I've got nothing against the idea, but I've lost my focus. Everything is a little blurry. My head is spinning even though I haven't been drinking all that much. I begin to sweat. Then I begin to shiver. Then I'm sweating again. So I go home.

Luckily it's not far from my front door to the sofa. I'm pretty sure I can't even make it to the bedroom. I know if I bend over I'll fall over and won't be getting up for a while, so I manage to wrench my shoes off with my feet, standing up, weaving precari-ously. I fall onto the sofa and lay there for a few minutes. It seems like it takes another hour to get my legs up there with me but I do.

There's a decorative, Indonesian blanket over one of the arms and a couple of pillows. I pull the blanket over me, cling tight to one of the pillows and give in to the chills, then the sweats, then more chills.

I'm in and out of consciousness. At one point I think I should get up and turn off the light but I can't make myself do it. Then there he is, sitting on the coffee table next to my head. This time I'm pretty sure I know how he got here. He reaches a hand out to stroke my hair. I'm sweating at the moment so it feels cool and refreshing.

"Malaria?"

"How'd you know? Damn stuff keeps coming back. Just for a night or two, but it's pretty intense. Who are you anyway?"

"What's it matter?"

"I keep forgetting to ask. Are you a ghost, or what? Are you really here or just in my head? Can you carry stuff?"

"Not much difference really. In your head, here, we're talking aren't we? Why do you want to know if I can carry things?"

"I could really use a glass of water and I don't think I can get up."

"Sorry, wish I could help but I can't."

"What about poltergeists? They move stuff around don't they?"

"You don't believe in that crap do you? I'm disappointed, I thought you were a skeptic."

"Don't worry, I don't believe in you either. But we're talking so I thought I'd ask."

He chuckles and strokes my forehead. "Atta boy."

The chills come on again bad. I close my eyes, clutch the blanket and pillow tighter and shake for a while. When they ease off I open my eyes again and he's gone. No surprise in that. No matter how real he seems, I know he's not really there. I've talked to myself since I was a kid. After I got malaria five years ago it took on form. Sometimes he's there to talk with even when it doesn't feel like I've got a fever, when I'm stressed I guess, or dreaming. If it happened too often I'd be worried about it.

Everything's calmed down for now and I take advantage of the lull to chase four aspirin with two glasses of water. I don't know if I ought to turn up the air conditioning for when I start sweating again, or pile more blankets on the bed for the chills. I do both, take my damp clothes off and get under the covers.

I must've gone to sleep sometime during the too long night because it's all over when I wake up. I feel depleted, but from past experience I know I'll recover by late afternoon. I strip the soaked, salty sheets off the bed, take a very long, very hot shower and make myself a cup of coffee strong enough to walk across. I drink a lot of water and eat some bread and cheese and I'm beginning to feel human again by the time I get a taxi to the jetfoil.

I have a beer, then sleep a little on the ferry and get to Macau at noon. The Darling Sauna's across from the terminal. The same building's got a couple of restaurants, a bowling alley, a casino, another big massage palace and four nightclubs, including the Starlight. I'm in need of some pampering and it's convenient.

Darling's just opening when the elevator lets me out in front of the fish tank. Brightly colored tropical fish swim lazily around similarly brightly colored coral in a wall-sized aquarium. It's a wonder that they don't all eat each other. I guess they're well fed. They're also almost all illegal, endangered species smuggled from Indonesia and the Philippines.

Through the glass and the clear bubbling water I can make out movement in the other fishbowl, the one where the Thai women sit.

A different set of gangsters, Chinese triad gangs, bring women from Thailand, and lately Vietnam as well, to Macau. A few of those women work in nightclubs but mostly they sit behind big glass walls in massage parlors. They wear what look like nurses uniforms with bright red numbers pinned to their chests.

They watch TV, play cards, groom themselves and each other, chat or just sit staring vacantly until a customer, who they can only barely make out in the gloom on the other side of the glass, selects them.

Some of them can actually provide a pretty good massage. But that's not what most of their customers want.

That is what I want at the moment. At least.

I notice that number 24, the girl with the long dyed yellow-blonde hair who gave me her card in the café last weekend, is working. I ask the man behind the desk if she gives a good massage. I don't know why I bother asking, what's he gonna say? He says yes of course, "she give number one massage, strong girl."

She smiles when she comes out from behind the glass and sees me. "I remember you. Why no come last week?"

I apologize for that and for forgetting her name.

"Nuoy, same *nit nuoy, nit nuoy*."

I speak almost no Thai but I do know that *nit nuoy* means 'a little bit.' She's not all that little, about average height and weight for a Thai girl, so who knows what it means. She takes my hand and leads me down a long hall, around a corner and down another long hall, down some stairs and through three more long halls. Just how big is this place anyhow?

We finally get to a room and it's immaculately clean and well equipped for anything that might loosely enter into the working definition of "massage" in this sort of place. The walls and ceiling are covered with mirrors. There's a black porcelain Jacuzzi big enough for three or four people, a massage table, a large round bed with shimmery satin sheets, a big cushy chair with soft arms and what looks like a trapeze hanging over the bed. Two lamps with deep red shades softly light the room.

Sad, mournful music is playing over a hidden speaker; a deep drum, an electric guitar, something that sounds like a tenor flute and a warbling voice with a slight harsh tinge at the edges. It doesn't sound anything at all like the blues, but it has that feel to it. I ask Nuoy what it is.

"You no like? I ask change." She steps toward a telephone on the wall next to the bed.

"No, please, I do like it. It's very beautiful. What's it called?"

"Name music *mor lam sing*, is music Lao."

"What's it about?"

"Is song young girl live farm, little rice, no job. She go Bangkok, big city, work bar. Then she sick, no more can work. Go home die. Everybody very happy, she give money family then go better life."

I guess it is the blues after all. It's just the sort of poor people's misery they sing about nine thousand three hundred miles west of the Mississippi River. "That's a very sad song."

Nuoy smiles at me and shakes her head. "Is bullshit song. She stupid girl get sick. You use condom, okay?"

I nod my head yes but it doesn't make me feel any better. At this point I'm not so sure anything's going to get hard enough to slip a condom over anyhow.

But it does. Nuoy fills the Jacuzzi with hot water and some slippery, scented oil. She slides all over me like a playful wet seal while the bubbles churn and froth around us. Then she dries me off, leads me to the bed and demonstrates that she does give a good massage. I'm on the verge of sleep when she starts waking me up with her fingertips and mouth. Before long I'm asking her to show me what the trapeze is for. I like it. Every bedroom should have one.

Afterwards I pour my very relaxed self into a taxi and go to the hotel where I lie down for a nap. I think I'm dreaming about flying when a knock at the door wakes me up. I wish I could remember it, but I'm not very good at holding onto my dreams. I get up and they're gone.

The knocking isn't gone though. It's getting persistent. After I left the Darling I checked into my hotel, went up to the room and fell asleep pretty quick. I'm still a bit groggy. I shout out something. I'm not even sure what it is. I wrap a sheet around me and go to the door.

It bangs open when I unlock it, straight into me. I put my hand up to my face and almost immediately something slams me in the stomach. The air explodes out of me as I fly back. I don't remember anything for a little while after that. I'm sorry I can recall what happens next.

I come to on the floor. My face and hair are wet, there's a terrible crushing weight on my chest, and my arms are pinned to my sides. I blink my eyes open and Boorya, Storm, comes into focus. She's sitting on my chest. This isn't what I'd hoped for.

She sees I'm coming to, reaches behind her and grabs my crotch. She isn't squeezing it that hard to be friendly.

"*Ty menya uvazhaesh?*"

"Huh? I, I don't speak Russian. Sorry."

She squeezes harder and I want to yell but I also want to disappear into the floor so I keep my mouth shut.

"*Mandavoshka! Yob tvoyu mat'!* She slaps me hard in the face with her other hand and I feel like I'm about to black out again. I don't.

I hear a chuckle from somewhere behind her. I can't see who it belongs to. He has a soft, deep voice. "That is right, you do not speak Russian. I will make translation. Storm, she want know, do you give respect? She say you are cunt bug. How you say? Lice, crab lice in the cunt. I do not know, maybe her cunt, maybe you go into the cunt. Then Storm say she fuck your mother. I see her fuck mother before. Storm have very big *khuy*, dick for woman. She make from steel. Maybe sometime she fuck you with big *khuy*, you lucky man."

I'm looking up and into her eyes and she's smiling down at me. Her eyes are soft, almost caring. She's loosened her grip on my crotch and she's gently stroking it. It's getting hard and I don't want it to. This is embarrassing, and stupid. You'd think having an Amazon killer sitting on my chest would be enough to keep my dick soft, but it isn't. She has good hands. The sheet that covers me must be well tented by now and she's smiling brightly, licking her lips. She knows she's got me.

The voice comes from behind her again. "Ah, I think Storm like you. I can see you like Storm." He switches to Russian and barks out a couple words. Storm reaches further down and grabs my balls. She squeezes them hard until I can't stand it. I think I hear myself shriek. My brain feels like it's snapping on and off with the pain, my eyes go wild and wet and out of focus. I don't lose consciousness but I lose all sense.

When I subside she's towering over me. One of her stiletto-heeled boots is on my chest, threatening to impale me if I try to get up. I can look straight up past the boots, past the fishnet stockings into her short skirt where I can see she isn't wearing underwear. She shaves, or waxes or something and I'm getting a full, gyneco-logical display. Under the circumstances it's not exciting.

She sees me looking, spreads her legs further apart and squats down just in front of my chin. "This cunt Russian woman no for you. You no talk girl The Roman. You no fuck girl The Roman. No go Starlight disco. You understand?"

I nod my head yes. She moves her crotch up and plants it over my nose and mouth. It's wet and salty and she shoves it down on me hard, suffocating me, pressing hard enough that it feels like she's trying to break my nose. Squeezing my head with her thighs. It hurts, and I can't breathe and I'm trying to kick my legs, she's got my arms pinned. It's embarrassing and frightening at the same time and it's not any way I want to die. I can hear her muted laughing.

She keeps laughing when she gets up and goes out the door. I can still hear her laughing as she walks down the hall. I lie there and stare at the ceiling for a while, then I close my eyes and feel myself drifting away, passing out maybe, or falling asleep.

I hear a soft chuckle from the chair behind me. Please don't let it be The Roman. That's who must've been speaking earlier. I twist my head around and there he is again. I don't feel like talking. I don't want to listen. I just want to lay here, blank to the world, but I can't help myself.

"That is some woman. They just don't make a lot of 'em like that. At least none that I ever met before. Not to mention, those people have really foul mouths. Whatever happened to the beautiful romance of the Russian language?"

"Can't you do anything? Isn't there some way you could have helped?"

"Hey, I told you, I couldn't even bring you a glass of water. Whaddaya want me to do, put on a white sheet and say 'boo" or something? I'm not a ghost anyhow."

"So great, all you do is watch what happens then show up and make snarky comments about it. Fat lot of good that does me."

"I'm company aren't I? Would you rather just be lying there alone, afraid, stewing in your juices?"

"Okay, okay. I wonder how they knew I was here or that I'd been asking questions?"

"Pretty obvious isn't it? That girl Yana."

"But why?"

"Why d'ya think? You don't want to get a guy like The Roman mad at you. She was afraid he'd find out somehow and if she hadn't said anything it might be the last thing she didn't say."

"So how'd he find out I was back here?"

"Who knows? Maybe your little friend Sasha told Yana you were coming back. Maybe he's got people in the hotels looking out for guys like you. I don't know everything. I do know you'd better do what that Storm woman told you. So what if she doesn't wear panties, you don't want to see her again."

There's a knock on the door. I open my eyes and he's gone. I don't want to get up to answer it. Storm left the door open so I just yell out for whoever it is to come in. If it's Storm or The Roman coming back to finish me off they'll find a way in anyhow, so they might as well get it over with. If it's anyone else, I must look ridiculous lying on the floor half-wrapped in a sheet, but I don't care.

Sasha steps in and locks the door behind her. She doesn't seem in the least bit fazed at the sight of me. She lies down on the floor by my side, kisses me hello and looks at me.

"I see Storm and The Roman leaving the hotel. I hide so they do not see me. Were they here? Are you hurt?"

"Only my pride. Well, that and my nose. I don't think it's broken but it's sore."

"What is happening?"

I tell her. She wants all the details. When I'm done I can't tell if she's concerned or amused. Then she looks like she's going to spit.

"Storm, she is *choknutaya*, crazy *zasranka*. She sit on your face, in Russian I say it is like she has made a shit on you. I already kiss you. Now I will go wash my mouth. You come and wash your face."

We end up in the shower. Sasha eases my pain.

| |CHAPTER **FOURTEEN**| |

I f Sasha doesn't go into work she has to pay the club twenty five hundred dollars. That's three hundred and twenty U.S. and as much as I want her company for the rest of the evening, I can't afford it. Once again she tells me that she'll try and come to my hotel after the club closes, if, that is, someone hasn't rented her for the whole night. If they do, she'll try to call and then come to my room around ten the next morning.

I'm not sure if I have to pay her the five hundred for what we did in the shower. It's not Sunday. I slide the money into the top of her purse when I know she's watching. She doesn't say anything. Neither do I.

We go for an early dinner, to a small restaurant run by a family that left Mozambique when it gained its independence from Portugal in 1975. The place is famous for its "African chicken," a spicy grilled bird that is best washed down with a lot of near-frozen beer. We eat while talking about music. The restaurant has a big collection of tapes from West Africa. Sasha comes here often. She knows a lot about the bands and the musical styles. If she ever saves up enough money she wants to travel in Africa. I didn't expect it and it adds to the list of things I like about her.

We finish dinner with a few shots each of homemade *aquardiente*. It's strong enough that you don't want to light any matches near your mouth for an hour or so after drinking it.

Sasha's eyes are slightly glazed. Her drinking seems deliberate, like preparation. "Is work better when you're drunk or sober?"

She hoists her glass at me and winks. "Drunk, of course, but not so much drunk. I need to feel good, to have energy, but not to be so drunk as the men I am with. It is no good if I am stupid. It is better when the man is stupid."

If I'd thought it over, I would have guessed that. I wonder how I fit into it? Am I one of those stupid men? I don't like the thought.

We wobble through town, stopping in shadows a couple of times to kiss and run our hands all over each other. Three hundred and twenty bucks seems like less money all the time. Luckily we get to the Lisboa before my hormones can trick me into paying it. I watch the lushly rounded back of her ascend the escalator.

I walk back through the casino trying to figure out how to keep myself amused for the evening. I stop in the coffee shop for an espresso and entertain myself watching the parade of floozies glide by. There are a lot more Russians than usual tonight and the Chinese girls look agitated by the competition.

I'm about to get up, pay and leave when I catch sight of Storm striding fast down the hall. I grab a menu from the counter and hold it up in front of me to hide behind. I can't help peering around it and I see that it's not necessary. The big woman's intent on something. She has her head set, her eyes straight ahead and she doesn't even cast a glance in my direction as she hurries by.

Okay, so maybe I am stupid. Or at least I can be. That isn't news to anyone who knows me. I throw money down on the bill and rush out the door to follow her. I've got nothing better to do and there's something about it that feels like a game.

I'm also plenty pissed off. I don't like being threatened. Where the hell do Storm and The Roman get off trying to push me around? They might think they own Marta and can do whatever the hell they want with her, and I hate that too. Maybe there's something I can do about it.

She's a ways ahead of me but is easy enough to spot as her platinum spikes stick up well above the herd. She's moving fast toward the casino. Then she cuts across it and her looks are startling enough that her passing actually diverts the attention of some of the gamblers from their cards. I can see their heads popping up and swiveling to follow her.

She bursts through a knot of Japanese tourists who have just arrived at the entrance on the other side. They spring back and out of the way like someone's tossed a grenade into their midst. She palms the heavy glass door to the side and legs it onto the street, where she pauses for a moment and looks around.

I won't risk following her if she gets into a taxi or a car. There's too good a chance she'll spot a cab tailing her. Besides, I don't know how to say, "follow that car" in Cantonese and by the time I could work out how to get it across she'd be gone.

She settles on a direction though, turns right and heads up the street at a bullish lope. Or maybe that's just how she always walks on those strong long legs. I don't know how she does it in her heels. I guess there's only about three inches of rise between the four-inch platforms and the seven or so inch stilettos, but the fact that she stays upright and doesn't stumble or wobble is one of the most impressive things about her.

I can hardly keep pace as she motors up the block past the one snarling and one resting lion in front of the Bank of China, past a row of all-night pawn shops and gold dealers and turns into an alley crowded on both sides with *dai pai dongs*. These particular food stalls cater to the greed and lust that fill the nearby casinos and brothels.

One serves coagulated pigs blood, sprinkled with chopped green onions and dried ginger. It's meant to make a person strong, alert, and smart. It's just what you need at the gaming tables. Another dishes up *congee*, a rice gruel that settles nervous stomachs. One cart offers grilled skewers of venison with small thimbles of deer penis wine, a combo that's guaranteed to give a guy sexual energy and stamina.

At the end of the alley are two competing stalls that serve snake. Men sit on wooden stools around folding card tables, a large, thick, chipped goblet in front of each of them and a big pitcher of slightly yellowish strong rice wine in the middle. Rough-hewn wood crates are piled high on every side.

A waiter takes an order then reaches into one of the boxes and pulls out a live snake. It looks like a cobra. He holds it up to the customer for inspection and when it meets with approval he whips out a knife, quickly slits the belly of the wriggling reptile and lets its blood drain into the glass. When it's about half full the waiter digs into the gash in its stomach, pulling out the bright green bile duct and dropping it into the goblet of rich red blood.

The customer fills the glass the rest of the way with the rice wine, and then swishes it around to mix it. He lifts it to his lips and chugs it down fast, taking an especially large gulp when the fresh organ reaches his mouth. Having drained his glass the customer hands the waiter a five hundred dollar bill and tells him to keep the change. The waiter, happy to see another satisfied customer, tosses the writhing, dying snake onto the gory asphalt, bloody and slippery with the entrails of dozens more. The customer scurries off to a nearby massage parlor where he can get down to business with what is reputed to be the mother of all hard-ons.

I don't know if this stuff works or not. I've never tried the snake blood, bile duct and rice wine concoction. Once, in Taipei,

I ate the venison and drank the deer penis wine. It's actually rice wine poured from a large jar in which a deer organ has been soaking for a while. Or so they say. I didn't look into the jar and I didn't think about it too much. It tasted pretty much like ordinary, if very strong, rice wine. I also didn't notice any special affects. The venison was good though.

Storm plows ahead straight through the dying snakes and the gore and doesn't notice it any more than she'd noticed the gamblers back at the Lisboa. I follow, skirting the edges, giving a wide berth to the serpents wriggling on the street and waiting in the boxes. I hate snakes and I don't like to get too near them. But I don't like to see them suffer either.

As she crosses the next street I think I know where she's going. "Nine Levels of Heaven" rises up in the middle of the next block. That's not really the building's name. It's called *Edifício* something or another in Portuguese, but it's better known for the kind of fun you can have there.

The first floor is just the elevator lobby and there's a kiosk where you can buy booze and if you are known and the right person is behind the counter you can buy a variety of other, illegal substances. The second floor is a pool hall with attractive women in skimpy dresses to rack the balls for you or beat you in games. The third floor is a sauna and massage parlor with deluxe facilities where you can get very high-quality therapeutic massages from beautiful women, finished off with no more than *dah fay gay*, which means "shooting down airplanes" and is the colorful local euphemism for a handjob.

The fourth and fifth floors are the Mona Lisa Sauna, one of Macau's largest fishbowl "massage" emporiums. The sixth and seventh floor are the Tonnochy Nightclub, known lately for its large selection of South American hostesses. The eighth floor is the Thai No-Hands Sushi Bar and Restaurant. It has small, private dining rooms in which naked waitresses sit on your lap and feed you. They'll do other things too; you just have to tip them.

I'd been there once for a friend's bachelor party. The ninth floor are the offices of Macau's government commission that regulates gambling and other vices. No doubt all sorts of interesting things go on in there.

My guess is right. Storm is heading straight for Nine Levels. I have to get there fast if I want to figure out what floor she's going to. Luckily I can see into the lobby and she's having to wait for the elevator. I lurk in the shadows outside until she gets into it, then move quick and watch as the counter above the door ticks up, finally stopping at eight. Maybe she's got a hot date for dinner.

I'm not even sure why I've followed her. It's a lot more exciting than most of the journalism I get to do as an editor of a business magazine. I don't know what's wrong with me but it's fun. I get off on the action.

But what do I do now? Kidnap Ed, take him somewhere far away and deprogram him out of loving Marta? That's hardly practical. Following Storm is just begging for trouble.

I don't know if it's stupid, brave or it's just that I don't have anything better to do at the moment, but I decide to play this thing out at least a little longer and see where it leads. I'm gonna need a date for dinner, or at least for cover, so I take the elevator up to the Tonnochy to check out a hostess for an hour or two.

Unfortunately it's a whole process. I can't just walk up to the desk and have them send someone out to accompany me upstairs. I get led to a booth. I go through the hot towel ritual. I accept the bowl of nuts, order a drink and reject the fruit plate. I ask for a South American hostess, figuring if that's the specialty, 'why not?'

Her name is Irna. She comes from Ecuador. She speaks passable English. Unfortunately she looks a little and acts a lot like Charo; all high-piled dyed reddish-blonde hair, way too much makeup and dressed like a gaudy chandelier. She's what I think of as a *cuchi cuchi* girl, loud and brazen and sort of embarrassing to spend much time with.

I was thinking of a subtle, quiet approach to my spying mission, but that's obviously impossible with Irna. Maybe that's not so bad. When Storm and whoever she's meeting with notice me, which they will as soon as Irna opens her mouth, they'll never believe I'm trying to spy on them. They'll figure it's just dumb coincidence and my bad taste that has led me to be with this particular woman in that particular place. Spies don't try to draw attention to themselves. No one could be that stupid. It's the old hide in plain sight tactic.

Irna erupts with joy or greed or something else noisy when I ask if I can take her out. She practically rapes me in our booth. I call the *mamasan* over and try to arrange a two-hour takeaway. There's a three-hour minimum. So I fork over nine hundred bucks.

When I tell Irna we're going to dinner upstairs she gives me a dirty look. "I no have the sex with Thailand girls. I no like them. You want two girl, I have the friend here. She is fun, like me."

I'm sure she is and I tell Irna that I'm sure she is. But I insist we go upstairs for dinner. "Maybe after dinner we'll come back and find your friend." What I'm thinking is 'no way.'

They don't get too many women customers in the Thai No-Hands Restaurant. When your waitress is part of the package deal, why would you bring along an extra? But the woman at the front desk is polite about it and asks if we want two waitresses. Irna pinches me hard. I say one will do.

As we're led past the private dining rooms, all closed off behind thick paper screens, I listen for Russian voices. I don't hear them until we get where we're going. They're coming from the next room and they're thick and loud with alcohol. I guess this is a stroke of luck.

The rooms are on a raised platform. The table, surrounded by pillows and backrest cushions is set over a well into which you dangle your legs. The front desk hostess leaves us with menus and is soon replaced by a very cute, little Thai waitress named Lek in loose-fitting silk. She looks a bit surprised to see Irna, but covers it well as she kneels by our sides to present us with hot towels. She takes our drink orders. Irna wants a champagne cocktail. I consider ordering a quadruple vodka but limit myself to a double and tell Lek to get something for herself as well.

As soon as she's out the door Irna is all over me, pushing me back against the cushion, running her hand up and down my thigh, kissing my face and neck and nipping at my ears. She coos loudly and makes clucking noises that she punctuates with what she must think are words of encouragement.

"Ooh baby, you are so sexy. I want you too much. I want you hard cock in my pussy. Ooh baby, you are so mucho macho man baby…"

It doesn't turn me on. It's loud and embarrassing and the Russian voices next door grow quiet, then I hear laughing. None of it deters Irna until the waitress comes back with our drinks. She looks embarrassed too, slowly shaking her gaze from my face to Irna and back. She doesn't know what to do. Under normal circumstances, at this point I'm supposed to help her off with her clothes and onto my lap and she's supposed to help me figure out what overpriced items to order from the menu. I pat the cushion next to me and tell her to keep her clothes on. Lek looks relieved, sits and takes a long slow sip from what I think is a tall lemonade with a booster shot of something strong.

The Russian voices next door have raised back into loud, jovial banter punctuated with the clinking clash of glasses after every few sentences. I'm beginning to think I understand a few words and phrases, at least the really foul ones that seem to constantly pepper the conversation.

It reminds me of one of the first times I understood, sort of, a conversation I overheard between two Cantonese teenagers. The entire exchange consisted of *"doo lay loh moh"* with only the rare other word or phrase thrown in. The southern Chinese language is one of the world's most tonal, but substituting the word "moth-erfucker" for almost everything stretches the use of tonality to new heights. Listening to the Russians in the next room trot out variations on "*tvoyu mat,*" which I'm pretty sure means the same thing, fills me with something; maybe even a little admiration for their ability to make sense out of the subtle bending and twisting of sounds.

English is supposed to be one of the hardest languages to master. Maybe it's just too big. Some people seem to communicate just fine with variations on one or two basic phrases.

Irna's got a few very base phrases of her own and she's using them in my left ear while emphasizing what she means by pawing me all over. It's irritating but I don't want to make her mad by rejecting her, at least not yet. Lek is watching us, both hands wrapped around the glass that she holds up in front of her mouth. I look at her and roll my eyes. She's gotta be wondering what in the hell she's doing here.

She puts down her glass looking like she's decided it's finally time to go to work. She claims some space on my thigh with a hand and moves in to nibble at my right ear. I know I should be enjoying all this attention but I'm not. As politely as I can, I ease the two of them off me, pick up the menu and say, "Let's eat. Whaddaya want?"

Irna quickly finds the most expensive item on the menu; it's a Japanese steak of some sort. Lek points to some sort of seafood salad. Of course it's the second most expensive dish. I smile; close the menu and say, "okay."

Lek looks very pleased; at least something is going right. I hope she gets a commission. She reaches behind her to the wall and pushes a buzzer. Another waitress shows up right away and seems a little confused to find three of us seated there, fully dressed. Lek gives our order in Thai, and then asks if we want more drinks. We do.

The voices from next door are getting louder. There are three of them if you don't count the soft, almost inaudible voices of two Thai waitresses. I'm pretty sure the bellicose one is The Roman.

It sounds like the voice that was in my hotel room. There's a sullen voice that sometimes eases into a snarl. It sounds familiar but I can't place it. Storm's voice pushes its way in occasionally. She sounds like she's trying to calm things down.

I'm trying to figure out what I'm doing here other than spending too much money on a dinner I don't really want with a couple of prostitutes that I don't want either. I can't understand what they're talking about in the next room. Even if I could, it's not likely to do me any good. 'You know Ray,' I'm thinking, 'sometimes you are one dumb fuck.'

That's when the vodka bottle comes crashing through the paper and balsa wood wall and shatters on the table in front of Irna, Lek and me. Its momentum carries the glass shards away from us and we three go flying back onto our cushions away from it. The voices next door are shouting. Someone, obviously, is pretty damned unhappy about something.

I pull my legs out of the hole under the table and turn around to see what I can. There's a bottle-sized ragged tear in the wall and the concerned face of a Thai girl is peering through it. In a moment a large hand pulls the face away and Storm pops into view. I don't have time to say anything before about half of the rest of her bursts through the wall, knocks me over back onto the table and grabs me around the throat. She isn't squeezing though. She just wants to make sure I know she can.

"Nice to see you too."

"What you doing here?"

I swivel my eyes left and right to point out Irna and Lek. They're at opposite ends of the room, slightly curled up and hugging themselves protectively. Storm looks at them, shakes her head, takes her hands off my throat, pats me on the cheek and laughs. "Russian girl better fucking, but now maybe you scare Russian girl. Good."

She moves back off me and I sit up. I can see past her, through the hole she made busting up the wall, into the next room. A stocky, hairy, shirtless man with a shaved head and a tattoo of a gladiator on his shoulder is pointing a gun at a man with his back to me. The man with the gun must be The Roman. I recognize the back of the other man's head; it's Gary. Two naked Thai waitresses are huddled and shaking together in the corner by the door. They look too scared to move.

Storm is smiling at me and I don't know if that's a good sign or a bad one. I hear the door to my room slide open and catch a glimpse of the back of Lek as she slips out. Other voices and footsteps are approaching. The Roman puts away his gun and spits out *"tvoyu mat"* in a tone that must make sense to Storm and Gary as they both almost immediately relax.

Storm pats me on the cheek again, gives my crotch a playful little squeeze and then pulls herself back into the next room. She goes over to whisper something to The Roman. He takes a hard look at me, then his expression softens and he laughs. He says something to Gary who also laughs. Moments ago I was sure someone was gonna get killed. Now everything's just fine. I think they must've bought it as coincidence that I'm here. Macau's a small place.

The doors to both our rooms slide open fast and we have an audience of Chinese bouncers dressed in black. Some of them carry *nunchuks*, those sticks connected by a short chain that Bruce Lee used to bop bad guys with in his movies. There's maybe twelve of them, all alert, rocked a little forward on the balls of their feet. A slender, impassively confident looking man in perfectly fitted black pants and t-shirt steps between them and leans just a little into the Russians' room. The Roman scoots around in the hole under the table to talk with him in a whisper.

So subtly that I would've missed it if I hadn't been watching for it, The Roman slips the man a large wad of cash. The man in black stands back, smiles and gestures for the bouncers to leave. He steps over to our room.

"The Russian gentleman is sorry for disturbing you. He has paid for your dinner and drinks and also for you to take out Lek for the evening. Please, we will now move you to another room."

Lek is standing by his side looking like she doesn't want to be there. *Cuchi cuchi* girl, Irna, is still curled into a cushion in the corner, looking wary and mussed. The Russians are looking at me through the hole in the wall, smiling but not in a way that makes me feel like they want to be friends. The naked Thai girls are hesitantly creeping closer to the men. No one looks like they've got much of an appetite left for anything.

I politely turn down the offer of another room and walk out of the place, Lek and Irna trailing behind. We're silent in the elevator down to the lobby. When we get to the ground floor I hand each of them five hundred bucks and tell them to go away. They're more than happy to.

| | CHAPTER **FIFTEEN** | |

I spend the rest of the night keeping out of trouble. I walk over to the *Militar* and have a quiet drink by myself. The place is nearly empty except for a couple of bone weary colonials shooting billiards in the basement recreation room. I nurse an *aguardiente* and watch them for a little. I've never been able to figure out the game. What's the point without pockets to sink your balls in?

There's a cricket match from India on the TV by the bar. That's another game I can't work out. It seems like the matches go on for days and the scores wind up lopsided; three hundred and forty eight to six and numbers like that. Players can hit the ball anywhere. There doesn't seem to be any boundaries. I watched cricket for three hours once with a Bengali friend who's a big fan. He tried explaining it. By the time I gave up I was more confused than when I started.

Walking back to my hotel through the Lisboa I briefly consider going up to the nightclub and seeing if Sasha's available. But I've spent too much money already. I'm running the gauntlet of whores past the coffee shop when I look in and see Ed sitting by himself with a beer and a cigarette. He's the one person involved in all this stuff who I haven't talked to yet.

He's at a table and I walk up and sit down across from him without being asked.

"Hey Ed." It takes him a few moments to place me.

"Oh yes, hello, you're Ray Sharp, you work with my brother." We'd met once before, briefly.

"That's me allright. You alone?"

"Yes. Just waiting for someone."

"Marta?"

"Ah, no doubt Frederick has mentioned my engagement. It does not make him happy."

"Is there anything that makes Fred happy?"

"He does hate being called that."

"I know, I can't help myself. I'm just an ugly Yank."

He smiles and tilts his beer at me. "He struck me once when I called him 'Freddie.' We were young. Care for a beer?"

I do. The waitress brings me a cold Carlsberg and a hot glass fresh out of the dishwasher.

"Fred tell you he asked me to see what I could find out about Marta and her boss?"

"Ah, that does explain what he has been telling me. I think he is trying to frighten me."

"You're not? Maybe you oughta be."

"These men are gangsters. They want money. Marta is of no interest to them, only the money. You are aware of my family. I have money but I live a simple life. Now I can use it for something that is very important to me. I can pay them whatever they want.

The money is of no concern to me, only Marta. I must free her from them and then we can be happy together."

"What if they won't let her go?"

"As I said, they are gangsters. What they do is unsavory, but they are in business. I will pay them more than they could hope to earn from her."

"I think you're underestimating these guys. Sure they're in business, but have you ever heard the word 'goodwill' used in evaluating a company? It means the company's reputation, how its customers and employees feel about it. It's a hard thing to put a number on, but it's one of the most valuable things almost any company's got.

"These guys, they've got, let's call it 'badwill.' They need their employees and customers to be afraid of them. Whaddaya think it does to their reputation if they let one of their best girls fall in love and run away with somebody? Even if it works, even if they let you buy her out of her contract, they'll just keep coming back for more."

"I will pay them enough that it shouldn't be a problem."

"No, it shouldn't. But have you met these people? Have you met The Roman or Storm? You don't deal with these people."

"Marta has asked me not to speak with them. She says that she will make the arrangements."

"If you're willing to spend all this money, why isn't she with you now? Why's she at work?"

"Ah, see, we are indeed being cautious. She must work until the arrangements are made. There could be problems for her if the same man was desiring her company every night."

"That'd bother a lot of guys."

"Do not think that it doesn't. It is agony to be here without her."

"It's gonna be a lot more agony if they kill her, or you. Why not just have her go back to Russia. Help her move to Moscow. Then in a year or two you can send for her. Even that might not work but it's got a better chance."

"She is a slave to these people. I won't have that. I will free her, then once she is free we will work together to fight this despicable practice."

He sounds naïve, but I might be doing the same thing if I was in his shoes. I'm at a loss for anything else to say. I hope it doesn't get to the point where Storm will beat some sense into him, but maybe that's what it'll take.

I finish my beer and get up to leave him alone. "How do you feel about cricket?"

"I absolutely loathe it. It is among the terrible things that the British Empire should have to make amends for."

I like this guy. I hope he doesn't get hurt. I hope it all works out well for him and Marta and they live happily ever after. But I have my doubts.

I'm wide-awake, heading for a crummy mood and feeling a little lonely. I want company. That's another set of things that make me stupid. Money won't solve those problems permanently, but it'll take care of them for at least a little while. I head up the escalator to the nightclub. I ask the woman at the front desk for "mommy June." Her voice crackles into her walkie-talkie and June materializes by my side in less than thirty seconds.

"It is so good to see you again. Let's see. Last time you were with Sasha. Did you enjoy her?"

"Yes, very much. That's why I'm back. Is Sasha available?"

She scurries away to see, then comes back out to lead me to a booth where Sasha's already waiting. Another sylph-like waitress takes our drink orders and drops off the nuts and fruit. I sit down and we have a long kiss. We break, and then Sasha moves back to look at me, holding my chin in one of her hands.

"Why are you here? I am happy to see you, but you are crazy. It costs too much money for you to always come here. I already say to you that I will come to your hotel later."

"I know, but I wanted to see you now. I wanted a friendly face." I tell her about my evening and get severely scolded for having followed Storm.

"You are crazy stupid. Maybe you will get yourself killed. Do you want to commit suicide? Tonight you are lucky. Next time maybe not so lucky."

I try shutting her up with a kiss. It takes a while but finally works. It's late, so it doesn't cost as much to buy her out for the rest of the night. She changes into a loose, knee length skirt, a billowy blouse and her walking shoes. Apparently we're going for a walk again.

We walk for a long while along the waterfront, talking and holding hands. We talk about music and painters and movies, although we haven't seen many of the same movies. She asks me more about Irina; how we met, what we like to do together, what do I think might happen in the future. I ask her about her hopes and dreams, what she wants to do with her life. I avoid asking about her love life. I'm afraid it might be a difficult subject. We talk like friends, two people who genuinely like each other and are getting to know each other better. My mood's improving rapidly.

We're passing the dark entryway to a government building of some sort and I pull her into it. We stand in the shadow, kissing and running our hands over each other. Sasha turns her back to me, lifts her skirt and pulls down her panties. She looks back at me and smiles. "*Eblya s periskopom.*"

I have no idea what that means, exactly. But I have a good enough inexact idea that I quickly unzip my pants and we fuck, quick and rough, watching the occasional car cruise by a dozen or so feet away.

When we finish I ask what she'd said. She laughs.

"It is more Russian slang, it means 'fucking with *periskopom*', I do not know the word in English."

"Periscope? Like in a submarine?"

"Yes, for seeing when the boat is under the water. In Russia it is hard to be private. So people sometimes are fucking in doorways, outside in the dark, but always watching because maybe other people are coming."

I might even learn to like Russian slang when I don't have people threatening me with it.

We walk for another half hour or so, taking a roundabout way back to my hotel. I don't have to ask if she wants to come up and spend the night. Even if we didn't like each other my cheap hotel room is quieter, cleaner and more private than her apartment.

She ends up staying with me for the rest of the weekend. I can't keep doing this. I'm paid well, but not that well. Saturday we have a good time exploring more of the city, ending up in an underground African bar near the border on Saturday night. It's a tiny, smoky, dark room throbbing with irresistible dance beats and sardine-packed with sweaty bodies in less and less clothing as the heat builds. It seems like she knows everyone there and can talk with all of them in at least snatches of their own language. We dance until it almost kills me, then spill into the street drunk and dripping to find another dim alcove in which to e*blya s periskopom*. By then it's Sunday morning and I don't have to pay her.

Back in bed together, just before I have to leave to get the ferry, things feel a little strained between us, a little awkward. Maybe it's that I'm about to go away again and what's going on between us isn't clear. Circumstances won't let it be.

Sasha's got her back turned to me, just touching me lightly with a foot on my leg. "Do you come back to Macau soon? What are we? What you are to me, I don't know. What am I to you?"

Damned if I know and I feel like an idiot trying to make any sense of it. "We're friends. I know that at least. Good friends. And I want you. Thinking about the rest of it Sasha, it doesn't help."

She goes with me to the ferry pier and gets teary when we kiss goodbye. Her visa doesn't let her come to Hong Kong. I tell her that I'll try to come back to Macau next weekend.

| |CHAPTER **SIXTEEN**| |

There's trouble in the Singapore bureau and I have to fly down there to straighten things out. Our correspondent, a young, likable Singaporean Indian guy with a degree in journalism from Northwestern in Illinois, has been caught plagarizing, again. The first time he got off with a warning. As much as I like him, I'd wanted to fire him then. There are at least a few ethical absolutes, even in journalism. The editor said "no." This time there isn't any choice and I've been sent to do the dirty work. I've also got to interview some replacement candidates so I'm going to be there for the whole week.

I call Irina and offer to pay for her ticket to meet me. It's just a little over an hour flight from Jakarta to Singapore. She does and the time passes a lot more pleasantly than I thought it was going to. We try to call Sasha a few times. I want to tell her I won't be in Macau this weekend and Irina, who's been teasing me about Sasha, wants to tease her about me. We can't get her, just her answering service. Neither of us think too much about that, those sorts of things happen all the time for any number of reasons.

By Thursday night I've finished my work. The firing went okay. He knew what he'd done and expected it. I just had to give him a dirty look when he asked if I'd write him a letter of recommendation.

The hiring goes even better. Janet Chang is so good that she's intimidating. She's got a double masters from Columbia in journalism and economics. She speaks Mandarin, Cantonese, Hokkien, Japanese, Indonesian, French, some Arabic and her English, at least her grammar, is probably better than mine. The only advantages I've got are about twenty more years of experience and I'm learning to swear in Russian.

Janet's also a lot of fun. She's one of the few creative, non-conformist Singapore natives I've met. Usually the educational system and social conventions manage to beat the spirit out of people like her. I don't know how she escaped it, but she did. I snap her up fast before one of the big boys, the *Wall Street Journal* or the *Financial Times* or someone like that can offer her the money she really deserves.

I ask her out to dinner to seal the deal and figure I'll impress her with the fanciest, most expensive sushi bar in town. *Asian Industry*'s picking up the tab and I invite Irina along. I'm not above the occasional creative expense accounting, although on most trips I save the company more money than I cost it with the occasional extra dinner guest. Unlike the other editors I usually stay in moderate-priced hotels and eat at food stalls or cheaper restaurants.

Janet doesn't like the idea one bit. "You must be joking lah! Eat your sushi in Japan. This is Singapore. The only really great food is at hawker stalls." She takes us to the roof of a parking structure where we eat the best Chinese seafood I've ever had. It costs less for the three of us than one small order of top grade tuna sushi at the place I'd planned on.

She and Irina are comfortable with each other from the moment we all get together, although Irina does dodge a question about what she does for work. The two of them spend a lot of the evening ignoring me, speaking in a strange patois of Indonesian and French. I didn't even know Irina could speak French.

After dinner Janet goes home and Irina and I walk back to the hotel. "*Yob tvoyu mat.* I didn't know you spoke French. What else don't I know about you?"

"*Khuy!* Never should I give to you name Sasha. If I want Russian boyfriend, always talk bad Russian language, I go back Russia."

"It's not Sasha, she doesn't swear that much."

"All Russian swear a lot."

"You don't."

"When talk other Russian, I too swear a lot. So, if no Sasha, where you learn swear?"

I tell her about Storm and The Roman and Gary, but they all seem so far away, like a dream I can only remember because I've already told it to someone else. Irina's heard of them before. Gary was her pimp when she was in Macau. She never met The Roman or Storm and never wanted to. They scared her.

"You no talk them more. You do, they kill you. I being very angry and I kill you too." She looks serious, serious enough that if they did kill me she probably would find some way to do it again.

I reassure her that she isn't going to have to kill me. I want to distract her. There aren't many dark alleys or shadowed doorways in Singapore, but I spot one. "*Eblya s periskopom?* I hope I pronounced that right."

Irina looks at me and shakes her head. "I know Sasha. That you learn from Sasha. We have good room. Clean, big bed. We go there okay?"

It's a lot more than simply okay. We spend most of the next three days there.

On the way to the airport I almost ask her again if she'll come to live in Hong Kong. But we both know the only way to do that is if we get married. Neither of us wants to get married. I've been lousy at it once before and she's pretty certain she'd be no good at it either.

"We meet again soon. Maybe you come Jakarta. Maybe we both go Bangkok. No fall love Sasha okay? Sasha only friend. Good fucking too but you no fall love."

I like Sasha. She's becoming a good friend, and yep, it is good fucking too. But that's as far as it goes. I explain it again. Singaporeans aren't big on public displays of affection and I'm sure Irina and I scandalize a bunch of them when we say goodbye.

When I get back to Hong Kong I try to call Sasha again. Her portable phone is still disconnected so I try her apartment. No one answers there either. I try a few more times over the next couple of days and still no answer. Wednesday night I call the Lisboa nightclub and ask to talk with *mamasan* June. I ask her if Sasha is working and she says she isn't. I ask if she'll be working tomorrow or Friday. She doesn't know. I'm starting to worry. I get back on the phone and book a seat on the Macau ferry for Friday.

Thursday at work Fred comes by my desk and wants another coffee. We go across the street again. This time I order a Coke.

"What's up? I ran into Ed in Macau last weekend. I tried to scare him, but I don't think it worked."

"No, it certainly didn't. The matter has become worse."

"He's one stubborn son of a bitch."

"Yes, I suppose thinking that you are in love will cause that sort of behavior."

"So what's he doing now that's worse?"

"He's taken leave of his firm and taken up residence in Macau. He is living with that woman in a hotel."

"Is he paying the nightclub, or her pimp?"

"I am not familiar with the arrangements. It is only apparent to myself and to his firm that he has taken leave of his senses."

"I'm going back to Macau tomorrow. What hotel's he in? I'll see if there's anything more I can find out."

Ed and Marta are shacked up at the Hac Sa Resort on Coloane Island, just a mile or so up the beach from Fernando's. At least I can get a good meal when I check up on them.

I'm worried about Sasha. By the time my ferry pulls away from the dock I've tried calling her three more times and the Lisboa once. She still isn't around. I called Irina Thursday night to ask if she'd spoken with her. She hasn't. She says it's too early to worry about anything. When she worked in Macau, a few different times a rich gambler paid for her company for as long as a week. She'd spent those weeks a prisoner, although in the lap of luxury. She laughed, said I probably wouldn't want Sasha anymore because she's no doubt getting fat sitting around a hotel suite eating chocolates all day. When I do find her though, Irina wants me to call and let her know. I think she's a little more worried than she's letting on.

I'm not convinced that things are okay. I've got an uneasy feeling in the pit of my stomach. I never get seasick. It's a calm day on the Pearl River Delta in any event. But I feel queasy the whole way to Macau.

| |CHAPTER **SEVENTEEN** | |

No one answers the buzzer at Sasha's apartment. I try to ask the old woman who runs the coffee shop if she's seen the Russian woman who speaks such good Cantonese. Either she doesn't have a clue to what I'm talking about or won't tell me.

The apartment where I first met Marta and Yana isn't far away so I walk over there. I don't know what number it is, just the building, but I'm hoping I can figure something out once I get there. I can't. There are forty-eight apartments in the building and the mailboxes are only labeled with numbers. There's a laundry across the street and a young Filipina is behind the counter. I ask her about the Russians across the street. She's seen them; sometimes they bring their clothes in. But she doesn't know what apartment they're in.

I go back across the street to the lobby and start randomly pushing buzzers. There's somebody home at almost every one, but once they hear my voice no one speaks English.

I know where to find Marta. I know where Yana works. I'm not giving up.

The taxi drops me off on the marble driveway at the ornate front portico of the Hac Sa Resort. It opened about six months ago and is the best place to stay in Macau if you want to get away from Macau. I can hear the thwock of tennis balls from the professional level courts around the side of the front building. I can hear splashing and children's shrieks from the pool. There's a para-glider being towed behind a buzzing speedboat out on the bay. It may be early afternoon, but the clink of crystal cocktail glasses shatters the tranquility of the bright, vaulted lobby.

Only the message machine answers the phone when I call the room. If they are there, I figure they're screening their calls. "Ed, it's Ray Sharp. Your brother told me where to find you. I need to talk to you and Marta. It's important; it's about a friend of mine, Sasha. Marta knows her. I'm in the lobby."

I sit down on a leather sofa and pick up the *International Herald Tribune*. Stock markets are up; housing markets are up, wheeling and dealing is going on non-stop, and a small vacant lot in Central, Hong Kong sold for nearly forty-five million U.S. dollars. Asia's economies have been going nuts since I arrived in 1989. That was six years ago. Sooner or later something's gotta give. I look at the paper and can't help but be pessimistic in the glow of all this good news. I get the feeling that the whole wide world is cruisin' for a bruisin'.

Maybe that's just today's mood. I'm usually a 'glass is half-full' kind of guy. I turn to the sports page and the Dodgers are in first place. That cheers me up. I always think they're going to go all the way.

"I know you can't be reading cricket scores. Not in the *Tribune*." I put down the paper and look up at Ed.

"Baseball, it's probably just as bad unless you're a fan. I thought you might be screening your calls. Thanks for seeing me." He sits down next to me.

"What's this about? Did my brother ask you to frighten me some more?"

"Yeah he did, but that's not what I'm here for."

He looks the question at me.

"My friend Sasha's missing. I'm worried about her. Marta knows her. I'm hoping maybe she's seen her or knows someone who has."

"A Russian hostess?"

"Yeah, why?"

"I hear these women disappear all the time. Why are you concerned?"

"She's a friend. We keep in touch. She introduced me to Marta and Yana and I asked them questions about The Roman. Then he and his bodyguard threatened me. I'm worried they found out about Sasha."

"This was at my brother's request, wasn't it?"

"Yes, but now it's got nothing to do with you. I just want to make sure Sasha's okay."

He takes me to his room. Marta's sitting on the end of the bed watching TV. She looks disheveled, unkempt. She doesn't light up the place like she did when I first met her. She frowns when she sees me. The blinds are closed, the floor's littered with room service trays. It looks like no one's been in to clean for a while. He sits on the bed next to Marta, picks up the remote and turns off MTV. I take the chair from the desk, turn it around and straddle it facing them.

"You two can't hide out here forever."

"I know, I know. We go out sometimes. I'm still paying the Starlight for Marta's time. I'm assembling the money to get us out of this."

"If you're paying them, then why're you hiding out? They've gotta know where you are, Macau's a small place."

"You're right, of course. It seems safer somehow. But I prefer not to speak of this, what about your friend?"

"Marta, you know Sasha, my friend who introduced us?"

She nods yes, then looks at Ed.

"I can't find her. I'm worried about her. Do you have any idea where she is or any idea who might know?"

"I not know. She friend Yana. Maybe Yana know."

"Can you give me Yana's phone number, or the apartment number where she lives? I don't want to go see her at the Starlight, it might get her in trouble."

"Yana move. Not know where go."

"Please, think, is there anyone who might know?"

"I here ten day. Talk nobody."

This isn't getting me anywhere. I give them my number at the hotel and also in Hong Kong, ask them to call if they hear anything, but I don't hold much hope for it. Ed walks me to the door.

"Look Ed, I know you don't want to hear anything more about this, but be careful, these people are really dangerous. I'm on your side, I really am. Your brother's being an ass. I have a Russian girlfriend myself, Irina. We're in love with each other. She lives in Indonesia now but she used to work in the clubs here. I know a little something about this stuff. From what I hear The Roman might enjoy killing you two even more than taking your money."

"I appreciate your concern, but please, I am an adult. I can take care of myself. Tell my brother not to worry. I hope you find your friend."

The door closes behind me and I hear the bolt being thrown.

The rest of the day I try Sasha's phone a few more times but no one ever answers. I don't have any choice but to go to the Starlight to find Yana and that's not good. I'm getting wound up and consider stopping at the Darling to unwind before I go looking for what's almost certain to be trouble. But I'm not sure how relaxed I can afford to be if I run into Storm or The Roman. I go back to the hotel and lie down on the bed to read.

I can't concentrate. What the hell do I think I'm doing? This all started out as a small favor for a colleague. I don't even like the guy, but...

Besides, I've got to admit it, digging into what's going on with Russian gangsters and brothels is a whole lot more fun and interesting than working on stories about farmers in Taiwan or even rapacious timber mill owners in Malaysia.

I keep hearing about how dangerous all this is, but there's part of me that just won't believe it. I'm a journalist, it's got to be more trouble to kill me than to ignore me doesn't it? Sure The Roman's made threats, but I figure he's just trying to scare me away. That makes me more interested. Hell, if I'm willing to give up before I find out everything, then why am I a journalist anyhow?

The least I can do is find Sasha. She's a friend. I like her a lot. And I've got to do it for Irina too.

So I toss and turn, wrestling with all my confusion over what's the right thing to do and what's the smart thing to do and not coming to any conclusions other than knowing I'll just keep blundering ahead. About ten I get out of bed, take a shower, get dressed and head for the Starlight.

If Storm's at the door I'm fucked. It's a quiet hallway and she can do whatever she wants. Once again I'm gonna need cover but I'm not sure what to do about it. I call Francisco and Tomas to see if I can talk them into going with me, but their portable phones are turned off. I walk through the Lisboa hoping I might run into someone I know. I take the escalator up to the nightclub and ask for June in the hope that somehow Sasha has come back and is at work. She isn't there. I poke my head into the *Militar* hoping someone I know will be in there. No one is.

I walk to the Starlight through the mostly empty streets lined with construction sites and new cookie cutter buildings. I walk slowly, like I don't really want to get there, which I don't, but I have to. I don't come up with any bright ideas along the way.

By a stroke of luck there's a group of five young Chinese guys in the elevator with me. They get off and knock on the door. I put myself as close to the middle of them as I can without making them too nervous. I'm barely breathing, trying to make myself invisible. I hope there's safety in numbers.

The door opens and I let my breath out. It isn't Storm. It's a Chinese *mamasan* who I've never seen. She leads the six of us to a table thinking we're together. I break cover and have her take me to my own table nearby. I want people around, even if it is too dark to see them.

Before she can go away I take her arm, palm a five hundred note into her hand and ask if Yana is available. She nods without saying anything. I sit and a waitress comes to fuss over me. I'm nervous as hell and order a double and a glass of ice water. I'm not sure which one I'll drink. I'm also hungry and quickly chomp down handfuls of mixed nuts.

The *mamasan* returns leading Yana. I slide back into the darker shadows, hoping Yana won't see me until she's already sat down. I don't want to spook her.

She slithers in next to me. I mumble "thanks" to the *mamasan* and put my arm around Yana to make sure she stays put when she realizes who it is. She's fidgeting. She seems a little nervous. With my other hand I pick up the candleholder and raise it between our faces. She isn't happy to see me. She's scared and shaky.

"You, go way, no want trouble, *puzharlooysta*, please go way. Storm no see. Go, now, bad here."

"I'm looking for Sasha. I'm worried about her."

"You no find. Sasha go way, no come back. You go way too."

"Please, Sasha's your friend, my friend, I'm trying to help. Where'd she go?"

"No, no talk, not know. Go way."

She tries to pull away from me but I hold on. I don't know why. I doubt there's anything more I can get out of her but it sounds like she knows something. I squeeze her arm tight and put my face up close to hers. I hate to threaten her; she's scared enough already.

"I'll get out of here as soon as you tell me what you know. Anything. Just give me a hint. If you don't I'll start making noise, a lot of noise and Storm's gonna know I'm here talking to you."

She's whimpering, shaking with fear and I'm feeling like an asshole for doing it to her but if she doesn't give me something to work with I'm at a dead end.

"Palace. Go Palace," she hisses in my ear before breaking away and hurrying out of the booth. If she's smart she's headed off to tell Storm I'm here. She probably can't keep it a secret and if they think she is trying to she'll be in very big trouble.

So will I if I don't get out of here fast. I throw a thousand dollar bill down on the table, that will more than cover it, and steam out of the club as quick as I can. The elevator light says it's on the ground floor. I don't want to risk waiting for it so I look around, find the stairs and run down them. Risking a fall and a broken neck is preferable to anything The Roman and Storm might come up with for me.

There's no line for taxis and I scramble into the backseat of the first one. I tell the driver to take me to the Palace and he turns to give me a funny look. I'm sure he knows where it is. I wave my hand at him and tell him to "go, fast."

There might be a massage parlor in Macau that inhabits a lower ring of hell than the Palace, but it's hard to imagine. I don't want to think about it. I've never been there but I've heard the stories. It's the Gulag of the local sex industry. When one of the local mob bosses - Russian, Chinese, Thai, it doesn't matter – wants to punish one of his girls, that's where he sends her.

It's a half block from the border gate, behind a high stonewall topped with shards of broken glass. My cab driver lets me out in front of it in just a little over five minutes.

If I stop to think I probably won't go in there. It's the kind of place from which you don't get out unless the people inside want you to. There's a buzzer by the iron door and I push it. I stand back to let myself be seen by the video camera set in the wall. There's a loud click as the door unlatches. I push it open and go inside.

There's a short walkway, no more than about ten feet long, leading to another door, this one set into a squat, windowless concrete bunker. It's brightly lit in front of this door and I'm scanned by another video camera before it also clicks to let me in. I walk into a small, bright waiting room, its walls lined with red folding card table chairs. At the other end is another door, with what looks like a ticket sellers window next to it. The window's made of mirrored glass. I can't see in, but I figure someone's on the other side looking out. I walk up to it.

A gruff Chinese voice spits from a small speaker above the window. "What you want?"

I talk back to the mirror. "A massage. Do you have Russian girls?"

"Yes, many girl, all country. Three hundred dollah." A drawer slides out of the wall under the window. I fumble in my wallet and put the money into it. It slides back and the door next to the window clicks.

I push my way in and I'm in another small room. This one is dark except for what looks like six small portholes in the wall in front of me. Beams of light pour out of them and cross the room to make circles on the opposite wall. A speaker somewhere in the room barks at me. "You say number girl."

The women must be behind the wall. I step up to peer through one of the portholes and there they are, maybe thirty or forty of them sitting on a stepped riser covered with filthy green carpet. They're about evenly split between westerners and Asians, all shapes and sizes, mostly young, some look too young.

They all look like zombies. Near as I can tell there's no TV, no one's playing cards, no one's reading. They aren't even talking among themselves. They're just sitting there with dead eyes and blank expressions. About half of them are sprawled, loose-limbed and listless. The other half look on edge, tensed, shivering with effort at self-control. They all wear blood red disks with numbers on a ribbon around their necks. And they're all naked.

A lot of guys fantasize about rooms filled with naked women. I have. This isn't that. This is scary. It's about as far as I can imagine from anything anyone sane would ever have a fantasy about. It makes me want to call the cops. Or the U.N. Or somebody, anybody who could do something about it.

It's hard to pick out individuals from the group. They look generic, like the self has been knocked out of them. At best they break down into types; blondes, brunettes, tall, short, thin, rounded. I don't see Sasha. I'm about to turn around, tell the voice it can keep my money, and get out of there as fast as I can, when I think I recognize someone. I think I saw her walk past at the Lisboa nightclub the night I first met Sasha. Maybe she'll know something.

"Eighteen. *Baat sahp*."

The voice repeats the number and I hear a door click to my left. A narrow beam of light comes from where it's cracked open. I push through it and into a dim hallway lined with numbered doors with red and green lights over them. The voice follows me.

"Go number six. Wait."

There's just enough space to step into room six and get onto the small hard bed that fills the wall facing the door. A dull yellow light spreads like fog from one bulb in the middle of the low ceiling. It smells dank and moldy underneath an acrid overlay of disinfectant. I'm nervous about sitting on the bed, much less taking off my clothes and lying on it. So I turn around standing and face the door, waiting for number eighteen to arrive.

She does in about a minute. She seems surprised that I'm dressed and gently pushes me toward the bed while closing the door behind her. "Take off clothes."

I sit down. "Wait, please, I want to talk."

She sits next to me. "No be shy. No talking. Only fucking. I sucking you same money. No condom, more money."

"What's your name?"

"No name here, only number, only fucking."

"Wait, no, please. I'm looking for Sasha. Do you know Sasha? She used to work at the Lisboa."

She puts a finger to her lips and reaches to unzip my pants. I put my hand over hers. "No want fucking?"

"No, I'm trying to find Sasha, can you help?"

She points at the door. "They spy. No fucking, I having problem."

I reach for my wallet, take out two thousand dollars, which has got to be a whole lot more money than she usually makes. "Here, I'll give you this. What do you know about Sasha?"

"You give money no fucking?"

"Yes."

"Okay, but pretend fucking, okay?"

She undoes my pants and fondles me while we make sounds like we're having sex. I can't get hard. That's a relief. I might have to hate myself if I could get excited in a place like this. She whispers softly in my ear.

"Sasha have big trouble with The Roman. He buy contract. She here one week, try run away. Storm catch her, take her Zhuhai. Maybe place name Imperial. Maybe Emperor. Very bad place. Give girl drug, make take too much drug, do many bad thing. You not say I talk you, okay?"

I assure her I won't. We make a few more noises. I wish her luck but it seems like a dumb thing to say. She's gonna need a lot more than luck.

On the way out, waiting for the four doors to click open and let me pass, I feel like I'm suffocating. On the street I take deep breaths but still feel pain in my chest. I look to the north, to the heavily fortified border gate to China. The lights of Zhuhai wink at me from just up the block. They look very far away.

| | CHAPTER **EIGHTEEN** | |

There's nothing more I can do in Macau and I can't get into Zhuhai without a visa. I need to go back to Hong Kong for that. I don't want to stay here any longer. I love this city, but not at the moment. I want to go home, crawl into my own bed, pull the sheets up over my head, maybe take a bottle of booze under there with me and just be gone for a couple of days.

That's what I do until Sunday morning when I get up long enough to call Irina. Once all the "I miss yous, I love yous and when will we see each other agains" are out of the way I tell her what I've found out about Sasha. Once the tears and the torrent of upset Russian subside, I ask if she knows anything about the clubs in Zhuhai.

If it wasn't for a lot of barbed wire, brick and electrified fencing overseen by automatic weapon toting border guards, Macau and Zhuhai would be one city. A "Special Economic Zone," like Shenzhen that is attached to the northern border of Hong Kong, Zhuhai is no longer the sleepy farm town it was as recently as seven or eight years ago. There are new tall buildings, resort hotels, fast food emporiums and traffic.

If it wasn't for the noise, pollution and construction it could be a pretty little city. Its streets are heavily lined with trees; there are plenty of parks. On one side there are wide, sandy beaches on the other a picturesque harbor.

There's also plenty of crime. Young women come from all over China to wait for their chance to get into Macau. They bide their time streetwalking in large, voracious packs. The going rate is a lot cheaper than it is in the Portuguese colony, so cost-conscious horny men cross the border in droves.

The police and the army in China control prostitution and brothels, at least on land. The navy runs several notorious "resorts"; islands in the South China Sea with casinos, restaurants serving endangered species and well-stocked with women from around the world.

The freelancers on the street pay off the local police and soldiers. The army, navy and police don't have any competition. Prostitution is illegal in China. When a woman doesn't pay off the right people, or is unfortunate enough to get swept up in one of the occasional "morality" campaigns, she's sent to a "re-education through labor camp." Pimping and pandering, by anyone who isn't in a position of power, is punished by death; one quick bullet through the back of the head. The family of the condemned is sent a bill for the bullet. That's supposed to be humane, at least they know what happened.

When I was in college I was a left-wing radical. I thought there were reasonable answers to the problems that plague the planet and that some of them had words like "socialism" and "communism" attached to them. Living near China got me over that pretty damn fast. Now whenever I hear anything with "ism" tacked onto its end, I think it's just another trick by which some small group of assholes is going to try and get over on everybody else.

"People's Liberation Army," "Workers Paradise," "Compassionate Conservatism;" it's all just window dressing for the same old brutal survival of the fittest, or the most heavily armed.

The older I get the more I don't trust big ideas. It's the little things, the simple things, the regular day to day stuff that makes the real difference in most people's lives. I still vote. I still figure that some governments are better than other governments, that more freedom is better than less freedom, that more opportunity is better than less opportunity; but I don't believe in miracles.

Irina's heard of both the Imperial and the Emperor clubs and I don't like what she's heard. The Imperial is in Zhuhai. It's exclusive and you need an introduction to get in. Its facilities are deluxe and the women are pampered but they're prisoners. It's also a slave market. Wealthy customers will sometimes buy one or more of the women and take them away.

She doesn't know much about The Emperor. It's on an island in Chinese waters, about thirty miles to the southwest of Macau and Zhuhai. It's supposed to be a really terrible place, the worst place a woman can be sent to work. Women go there and no one ever sees them again. That's all she knows.

I don't like it. I don't like my chances of getting into, or even more so of getting Sasha out of either of those places. If she's in the Imperial or the Emperor she's probably gone and it's at least partly my fault. I crawl back into bed and anesthetize myself with a liter of vodka.

The Spanish inquisition is going on inside my head when I wake up the next morning. I'm being tortured in there by my hangover and my conscience. What can I do? What should I do? Is it worth the risk? What's Irina going to think of me if I don't do anything? What's happening to Sasha? I can't concentrate on anything. I want to beat my head against the wall until the voices and the pain stop.

I stagger out of bed and try swallowing four aspirin with a lot of water. None of it stays down long. I must have passed out on the bathroom floor after throwing up, because when I wake up again that's where I am. My joints ache where they've been resting on the tile floor. My stomach and throat feel raw. My head hurts a little less. I can't think and I'm glad for that.

Slow-motion auto-pilot takes over and I lean against the stall wall under a scalding hot shower until the hot water runs out. I prop myself at the sink and this time manage to hold down the aspirin and water. I make myself a strong coffee and somehow keep that down too. I look in the mirror and am not at all surprised that I hate what I see. I consider going back to bed, but instead I bend and crack my arms and legs into clothes and go to the office. I'm moving very slowly. This must be what it's like to be a very old man.

Fred comes by my desk to ask if I saw his brother. I tell him I did and that it's no go. Ed just won't get scared off. He's actually bothered enough that he's genuinely nice when he thanks me for trying.

By noon I've had a couple more cups of coffee and am almost feeling normal. I remember Bill Warner, the guy from the consulate I met in the Lisboa coffee shop. I rummage around on my desk until I find his card. I run a gauntlet of three people, and have to give my passport number to the last of them before I get through to him.

"You agriculture guys have some pretty tough security."

"Well, you know, it's one of our most important exports. You calling about the latest food promotion? Got the press release and want a free lunch?"

"I'm not that kind of press. Actually I'm calling to see if I can buy you lunch, ask you some questions."

"On the record or off?"

"Most definitely off. It's personal. A friend of mine's gone missing in Macau. I hear she might've been taken to Zhuhai. I want to know more about it."

"What makes you think I'd know anything about that?"

"Zhuhai used to be a farm town didn't it? If you want I'll stop beating around the bush."

"Okay, okay, I'll see what I can find out. Can't do lunch though. Drinks? You might need 'em. What sort of friend is this anyhow?"

"A girlfriend. A professional one. Russian. She might be at a place called the Imperial, or another called the Emperor. That's all I know."

We agree to meet at a restaurant/bar/disco called Zuma Beach for happy hour. At two-for-one it's the only time it makes any sense to drink there.

The real Zuma Beach is just north of Malibu, along the coast in Los Angeles. The one in Hong Kong is a glitzy schizo mishmash of chromed high-tech and funky beach hut. The menu tries a little too hard, offering everything from Cal-Asian-Southwestern-French-Nouveau comfort food to what are possibly the best burgers in Asia. The bar serves a nauseating variety of drinks that require blenders. As the night progresses a disk jockey plays ever louder and throbbier tunes until finally half the tables and chairs in the place are whisked off the dance floor and it becomes almost unbearably crowded, as more people line up outside sucking up to the doorman.

Most of the nighttime crowd are expats and most of them are relatively young and British. Despite being a British Royal Crown Colony, since about 1990 there've been more Yanks in town than Brits. But a lot of the Americans are here with their families. They don't go out much to bars and discos. And the ones that do seem to prefer quieter, or more down-home sorts of places. There're also a lot of tourists who find their way into Zuma Beach and an increasing, but still minority part of the crowd are what one of the local newspapers calls "Chuppies," as in "Chinese yuppies."

It's expensive too. Dinner and a few drinks can set you back a hundred U.S. dollars per person or more. It's not my scene. But happy hour, if you get there early enough, can be relatively sedate and pleasant. For some reason it also attracts fashion models and visiting celebrities, so there's usually someone to look at.

I get there early and take a table behind a potted palm and a dance floor speaker. The music'll stay soft for the next couple of hours at least, so I'm safe 'til then. I order a double, since it's two-for-one I tell the waitress to pour them into the same tall glass and bring me the ice on the side.

I've seen her before. She remembers my drink but not me. That's okay. I've only been there a few times and never got up to anything memorable in the place. After bringing me the drink she sticks around to flirt. She's a cute, slightly plump Scottish girl with a thick accent I can barely understand. I'm not really interested, neither is she. It passes the time and I think she's hoping it helps raise her tip. It does.

Warner comes in and interrupts us. He sits down, orders a Sam Adams and eyes my glass. "That's some head start. You should be sober to hear what I've got to tell you. There'll be time for that later."

"Don't worry, be happy hour. This is a double and I'm no more than a couple CCs into it."

He gets his Sam Adams and touches my glass with the bottle, lifts it to his lips and takes a long, satisfied looking pull. He doesn't set it down, just lowers it and holds it in front of him. "You try this stuff? It's pretty damn good. Long as I'm having to promote our beer I'm glad it isn't Bud."

I take a handful of peanuts from the bowl on the table. "These your nuts too? They're stale." I eat them anyway. I need the salt.

"Not my patch. That's another section."

"I wish to hell I knew what we're talking about. This is the third time I've talked to you and I haven't got a clue."

"If you knew I'd have to kill you."

"I wish you'd at least smile when you say that."

He smiles, big and phony, takes just one peanut from the bowl, pops it in his mouth and swishes it around a little before chewing and swallowing.

"So I found out something about what you wanted. It isn't pretty."

"I didn't think it would be."

"The Imperial's in Zhuhai allright. It's in the basement of the Grand Imperial Resort, that's one of the new big ones on the beach side. We think it's owned by a P.L.A. general, but you could spend the next ten years wading through all the dummy companies before you'd be able to pin that down. It's famous for its swimming pool."

"That sounds wholesome enough."

"Yeah right. You have to be a member, or be brought there by a member and it's not easy, or cheap to join. Although I hear you can get a joint deal with one of the local golf country clubs for fifty or sixty grand."

"U.S.?"

"Yep. Hey, don't knock it, that's a lot cheaper than any of the country clubs here in Hong Kong and you don't get the fancy cathouse with one of those memberships."

"What's so fancy about the cathouse?"

"It's not just any old swimming pool. It's Olympic-sized, there's free bar service where they only pour the top-shelf stuff, there's A-list live entertainment, gourmet French and Chinese chefs and top-of-the-line Cuban cigars for the taking."

"Sounds swell."

"Yeah it does. And there's girls. A whole lot of them from all over the world and one more beautiful than the next. They'll do anything you want, either right there around the pool or if you're shy there's deluxe private rooms."

"Okay, so it's the world's fanciest whorehouse and it's owned by a Chinese general. I've heard a lot more sinister stories."

"Did I mention that they're all junkies?"

"Who?"

"The girls. That's how they keep 'em there. They're not allowed to leave. The place is heavily guarded. But after a few months, most of 'em probably wouldn't leave if they could."

"Holy shit."

"Nothin' holy about it. The other place's worse."

"The Emperor?"

He nods and waves at the waitress who's been keeping his second beer on ice. She comes to the table with it and I order another double, make that a quadruple. Happy hour has another hour to go and I might need to be carried out.

I drink more than just a couple CCs of my new drink before setting it down and looking up at him.

"The Emperor's not in Zhuhai. It's on *Haak Dou*, 'Black Island.' It's a tiny, rocky island thirty-two nautical miles, that's about thirty-seven miles on land, to the southwest of Macau. It's in the middle of major fishing grounds, but it's Chinese territory. There's a small naval base there."

"What makes it worse?"

"It's a brothel for S&M, sadism and masochism, mostly S. A customer can do anything he wants to the women there, anything at all. They're all junkies too. If he kills one by mistake it just costs more, a lot more. But knowing these people there's some loansharks around to arrange financing. It's a real chamber of horrors."

"Does the army run that one too?"

"Not sure, but my money's on the Navy. Same thing."

"Is there any way into these places?"

"Why, you got a thing for junkie whores or you feel like beating someone up?"

"You want my drink in your face?"

"No, look, I'm sorry. I know you want to find your friend, but what if you do? How're you gonna get her out of there? If they find out that's what you're there for, how are you gonna get yourself out?"

"I don't know. But until I know where she is I can't come up with any sort of plan."

"Listen, we'd love to close these places down, but we won't. We can't go to war with the Chinese army or navy over this. You can't either."

"You've got to know some way for me to get into these places. Where'd you get your information?"

"If I knew, I wouldn't tell you. Consulates are supposed to protect citizens, not get them killed. I'm sorry about your friend but you're just going to have to accept the fact that she's gone."

"What kind of fucked up thing is this? She went to medical school, she's a smart, educated person. How the fuck does this happen?"

"Beats me. I never thought I'd hear myself say this, but maybe a lot of people were better off before the red bastards lost control of the Soviet Union."

"Sasha was."

"That was her name?"

"That *is* her name."

"Sorry, but not for long."

| |CHAPTER **NINETEEN**| |

Somehow I get home and into bed and even have the presence of mind to drink enough water that the next morning I'm not in pain, just listless. In the office I try editing an article about U.S. companies hiring people in China and India to input their historic data into computers. It's badly written, dull and would be a welcome distraction except that Zhuhai keeps coming up. A lot of the work is done there. That gives me an idea.

I ask the research librarian, Jane, to work up a file for me on the data input companies in Zhuhai and slip in anything she can find out about the Grand Imperial resort and also, "oh just out of curiosity," Black Island. She's good and fast and everyone thinks I hired her for her very long legs and very short skirts, but I didn't. Those are just a bonus.

She gets back to me in about twenty minutes with a thick wad of papers. There's a lot about the input companies; a few pages of press releases from the Grand Imperial none of which say anything about the whorehouse in its basement; and one paragraph telling me that Black Island is a naval base with restricted access.

I wave the paperwork at Norman, the editor-in-chief, and tell him I think I ought to go to Zhuhai for a day or two; there's an interesting story to be had there. He tells me to go. I knew he would, I make him nervous.

Norman's another stuffy Brit, though one from a working class background he's trying to overcome. He spends a lot of time with Fred and has no idea that his truly upper-crust countryman makes terrible fun of him behind his back. If Norman was just the slightest bit nicer himself, it'd almost be enough to make me like him. But he isn't, and I don't. We have never, not even once, seen eye-to-eye on anything. I don't know why he hired me and I'm sure he regrets it. He's happy when I'm out of the office and I take advantage of that.

Back at my desk I reserve a seat on Thursday's nine in the morning ferry to Zhuhai. I'll need the rest of today and tomorrow to get my visa.

I do something I usually don't and call the general manager of the Grand Imperial to book my room at the "journalist rate," and to arrange an appointment with him. When he assumes I'm going to do a story about the hotel, I don't correct him. He wants to treat me to dinner and I don't say "no" to that either. I set up appointments with the managing directors of three data input companies, making sure they know I'm a VIP; "Deputy Editor of the largest circulation business monthly in Asia." I'm pretty sure one of those people is going to be able to get me into the basement of the Imperial.

Irina wants me to call her back when I find out anything more about the Imperial and the Emperor. I can't bring myself to do it. The new information won't do anything other than make her even sadder over the fate of her old friend. And I guess I'm afraid that she might blame me for it. At least for part of it.

Thursday morning I get the ferry. It's a gigantic, jet-powered catamaran that slides along closer to the water than the jetfoils. It's a choppy day and I can't do much of anything other than stew in my own ugly thoughts while the hull bangs and slaps underneath me. It's only ten minutes more to Zhuhai than to Macau and I arrive with plenty of time to check into the hotel before going to my first appointment.

The computer input company office looks just like any other huge typing pool. Fifty or sixty nearly indistinguishable heads are bent over keyboards in front of screens. At least it's relatively quiet, the soft click of fingers on plastic having replaced the striking clatter and bell rings of typewriters. I'm supposed to take pictures to go with the story, but there's nothing photogenic about the place. I find the best looking people who are closest to the few windows. With any luck the little natural light will prevent the humming fluorescent lights overheard from turning all the photos green.

Back in his office the managing director refuses to use an interpreter. He suffers from the delusion that he speaks English. He's almost entirely unintelligible. I politely pretend to be taking notes while I think about what I might do if I find Sasha, or what else I can do if I don't. I don't come to any conclusions.

When he finishes whatever it was he was telling me, he calls four of his other managers into the office and insists I take a group photo. I do, and then he invites me to lunch. None of them speak much English either, but I'm hungry, my next meeting isn't until two and who knows, maybe one of them can get me into the Imperial.

We walk across the street to an ornate restaurant where there's a private room reserved. Some food is already on the table when we arrive and more keeps coming. They pour me a tall glass of brandy and a chaser of beer before serving the same to themselves.

They shout something, lift their glasses in my direction and throw back the brandy, then they all look at me, waiting for me to do the same. I've still got two more meetings this afternoon but I don't want to risk alienating these guys.

I'm relieved that after the first glass we all slow down, simply sipping at the next and mostly drinking beer with our meal. I try making small talk but it's almost impossible, their English isn't up to it and my Cantonese and Mandarin are useless for almost anything other than swearing, taking taxis and ordering a few dishes I like in restaurants.

After some feeble effort at conversation I give up and they talk among themselves, keeping an eye out to make sure that I like the food. I do, it's excellent. Whenever it looks like my rice bowl is threatening to empty, someone puts something more on top of it. I notice that there is one dish, a large earthenware bowl from which they aren't serving me. When it rotates near me on the lazy Susan in the middle of the table I stop it and ladle some of its contents onto my rice. It's a meat dish. Their conversation stops. The managing director, who is sitting next to me, smiles, takes some himself and turns to me.

"No good for *gwailo*. No happy eat."

I bend over and take a sniff of it. It smells fine. "Don't worry. I like most things, it's not a problem."

This happens a lot. The first week I had a job in Hong Kong my Chinese colleagues took me out to lunch. They deliberately ordered a lot of food that they thought I wouldn't like and a couple of dishes that they figured were dull enough for my heathen tastes. It was a test and I passed it; sucking the meat off the bones of the stewed chicken feet, slurping my coagulated pig blood, nimbly picking up slippery slices of intestine with my chopsticks and chewing rubbery jellyfish with a smile on my face. After that they liked me and I could eat what I wanted for lunch.

Across the table two of the middle managers have put down their chopsticks to watch me. I overhear one of them say to the other, "*gau yuhk.*" I do know enough Cantonese to know that means "dog meat." I learned that to the amusement of one of the magazine's secretaries because if you say *gau* with a slightly higher-pitched and longer rising tone, it's nasty slang for "penis."

I take a bite. It tastes a little like goat. There used to be a pretty good taco stand that served goat near my house in Los Angeles. This reminds me of that and I like it. I smile and look around the table. "*Gau yuhk, ho lawn ho seck-ah.*"

Everyone looks a little startled to hear me saying that dog meat is "very fucking good food," then they laugh, long and hard. After that, across the language barrier, we're all pals. Using a few words of English here, a little Cantonese there, sign language and drawing on the tablecloth we somehow manage to talk more than we had when we were trying to be polite.

By the time the lunch party breaks up so that I can hurry to my next appointment, two of the managers, Wai Lam and Albert, have invited me to the Imperial that night. My first meeting of the day couldn't have gone any better.

The next two meetings aren't fiascos, exactly, just dull. I get more than enough to put together an article that is only marginally more interesting than the one I was editing at the start of the week. I'm glad I'm really here for other reasons. This type of journalism is nowhere close to as interesting as poking my nose into the goings on of gangsters. I get back to the hotel by four-thirty. I want to rest before the evening's festivities.

It's impossible. Despite a "Do Not Disturb" sign on the door and a "No Calls Please" request on the phone, there is a constant parade of people wanting to know if I want something. Mostly they want to know if I want them. I keep count; in two hours, eight young women and two young men knock on my door selling sex. After I say "no" and close the door I can hear them knocking their way further along the hall. I unplug the phone after the sixth call in which the only English the person on the other end can speak is "fucking" or "sucking."

I don't know why I'm surprised. This happens every time I stay in hotels in China. I guess it's their idea of really good service. In five star hotels around the rest of Asia the over-abundant staff pester you constantly also, but to turn down your bed, change your towels, freshen the fruit bowl, make sure the TV is working properly, things like that. Even in Bangkok, which is famous for its sex-industry, you have to go out looking for sex; it doesn't just come to you. I guess all the years of repressive communism have left China with a lot of catching up to do.

I give up by six and go down to the lobby bar where I nurse a drink until I meet the general manager at seven. He's Swiss, named Hans, just three years out of some "world renown" school for hoteliers in Geneva. He's tall and prissily dressed in a gray wool suit with green piping. I have to look twice to make sure he's not wearing lederhosen. He looks like he washes his hands a lot, with perfumed soap and very hot water. He confides in me that it's just a matter of months before he's brought back from exile to run a "more suitable establishment" in Europe. He asks if I have any complaints. I tell him I wouldn't have minded an undisturbed nap.

"These Chinese, they are primitive. They have a great civilization yes, a great history, no? But they have forgotten. They have no concept of service, some of them are savages."

He says that in the nicest way, figuring I share his brutish sentiments. Maybe I even do, a little, in a knee jerk kind of way, but I'm not about to admit it to him or anyone else. I do my best to smile and keep the conversation light.

A light dinner would be nice too, especially since lunch had been huge. But Hans is very proud of his fondue restaurant. Either that or he wants to give it some business. We're the only people in there. Chinese don't eat much cheese and a bubbling vat of it is brought to the table with hunks of bread that the Chinese don't eat much of either.

He wants to impress me with his hospitality. A complimentary press clipping or two will look good stapled to his resume. Unfortunately he seems to think I can be bought with a very expensive bottle of thick, cloying red wine along with the cauldron of hot white, oozing fat in front of us.

One glass and three dripping, viscous chunks of bread into dinner I excuse myself to go to the men's room. I consider making a break for it, out of the hotel and across the border to Macau, but I just splash a lot of water on my face, paste a smile on and head back to the table.

I beg off the chocolate fondue, the schnapps and the tawny port, managing to cut through the end of the meal with a very strong double espresso and a truly remarkable snifter of twenty-five year old single malt scotch. Hans seems a bit disappointed when I tell him that I'm meeting some people after dinner. When I tell him where he becomes curt and formal and makes it clear that his management is not associated with the "club" in the basement.

Wai Lam and Albert are waiting in the lobby at nine-thirty. They look like the Laurel and Hardy of China. Wai Lam is short and round with the merest wisp of a mustache and unruly hair that looks like it's been cut around a bowl over his head. In spite of not having a Western name, he speaks more English than Albert who is tall and skinny with a very short buzz cut topping him off. They look a little nervous standing, waiting for me to walk up to them, rocking their weight from one foot to the other. When I say "hello" they nod in greeting, both of them clap me on the back and turn me in the direction of the elevator.

We're only going down one floor, but I can't spot a staircase. There's got to be some other way in and out of the place and I'd like to know where it is, but I can't see one. The elevator lets us off in a mirrored waiting room with a couple of plush sofas. We remain standing. Before long one of the mirrors swings open silently from floor to ceiling and a tall, elegant Chinese woman of indeterminate age in a very expensive black dress and carrying a clipboard totters out on stiletto heels. She greets Wai Lam and Albert by name and gives me a hand to hold. It's so cool I wonder for a moment if she's a vampire. It might be refreshing if I wasn't so nervous. I worry if my hand is sweating.

She speaks in Mandarin with the guys, then turns to me holding out the clipboard and one of the sort of overpriced fountain pens that people get for college graduation gifts. Her voice in English is measured, soft and sibilant with a pleasantly mannered Beijing accent. "Please, welcome Mr. Sharp. We are always happy to accomodate the honored guests of our members. We do, however, please ask you to fill out this small form. Perhaps in the future you will become one of our members."

The form's in Chinese, Japanese, Korean, Thai, Malay, Arabic, French and English but it doesn't ask for anything more than my name, address, employer and who's my host. There's some sort of boilerplate legalese at the bottom. I skim the fine print. It just says I agree to abide by the rules of the organization. If I insist on knowing what they are, they can provide me with a copy. I don't need to know the specifics; it shouldn't be too tough to figure them out as I go along.

I sign the form and hand it back to the hostess. She takes my hand again. "I am certain Mr. Sharp that Wai Lam and Albert have explained our club to you, but please remember that we do not use money here. You may safely leave all of your valuables in the dressing room and indulge yourself as you desire. If you have any special requests, please do not hesitate to inquire of one of our staff."

She sweeps the mirrored door open again and gestures us inside. We file into a long narrow hallway with raw silk covered walls on which hang classic Chinese erotic prints and scrolls. I move along slowly, admiring the collection. I stop in front of a very large embroidered tapestry of an Imperial Court orgy scene. It's lit beautifully. It's as vibrant and colorful as a perfectly exposed transparency on a light table. Just about anything sexual that people can do to and with each other or themselves is being done in perfect, hand-stitched explicit detail.

I feel the soft, cool hand of the hostess on my arm, her light breath on my neck as she moves up to stand next to me, one hip gently brushing my leg. "It is beautiful, is it not Mr. Sharp?"

"Yes, I've never seen anything like it."

"It is from the Ming Dynasty, perhaps six hundred years old."

"It looks perfect, new."

"Yes, we are very proud of this piece. It is possibly the finest like it in existence."

"A lot of what they're getting up to looks pretty modern to me."

She smiles and leans a little further into me. "Indeed Mr. Sharp, the pleasures they are enjoying are timeless."

There's proof of that once I get out of the locker room and into the high-vaulted chamber that holds the famous swimming pool. Wai Lam, Albert and I are wearing towels. They look like they're not sure if they need to keep me company or not. I let them know that there's no need and that I will no doubt run into them later. They scurry away in opposite directions around the pool and disappear into alcoves at the far end.

The room is enormous. A series of huge, but delicate looking arches, maybe fifty or more feet tall support a softly glowing ceiling dotted with shimmering stars, the moon and the planets. The swimming pool underneath the ceiling is at least Olympic-sized, probably larger and around its edges are other pools, bubbling Jacuzzis and rocky grottoes, tropical waterfalls cascading into pools and brown, green and red mud baths that give off faint, pleasant mineral odors.

At the far end of the pool there are café tables and a bar. A bandstand is tucked away in a corner of it and there is a small jazz combo with a sylph-like singer sheathed in white and diamonds. She's crooning a torch song in Mandarin. It wafts across the room on the lightly chlorinated air currents reminding me of the soundtrack to a movie about Shanghai in the nineteen-twenties.

There's a light tinkle of voices speaking a blend of languages. There are about a dozen men and perhaps three times as many women. About half the men are modestly wrapped in towels; the others are acting out scenes from the tapestry I'd admired. Towels would only get in the way.

The women are all naked and beautiful. A few of them are floating on inflatables in the pool, others sitting on pads around its edges. The rest are scattered around the place; in the other pools, on chaise lounges along the sides, at the tables and bar at the far end.

Two women approach me. One of them is Japanese and tells me her name is Kiko. She's got shiny black hair to the back of her knees and a hairless, boyish body that glistens with oil. The other, Gail, is blonde, buxom, tall and greets me with a harsh Australian accent.

They're both available for anything I want, but it's only briefly tempting. They're sexy at first, but then they begin to seem like Stepford wives; detached, listless, their eyes dull and empty. I excuse myself saying that I just got here and want to break myself in slowly. I pad softly around the pool to the bar, fending off a few other advances along the way.

There's only one stool left at the bar and I take it. The bartender is Thai and once she's settled me with an icy vodka she wants to know if she can serve me in other ways underneath the counter while I drink. Her glazed eyes look off at something in the distance, but she licks her lips while she makes the offer. It's also not tempting. I suppose it ought to be, but it isn't.

"Just the drink for now thanks. Maybe later."

An American voice to my left speaks up. "First time here?"

I swivel on the stool to look at her. She's about the color of an espresso, with a short pageboy cut of thick, softened hair. Her eyes are large and sad, a little bloodshot but with a remnant sparkle somewhere deep in there. I try to be subtle about making a quick scan of her body. She sits ramrod straight, small, perky breasts with long nipples poking out in front of her. She catches me looking and uncrosses her legs.

"Should I stand up and pirouette?"

I'm not sure if she's serious or not. I'm sure I'd probably like that but I'm just as sure I'd be too embarrassed to say "yes." Instead, I must look confused.

"You've gotta be an American. You guys are always shy first time you come here." She gets up and slowly turns around for my inspection. She's got, as they say, legs up to here and a high riding bubble butt. Her skin looks flawless.

She sits back down and reaches out to stroke my crotch through the towel. "You like what you see?"

"Yeah, well, how could I help it?"

"I can help you baby. What kinda help you want?"

She is very sexy and somehow seems to have held on to a scrap more of her personality than the other women I've met. She's almost enough to make me forget why I'm here, but not quite.

"Later. Let's talk first. What's your name?"

She rolls her eyes at me and snorts. "We don't need names here honey. What's the point?"

"I'm Ray. Come on, what do I call you?"

"Please, don't press it sugar, just call me 'honey' or something, okay?"

"You got it. Where're you from, honey?"

"Nowhere baby. Why so many questions? I'm here, you're here, we can get busy together and that's all you gotta know sugar. I don't answer no questions."

"I'm looking for somebody."

"You found me hon, don't you like dark meat?" She stands up again and steps back for me to get a better view of her. "Want to take another tour?"

I reach out to take her hands, then turn her arms to take a look at the inside of her elbows. If she's a junkie, she doesn't stick needles there. She gives me a stern look.

"What're you lookin' for?"

"I've heard some things."

"Keep 'em to yourself. This ain't no place for questions. The people who run this place're smarter than that. Too smart for me. Too smart for you. You don't want to get us in trouble now, do you."

"I'm still looking for somebody, a friend of mine, a Russian girl." I describe Sasha.

"I ain't seen her. There's eight or nine Russian ladies here, but she don't sound familiar. You wanna get with one of those Russian ladies you go right ahead. I'm all done answering questions." She starts to turn away. I hold onto her wrists and turn her back to me.

"Look, I'm sorry, I don't mean to cause you any problems. You're very sexy and I'd love to get together. First I've gotta look around some. Could you point me in the direction of some of the Russians? I'll go talk to them and come back. Where will I find you?"

"Where d'ya think you're gonna find me fool? I ain't goin' nowhere. If I'm busy later, too bad."

She looks around. She points to two tall blondes who are sitting on opposite ends of a short, fat Asian man on one of the chaise lounges. "Those girls're some Russians but they look busy to me." A little ways further down three women are talking. One's in the water, holding onto the edge, the other two are sitting, dangling their legs into the pool. "There're some more. Now get outta here and come back when you're ready for some real woman."

I walk over to the three women. When they see me approach the two on the pool deck move apart and pat the space between them by way of invitation. I sit down and dangle my legs into the water. The one in the pool rests her forearms above my knees and looks up at me, slowly treading water.

"Hey ladies, how're ya doing?"

They look at each other and quickly confer in Russian. The one on my right, a redhead with dull green eyes and pouty red lips, is either the only one who speaks any English, or the only one who will.

"You America?"

"American, yeah."

"You like Russia girl?"

"Later. I'm looking for someone. Sasha, a Russian girl. Maybe you know her."

She looks down at the woman between my legs and says something to her, then reaches over and unknots my towel. The woman in the pool boosts herself a little further up my thighs and plants her mouth on my dick. The other two lean into me and start rubbing their breasts over my chest and arms, kissing my neck, nibbling my ears.

They're trying to distract me and it's working. There's something mechanical about it, something I don't like. But it still feels good. I'm just about to give up and get into it when the redhead lifts one of her feet out of the water and I get a good look at it. There're crusty scabs between the toes, dozens of slightly swollen and angry looking dots along the veins of the ankle. I shove myself forward to grab her foot. That dislodges the woman from my crotch; she falls back into the water. The other two lose their balance and sprawl out next to me. I lift the redhead's foot and take a closer look. I put it down and grab for the calf of the woman on the other side of me. Her foot's the same.

I don't want to think about what the owners of this place might do once a woman's veins in discreet places all collapse. Warner was right. Well why wouldn't he be? Isn't the C.I.A. supposed to know these sort of things? I'm not thinking about giving myself up to the pleasures of the place anymore, I just wanna get out. I pull my feet out of the water and am getting ready to get up and go.

I hear yelling in Russian and Chinese, maybe something in English. I hear the slap of shoes on the pool deck. As I'm turning to see what's going on, rockets burst in my skull. I see bright flashes of light and color. I hear crackling sounds. Then everything goes into slow motion, or at least I think it does. It's all gone black and I can't see anything so all I've got is the sense that things are slowing down. Then they just stop.

| |CHAPTER **TWENTY** | |

Something's digging into my back and it's really uncomfortable. Somebody's talking really loud. It's dark but I don't know if that's because I've got my eyes closed or not. I don't want to open them. I'm afraid of what I'll see. I'm afraid of what I might not see.

Something smells really terrible. It hurts my nose when I breathe. I try taking a breath through my mouth but that's even worse. The air slices me like a thousand little paper cuts on my lungs. I start coughing and the pain is almost unbearable. But the loud voices stop.

Wood slides over wood and there's a deep thunk as something is thrown down. I still have my eyes closed but there's light now on the other side of the lids. The voices come back. They're chattering in a Chinese language. It's not Cantonese or Mandarin. I'd recognize those.

Something, someone comes and squats next to me. I feel hands on my arms, wrapping around my back. I'm squeezing my eyes shut. I don't want to know what's going on.

I'm being lifted. Pushed from the bottom and pulled from the top. My body edges over the lip of something into fresher air and brighter light. I take deep breaths and they spear me with pain but they don't smell so bad. I curl up and roll with the agony of it.

After a while, it seems like a long while, I roll onto my back and kick my legs out straight flat in front of me. I risk opening my eyes.

There're faces, five of them, all Chinese, three men and two women. They're looking down at me with as close to a universal expression of surprise and concern as I can imagine. I don't know what to say to them. I don't know if they'll understand anything if I do.

In Cantonese you can say *joh sahn*, which means "good morning." But hardly anyone really says it and I don't know what time it is. There's a way of saying "hello" in Mandarin, but I can't remember it at the moment.

It takes me a couple of tries to sit up and I have to bow my head and hold it tight in my hands for a few moments to clear it after I do. Then I look up at the five Chinese people who are still looking down at me. They've moved back a little, to a safer distance.

What most Cantonese say in greeting is, "have you eaten yet?" It's going to sound really stupid under the circumstances, but if I can get them laughing at me I figure it'll be harder for them to hurt me. At least I hope so.

"*Lei sihk mm sihk fahn-ah?*"

They don't laugh. They look at each other then start talking among themselves again. Finally one of the women steps toward me and squats down to look me in the face. She's short, strong and burnt dark by the sun. She looks like she's in her mid to late thirties, but she also looks like someone who could be prematurely aged. She's wearing a faded yellow baseball cap with an elephant stitched onto it. I recognize it. It's from a baseball team in Taiwan. Her face is dirty, covered with soot, but she's wiped an area clean around her eyes and they sparkle out at me.

"*Ngoh sik Gwongdungwa. Matyeh?*"

So she speaks Cantonese and wants to know "what?" If I actually spoke Cantonese and knew what, I could tell her. I'm fast running out of vocabulary.

"*Mm gee doh. Ngoh bindouh-ah?*" I tell her I don't know and ask where I am.

She turns to the other people and says something that makes them laugh. She turns back to me, sniffs around my mouth and says, "*djoi-yu.*" She thinks I'm drunk. I wish I was.

"*Mo, mo djoi-yu. Ho mahfaahn.*" I'm not sure that'll get the point across, but I think I've told her I'm not drunk and that I'm in trouble, "very trouble" actually.

It's taken a while but I'm beginning to figure out where I am. I'm sitting on wood boards and they're shuddering slightly. The horizon is bobbing and weaving. At first I thought that was in my head, now I realize I'm on a boat. I get up on my knees to look over the railing. I can see a couple of small islands in the distance, nothing that looks comfortingly like the mainland.

The woman in the elephant cap puts a hand on my shoulder and repeats, "*matyeh?*"

"*Ngoh Meihgwo. Mgoi, bindouh-ah?*" I tell her I'm an American and ask where we are again, or where she's from, I'm not sure.

"*Ngoh Hainan dou.*" She's from Hainan Island. That's a start. She pulls up on my arm, wanting me to stand up. With some help from her I do and she points out the sights. To the left and behind us over the horizon is Macau and Zhuhai.

To the left and just a little in front of us is a tiny, barren rock that she calls *Gwoyahn dou*, which means something or another I don't understand Island. To our right are a few rickety old fishing boats, their nets spread out behind them. And beyond them I can see two gently rounded rock peaks on another island. That island's called *Hung dou*. She looks embarrassed when she says it and the men laugh, so I can guess what its name means. Far ahead of us and to the right, just barely poking over the horizon is another island. *Haak dou*, she says, adding something about *haa*. Apparently she knows it as a good place to catch shrimp.

I can't see it clearly but we're headed in that direction. Sooner or later I'll get a better look at Black Island. I'm just not sure I want to.

The boat I'm on is an old Chinese junk made of tar soaked planks of teak, with a high slanted back and front and a low flat area in the middle. It's broad and flat at the bottom, but even so it pitches and rolls in a way that makes me very glad I'm not prone to seasickness. It's got masts for sails but it's powered by a belching, coughing, spewing diesel engine. It's a shrimp boat.

I must've been knocked out, and maybe drugged last night in the Imperial. Someone broke into the locker I'd used, dressed me, carried me out of there and tossed me in the hold of the boat. I guess they didn't like the questions I was asking. I suppose I'm lucky. I'm still woozy and my head feels like a spike's been driven through it, right behind the eyes. They could have done a lot worse.

The woman brings me a mug of hot water. I thank her and introduce myself. She points to the crewmembers and assigns them all names that I immediately forget. Except for hers, it's Mei Ling. With my few words of Cantonese, sign language and the help of a calendar I gather that they plan to be out at sea just overnight. They can take me back to Zhuhai tomorrow.

I've got to admire the honesty of whoever dumped me on the boat. They've left me my wallet. I get it out and offer money to the woman, indicating that it's for everyone. She refuses it. She points me to a small cabin at the back. There're mattresses on the deck and a couple of large buckets of water with washcloths and soap. I go to clean up, but I don't want to lie down so afterwards I lean against the railing and watch the water.

Black Island is getting bigger on the horizon and I wonder if I'm being taken there. Even though there's plenty of other fishing boats around, it'd be easier to get rid of me there than it would have been in Zhuhai. A foreigner disappearing in a Chinese city would raise a ruckus. One lost at sea in restricted waters near a naval base might not be worth the trouble of looking for.

The crew has better things to do than to keep an eye on me. I'm not about to jump overboard and swim for shore. I explore the boat while they busy themselves with nets and ropes and filling barrels with seawater. I'm not sure what I'm looking for. Something to use as a weapon in case I'm attacked again might come in handy. There's plenty of knives and gaffing hooks and pieces of wood that could make a club. But my guess is that any one of the crew can fight with that stuff better than I can. Besides, there's five of them.

There's also no radio, no way to contact the shore or other boats. I'm stuck.

Other than looking out over the water or watching the crew at work, there's nothing to do. *Moby Dick* is one of my favorite books, but life on this shrimp junk is a whole lot less interesting than it was on the Pequod. No one's even steering the boat. The sea is calm and the wheel's been tied in place. The boat chugs along slowly in a relatively straight line. The water barrels are full and now everyone's sewing, mending the enormous net that's wrapped around a long wood cylinder with handles to turn it at either end.

I sit next to Mei Ling and watch as her fingers work over the mesh. I'd offer to help, to have something to do, but I'd just slow her down. I could use a cup of coffee but there's no Mr. Starbuck on board to make me one. I can't tell who's the captain either. There's no Ahab clumping along the deck shouting orders. Everyone just seems to know what to do.

I'd rather have something mindless to do than to just sit here and think. Thinking sucks. I don't really know what's happened to Sasha, but what I figure's happened gnaws at me like a hungry ghost in my stomach. I need to know. I can't just leave it the way it is. Even if there isn't anything I can do about it, even if knowing ends up hurting worse than anything yet. I need to know.

I'd left my watch in the hotel room and no one on board seems to have one either. I think it's mid-afternoon when we drop anchor about a mile out from a small bay on Black Island. We're over some sort of shoal. I can see rock peaks in the water just a few feet underneath us. There's a lot of kelp and seaweed and the water's clear enough that I can see large fish rainbowing in the sunlight when they come close to the surface.

I pick up the binoculars that hang from a peg by the wheel and take a better look at the island. It's long and low, fringed with white sand beaches and without much foliage. I can just make out the top of a stone building over a small ridge directly across from us. I scan the horizon and see only a few other fishing junks, some moving and trailing nets, others just bobbing in the water.

Mei Ling comes up the three steps of the ladder to the wheel deck. She takes the binoculars from me and slowly looks around us in a full circle. She hangs them back on the peg and turns to me, making a gesture like she's shoveling something into her mouth. "*Sihk fahn-ah.*" It's time to eat.

That's good because I'm hungry. I'd be happy to eat some fresh shrimp or fish but it hasn't been caught yet. Instead, some sort of canned, macerated pork is sliced over bowls of rice and sprinkled with flakes of dried cuttlefish. I take a bite and do my best not to grimace when they watch me eating.

I'm not sure what they're expecting, probably for me to not like the food, which I don't. But I hate living up to expectations so

I smile, pat my stomach and make a contented sound. They laugh, then one of the men hands me an open Budweiser beer can.

I don't like Bud, especially not warm, but it's gotta be better than the scalding water they're all drinking. I start to tilt it toward my mouth. Everyone's watching. What's so fascinating about a thirsty man drinking a beer? Just before I get it to my lips Mei Ling reaches out and stops me.

"*Mo bejau, laahtjiu-jeung.*" I take a sniff and the odor almost knocks me out all over again. My eyes start pouring water, my mouth floods with saliva. She's right. It isn't beer, it's chili sauce, and from the smell of it more potent than any I've ever come across before.

I dribble a tiny dab of it onto a finger. It's bright yellow, it looks radioactive. It's thin and oily with what looks like grains of sand in it. It feels hot on my fingertip. When I hold the finger up to take a closer look, tears cascade out of my eyes and I feel like I'll be uncontrollably drooling any minute. Do people really eat this stuff?

Everybody's laughing loudly now. Talking loudly. The other woman, she looks like she could be any age between seventy and a hundred and twelve, takes the can from me and pours about a spoonful of the sauce onto the side of her rice. She touches it with the tip of a chopstick, then picks up a piece of the meat and pops it into her mouth. She swallows then imitates the contented sound I made earlier. Everyone laughs harder.

I hold my hot sauce coated finger up and stick out my tongue to take a small taste. Someone tosses a grenade into my mouth, one of those hot, blinding flash ones. My head starts to tingle, my ears start to ring, and my nose starts to run. Niagara Falls has routed itself through my eyes. I'm about to drown on the liquid that's running in a torrent through my mouth.

The strangest thing is, I like it. It's delicious. Besides all the searing heat and pain and confusion, there's something else going on in there, in my mouth, something wonderful. The flavor is sweet and rich and complex, like a blend of exotic tropical fruits with a ferocious bite. As the initial violence subsides the taste takes over and puts me at ease. It's calming. I feel tranquilized and happy.

I've read articles. I know why I feel this way. Endorphins, everyone's favorite drug, are binding themselves to my neuro-receptors in an attempt to fight off the pain. And endorphins are a lot like heroin. And even though heroin screws up their lives, plenty of people still like it; love it even. And endorphins don't even screw up your life. They're not illegal and they're good for you.

I reach out for the Budweiser can and pour a lot of the sauce down the side of my rice bowl. Everyone laughs. I laugh. They're startled by how much of the stuff I end up eating.

About an hour later they're letting out the shrimp net. I'm doing what I can to help, making sure it isn't tangled as it spools off the end of the boat. The old lady is at the wheel, moving slowly forward to make sure the net doesn't float back in on top of itself. She cries out something and everyone looks up.

There's another boat coming toward us, a Chinese Navy patrol boat. It's better if they don't see me. Mei Ling points at me then at the hold. I climb down into it and squat behind a cluster of barrels as the Navy pulls up alongside us.

I hear shouting, but it sounds friendly enough. I'm sweating with the heat in the hold and the jitters. If they're going to turn me over to the authorities, this is when the crew of the shrimp boat will do it.

They don't. The patrol boat powers away and I stay below until Mei Ling comes to get me.

When I emerge the Navy boat is almost out of sight around the far end of the island. One of the men is watching it through the binoculars. When it disappears he lets them drop on their string around his neck, then he spits and yells out something that's obviously a curse in the direction it's gone. He turns and stares at me. He rolls up his sleeves and holds out his arms for me to inspect.

They're horribly scarred and crudely tattooed with rough, thick black Chinese characters. He turns around and lifts his shirt. His back is a raised hash of slash marks. He turns to face me, reaches out with his hands to grip my shoulders, looks at me long and hard, then smiles and goes back to his work.

Before long the net is fully let out and all there is to do is cruise in lazy circles sweeping up shrimp.

When night comes the crew hangs lanterns over the back end. I look down into a swirling mass of sealife attracted to the light. After a couple of hours I help haul the net back into the boat. It's heavy with the catch.

We shovel the shrimp into the barrels, toss the larger fish into different barrels and throw back the small fry. When everything is loaded the old woman steers the boat closer to shore, to the outer edge of a small bay. I can see a light on the island. I take out the binoculars and in the light of the moon can see that it's coming from the top of the stone building I'd seen during the day. It doesn't seem so far away.

I get an idea. It's a dumb one but I can't get it out of my head. The boat I'm on has a small rowboat, a dark green rubber dinghy really, but it'll get me to shore. It takes about twenty minutes to get the idea across to Mei Ling; to make her understand I want to borrow the boat, row into shore and come back before sunrise.

She wants to know why. She thinks I might get into *mahfaahn*, trouble. I can hardly draw at all and when I find a pencil and paper all five of the crew get another few laughs out of my attempt to explain with pictures.

Finally Mei Ling gets it. "*Lei pahngyauh mahfaahn?*"

Yes, my friend's in trouble. I'm glad she doesn't want to know what I'm going to try and do about it. I don't know myself.

The five crewmembers go into a huddle. The man who'd shown me his scars does a lot of the talking. When they break up, two of the men go to the small rubber boat and untie it. They lower it into the water, making sure the oars are in place. Mei Ling, the old lady and the scarred man disappear into the small cabin.

I'm stepping over the railing of the junk when the three of them return. Mei Ling has an old Army canteen. She's filled it with water for me. The man's holding a gun. It's a small revolver. Its barrel is dull with a patina of rust; the trigger guard has snapped off, its grip is wound with black electrical tape where the wood's fallen off. It's a six-shooter. He clicks the magazine open and shows me it's loaded, with three bullets. He presses it into my hand, pushes it against my chest and says something in his Chinese language I don't understand.

| |CHAPTER **TWENTY-ONE** | |

t's quiet on the water and luckily it's a calm night. The moon is directly overhead and a little more than three-quarters full. There's just a few wispy clouds and a glittering rice bowl of stars. When I was in college I'd lived by a lake. I had a small rowboat and used to spend a lot of time out on the water. It doesn't take long before my body remembers how to row and I settle into a steady comfortable rhythm. It would be beautiful, peaceful, relaxing, if I didn't have any idea of what I might be getting myself into.

Earlier in the day one of the men on the boat drew me a rough map of the island. The boat pier's on the opposite side from where I'm headed, the Naval base is on a spit of land that's out of sight around to the left. The only building that he knew about, other than on the base, is the one with the light. I've set my course straight for it.

It takes me about a half hour to get to the beach. I pull the dinghy up onto the sand behind some rocks, hoping it's out of sight. I don't hear anything other than small waves and rolling pebbles. I can see the light on top of the building and I move slowly in that direction. I've got the canteen on a string over my shoulder. The gun's tucked under my shirt at the small of my back. It's a little uncomfortable. The fact that it seems like a good idea to have it isn't comforting either.

The beach slopes up and as it gets further away from the water becomes covered with scrub brush. I hope there aren't any snakes. This is exactly the sort of place I figure they like. I'm terrified of snakes and I'm having a very hard time forcing myself to keep quiet. Noise scares them away and I'd like to be making more of it, but I know that isn't a good idea.

I get to the top of the ridge and look out across a wide field. The building I'd seen is at the far end of it, on a slight rise. There's a large, bright light on the roof and dimly lit windows on what looks like the third floor. I don't see any windows at all below that. It's fortress-like, forbidding. Why the hell am I here? Just what was I thinking?

I move into the field, listening for anything that might give me the excuse to flee back to the beach and the boat. About halfway across, the foliage stops and I'm on a neatly manicured lawn. I stop and crouch down. If someone looks out from the building they can probably see me, or at least see some sort of movement. I crabwalk back into the brush and take a look around.

Over to the left there's a long, low stone building. I can just make it out in the moonlight. It's near the edge of the lawn. If I can get to it through the brush, it will get me closer to the big building without breaking cover.

I bend low as I walk. My knees are killing me, but better them than somebody else. Getting closer I can see that it isn't exactly a building, at least not a fully enclosed one. It's sort of a giant, permanent lean-to, divided into stalls. It might be a stable or a kennel. As soon as a dog barks I'm out of here.

I like dogs. My family always had them when I was a kid. But right now they're something I can do without.

The sidewall of the lean-to is old stone, huge, rough-hewn blocks of it mortared into place. It's not a hot night but I'm sweating like crazy. When I lean up against the wall it's cold, almost icy. It startles me.

So does a noise. Was it a cough? A voice? I freeze in place. I'd stop the beating of my heart, the slushing of my blood through my veins, if I could. I turn my head very slowly one way, then the other, hoping that will help my ears pick up sound.

Crickets are chirruping and I wish they'd shut up so I could hear better. There's a stream somewhere and the water lightly rattles over rocks. A bird chitters in the distance. Any moment I'm going to imagine I hear an owl hoot and a wolf howl.

I'm about to move when I hear it, a low moan. I stay frozen and the moan rises and falls, finally settling into a soft whimper. It sounds like a woman, a miserable woman, sadder than any I've ever heard before.

I pull out the gun; poking it in front of me as I squat as low as I can and duck walk as slow as I can around the corner of the wall. There are eight stalls with dirt and remnants of hay on their floors and metal gates at the front. It must be a kennel. The stalls have very low ceilings; a horse couldn't stand in one.

I freeze again, ready for a dog to wake up and start snarling, barking. Ready to run. But I don't hear anything other than the whimpering of the woman. The sound is coming from the second stall from the far end. I edge my way closer to it, looking all around. I don't see anyone or hear anything else.

I go back the way I came and around the back of the lean-to. I want to approach from both sides, make sure no one's around. It takes me another ten minutes before I get to the front of the stall where the sound is coming from. I freeze there, squatting, the gun in my hand and as ready for trouble as I can be.

The gate in front of the stall is made from strung razor wire and is chained shut. There's a terrible stench of shit and piss and body odor that pounds on my nose trying to get in. It's dark in the stall. I can just barely make out a slightly darker form lying on the floor against the back wall. The form is twitching. I can see the movement. It's still whimpering.

"Psst, hello, hello." I keep my voice to a whisper and look around while talking.

The whimpering stops. I hear a metallic rattle. It sounds like a chain.

"Hello, hello, who's there?" It's a frightened sounding, quiet female voice. The dark form the voice belongs to is up off the floor. She's moving, crawling toward me. The rattling noise follows behind her. I can't see anything clearly until there's her face, just inches from mine, separated from me by the slivers of honed steel.

"Please mister, I'll be good. I'll be a good girl. I won't be any more trouble. I'll do anything you want, anything they want. They can do whatever they want with me. I'm worthless, just a piece of shit, just a toy for them, for you. Please mister, you gotta let me out. I'll be good. I promise."

My eyes are adjusting and she's coming into better view. I think she used to be beautiful. There isn't much of that left now. Her hair is matted and soiled; it's impossible to tell what color it might have been. Her eyes are dark, listless pools and the rest of her face is almost as dark, swollen and bruised. She's got a tight, thick metal ring clamped around her neck and I can see a chain leading away from it into the dark behind her. I guess she's naked, but she's fully covered in scabs, bruises, cuts and filth. The reek of her this close makes my eyes water.

She's trying to rub away her tears and the snot from her nose, trying to wipe some of the grit off her face. I realize I haven't said anything. I don't know what to say. She reaches out to me, trying to stretch a hand through the razor wire, but pulls it back, sliced and bleeding.

"I, I, I'm Ray. I'm looking for someone. I want to help you if I can. What can I do? What's your name? Where're you from?"

"Name? From?" She starts whimpering again, begins to fall to the ground but the chain attached to her neck won't let her get all the way down. She gasps as the collar bites into her, and then scuttles back a little to where she can sit.

"Help me, you've gotta help me. If I stay here I'll die. I was beautiful once. I can be pretty again, I can. I'll do anything you want, anything. I'm not bad, really I'm not. I'm a good girl. I can do anything you want. You've gotta help me." Her voice is American and is on the edge of cracking. She's either crazy or on the verge of falling over that ledge.

I don't know how I can help her. I finger the chain and the lock on the gate and there's no way I can get them open. I've seen people shoot locks off in movies but I'm pretty sure the little gun I've got won't be much use. Even if I do open the gate, how am I going to get the chain off her neck.

"Are you thirsty? I have water." It isn't much. Under the circumstances it isn't really anything, but I've got to do something.

I take my shirt off to wrap around my hands for protection as I pull the gate open just far enough to squeeze the canteen through and hand it to her. She yanks the cork out with her teeth, throws her head back and swallows nearly all of it, making loud gulping noises. When she's almost done she stops and pours the rest of it on her face and rubs it around hard with her hands. She moves forward again so I can see her. She doesn't look any different.

"I can be pretty again. I can be pretty, see. I need a shower, makeup, nice clothes. I can go shopping, yes shopping. You'll see, I'll do anything you want, anything. Help me, you've got to help me."

"I don't know what to do. I don't know how I can get this gate open or your chains off. Where's the key? Do you know who has the key?"

"Key? Yes, the key. The tall mistress has it. The Russian mistress. You've got to help me. You've got to get me out of here. She'll kill me. She'll leave me here and I'll die. I don't want to die."

"This tall mistress, does she have a name?"

"Mistress Storm."

I was afraid of that.

| |CHAPTER **TWENTY-TWO** | |

What I should do is get the hell out of here. Getting myself killed isn't going to help anyone. I'm not sure if anything else is going to help anyone either.

I don't know what my problem is but I just can't seem to let these sorts of things alone. In one way or another I've always taken leaps into stupidity because of wanting to do some good. I was a student radical when I was young. I thought revolution would make the world a better place. It didn't. It almost never has.

I became a reporter, inspired by H. L. Mencken's description of the purpose of journalism: "to comfort the afflicted and to afflict the comfortable." But despite my best efforts the corruption and brutality I tried to uncover didn't stop; if anything, it got worse.

So somewhere along the line I got cynical, or realistic depending on your point of view. Big change, I realized, is almost always bad change. The little people, who are most of us, almost always get trampled underfoot by the big people, the big events and the big ideas.

Like most people I can ignore almost anything that isn't right in front of my nose or biting me on the ass. But now here's this woman in the cage. I don't know her name. The very stench of her is like a physical assault. I probably can't help her and whatever I try will probably be dangerous for me. But I just can't leave it alone.

What's fucking wrong with me? I've gotta see a doctor about this. Maybe there's some sort of operation I can have or a drug I can take to keep me from even considering what I'm about to do. In the meantime though, I'm here.

She wants my help, but she doesn't want me to leave her there. I don't know how I can explain anything to her, or if I should bother to try. She's barely coherent. That's no surprise considering her circumstances. I try to explain that I have to leave for a little while to try and find a way to get her out of here, but that I'll be back. She's way beyond believing anything anyone says to her and I can't blame her. She's gone back to the far corner of the cage and is whimpering again when I move away into the field.

There's no cover so I stay as low as I can and move slowly as I approach the main building. As I get near I can hear organ music, it's not a cheerful tune. The only lights I can see are the dim ones on the top floor and the bright one on the roof. There's a door, set into an arched stone entry at the left side of the building and what looks like a hatch leading down to a cellar at the right side. Before I try either I move around the building, I want to see what's on the other side.

The front of the building looks pretty much the same as the back, except that there's a long driveway cutting through a lawn that slopes down to the water. A sleek motor launch is tied up at a short pier. It looks fast and expensive, the kind of boat I've seen the bad guys running guns in on TV. There's a small guardhouse at the entrance to the pier, I can't see anyone in it. I don't see any people anywhere and I can't see anything through windows on the ground floor. The front entry looks the same as the one in back, only with a light mounted over it.

I creep back around the way I came. I'm not sure why I think I'll have any better chance of getting into the building unseen that way than the other, but it seems like the thing to do. The cellar hatch seems like an even better idea, especially when I discover it isn't locked.

The gun makes me feel a little more secure. There's no good reason for that, I've never shot anybody and don't know if I can do it. For that matter this thing's so clunky and old, for all I know it'll blow up in my hand if I pull the trigger. I take it out and hold it close to my side as I open the hatch with the other hand.

It's pitch dark down there. I can just about make out the first and second steps. If I can't see anything once I'm inside I'll have to go back and risk the ground level door. I feel my way down the steps. There's seven of them. I stop at the bottom, waiting for my eyes to adjust, if there's anything for them to adjust to.

There is. Straight ahead of me there's a door with faint light coming out around its edges. I slowly shuffle my feet forward to avoid tripping over anything.

Every sound I make seems unbearably loud. The soft scrape of my shoes on the stone floor, the rustle of my clothes, my breathing, the churning in my guts, the thumping of my heart. I stop at the door and put my ear against it.

There's the organ music filtered through the building's floors and walls, coming from some upper floor. There's a low hum, like a large fan or an air conditioner or a refrigerator. I can't hear anything else.

I try the doorknob. It turns but the door only opens a little, it's latched with a simple hook and eye on the other side. The gap isn't quite enough to get a finger through so I fish my drivers license out of my wallet and unhook the latch with it. The door creaks as it opens and I freeze in place for what feels like a long time.

No one's coming. The sounds from the building haven't changed. I let my breath out and move into the room. It's a kitchen, dimly lit by one small bulb over an old, sparkling clean gas stove. The hum comes from behind a large wood and metal door with a heavy-duty handle. It's probably a walk-in refrigerator or freezer.

I look around for a knife, something to add to my meager arsenal. There's a big cleaver, it's shiny blade biting deep into a thick, well-oiled wooden block. I wrestle it out but can't figure out what to do with it now that I've got it. I want one of my hands free. I'm afraid to put the gun away anywhere I might have to waste even a second getting to it. The cleaver's sharp. I don't want it near my skin so I can't just stick it in my belt. It's too heavy to hold in my mouth, pirate-style. I carry it with me anyhow. I can ditch it later if I need to.

I almost laugh, thinking that this is a problem you don't see much in the movies. I'm also right-handed and either the gun or the cleaver's going to have to go into my left hand where it won't be nearly as effective. I put the gun there. Pulling a trigger has got to be a lot easier than chopping somebody. I just hope I don't have to do either.

There are two doors that look like they might lead out of the kitchen. The first one I open is a pantry. The second opens onto a hallway lined with doors, each with a small square hole covered in wire mesh. Light shoots out of the holes, lighting the hallway with beams.

I move as quietly as I can to the first door and look in. A white-hot naked bulb in the middle of the high ceiling lights the small square room. There's a naked woman, curled up on the cold flagstone floor in one of the far corners. There's a metal bowl with bits of food still in it, and another one with water. She's chained to the wall, just like the woman in the cage. She doesn't look up when I look in. She might be asleep, or she hasn't heard me, or she's beyond caring who's at the door. I can see enough of her to know she isn't Sasha.

There are sixteen doors in the hall, eight on each side. Five of the rooms are empty; the others all have one naked woman in them, chained to the wall. All but two of the women have their backs to the door and either don't see me or don't care. They're a mix of ethnicity, hair color and build. Almost all of them have scars, scabs and fresh cuts on their bodies. One is missing both her legs. The stumps are neatly bandaged.

Two of the women are sitting with their backs against the walls of their cells. When I peer in they're staring straight at me and I pull my face back fast. When I don't hear anything coming from them I look again. Their eyes are open but vacant. Maybe they're seeing something. If they are, it's something I hope I never see.

Sasha isn't there. I consider trying to talk with one of the women, to ask some questions, but I don't want to risk it. The cells are close together. If I start talking to one of them, some of the others will hear me and they might make noise.

There are stairs leading up at the far end of the hall. Like everything else they're made of stone. At least I don't have to worry about floorboards squeaking as I creep slowly up them. At the top there's another wooden door. Light is coming from behind and underneath it and the organ music has gotten louder. There's a little more than an inch of space where the door doesn't meet the floor, so I bend down to see if I can see anything.

I can see table legs, the base of a lamp, the bottom of a leather sofa and a red Oriental carpet. I don't see any shoes or feet and I don't hear anything that sounds like people. So I stand up and try the door. I open it just a crack and don't see anything in that field of view. I open it a little more and still don't see anyone. I open it enough to step through, close it behind me and quickly hunker down behind the sofa, my back to a wall.

My fists are clenching spasmodically with fear. It's a good thing my finger isn't on the trigger of the gun. Shaking, I put it and the cleaver down, then curl into a tight ball, hugging my legs to my torso, trying to get a grip or to disappear. It can't be more than a minute or two, but it feels like hours before the shuddering subsides.

I get hit with a wave of exhaustion. I'd like to stay here, hidden. Maybe stretch out behind the couch and take a nap, wake up refreshed and get the hell out. That might be the smart thing to do, but I've already started doing the stupid thing and I can't stop. I've got to see it through. I pick up the gun and cleaver, stand up and come slowly out from behind the sofa.

There's no one in sight. I came up the stairs into a large sitting room. Other than the very soft black leather furniture and several extremely fine oriental rugs, there's a lot of art. Erotic art, I guess, if you're into rough trade. The Marquis de Sade would spring a boner for sure in this room. I'm not him.

The smoking room, or den, or whatever the hell those rooms are called is through an arched doorway. It's dark and plush, the walls lined with the same sort of shiny silk fabric that old-fashioned smoking jackets were tailored of. Iron pedestals hold up cut crystal ashtrays. A wheeled trolley holds an array of rich golden brown liquids in decanters that match the ashtrays. There's also a bottle of water and I'm thirsty. I put down the cleaver on the seat of a chair and take a few gulps.

Picking up the cleaver I notice the chair it's on. It's covered in the softest fur I've ever felt. Its color matches the richest, warmest looking booze in the crystal bottles. It's a magnificent piece of furniture and it makes me mad. I stick the blade of the cleaver into the material at the top seatback and run it down to the cushion. The covering splits open, cotton batting spills out and I move into the next room smiling.

Sure it's juvenile. But it makes me feel better.

There's a gigantic empty ballroom with a small stage at one end and stacks of folding chairs at its sides. That's all there is to one side of the building.

Moving back, I come to a high, vaulted reception hall with a sweeping staircase leading up. It's lit by a hideous chandelier made of welded together medieval weapons. I move quickly through it, ready to run out the door if I have to.

The other side of the building is a mirror image of what I've just explored. The ballroom and the smoking room are almost identical. I slit the back of another fine chair to even things up.

The sitting room is something else. It's overstuffed with more of the same sort of art and there's more plush black leather furniture and oriental carpets. The spiked iron cage hanging from the middle of the ceiling is different. I notice that the spikes are reversible; they can be pointed out or in. I guess it depends on how you feel about your go go dancer.

Around the room are several iron armchairs with restraints on their armrests, legs and set into their backs. They also have holes in their seats. Underneath the chairs are small hydraulic lifts with little trays attached at the top. An enormous stainless steel dildo is mounted on one. A small stone bowl sits on another. I look into the bowl and it's filled with gray ash from burnt out coals.

There's a fireplace tall enough for me to stand up in at the far end of the room. Metal rings are set into the stone around it. There's a spit inside of it, with a long, horizontal metal cage attached. I can see the chain leading from one side of it up to where there must be a motor that turns it. I don't want to think about it.

"Do you enjoy roasted meat Mr. Sharp?"

I've heard the voice before. It's The Roman. Storm is no doubt around too. I'd put the cleaver down on one of the chairs. The damn thing was getting heavy. The gun's in my right hand and in front me. There's a chance they haven't seen it. I try to keep it hidden as I turn.

"I like it just fine. Is it dinnertime? I am a little hungry."

"Soon you will no longer be hungry Mr. Sharp. A dead man has no appetite."

"That's pretty corny. Can't you come up with something better than that."

"*Der'mo-muzhik*, you are a shit-man, you are nothing Mr. Sharp." He turns his head back toward the door. "Storm."

She strides in and stands towering over him in her tall boots and her spiked hair. She smiles when she sees me. It's not a friendly smile. The Roman points at me. "*Poshol v pizdu*." He switches to English, I guess for my benefit. "Have fun my sweet, and make him suffer before you kill him." Her smile gets even broader, and very toothsome.

I'm not sure how she's planning to kill me, but she steps my way and doesn't have a gun. At least not in her hand. Neither does he. I try to imitate Storm's smile but it makes my mouth hurt. I give up trying and bring out the gun. She's still far enough away that it stops her in her tracks. I'd have time to shoot her if she charges me.

The Roman moves quick to his right. He's trying to come in on me from the side, keeping some distance between him and Storm. She starts toward me again and I point the gun right at the middle of her. "Stop. I'll shoot."

She stops. She doesn't know that I'm a lousy shot and I'm not even sure the damn thing's gonna work anyhow.

He doesn't. He keeps coming. He's close enough to reach a hand out and make a grab for the gun. I pull the trigger. Blood erupts from his hand. He stops. I step back. He looks at his hand, then me and he looks shocked. He can't be as surprised as I am. My stomach turns. My knees want to buckle but I fight them off. I hold on inside, doing my best to look like I'm in control.

I move around so I can cover the two of them at about the same angle. I've got to do something fast. I don't know if anyone else has heard the shot. It's a small gun. It was close to his hand when it went off, but its pop sounded loud to me. "Both of you, get in the middle of the room, keep together."

They do what I tell them. He's gripping his hand at its base, trying to stop the bleeding. This is almost fun. I can see why people like guns. I tell Storm to sit down in one of the iron chairs. I tell her to bend over and strap her legs to the chair with the restraints. When she does I tell her to strap one of her wrists to the armrest. She does that too. I have The Roman strap her other wrist. He's awkward with the one hand but he does it. Shooting someone's a good way to convince them you're serious.

I keep the gun on The Roman and walk over to make sure the restraints are tight. They are, but I tighten them some more. Storm spits at me and swears a blue streak. I'm trying to think of anything I can say back, something really vile in her own language. But nothing's coming to me at the moment. I'll have to practice more. I ignore her.

When Storm's strapped down I have The Roman sit on the chair with the dildo under it. I consider telling him to take off his pants first. Then we can have some real fun. But that's just me being nervous, making jokes to keep myself calm. Or maybe it's the gun going to my head. I don't mention it and he sits down with his pants on.

I have him go through the same routine as Storm, but when it gets to the final restraint I have to do it myself. I hold the gun behind his head and cinch up the final strap. I step back to admire my handiwork.

"You two make a lovely couple."

Neither of them say anything. They aren't yelling either so I guess there aren't any guards within earshot. I've been lucky so far. My two remaining bullets aren't going to get me very far if shooting breaks out.

The woman in the cage told me that Storm has the keys. She's wearing a short leather skirt and it has the only pocket I can see on her. I pat the outside of it and there's nothing in it. "Where do you keep the keys?"

"*Ebi tvoyu mat.*"

I grab her by the chin, hard and look her in the face. "I'm not going to fuck my mother, but I do want the keys."

She coughs up a big one and spits it in my face. I want to slug her. I pull my hand back to do it, but something stops me. What's wrong with me? I just shot a man, Storm was going to kill me, and I can't bring myself to hit her. The moment passes while I wonder at my reaction. Instead, I use my hand to wipe off the hot, viscous wad of gunk and then gently baste her cheeks with it, making sure to keep my fingers away from her mouth.

A torrent that's even hotter, more viscous, more vile hisses out from behind her teeth. It's words, really nasty words I'm sure, and it's impressive. I stand back and take the full force of it. The words baste me and make me feel like I need a shower.

I step behind her, pick up the cleaver from the chair and cut a long strip of leather off its arm. I step up close to her, reach down and massage her neck muscles. I knead her hard; the way I like it when I'm tense. I lean over and whisper in her ear. "Chill out hon, one day when we're all friends again, I'll have you give me a language lesson."

She opens her mouth to say something and I slip the strip of leather over and into it. I wrap it tight around the back of her head and tie it in place.

I go to cut another strip of leather. The Roman's been watching. I walk up to him wondering if he's going to just let me gag him or if I'm going to need to come up with some sort of trick.

"Mr. Sharp, if you want to live, you will kill Storm and also me. Then maybe you will live, maybe you will not. If we live, you will die." He deliberately leaves his mouth open when he finishes talking and I quickly gag him too. I don't see any reason to say "thanks."

I can't resist squatting down in front of the chair to figure out how the hydraulic-dildo gizmo works. There's a button at the bottom of the metal penis. I push it and the head starts slowly rotating. I push it again and the whole thing starts vibrating heavily.

There's a toggle switch at the base of the lift. I flip it up and the dildo slowly rises toward the hole in the chair, stopping hard, butted up against the bottom of The Roman. I watch while his crotch begins to jiggle uncontrollably. It's a shame I didn't follow my impulse and have him take off his pants.

I look at his face. If he had machine guns behind his eyes I'd be shot full of holes. I look at Storm. It seems like she'd be smiling if she could. Her eyes sparkle. For her sake I hope The Roman doesn't see her. I toss her a wink, pick up the cleaver and the gun and walk out of the room closing the door behind me.

| | CHAPTER **TWENTY-THREE** | |

Here isn't anywhere else to go but up. I've seen the first
floor. The stairs are carpeted over the stone and I take them
quickly, not worried about them creaking. At the top, hall-
ways lead both directions. I don't think there'll be anyone on the
second floor, otherwise The Roman and Storm would have made
more noise to attract attention, but I poke my nose into all the
rooms anyhow.

The rooms are empty except for the equipment. It looks like
a well-furnished, deluxe gym; one where the people getting their
workouts are strapped to the steel bars, weights and pulleys until
they're done. I've always had a hard time disciplining myself in a
gym. Something like this might work.

The display cases and holding racks filled with whips, chains and various tools that look like they'd be more at home in a metal workshop, make it plain that this isn't any ordinary fitness center.

I go back to the staircase. There's life on the third floor, at least the sounds of it. It doesn't sound like any life I want to live. From behind the first door on the left I hear what I think must be the cracking of a whip punctuating a constant low moaning. I fight the urge to bust in and break something, or someone, over my knee. I've gotta figure out what's going on all around me before I make any moves.

Along the hall most of the rooms are empty. A harsh, hot, putrid odor of seared flesh is coming out from under the door of the last room. I can hear the thrum of something like heels kicking up a fuss on wood and a muffled voice. I back away quick before doing something stupid.

Down the hall on the other side of the staircase two of the rooms are also occupied. The thwack of something that sounds like a paddle is coming from one, just a low, dull, rhythmic "uh, uh, uh" from the other.

I go back to the staircase where there's a door. It's very heavy, thickly padded with something on both sides. It takes a lot of effort to get it open. A slight whoosh of vacuum packed air escapes when I get it cracked. It swings noiselessly, almost effortlessly after that.

It's like walking into a giant freezer. The air hits me with an Antarctic blast. The stone steps leading up aren't carpeted and I can feel their chill through my shoes.

That's nothing compared with the chill I feel in my marrow when I get to the top.

I'm in the attic of the building. It's heavily insulated and there are two huge cooling units, one at each end, pumping out a dense fog of near-frozen vapor. In the middle of the room, directly in front of me, is a large wooden wheel, like a wheel of fortune in a carnival. Two thick beams cross it at right angles to each other. It's tilted at about a forty-five degree angle and there's a naked woman pinned to it face up, her arms and legs spread at right angles to her torso, her head hanging limply down. I can't see what's holding her to the cross.

There are two people in front of her, their backs to me. They're dressed against the cold in heavy, padded suits. There's a charcoal brazier in front of them and they're each holding onto something that's thrust into it. They're not toasting marshmallows.

I've got to do something quick before I freeze in place, from both the cold and the fear. I put down the cleaver and try to hold the gun steady in front of me with my shaking hands. "*Yob tvoyu mat.*" I have no idea if they'll understand that, but I might as well use some of the foul Russian I've been learning.

It gets their attention and they turn around. The one on my left turns around fast. He's got a glowing red poker in his hand and either he hasn't seen the gun or he doesn't take it seriously but he starts coming at me. He's grinning and looks like he plans to run me through. I lift the gun to make sure he sees it but he keeps coming. I can feel heat on my face and see the blurry point of the poker when I pull the trigger.

He looks startled and drops his weapon. A small red flower blooms in the middle of his chest and he crumples to the floor. I think I may have killed him and I don't like the thought. But I don't have time to think about it. I've gotta keep an eye on the other guy.

He's playing it smart. He's left his poker in the fire and raised his hands over his head. I motion him further away from the fire. I keep the gun on him and look around. There are two chains with some sort of cuffs dangling from the ceiling in front of one of the cooling units. I point him over there and he obeys. I can barely hold the gun in the cold but I'm trying my best not to let him know that.

It's a juggling act to hold the gun and get his hands locked into the cuffs. Luckily he's afraid enough of me at this point that he doesn't try anything. I try speaking to him, but he's Chinese and just looks at me blankly. When I've got him secured I go over to look at the man I shot.

He's a white man, but I can't tell where from. I rifle through his pockets but they're empty. I can use his coat and gloves. He doesn't need them anymore. He's dead. The coat's got a bloody hole in it but I don't care. It's small for me, but I can still squeeze into it.

I go to check the woman on the wheel. She's unconscious but alive. Her body charred in places, blistered in others. The blisters have erupted from the cold, and then congealed into a horrible white paste. I still can't see how she's attached to the wheel.

I leave her there to see if I can turn off, or down, the coolers. I find a switch and a thermostat. I don't think I should turn them off. The room may be soundproofed but the humming of the machines can be heard and felt in the background throughout the building. If it stops all of a sudden it might attract attention. I turn the temperature up on them, but not so far as to disrupt the hum.

The woman is coming to. I can hear her moaning. The charcoal brazier is on wheels and with my foot I move it closer to her, hoping to give her a little warmth. When it gets close enough that she begins to feel the heat her eyes snap open and she starts screaming, a horrible, piercing, unearthly shriek that's even more terrible than the moaning.

I go and stand next to her, where she can see I'm not one of the two men who were torturing her. I want to calm her, reassure her, soothe her, do something, anything to make her understand that I'm not going to hurt her, that I'll help her if I can. I don't know what I can do. I feel like I should touch her. Isn't a touch reassuring when you're in pain and frightened? But I don't know if I should.

I do anyway, lightly stroking her hair, trying to smile at her, making soft shooshing noises. She stares straight at me, straight through me. I can't tell if she's seeing something far away or no further than the surface of her eyeballs.

Finally, when the heat doesn't get any worse, when my voice begins to break through, she stops screaming and starts crying. Only her head moves, her body lightly quakes.

While she cries I try to figure out how she's stuck to the cross. If I can figure it out maybe I can get her loose. She's adhered to it somehow, not tied or strapped to it. At first I think it might be that they wetted her skin and the beams and held her there until she froze solid in place. But as cold as it is, it's not quite cold enough for that. There's a bucket of water near the brazier and it's slushy, not ice. All I can finally figure out is glue. Unless I can find some sort of solvent to use on it, there's nothing I can do without causing her a whole lot more pain.

The wheel she's on is attached to a metal framework. I look it over and find a small hand crank, folded down on its side. When I unfold and turn it the wheel slowly begins to lower to horizontal. That'll help some. Not enough, but it's better than nothing.

When she's lying flat I go to the Chinese man and wrestle the coat off of him. I have to undo one of his hands at a time to get it off and I'm worried that he might try and attack me, but he's cold and complacent.

I take the coat and drape it over her. I move the brazier a little closer and this time she doesn't scream. She just looks at me through narrowly slitted, tired eyes.

I stay there next to her, lightly stroking one of her hands with just a fingertip, trying to reassure her but I still have no idea what I can do. She's Asian, maybe Vietnamese. Using sign language I try to get it across that I'm not going to hurt her, that I'm going to have to look her over more carefully to see if there is anything I can do to help her.

My inspection leaves me feeling more helpless than ever. Her arms and legs are either broken or severely dislocated at the shoulders and hips. If I do manage to get her off the wheel the only way out is for me to carry her. The pain that will cause would most likely send her further into shock. That alone will probably kill her.

I tuck the jacket tighter around her and go back to stroking her hand. She's trying to speak. I lean down to put my ear near her lips but even if I could hear her clearly I can't understand her.

I try a few words of Cantonese and she doesn't understand them. All I know of Thai is how to count, the names of some types of food and a few flirtatious words and sentences I've learned in bars. I try counting to ten, just to see if she recognizes it. She doesn't. Indonesian doesn't work. A couple of words of Mandarin don't do anything. "Good morning" and "thank you" in Japanese don't get me anywhere. And the name of a spicy Korean soup that I like a lot doesn't do anything either. I try some French and some Russian. Some Vietnamese, especially older ones, speak those languages, but they too draw a blank. I smile and revert to what I hope are comforting sounds.

She closes her eyes in a little while and seems more at peace. I think maybe I can cut her off the cross. I'm still not sure what I can do with her once I get her free, but I've got to try. So I go pick up the cleaver and try sliding it gently under her. I don't want to cut her skin, but even if I have to, maybe she's cold and numb enough that it won't hurt so much.

But it does. Her eyes shoot open and she screams when I try wiggling the blade forward just a little under one of her legs. I stop and pull it back. I put it down on the floor. I don't want her to see it because it might scare her more.

She stops screaming and starts quietly crying again. I go back to stroking her hand and mumbling soft nothings to her. I don't know what else to do. She closes her eyes and it seems like she's falling asleep or under.

I move away to search the room, to see if there's anything I've missed, anything I can use to help her. I'm not finding anything when I hear a soft coughing, a slight choking sound. I get back to her in time to hear a faint gurgling, see spittle bubble out of her mouth, see her face go slack. I don't know if it's my imagination or what but it just looks like someone turned off the lights behind her eyes. I feel around her neck for a pulse and there isn't one. I put my ear close to her mouth, her nose, to see if I can hear or feel any breath and I can't.

It won't be too long before she's as cold as the room. I stroke her hair lightly and bend over to kiss her chilled forehead. It's as close as I've ever gotten to a prayer. I don't know why but I tuck the jacket even closer around her.

I pick up the cleaver and walk over to the Chinese man who's standing, shivering, his hands cuffed to the chains from the ceiling. He looks wild-eyed when he sees me holding the cleaver and I wave it at him to frighten him more. He doesn't know there's no way I can bring myself to chop him. I wish I could.

Instead I walk past him to the cooling unit on his side of the room and I lower the thermostat to its coldest setting. I walk to the other side of the attic and do the same with the other unit. I feel like I'm wading through a blizzard to get back to him. I look him in the face for what feels like a long time. I don't say anything. I just squat down and yank off his warm pants. He's left wearing a thin shirt and his underwear. He's struggling when I leave. He's lucky. I've read that the last stages of freezing to death can actually be pretty pleasant.

| |CHAPTER **TWENTY-FOUR** | |

My whole body prickles nastily as the warmth of the third floor seeps back into it. I wait at the top of the stairs, the attic door closed behind me, to regain full feeling. I don't know how long I've been up there or how late it's getting to be. I figure I've gotta be quick if I'm going to do anything and get away. I rub my hands together and rub them all over my body to speed up the warming process.

I'm still slightly chilled when I go to the first door; the one where I'd heard the whip and the moaning. It's quiet in there now. I open the door slowly and the room's empty. I move down the hall to where I'd smelled the burning flesh. That room's empty too. On the other side of the stairs only one of the rooms is occupied. I can still hear a rhythmic "uh, uh, uh" coming from it, but it sounds slower and deeper than it had when I first heard it. I move through the door gun first.

There's a woman intricately trussed up with ropes, dangling from the ceiling. A naked man is sitting in a plush leather chair in front of her, looking into her eyes. He's more surprised by the gun in my hand than I am by the penis in his.

He wilts when I step up and show him the ugly hole at the end of the gun barrel. He whimpers something, it might be in German; maybe even English, but I don't care what he says. I slug him hard on the temple with my hand wrapped around the butt of the gun. He goes goofy eyed. I slug him again and he goes out.

I go to the woman. She looks at me with wide, hard eyes. She's got a ball gag stuffed in her mouth. I reach behind her to undo it. The ball falls out and she starts working her mouth, trying to get feeling back into it.

"I'm gonna get you down. Hold on, I'll be as quick as I can." I look around and see that she's held up by a rope and pulley. The rope is secured to a hook in the wall. I undo the rope and lower her as gently as I can to the floor. She rolls onto her side, wincing with pain.

It's the most complicated batch of knots I've ever seen. She lays still while I untie the ones I can work out and cut through the others with the cleaver. When she's free she stays on the floor and stretches, groaning with the effort.

The guy on the chair is still out cold. I look around and see his clothes, neatly hung on pegs by the door. I get his shirt and pants and bring them to the woman on the floor. I help her stand up and hand them to her.

"Thanks." It's clear English, but with a thick Japanese accent.

While she's dressing I take the rope and tie the man up with it. I stick the ball gag in his mouth and tighten it behind his head. I wrestle him off the chair and prop him up in a corner. When I'm done and turn around, the woman is sitting in the chair, holding the cleaver.

"Who are you?"

"My name's Ray. I came here looking for a friend who's disappeared."

"Have you found her?"

"No."

"What is her name?"

"Sasha. She's a Russian girl."

"Brown hair? Not tall? Big bosom?"

"Yes."

"I am sorry."

I don't like the sound of that. "Sorry for what?"

"She was here before. One week ago the big Russian woman and the Russian man took her up there." She gestures above us with her eyes.

I sit down heavily and put my head in my hands. It takes a while and an effort but I look back up at her. "Is she?"

"When a girl goes up there, we never see her again. I think your friend is gone."

I drop my head into my hands again. Is this my fault? What the hell have I done? Sasha would probably still be alive if she'd never have met me. I can't think about this. If I do I'll just stay here, curl up on the floor and wait for them to find me.

I look at the Japanese woman. She's looking better than when I first untied her. Every now and then a slight grimace passes across her face, she must be in pain, or at least very stiff, but she looks okay. She's not looking at me with sympathy, or much of anything else. Just looking at me, waiting to see what I'll do next.

"What's your name?"

"Hiroko."

"How long've you been here?"

"Three weeks."

"How do we get out of here?"

"I do not know."

"Are there guards, security?"

"Tonight not so many. One guard inside, one outside, the Russian woman and the man. Not so many customers today."

"Do you know where all the keys are?"

"There is an office on the ground floor."

"Can you walk? Let's go."

"What about him?" She nods toward the tied up man in the corner. He's now awake and watching us.

"He's not going anywhere, we'll just leave him."

She gets up and I move toward the door. She moves slowly, stiff-legged toward the man in the corner. She's still holding the cleaver and he starts to struggle with his ropes as she walks toward him. I move quickly to stop her. I take her by the arm. She turns and brandishes the cleaver at me. Her voice hisses out of firmly set lips. "I will not kill him."

I let go of her and she squats in front of him. She grabs his face with one hand, digging long fingernails into his cheeks. She lightly runs the cleaver blade along his forehead. It opens and blood cascades down over it and into his eyes. She moves down and grabs one of his feet and before I can move to stop her she severs the Achilles tendon. She holds his face and slaps it as he squirms in pain and fright.

She falters a little trying to stand and I put out an arm to help her up. She takes it and rises to face to me with a smile. "He will not forget me."

"No, I guess he won't. Let's go."

The building's quiet except the hum from the attic. We move cautiously along the hall. At the top of the stairs we stop. I turn to Hiroko who's close behind me, still holding the cleaver.

"Where's the guard?"

"He has taken the others downstairs to their cells. That pig had paid for me for all night. The guard won't be back upstairs until morning."

"Where do you think he is?"

"He stays in the hall with the cells."

"What about the outside guard?"

"I think he stays at the pier, in a small building. I don't know where the Russian man and woman are."

"That's okay, I do. I've got them tied up and gagged downstairs. They won't be a problem."

She gives me a look and I can't tell if it's admiring or skeptical. I have other things on my mind to worry about.

We move down the stairs to the ground floor. The office is behind a metal door in an alcove just off the entry hall. I'd missed it when I first looked around. It's also locked. It isn't the sort of door with a lock I can pick or that I could kick open like in the movies.

I look at Hiroko.

"I think the big Russian woman must have the key. When she is here, she is in charge."

I'd checked Storm's pocket and the key wasn't there, but I hadn't searched the rest of her. Hiroko won't go with me into the other room to look. She's afraid that if they see her helping me, then they'll kill her for sure if we can't escape from the island. She's probably right, so I go alone.

The Roman and Storm are where I've left them. He's more agitated than before. He's almost too distracted to even look at me when I walk in. A metal dildo rattling your crotch for an hour or more will do that. She doesn't look relaxed, either. But she does look resigned, waiting for an opportunity to get loose. She stares daggers at me when I walk in.

Sasha's dead, they did it and I want them to suffer. I walk quickly up to The Roman, poke the gun up to between his eyes and cock it. He stops squirming and his eyes go very cold. I press the barrel hard against him. I scratch his forehead with it. I run it around his head, poking it into his ears and finally screw it into his left nostril. I pull it out hard and his nose starts bleeding. I turn it around and hit him with the bottom of the grip like it's a hammer. He goes groggy, his head goes limp and moves around on his neck, but he doesn't go out. He shakes it to clear it and as much as he can through the gag he's smiling at me when he comes up. He knows I'm not going to kill him. I hate it that he knows that. I can't stand to look at him anymore.

I haven't gone through his pockets. I don't know what I might find in them, but figure I'd better look. There's nothing in his shirt pocket. It's a little tough getting my hand into his jiggling pants pockets. All I find is a money clip, fat with bills. I take it. There's got to be someone with a better use for the cash than him.

I move over to Storm and she can see that I want to hurt her. She tries moving her head back and out of the way. I'd wanted to hit her earlier and couldn't do it. Now I can. Her nose breaks with a satisfying snap when I slam it from the side with my palm. Her eyes stream with water, but she's an old hand at this. It isn't long before she's tilting her head foreward to let the blood flow out, then back to stop it once the flow slows.

Finally she straightens her head to stare at me and it's a look that says if I don't kill her now I'm going to live to regret it.

I already regret it. I'm sorry the gun doesn't have two bullets left because I don't know which of them I want to kill more, or first. I've got to hurry up and get out of here.

Storm's pocket was empty when I searched it before. Maybe she's got a key hidden somewhere else. I rummage around under her clothes for it. She's wearing a necklace. It hangs down between her breasts. They're big and damp with sweat and rock hard like bad fakes, but I'm not in any mood to think it's fun fishing around in there. I yank the leather cord hard and pull it off her neck and throw it into the fireplace when I see it's nothing more than a religioius medallion.

The only place left to check is under her skirt and I squat in front of her. She's not wearing underwear again and once again I don't care. I do see something a little shiny against her skin, just below her belly. I reach up and grab it. There's a small chain with a key on it. The thin gold strand breaks easily.

I stand up and dangle the key in front of her face. "Fuck you, bitch."

She's squirming against the restraints, trying to shout at me through the leather gag. I stand back and look at the two of them. Maybe I ought to shoot at least one of them. But which one? I guess it'd have to be The Roman. He's the boss. But I'm not out of here yet and I might still need the gun.

Who am I kidding? I can't do it anyhow. I'm sorry Sasha. I'm sorry Irina. I'm sorry for the woman in the attic, but I can't do it. I've just got to get out of here and do what I can do.

Hiroko's still by the metal door. I wave the key at her and she smiles at me. Inside the office is very tidy. There's not much in it, just a desk and chair, a phone, a clock and a laptop computer. It's getting late, just a couple of hours before sunrise.

The top drawer of the desk is empty. The large bottom drawer has a combination lock on it. It's heavy steel and there's no way I can get it open. I turn on the computer to see if there's anything I can get from it. It's password protected and I can't get past the first screen. I turn it off, unplug it and take it with me. Out in the hall I hand it to Hiroko.

"Stay here, I'll be back in a moment."

She nods and clutches the computer to her chest.

I go back into the room with The Roman and Storm. I'm not sure what more I can do. I turn off the dildo under The Roman, hold the cleaver up near his throat and take off his gag. He spits at me and works his mouth trying to hock up another. I move behind him, still holding the cleaver.

"Where're all the keys?"

"*Yob tvoyu mat.*"

I lean down to his left ear. "Listen to me shithead, you're tied up and I'm getting tired of all this. You killed my friend. I've got a gun and a cleaver and I'll fuck you up bad if I don't get what I want."

I don't like it that he laughs. "You big fucker man. You think you are *ubivets*, killer, big dick. Hah! *Vy chistiy impotent*, no hard-on man. *Mat' tvoyu v grob.* I fuck your dead mother."

He knows I won't kill him. He probably even suspects I won't hurt him too bad or I would have done it already. It's the advantage that guys like him always have over guys like me. I remember what Hiroko did upstairs and I give him a nice little slice on the forehead to go with the one from the gun barrel. The Roman just blinks the blood out of his eyes and laughs even more.

I'm sick of it. I gag him again, turn the dildo back on and go over to stand in front of Storm. I don't know what to do though. I can't imagine I'll have any more luck with her.

I stand there and it looks like she'd be laughing too if she wasn't gagged. I lean down and put my face right up in front of hers. I can't speak. I want to say something, anything to scare her, hurt her, to make myself feel better, but there isn't anything to say. I reach out and twist her broken nose, turning it almost all the way around. I can see that it hurts, it's gotta hurt a lot. Her eyes start watering again and she clamps down hard with her teeth on the gag.

But it's not enough. Nothing's going to be enough and I'm fed up with trying. If I can't kill her and The Roman I've got to leave them here and get out, fast.

I cinch both of their restraints and gags as tight as I can, then I walk out.

Hiroko's still waiting, hidden behind a doorway leading off the entry hall. We go to the door that leads down to the hallway lined with the women's cells. I begin to open the door, to go down the stairs when she stops me.

"The guard is always there when he isn't upstairs. He has a machine gun."

"I didn't see anyone when I came in."

"Maybe he was away for a minute or two, but there is always a guard there."

"You sure it's just the one?"

"Yes, when the Russian man and woman are here, the other people go away."

"Does the guard have keys to the cells?

"I do not know. Not all the time."

We get lucky. He's snoozing in a chair, his back turned away from us when we come up behind him. I knock him cold, get his gun, tie him up, gag him and search him before he can stir. But he doesn't have any keys. The cell doors are too sturdy, the locks too strong. There's nothing we can do without a key or the right tools and enough time. We don't have any of that.

Neither of us wants to leave the women in the cells but we don't have any choice. If we get away, maybe there's something we can do for them. Hiroko and I get out through the kitchen, then back across the field. She's moving slow, still stiff, but loosening up quickly.

I don't know what to do about the woman in the cage. I still don't have a key, or anything else I can use to get her out. It might be worse if I go to her again, if I give her false hope and then can't do anything for her. Or it might not. I don't know. Hiroko and I stop up against the sidewall of the low building and I ask what she thinks.

"Leave her. You cannot help her. You have no key. You cannot break the chains. If tomorrow the guards see that someone has tried to break the chains they will kill her. If we escape, maybe someone can come back. Maybe someone can help her. You cannot help her, not now."

I wish she wasn't right, but she is. We head off through the brush, back to the beach to the skiff.

It's where I left it. The tide's gone out. The moon is low and it's much darker than it was when I rowed ashore. That's good in one way and bad in another. It'll be harder for anyone to see us. It'll be harder for me to find the shrimp boat.

I drag the rowboat across the rocky, exposed mudflats. Hiroko isn't much help; she's not strong and the wet muck we're slogging through is giving her a hard time. We finally get to the water. I help her into the boat. She sprawls in the front of it, leaving little room for me to get in and work the oars. But I do.

The laptop computer is safe, at least for now. I ask Hiroko to hold it, to keep it dry, above the puddles of water at the bottom of the boat. If there's anything useful in it, I don't want to risk getting it wet. I'm now better armed. I've got the pistol the man on the boat gave me and the Chinese AK-47 I'd taken off the guard. None of that is going to do us any good if The Roman, Storm, the guard, the guy who'd been in the room with Hiroko or the men in the attic are discovered any time soon. I might be putting the people on the shrimp boat in danger if we can't get out of these waters fast enough.

If, that is, I can find the shrimp boat. I've been rowing for about twenty minutes and haven't seen it yet. I stop for a moment and look carefully around us. The light on top of the building on shore is still on and there's a very faint glow to the east, in the direction of Hong Kong. Maybe it's the city, but more likely it's sunrise. I've gotta find the shrimp boat, and soon.

I keep rowing away from the island, in the direction I remember coming from last night. Was it only last night? Maybe I'm asleep. Maybe none of it ever really happened. Maybe it's some unendurably long nightmare.

I'd pinch myself if I could stop rowing long enough. I want to stop rowing, just lay down, my feet up near Hiroko's head and go to sleep while the boat drifts on the current. Maybe if I fall asleep I'll wake up later and it all will have been a bad dream.

I pause long enough to rub my eyes, hard, and when I open them again I think I see a small point of light not too far away and ahead of us. It might be a tracer left from rubbing my eyes but I blink a few times and it's still there. I row for it. The sky to the east is definitely lightening now and it seems like I'm racing it. This small boat needs to be off the water and out of sight before anyone can spot it from the land.

My arms and shoulders burn, my back, legs and neck ache with tension and strain. My head is filled with racing thoughts moving so fast I can't grab hold of any one of them long enough to make it make any sense. I just know that they're terrible thoughts. My brain is ripe to the bursting point with horror.

Sunrays are beginning to skewer the horizon, the water is taking on color and the sky is going from black to gray to purple to dark blue. There're gulls overhead, their squawks sounding like The Roman's laughter. They're taunting me. My fear of them helps push me forward.

There's the boat. It's not far. Why hadn't I seen it more clearly before this? In just a minute the skiff is knocking up against it. The sound of wood on wood is comforting somehow. My heart slows. The vortex in my head eases and my ears fill with the chatter of friendly Chinese voices.

I manage to stand, to steady the skiff while two of the men from the boat come down and lift Hiroko onto the deck. One of them leans back down to give me a hand. I pass the pistol and the automatic rifle up to him and then he gives me his other hand.

On deck the old woman has come out with a blanket and wrapped it around Hiroko. The young woman has two mugs of steaming hot water. She waves them at us and then beckons us to follow her to where the mattresses are laid out on the deck under the overhang. We sit and she hands us the mugs. She squats in front of Hiroko and starts talking to her in Chinese. Hiroko looks at me, not sure what to say.

The young woman looks at me and switches to her pigeon Cantonese. "*Pahngyauh?*"

She isn't the friend I'd gone ashore to find. That friend is gone, forever. But I can't explain that. I've rescued Hiroko. Maybe saved her life. That attaches us to each other. We're more than friends, I think.

I nod my head. "*Haih.*"

"*Mahfaahn-ah?*"

"*Ho mahfaahn.* Sorry. *Heui faaidi, ho faaidi.*"

She looks at me like she doesn't quite get it. I know she understands "a lot of trouble," but I'm not sure she got "go fast, very fast." I gesture for the pencil and paper and quickly draw a very primitive picture of the island, the shrimp boat, then another, bigger boat coming toward us with guns.

That worries her. I don't blame her. She goes to confer with the men and the old woman. Hiroko is quiet, looking on, sipping her hot water.

The men and the younger woman start busying themselves about the boat. The young woman throws open a chest and pulls out towels. She starts drying off the skiff, making it look like it hasn't been off the boat. The net's out for the early morning catch, but the men start reeling it in. The old woman comes and gestures to us to follow. We do, into the farthest, blackest corner of the hold. I help her wrestle a few barrels, sloshing with water and shrimp, in front of us. The old woman goes away and I hunker down in the wet and dark with Hiroko.

| | CHAPTER **TWENTY-FIVE** | |

We talk in whispers. She asks about my friend Sasha and I tell her what I can. What I can stand to tell her. She tries to be comforting, but there's no comfort in it. It's a half-hearted effort anyhow. After what she's been through there isn't much empathy left in her. At least not for now. Maybe it will return gradually, like feeling to a numbed limb.

I change the subject. Hiroko is twenty-two. Her father's a banker in Osaka.

"Where'd you learn English?"

"My parents send me to boarding school in Switzerland. It was terrible, so boring. I run away and come back to Japan."

"They must have been mad."

"I don't go home. I go to Tokyo and start to find a job."

"What'd you do?"

"I am very lucky, I have a very good skill. I am, what do you say, I can twist my legs and arms in many positions."

"Double-jointed?"

"Yes. In Japan many people, they like bondage. It is an ancient art. The people who do it have much skill, it takes many years of practice. A girl like me, double-jointed, is very popular."

"Is it a sexual thing? Do they have sex with you when you're tied up?"

"No, I do not. Some girls do. I was in many movies. I am a big star of the bondage cinema. Sometimes I would be naked, and maybe for some men that was sex, but they never touch me, other than to tie me up."

"How'd you end up in this mess?"

"I go on tour, to different countries, to clubs and sometimes private performances. Six months ago a very rich man from Malaysia sees me at a gallery in Bangkok."

"What do you mean 'gallery?' Like an art gallery?"

"Yes, same as art gallery, many performers. I am the star. I am bound in eighty-eight knots and hanging from the ceiling."

I've heard about this sort of stuff. I'd never seen it until I rescued Hiroko. I don't get it, but I resist saying so.

"The man from Malaysia asks me to stay with him for three-months. He lives in a very big house near Kuala Lumpur. He will pay me a lot of money and does not want sex. He wants to practice bondage, that is all. After three months he will fly me back to Tokyo on his private airplane. It is very much money, more than I usually make in two years."

"It sounds strange to me. Weren't you scared?"

"Maybe I was scared a little, but this is not so unusual in my work. It was good. He was very kind, he has great skill and I learn many things I can use back in Japan. He is true to his promise also, he does not want to have sex with me.

"But then three months end and he will not let me leave. He keeps me in prison, locked in a small house behind his house. He still wants to tie me up and I fight with him. I yell and scream. He puts drugs into my food and when I wake up I am bound tighter, harder, sometimes with wire, sometimes with rough rope.

"One day I find a pencil. Then I hide my food and pretend to be asleep when he comes to get me. I stab him in the hand with the pencil. He hits me and I am unconscious. When I wake up again I am in a small box with only holes to breathe. I cannot see. It is shaking and there is a noise like I am on an airplane.

"When they let me out there are men in uniforms, Chinese army I think. They put me into a cell with other women and every day they come and inject us with drugs. I think it is heroin. I have never tried it before, but that is what one of the women says. It makes me feel very good. It is the only thing that feels good.

"Maybe two, maybe three weeks later, I do not know time anymore, they take some of us to a boat and bring us here, to the island. Since that time I only want to die."

I want to comfort her but I don't know how. I'm afraid to touch her, I'm sure she doesn't want to be touched. I know that anything I say can't make any of this better. We sit in the dark, apart. The whole world seems harsh to me at the moment. Hiroko starts sobbing, quietly but steadily and it goes on for a long while. I reach out and start to put my arms around her, to pull her to me, to stroke her hair and say something to soothe her pain. But she senses what I'm doing and shifts back, away from me.

I could use some comfort too. But neither of us is going to get it now. Maybe later. I hope so.

I try to concentrate on the sounds from the deck, the splashing of the water against the hull. I close my eyes and the rocking of the shrimp boat must've lulled me to sleep because I come out of it with a start when I hear a heavy thump.

There's a crackly Chinese voice over a megaphone somewhere above and the sound of heavy ropes being thrown on board and dragged across the deck to where they can be tied. Then there're footsteps. We're being boarded.

I hear talking and the crash and bang of things being overturned. They're searching the boat. I don't know who they are. There's nothing I can do. I can't see Hiroko in the dark but I know she's heard it too and has got to be as frightened as I am. Maybe she doesn't want to be touched but I don't care anymore. I edge over to where she is and put my arms around her. She burrows as deep as she can into me and we dig ourselves as far as we can back into and a little behind the dark, oily timbers of the hold.

Booted feet come down the steps. It sounds like just one person. The beam of a flashlight moves around in the dark. We're well hidden behind the shrimp barrels. They look like they're shoved up against a wall, but if he moves one of them, or even carefully looks behind it, he'll see us.

Hiroko is shaking and I'm afraid she'll start making noises. I clamp a hand over her mouth and she bites down hard on one of my fingers. She's got sharp, young teeth and it hurts like hell. It takes everything I've got to avoid crying out.

The footsteps are getting nearer, the beam of light plays over the timbers close on either side in front of us. I'm afraid to hold my breath because when I let it out it will make a sound. I concentrate on steadying my breathing, slowing it, making it as shallow as I can. I try to ignore the pain in my finger, it helps that it's starting to go numb.

The footsteps stop no more than the width of the barrels away from us. Light paints the darkness just a foot or two over our heads. I can hear the searcher breathing. Then he stops breathing, stops moving. He's listening. I try to will myself unconscious, nearly dead so that there isn't even the sound of my skin shedding its dead cells.

It doesn't work. It doesn't work so bad that my nose starts to itch. It feels like I'm going to sneeze and that might be fatal. I bury it as deep as I can into the nape of Hiroko's neck. She stirs, slightly, I don't think she likes it, but she knows this isn't the time to do anything about it. At least her teeth let up a little on my finger.

The light shines down on top of the barrels, strikes the silvery shrimp that cover the surface and is reflected in small rainbows over the ceiling of the hold. Some of it spills down on us and I can make out the outline of Hiroko's head nestled in my chest. Her black hair has a lacquer sheen and I think it's not such a bad sight if it has to be one of my last.

I'm tensing my muscles, figuring that if I'm going down, at least I'll go down fighting. My right foot's asleep and I flex it. It tingles painfully. My stomach churns trying to hold the pain inside, to prevent my whole body from squirming. I doubt I'll be able to get out from behind here before whoever's on the other side shoots me. I'll wait until the last moment. The moment when the flashlight finds us.

I don't have to wait long. A voice shouts down into the hold and I hear the person on the other side of the barrels turn to it. Then the footsteps walk away and I hear them going back up the steps. I take my nose out of Hiroko's neck and risk enough of a sniffle to hold back the sneeze. She lets out her breath and pulls her teeth out of my finger. There isn't much room for it, but our bodies slump, puddling in place.

Before long we hear the footsteps on deck crossing to the side. Then the scrape of the ropes being dragged over the boards the other way, a few last shouted voices then the deep rumble of an engine somewhere just beyond the timbers we are laying against and under the water. Then a throttle opens and the rumble recedes.

I can't see her, but I can sense Hiroko turning her face up at me. I find her forehead with my lips and leave them there while she shakes and cries.

Maybe a half hour later, lighter footsteps come down the steps. It's Mei Ling, the younger woman. She starts trying to pull the barrels out from in front of us. I push from the back. When we get a couple of them out of the way, Hiroko and I crawl out from behind. I can hardly see the woman, just her silhouette against the faint light that filters down along the steps into the hold.

She holds out a hand to help us up. I stand and ask her what's up.

"*Di-mah?*"

"*Syuhn heui, moh-mun-tai.*"

I turn to Hiroko. "She says that the boat's gone and there's no problem. We're okay now."

"Where are we going? How will we get off this boat?"

"They'll take us to Zhuhai. I'll call my office in Hong Kong from there; have them call the Japanese consulate. We should be okay."

The trip back to the mainland is uneventful. I do what I can to help around the boat. I've made them cut their shrimping short and no doubt that costs them money. I'm not sure why they helped me. It was a big risk on their part. But then fishermen everywhere are a fiercely independent group of people. And from the scars I'd seen on the back of the man who loaned me the gun, I guess that the people on this boat don't have much reason for warm feelings towards the Chinese navy, or government.

When we tie up at the dock in Zhuhai, I get out The Roman's money clip. The younger woman and the man with the scars refuse, gesturing for me to put it away. The old woman and the other men eye my money hungrily. I hand the wad to the old lady, keeping back a hundred dollar U.S. bill for myself. Her eyes widen, it's more money than she'd normally see in a year. I wave my hand in the air, taking in the whole boat. I point to the net and hold my fingers close together. I hope she gets it that I'm apologizing for their having come back with only a small catch. One of the younger men hands me the AK-47 I'd taken off the guard. I laugh. What the hell am I gonna do with that? I insist he keep it, waving my hand again to indicate it's for the boat.

The Grand Imperial isn't far away but I'm not sure it's safe to go there. I don't know if The Roman and Storm are connected to the nightclub in its basement or not. I could have been knocked out and gotten rid of just on general principle for asking too many questions. Or not.

There's another, smaller hotel closer to the dock. Hiroko and I walk to it, to find a telephone. I get through to Hans, the general manager at the Imperial.

"Mr. Sharp, are you allright? We have been concerned for your safety. Your office has been telephoning."

"Yes, thank you. I'm fine. I had a little trouble but it's taken care of. I'm at a small hotel near the harbor. I think it's called the Seafront Garden. I need you to do me a favor."

"Certainly, I am at your service."

It takes a bit of explaining but Hans agrees to collect my stuff from his hotel and bring it to me here, discreetly. The Roman's hundred dollar bill comes in handy for convincing the registration desk to rent a room to Mr. and Mrs. Jones without seeing our passports.

A half hour later Hiroko's taking a hot bath and the Swiss general manager's at the door with my suitcase, a large envelope and a sheaf of phone messages. He hands it all to me.

"I'm afraid Mr. Jones, that your room was broken into. Did you have a computer with you? If so, I am very sorry but it was stolen."

"No, no computer, just the suitcase and a small camera bag."

"Then I am afraid your camera has been stolen. Are you in trouble Mr., uh, Jones?"

"I don't know. Maybe. Do you know what happened the other night in your club?"

"I told you Mr. Sharp, it is not my club. I avoid knowing what transpires there."

"Okay I won't tell you. But it's why I'm here."

"Please, Mr. Sharp, I hope you have no complaints about the service at our hotel. Please let us make it up to you if you do."

"No, you've made it clear you've got nothing to do with the nightclub. I just have to keep a low profile while I'm still here, I don't want anyone to know where I am. Please don't let anyone know you saw me."

"It is all very mysterious, but of course Mr. Jones, you can count on my discretion."

I can't tell if he's angling for a tip. As the general manager of a hotel I think he'd be above that sort of thing, but you never can tell. I start to open the envelope that he'd given me with my passport and cash from the safe deposit box in his hotel, but he puts out a hand and stops me.

"Please Mr. Sharp, do not insult me. That is not necessary."

I smile, thank him, tell him I'll recommend his hotel to anyone I know who needs a place to stay in Zhuhai and close the door on his back.

I look over the phone messages. They're all from my office, starting about midday yesterday. I'll call in later, or tomorrow.

It's hard to tell if I'm sleepier than I am hungry. Hiroko comes out of the bathroom in a robe. I ask if she wants to eat and she shakes her head "no." She's about to fall asleep. I go into the bathroom and take a shower. When I come out she's already in the bed, under the covers. I go to take the pillows from the other side and put them on the floor. I can sleep on the carpet. At this point I can sleep anywhere.

"No, it is your room. It is a big bed. We can both sleep here."

"You sure? I'd think you'd've had enough of men anywhere near you for a lifetime."

"The men on the island, most of them did not want sex. They only wanted to tie me up, sometimes beat me, sometimes other things."

I get into bed. It's a king-sized bed and I stay far away on my side. I turn to look at her and she smiles. "You are good to me. I will not bite you."

"I'm more worried about you thinking I'll hurt you. I won't."

"I know that you won't."

"What about the heroin? Are you going to be okay? If you begin to have withdrawals, it's not like I can order some from room service. Maybe I can find some other sort of pain killer if that helps."

"I don't know. I am small but I am strong. Now, my stomach hurts a little but not too much. I just want to sleep."

"Me too, but if you need anything wake me up or call room service or whatever."

She smiles and holds out her hand. "Please come a little closer to me."

I do, but not too close.

| | CHAPTER **TWENTY-SIX** | |

I t's morning and Hiroko's bundled into my arms, pressed tightly up against me. She's sleeping like a little girl, one of her thumbs stuck into her mouth. She looks peaceful, at least for now.

I'm drowsy and warm, dreamy.

"She's a good kid. You did a good thing getting her away from there."

I poke my head up and he's sitting on the edge of the bed. I speak softly. I don't want to wake her.

"Yeah, right. I got Sasha killed and I couldn't get the others out of there."

"Getting yourself killed wasn't going to help anyone. Maybe you can go to the police."

"Which police? The Chinese police aren't gonna fight the Chinese navy and you heard Warner, the U.S. isn't gonna risk an international incident."

"You can try. You're a journalist, write about it, cause a rumpus. Isn't that what you're supposed to do?"

"Fat lot of good it's gonna do."

"Who knows? You're not going to let it rest anyway."

"No, you're right, I can't. I never killed anyone before though. I never hurt anyone like that. I don't know how I feel about it."

"Those guys killed that girl, tortured her to death. They got what was coming to them."

"It wasn't up to me."

"Sure it was. If you hadn't've been there they'd have gotten away with it."

"The girl'd still be dead anyhow. I couldn't bring Sasha back. I couldn't even help that woman in the cage. I told her I'd be back. I lied to her."

"At least you got one person out, that's better than none."

"I guess."

"What do you mean, 'I guess'? You did a good thing; you can do more good things. Don't be a jerk."

Hiroko stirs. I don't know if she's waking up or not but she pulls my arm tighter across her and slides her butt back against me. I look up at him again and he's smiling and fading away.

I must've gone back to sleep, or maybe I wasn't awake. The conversation seemed real enough. Later I wake up. I know I've got to do something to get Hiroko and me back to Hong Kong. I've got to do something else too, something about Black Island, something about Storm and The Roman. I'm just not sure what it is. My stomach's rumbling with too many things. I'm sad, I'm pissed off, and I'm also feeling guilty and that makes me even sadder and angrier.

I call Jane, the research librarian for my magazine. I don't want to talk with Norman, the editor, he'll ask too many questions that I'd rather answer in person. I'm not sure how I'm going to answer them anyhow. I ask Jane to let him know I've had some trouble and I'll be back in the office tomorrow. I also ask her to dig up whatever more she can on Black Island, to look through the Chinese sources as well and translate anything she finds.

"Does this have anything to do with the trouble you got into?"

"Yeah, but keep it quiet. I don't know what I'm gonna do with it, but it could be something big."

We hang up and I call the U.S. Consulate. I'm planning to just leave a message, but Bill Warner answers his direct line. "What're you doing at work on a Sunday?"

"It's Saturday night back in D.C."

"Yeah, my point exactly."

"Whaddaya want? I just came in to clean up a couple things. I was about to go home."

I give him the short version of the last couple of days. He isn't impressed.

"Man, do you have a death wish or what?"

"I'm here aren't I?"

"For now. I'd steer way clear of Macau and I'd take the next boat out of Zhuhai if I were you."

"I've still gotta help Hiroko. Know anyone at the Japanese consulate?"

"Shit, this is what I get for talking to a guy in a casino coffee shop."

"Hey, it's your job to help guys like me."

"If you say anything about truth, justice and the American way I'm hanging up."

"Look, really, can you be any help here? We know some stuff about Black Island. You can debrief us."

"Okay, lemme see what I can do."

"One other thing, we may need some protection. The Roman probably has some pals in Hong Kong."

"Yeah, I already figured that out."

"Thanks. I owe you a beer."

"You owe me a helluva lot more than that."

Bill must have good connections. By noon Hiroko's got an exit permit for China and a transit visa for Hong Kong. They were faxed to an office somewhere in the city and delivered to the hotel. By two-thirty, as we walk out of Hong Kong immigration and customs, Warner and a couple of burly Marine guards greet us at the terminal and whisk us off to a secured section of the U.S. consulate building.

I'd warned Hiroko about this ahead of time and she goes with a woman from the agricultural section down a hall. Warner guides me into a small room that's filled almost to its edges with a table and chairs. There's a big mirror on one wall. I go up to it and try staring through it.

"So Bill, is this like a cop show on TV? Is the lieutenant behind the glass?"

"Don't flatter yourself. I'll just record this and then you can get out of here."

"Where to? I'm not sure I ought to go home."

"We've got an apartment you can use, at least for a few weeks, but you can't hide out there indefinitely. We can't assign you bodyguards, anything like that. Sooner or later you're gonna have to come out of hiding and I don't know what to tell you about that. Be careful."

"My tax dollars at work. Thanks."

"Don't mention it. You think the girl's gonna be okay?"

"Yeah, she's tougher than she looks."

"Bondage videos?"

"She's double-jointed, has a lot of fans back in Japan."

"I guess I'm old-fashioned, I don't get that stuff."

"Me neither."

"Glad we got that straight. Now sit down and tell me about it, slow, with every detail you can remember."

I give him the computer first, tell him I have no idea if anything useful or interesting is on it, but make him promise to give me the details if they can crack the code. Then I tell him the rest. He coaxes details out of me that I didn't even know I remembered. When I get to the part in the attic, I pause.

"Can I ask you something off the record?"

He smiles and turns off the tape recorder. "I thought that's what guys like me are supposed to say to journalists. What?"

"I'm not saying I did, but I might've committed a crime."

"I won't know until you tell me about it."

"Yeah, well, I don't want to admit to anything that might get me put away."

"This crime you might have committed, did it involve any other Americans?"

"I don't think so."

"If you're worried that we're gonna turn you over to the Chinese for something you might've done in a whorehouse, maybe I ought to call it a 'horror' house, run by gangsters on one of their islands, don't."

So he turns the tape recorder back on and I tell him. When I'm done with that part of it he turns the machine off again and looks at me. "I didn't say this, but don't sweat it. You did the world a favor getting rid of those guys."

"So why don't I feel any too happy about it?"

"You'd be really screwed up if you did."

I finish the story. At the end he snaps off the machine and stands up. "I'll go see if your friend is finished. It's good you got her out of there. You're both lucky."

"What about the rest of them?"

"Don't hold your breath."

"Isn't there anything we can do? Hell, even the Chinese government can't want this sort of thing going on."

"They don't, but we're a long way from Beijing. The army and navy's what keep all those old guys in power. They don't want to piss 'em off."

"So they just let 'em get away with anything they want?"

"So long as it's discreet. They don't want to hear about it."

"What if they can't help but hear about it?"

"Then they might do something, or they might not. But if you're thinking what I think you are and this hits the headlines, those girls'll just disappear. They won't stand a chance."

"They don't anyway. Closing down that place has gotta be a good thing."

"Yeah, it will be, it'll take 'em a week or two to open a new place and they'll beef up their security."

"You're pretty cynical."

"It's my job, I'm realistic."

"Isn't there anyone who can do anything? An international anti-slavery group or women's group or something?"

"There are, but I doubt there's anything they can do either. You can write it up and send them a report. They can file it."

"That's it? There's nothing anyone can do?"

"I'm not sure. Now it's my turn to ask, off the record?"

"Okay."

"I might know someone to talk to in Chinese intelligence. No guarantees, but with some of what you've given us, maybe I can get a rise out of him."

"You've gotta try."

"I know. I will. But don't write this story, not yet. If this hits the papers before I get through to him, or before he can do anything about it, if he can do anything about it, it's not gonna work. He'll just pretend he never heard anything about it."

"How long?"

"No idea. Give it a week, then check in with me and I'll let you know what I know."

| |CHAPTER **TWENTY-SEVEN** | |

t's one hell of a slow week. Hiroko stays with me in the Consulate's small one-bedroom apartment for the five days it takes to get a new passport and money sent to her for a flight home. We stay inside the whole time.

The first morning I've got to come up with some sort of excuse for having disappeared for a couple of days. I call Norman and tell him a story about having been taken to a nightclub by some guys from one of the companies I'd visited, being mugged, knocked out and spending the missing time disoriented. I don't think he buys it, but he doesn't make an issue of it either.

I offer to take this week off without pay, but he agrees to let me spend the week working from home. He doesn't even question why I've got a new phone number. I don't know why I don't want to tell him the truth, at some point I'm going to have to try and talk him into letting me write up the story for the magazine. I just have to come up with a business angle on it first. It's not going to be easy. Stories that make China look bad make him very nervous. I don't like that, but I can't really blame him. In the meantime I don't want him shooting off his mouth to anyone else about it.

So I keep him off my back by writing the story I'd gone to Zhuhai to get. It's just the way he wants it; full of optimism, yet another bright spot for the booming Asian economy, and all backed up with dubious statistics that've been parroted to me by executives with high stakes in making their companies look good. He can't fault me for the lack of photos; my camera was stolen. He's just glad I'm not trying to get the magazine to buy me a new one.

I also write up the story of the island and what I know about The Roman and Storm, but I don't know what to do with it. I stick it in an envelope with notes on who to give it to and mail it to Jane at work. I call her first and ask her not to open it unless something bad happens to me and I can't take care of it myself. She has a lot of questions. I put her off, telling her I'll answer them all later, not now.

The week crawls by slow, boring and expensive. Hiroko lounges around all day, leafing through magazines, watching the trashy local television, calling friends in Japan, sleeping and eating. Japanese food is pricy in Hong Kong and that's all she wants to eat. She must not have had time to get very addicted to whatever it was they'd been poking into her because although her stomach hurts a little the first day or two, she's hungry all the time. There's a Japanese restaurant in the basement of the building. For a price, a high price, they'll send food up in the elevator. She doesn't have any money of her own.

I've been sleeping on the couch. I'm surprised Friday morning when I wake up on my back and Hiroko's sitting on top of me naked. She's rubbing one hand over her breasts and has my dick in the other, about to pull it into her. She's looking somewhere at the wall above my head or beyond that. I start to say something and she takes the hand off her breasts and covers my mouth.

"Don't talk, please, do what I ask you to, okay?"

I nod my head yes. I'm a little disoriented, having a hard time getting into it. I can't help but think of Sasha and I come close to stopping her, pushing her off me. I don't really feel much of anything but I respond. I guess it's a reflex. She doesn't ask me to do anything, she just does it to me. She pushes and pulls me to where she wants, grabs my hands and puts them where she wants, holds my head and puts it where she wants. We aren't having sex together; she's having sex with me.

It's not good really, not bad either, just a little sad, fraught, maybe a bit desperate, at best therapeutic.

Afterwards she's dripping sweat on the sofa beside me. I turn on my side to look at her.

"Are you okay? I didn't think you wanted to do that."

"I'm sorry. I wanted to do it to you. I wanted to be in control, to remember that I can be in control."

"Don't be sorry. I'd be a fool to complain. Let me know if you want to be in control again, anytime." I'm not sure I really mean that, but it seems like the right thing to say.

She smiles sadly at me. "Do not be angry with me, but I think I have had enough. Now we will only be friends, if you want."

"Yes, I want." I reach out tentatively, not sure if she wants me to touch her anymore. She scoots over and snuggles next to me. We lay there, wrapped in each other's arms and our own sad thoughts.

The first time we leave the apartment all week is a couple hours later when I take her downstairs to get a taxi to the airport, I'm relieved to say goodbye. So's she. We just don't have much to say to each other. Saving someone's life doesn't necessarily give you a lot in common with her. She's never said so but I imagine I remind her of something she'd rather forget. We say we'll keep in touch. Maybe we will, at least for a little while.

All week Jane's been ferrying paperwork for me back and forth to the office. She comes by after work on Friday and insists I go out with her for a drink. I'm about halfway through telling her why I'm not sure that's a good idea, when I change my mind. To hell with it. I'm going crazy in this place.

We go to King's Cross, a British-style pub named after a sleazy neighborhood in Sydney, Australia. It's three steps down from the street on Lockhart Road, the main drag of testosterone and cheap perfume-laden Wanchai. It's the neighborhood made famous by the book and movie *The World of Suzie Wong.*

It's still sort of a red-light district, but it's flirting with respectability. New, swank, trendy bars and clubs front the street alongside the go go bars, hostess nightclubs, topless bars and massage parlors.

Wanchai's still just low rent enough, however, that it's one of the few places on Hong Kong Island where you can find moderately priced drinks. That is, if you're not buying them for one or more of the hundreds of Thai and Filipina bargirls who ply their trade in the area's traditional establishments. A beer for yourself or a friend might set you back twenty Hong Kong bucks or so. But dare to buy a shot glass full of cold tea or a champagne flute filled with ginger ale for the girl in the day-glow bikini who's running her fingernails high along your thigh, and that'll cost ten, maybe twenty times as much.

A bit of advice, if you're ever in one of those places don't run a tab. Pay for your drinks as they come. A few months ago a friend and I were nursing our beers in the Carnival Club and watching a couple of British lawyers buying drinks for the bargirls. They had a swarm of maybe a dozen chattering bikini dancers around them. They bought everyone drinks. They bought the *mamasans* drinks. They offered to buy us drinks. The red plastic glass in front of them was filling with little slips of paper. After about two hours they asked the bartender to total up what they owed.

Their bill came to twenty-eight thousand Hong Kong dollars. That's just about three thousand six hundred U.S. They weren't happy. They tried to weasel out of paying. A couple of unusually large Chinese men, in expensive suits with the sleeves rolled up showing identical tiger tattoos, came out of the back room and stood uncomfortably close on either side of them. The bartender politely suggested that they might want to hand over their credit cards. They did.

King's Cross isn't one of those places. It's just a pub with a mixed clientele of expats and Hong Kong Chinese. It's as good a place as any for a drink, if you can stand the smell. Some moron thought it was a good idea to carpet the place. It wasn't. It's a bad idea for any pub, but a worse one below street level. Between rain-water flash flooding in from the sidewalk and spilled beer; I doubt the carpet's been dry since the day it was laid in the mid-1960s.

Everyone who walks in gets drunk as fast as they can. It's the best defense against the mold, mildew, rot, deep fat fried food, stale booze and cigarette stench that bleeds off the walls, ceiling and especially the floor. Jane and I find a table in a corner near a fan and each order a double shot and a beer to wash it down with.

Jane's half-Chinese and half-Australian, tall and rail-thin with a short, boyish-cut mop of lightened hair, big-framed bright red glasses and known for wearing the shortest skirts in the territory. She used to look embarrassed and would change the subject when I would ask her anything about her life outside the office. One night we were the last two left standing after a company holiday banquet. We hit a couple of bars together. At one of them we ran into a short, plump Irish woman named Sylvie, Jane's girlfriend.

Hong Kong is not one of the world's easiest places to be gay, especially a lesbian. Like China, the territory has long had the usual stupid laws against homosexuality. But the laws specify "male homosexuality." It's unimaginable to a lot of people that women would ever do such a thing, so why even bother to ban it? It seems strange in a culture with a long tradition and varied menu of erotic art and literature. But I guess like a lot of tradition and history, people only take from it what makes them comfortable.

Every now and then I try to talk Jane into coming out of the closet. How're people ever going to change if they're not confronted with their prejudices? But it's her life, not mine, so I've helped her keep it a secret. We're pretty good pals. Drinking buddies. She can drink me under the table.

I knock back my vodka and about half the pint of Carlsberg.

"Slow down there mate. I'm not hooking up with Sylvie 'til later, I wouldn't mind some coherent company for at least an hour or two before that."

Jane's mom's the Australian half and she's had a strong influence; her English is perfect, if maybe a little Aussie from time to time.

"Just needed a jolt. I hereby promise you at least ninety minutes of complete coherency and another hour or so of semi-coherency. That gonna be enough?"

"Your liver mate."

I wave my empty glass in the air at the waitress and hold up two fingers.

"So Ray, mate, what's the skinny on this Black Island? There weren't much to find, but what was there's got me a bit curious. It ain't a business story, 'less I'm missin' something."

At the beginning of the week I'd asked her to find out whatever else she could about the place. She'd done some digging into the Chinese newspapers. I swear her to secrecy then give her the semi-short version; just fleshed out enough that by the end of it she's shaking her head back and forth slowly and has pulled down her glasses to look at me over them.

"I thought you promised me you'd be coherent. You've gone troppo mate, or as my dad would say, '*chee-seen gwailo.*'"

"Your dad thinks all us ghost people are crazy. He married your mom. What's that make him?"

"We're not talkin' 'bout my dad."

"Yeah, you're right. But…"

She waves a hand in front of my face. "But what?"

"Sasha's a friend, was a friend. I had to try and do something."

"Do what? Get yourself killed? Get real here mate. You liked her, that's just fine. You feel sorry for her, that's cool too. But you di'n't know her all that well didya? It's got nothin' to do with her bein' a pross, but why's she worth getting' yourself killed over?"

"There's something else, but it's gonna sound stupid."

"This is all stupid so far, so toss it on the barbie, I'll see if I can swallow it."

I take a deep breath and a slug of my vodka.

"It made me feel alive, more than I've ever felt before."

"Don't go simple on me mate. Romance is always like that, in the beginning at least."

"No, it's not just that. Sure I was happy when I was with Sasha, she meant a lot to me. But it's more than that. It's like I had a mission, a calling, like I was trying to do something that meant something for a change. It was exciting, even when it was scary. It made my brain feel clear and sharp, it put me on edge and I loved it. It was more exciting than anything I've ever done before. And maybe, just maybe I could do some good."

"So you're the legend on the white horse, ridin' to the rescue of the fair maiden."

"I guess you could say that. Stupid, isn't it?"

"Yeah it is. I don't think I can swallow it whole, but I can get it down well enough with a few bites."

"What the hell does that mean? Speak English wouldya? My Australian isn't so good."

"Means 'I catch your drift.' That American enough for ya?"

"It is. I'm not even sure I get it myself though. I'm not sure why you would."

"If playin' hero is so bonzer, what're you doin' in this job? Y'oughta be workin' for one o' those scandal rags, or with a crowd o' do-gooders, or for some investigation outfit or somethin'."

"Bonzer?"

"Learn the lingo mate; good, great, fabulous. You coulda figured it out from the context if you weren't so dense."

"Jeez Louise, what'd I do to deserve this? I been coherent enough, long enough for you? Can we talk about something else and get serious about getting drunk?"

"Whatever you say. I'm meetin' up with Sylvie at Lan Kwai Fong later. If you can still stand up by then, why dontcha come along."

We hit a few more bars. I pace myself through another few hours of drinks. At one point Jane and I share a large, slippery plate of *Chiu Chau*-style rice noodles with hunks of stewed, fatty beef at a small street stand that's famous all over town. With enough chili sauce it's pretty good.

I should be nervous that The Roman's got people out looking for me, but I'm not. Maybe it's just that I'm drunk. Maybe it's the false security of the crowds that are always around in Hong Kong. Maybe I'm being fatalistic. I don't know, but it feels really good to be blowing off some steam.

We meet Sylvie at about one at Handover. I don't know what they'll call the place after July 1, 1997 when the British hand Hong Kong back over to China, or what the place'll be like. For now it's the premier, omni-sexual, Eurotrash disco and pick-up joint in town. It's not my scene.

It's not Jane or Sylvie's either so I'm not quite sure what we're doing here, other than it's one of the few public places they feel comfortable being affectionate with each other. The only reason we even get in is that it's too early. Handover's dead, waiting for the two a.m. crush of scenesters. At least we're parked in a choice booth. It's a good people-watching spot, when there are people to watch.

I lean back against the leather banquette and slowly sip my over-priced drink. I'm tired. My body feels used up. I close my eyes to rest them but my brain won't shut up and then he's there again and we're talking.

"What the hell are you doing out in public? Isn't there some foaming at the mouth angry Russian who wants to kill you?"

"Yeah, I know, but I can't hide forever."

"Maybe you should leave, move back to the States or something."

"I'm not gonna let that bastard chase me away."

"So you're just gonna let him kill you?"

"Not if I can help it."

"Who do you think you are, Sam Spade?"

"It'd be a lot more interesting than business journalism, all that bullshit I had to write about how everything's so great in Zhuhai."

"Yeah right, and it's kind of romantic, makes you feel important, sexy. Grow up."

"It's the way I grew up, back in the late sixties, early seventies, it was all free love and revolution."

"Whores and Russian gangsters? This is a long fall down from that."

"Hey, isn't that what growing up's supposed to be about; realism, lowered-expectations?"

There's an elbow hard in my ribs and I open my eyes. "Hey mate, havin' a kip? Who're ya talkin' too?"

"Was I?"

"You were mutterin' something. Sounded like a conversation from this end."

"I must've nodded off."

"Must have. Let's get you a coffee, an Irish coffee."

"You're a bad influence."

The rest of the night goes like that, not so-witty repartee as we get more and more plastered on high-priced booze. At one point a short, nerdy looking guy in his mid-forties or so comes into the now-heaving place flanked by two huge brutes with dark glasses and earpieces trailing wires down into their collars.

Sylvie leans across Jane to get to my ear. "There go your chances for the night fella."

"Why's that?"

"Dontcha' know? He's the bleedin' King o' Sweden. Howya gonna compete with that? I mean, he can shimmy up to any bird in the place and just whisper in 'er ear, 'howya doin' hon, I'm the King o' Sweden.' And he won' be lyin'. You reg'lar blokes don' stand a chance."

Not that I was looking to pick anyone up anyhow, but she's got a point. I watch as all the men edge away from the trio and the women sidle in their direction. The King of Sweden, if that's who he really is, ends up leaving with two tall blonde models in town from New York for a fashion shoot. I don't get it. Why's a guy from Sweden come all the way to Asia to pick up leggy blondes?

Not long after that Jane and Sylvie help me up and out to the street. They flag down a taxi and pour me into it. I think they're headed somewhere else, dancing or something. I just manage to cough out my address and slump into the backseat for the ride home.

| |CHAPTER **TWENTY-EIGHT** | |

Saturday's a write-off. I'm hung over and even if I wasn't
I'd be too tired to do anything anyway. Outside it's pouring rain, there's a typhoon somewhere between here and
the Philippines, and it's the perfect excuse to just spend the day
in bed with a book. It's hard to concentrate though, my brain is
chattering with thoughts of what I could have done different,
what I should do now. Late in the afternoon Jane calls to check
up on me, make sure I got home okay and haven't found any
new trouble to get myself into. I assure her that I'm safe and
snug in bed.

I still haven't called Irina to let her know what I've found
out about Sasha. I'm putting it off until I feel more up to it. I
don't know if I'll ever feel up to it. How do you tell someone
you love that you've managed to get one of her friends killed?

I wish she was here, but it's almost impossible for her to even get a tourist visa.

At some point I drift off to sleep, but not for long. I wake up with a start, my chest pounding, something screaming in my brain. Another nightmare, there's been too many of them lately. I can't recall the details. I just know it was bad. It's evening and I figure Irina will be out. I can call her and leave a message.

She answers the phone. I manage to croak out a greeting.

"You no sound good. What problem?"

"I've got bad news about Sasha. I think she's dead."

There's a long silence. I can hear heavy breathing, then crying and then a couple of deep breaths. She doesn't speak for a minute or more.

"*Shto*? What happens?"

"I don't know exactly, but I think Gary sold her contract to The Roman. She made someone mad and they took her to Black Island. I talked to someone who saw her there. Then she disappeared."

"Why dead?"

"I went to the island. I heard things, I saw things. Really bad things. I'm pretty sure she's dead."

"Who did this?"

"The Roman and Storm, his bodyguard."

"Call police?"

"There aren't any police. It's a Chinese naval base. I'm still trying some other things, but I don't think there's much anyone can do."

"She was good girl, smart, good friend."

"I know, I…"

"Is *dermo*. Shit. I hate Russia. I hate fucking man. I hate communism and capitalism and Yeltsin and fucking mafia and…"

I hold the phone a little away from my ear and listen to her spit out a litany of everything she hates and a lot of it's stuff I hate too.

About half of what she says is in Russian and I can't understand it, but I'm pretty sure I don't dispute it either.

When she runs out of steam and I can hear her sobbing I want to say something comforting but there isn't anything to say. If she was here I could hold her. I could let her pound her fists on my body if that would help. I could let her smash all my dishes, break my windows, anything. But she isn't here and there's nothing I can do.

Irina's sobs decay into sniffles and finally her cracked voice. "No can talk more now. Talk tomorrow, okay?"

The rest of the night I can hardly do anything. I can hardly think. I can't sleep. I can't even follow the crap that the remote makes dance across my TV. I can't get comfortable and I pace around my apartment, straightening things, getting glasses of water, staring out the windows at the downpour. I pour myself a drink, a big stiff vodka, take one sip and spit it out, dump the rest back into the bottle.

I guess I must've curled myself into a ball in my armchair at some point, because that's how I finally wake up. My back and shoulders are killing me and it takes an enormous effort to straighten out. It's not raining anymore, sun is crashing through a window and I'm encrusted with dried sweat.

I'm still tired. I feel like I'll be tired for the rest of my life. I'll just have to get used to it. I take a long, hot shower. I drink three cups of walk-on-it strong coffee. It's Sunday, a week since I talked to Bill Warner. Maybe he knows something.

He's not in his office. Maybe he's at the American Club, a lot of the consulate people are there on Sundays.

The club's on the south side of Hong Kong Island, on a cliff overlooking the water. It's got tennis courts, a big swimming pool, a gym, a bar with giant screen TVs that seem to always show American sporting events, an enormous Sunday brunch buffet in the restaurant and a poolside barbecue. It's a nice perk for corporate executives and ranking government functionaries. Membership is too expensive for the rest of us.

Roundtrip in a taxi, on a nausea-inducing twisty road, is going to set me back about fifty bucks U.S. I don't want to go out there unless I know I'll find him. I call and have him paged.

Three minutes go by before someone else gets on the phone, says that Mr. Warner's on the tennis court and said to ask if he can call me back after "he wins his game." I tell the messenger to let him know who called, to tell him he's a "cocky bastard," and that I'll show up there to let him buy me brunch in about an hour.

Forty minutes later I'm standing at the grand entrance to the club, my hands on my knees, trying my best to not throw up. The cab driver thought he was a racecar driver and he didn't understand the concept of slowing into the curves and accelerating out of them. Either that, or he was just venting his anger. This time of day people go to the American Club, most of them in their own cars, no one's leaving the place yet. He isn't likely to find a fare back to town.

When I recover I walk up to the front desk and have Warner paged again. He shows up a minute or so later in damp tennis whites, twirling a racket like it's a baton.

"Where do you get this kind of energy on a Sunday morning?"

"Clean living. I wasn't out until three-thirty or so Saturday morning swilling booze and envying Carl Gustav. You're in pretty sorry shape if you're not recovered by now."

"So that really was the King of Sweden? What're you doing spying on me anyhow?"

"I'm not saying."

"About the king or the spying?"

"Either one. I can keep a secret. It's why they pay me the medium bucks."

"You need a shower."

"You got here early. I'll sign you in; you can grab a table by the pool. I hate these big brunch deals. I'll be out in ten minutes or so."

They make good, strong Bloody Marys at the American Club. I'm halfway through one with a double shot of vodka when Warner finds me under an umbrella as far from the screaming kids in the shallow end of the pool as I can get.

A waiter comes over to the table and Warner says he'll have one of what I'm drinking and a double espresso.

"What happened to clean living?"

"They actually use fresh tomato juice here. Who the hell ever heard of that? Plenty of nutrients and they say booze is good for your heart."

"And I thought it was only good for the soul."

"Jury's still out on that one."

"Speaking of which, hear anything from your Chinese pal?"

"And I thought this was simply a social visit."

"Look Bill, maybe sometime it will be. You seem like a pretty cool guy for a spook. We can hang out sometime, hit some bars down in Wanchai or something, knock some balls back and forth, whatever. Right now though, I've got other things on my mind."

"I guess you do at that. I'm sorry, but it doesn't look like my contact can do anything."

"Can I ask why?"

"You can ask. Better yet you can guess. I can look surprised if you get it right."

"I always wanted to play this game. It's so, I don't know, Woodward and Bernstein and Deep Throat or something."

"It's all I've got for you. It's more than I should."

"High-ranking source at the C.I.A.?"

"Unnamed sources full stop. Leave the agency out of it."

"That'll go over big."

"I feel your pain. It's as far as I can go."

"Okay, so let me guess: Beijing's worried about unrest in the south. The Guangdong government even refused to send more tax money to the central government the last couple of years. The old guys up north are terrified that the slightly younger guys down here will get uppity, so they'll leave the army and navy alone to get away with pretty much anything so long as they stay loyal. The police, and even the Security Bureau guys have been told to keep their hands off."

Warner jerks his head, widens his eyes and throws his hands up in the air.

"Stop hamming it up. I get it."

"Just wanted to make sure."

"And we can't do anything about it because that might fuck up relations with China and fifty billion dollars of trade isn't worth risking over a few junkie whores?"

"How many women did you say were there, fifteen or sixteen?"

"Yeah, right, so at a little over three billion bucks per junkie whore, it just wouldn't be cost-effective."

"Sorry, it's not my call. You gonna write the story?"

"My rag doesn't do that sort of thing. I'm not sure what I'll do."

"Well, like I told you, if you write it, it'll inconvenience them for a little while. They'll probably just kill the women they've got now and then start up somewhere else with a new batch."

He's right and I hate it. Irina's list of everything she hates runs through my head, then I add to it while we sit in silence for an uncomfortable few minutes.

"You get anything off the computer?"

"Just a bunch of numbers, must be their accounts. They make a lot of money. That's not news."

"Guess not. Send me the specifics though will you?" I get up to go.

"Don't you want lunch? Good burgers, even pretty good ribs."

"I'll take a raincheck. My appetite's shot."

I call a cab from the front desk and it takes a while for it to get here. About halfway home I have the driver pull over so I can lean out of the backseat and puke up what little's in my stomach.

The phone's ringing when I get back to the apartment. It's Irina. I tell her to hang up and I'll call her back. It's a lot cheaper calling from Hong Kong to Jakarta than the other way around.

"Feeling better?"

"No, no so much. Very angry, very depress."

"Yeah, me too. I talked to the person who I thought might be able to do something. He can't."

"Is only whores. Why anybody do anything?"

"It's a little more complicated than that, but not much."

"Why you love me? I only whore too."

That's a whole lot more complicated than that. "One's got nothing to do with the other. I love you, the other thing, that's just something you do."

"Is all only me Ray. All same person."

"I know, but there are a lot of parts to you, that's just one of them."

"You like me be whore Ray? You want me be whore?"

"No, you know I…"

I can't think. I don't know what to say. Add logic to the litany of things I hate. I've never been tongue tied with Irina before. I mumble a few things, she mumbles back. We mumble our love and desire for each other but for the first time ever it feels strained, like we're going through the motions.

While we speak I've been looking out the window. An almost continuous dirge-like drumbeat of thunder's accompanied clouds as dark as my mood into view over the harbor. The rich gray is accented with green, the type of green that says something's coming, something's building up, get out of the way or be prepared. What little water traffic is still out on the chop is making rapidly for the typhoon shelters. In the lowering space below the clouds, everything is taking on a faint glow. What little light remains picks up colors, highlighting contrasts when a ray of sun struggles through and gets trapped, bouncing around off the heavy moisture in the air.

I hang up the phone and can't stay in the apartment. The walls have closed in on me. I can't let The Roman trap me in this place. If he's going to kill me, he'll kill me, but I can't let him get away with having me lock myself up first.

It occurred to me earlier, when I was talking with Warner, that he's having me followed. How else did he know when I got home the other night and what I did? But if he is, he isn't now. I'm pretty sure of that. I don't care.

Outside, walking, just aimlessly walking, is barely enough better than it was in the apartment. The air is swollen with water. Even though it isn't raining I can throw a hand out in front of me and bring it back wet. Winds are picking up. I feel like I'm being slapped at with damp towels.

I pass through Hong Kong park on my way down the hill. The animals in the zoo are all hiding behind rocks, in their pools, behind shrubs or burrowed deep into their enclosures. Palm fronds are snapping in the gale, tree trunks moaning as they bend. A few people pass, hunched over against the wind, scurrying home before the torrent strikes.

I don't care. It'll feel good to get soaked, lashed by gusts, bombarded with jets of water. Maybe a funnel cloud will swoop down on me like a hawk on a mouse and carry me away to somewhere that makes more sense. Or maybe it'll just consume me and oblivion will be enough.

Down on Connaught Road the last trams, hurrying to the safety of their station, are swaying on the tracks, sparks popping from the wires overhead.

It's beautiful and I'm not afraid. The snapping of electricity above me, in the nearing distance sizzling out of the clouds, hissing in the air that pounds at me from all sides, everything's juiced. It's beginning to rain and the water droplets sting like a swarm of angry bees. The wind shoves me hard from all sides, as if I'm in a stampeding crowd that can't decide where it wants to go.

It's power that doesn't take sides, that doesn't give a shit about me, about The Roman and Storm, about Sasha and Irina and the women on the island or anybody anywhere for that matter. I stand still in it for a minute, feeling it, welcoming it. I want Irina here with me, Sasha, someone.

I start to cry. That's something I don't do very often. It's been welling up in me the past few days. But the tears don't get far down my face. The wind whips them away and replaces them with water, just plain water. I laugh at that.

I don't laugh for long, but long enough that when I stop I'm settled, at ease. Something about it, about all the shapeless violence forming around me, is soothing.

Queensway Plaza looms up into the clouds in front of me. It's covered, all twenty-five to thirty floors of it, with bamboo scaffolding. They're cleaning it, or putting in new windows, or painting it or tearing it down to build something just like it only taller. But now the scaffolding is shivering, the bamboo hums and whistles as it begins to shake loose from the nylon strips that tie it in place.

The top floors have already broken apart. Long, tan spears fly through the sky above my head. Several break apart against the thick shatterproof glass façade of the angular, dimpled Lippo

Center across the street. One skewers the grassy slope in front of Flagstaff House, no more than ten or so yards from me.

It's getting dangerous out here. I'm not afraid, but I'm not stupid either. I can make my way through covered walkways into Central, and from there it's just a long uphill block to the relative safety and warm alcoholic embrace of the Foreign Correspondents Club.

I want company. I don't even care who it is.

| |CHAPTER **TWENTY-NINE** | |

S usan's almost alone in the bar, nursing a beer and picking at a bowl of peanuts. She's a whole lot better company than I expect, or deserve.

"Why aren't you at home?"

"I couldn't take it. Soon as it looked like we were gonna get a typhoon eight warning, my roommates ran to the video store and came back with five women-in-prison movies. Who even knew there were five of them?"

"Sounds bad."

"I would've thought most guys would be into the shower scenes."

"Not lately."

"What's wrong? You seem down."

I look around and see that the storm shutters are all pulled tight over the windows. There's a skeleton crew manning the place and just two tables of other lost souls in from the storm. I feel like telling her the story, but if we stick around here much longer we'll get trapped by the weather. I don't mind that. I don't know if she does.

"If you're gonna go home, you'd better go now. It's already pretty nasty out there."

"Nah, I'm gonna ride it out here. Long as the beer's cold I'll be okay. You?"

"Might as well. Let me get a drink, then let's retreat to a table. I'll tell you the sordid saga."

I give her the long version. We're not going anywhere and I'm not in the mood to pretty it up. The long tall Texan is gape-eyed when I finish.

"Holy shit. And I left the house 'cause of some women-in-prison flicks."

"Don't think I'll be watching any of those for a while."

"I'll bet. What're gonna do about Irina?"

"I don't know. I wish I did. I might not have a choice about what to do if she blames me for getting Sasha killed."

"But you didn't. Those people are monsters, anything could've set 'em off."

"I'd like to look at it that way. It'll take some work."

She changes the subject. That's nice of her. The metal shutters on the big windows rattle and clank. The bartender goes upstairs to take a nap, leaving us to our honor with the drinks. It's impossible to know how long this thing's gonna last, so we take our time. Later, no one's in the kitchen so we make ourselves sandwiches and write them up on our tabs.

It's all typhoon all the time on the TV, so that gets dull fast. The people at the other two tables are playing cards. They invite us to join them but we aren't in the mood. We just sit at the bar talking. It's comfortable, easy, and we're getting pretty drunk.

"So Ray, if you don't want to talk about it just say so, but what about the women on the island? Is there anything you can do?"

I smile and hold up my nearly empty glass in reply. Susan crawls over the bar to fill our glasses, then stands across from me, leaning on her elbows looking at me.

"I wish I knew what would help. I should write the story. Even if it only inconveniences those bastards, isn't that better than nothing?"

"I guess. But then it might get the women killed."

"They might be gone already. They probably are. The people who run the place know I've been there. I'm pretty sure they know I'm a journalist."

"Shit."

"Fucking shit."

"What's the deal with your colleague's brother? That's how you got into this to begin with isn't it?"

"There's nothing I can do about that. He and his Russian babe can't stay holed up at the *Hac Sa* forever. And I don't think The Roman or any of those other guys are gonna let him buy her out of her contract and live happily ever after."

"Isn't there anything they can do, somewhere they can go?"

"How? It's almost impossible for a Russian woman to get a visa to go anywhere. She has to leave Macau through China and there's no way she could do it without the mafia guys finding out. She doesn't have a passport in any case, The Roman's got it."

"Shit."

"Fucking shit."

We finish our drinks in silence. I get another. She says she'll have one too. The metal storm shutters are still clanging. The card players have stopped, they're just sitting around chain-smoking, slowly sipping drinks, not talking, looking sullen.

There's a big, wide sofa in the downstairs bar. I'm getting tired so I tell Susan I'm going to lie down. We end up putting the cushions on the floor and lying down next to each other. There's a moment when we're talking and our faces are close to each other that it almost seems like something could happen. A typhoon would be the perfect excuse; we were drunk, we were trapped inside with nothing else to do; it's almost like the fantasy about being stuck in an elevator.

But instead we just drift off into a drunken sleep for a couple of hours. When we wake up it's quiet outside. We're a little awkward with each other, but not too much. Back upstairs the shutters protecting the glass front doors have been pulled open. It's not raining, not windy. It could be the eye of the storm or it could be that it's passed through. We kiss close-mouthed, but more than just a peck, mashing our lips softly against each other. We say we'll see each other soon, and then walk through the quiet, littered, wet streets in opposite directions home.

I'm not sure what time it is. It's never really dark in Hong Kong. There are only a few shadowy spots where you can't read in the ambient light shed by the city, at least on the north side of Hong Kong Island or the tip of the Kowloon Peninsula. The sun rises out beyond the hump of the mountains and until its rays creep far enough into the harbor to see, you don't know that it's morning.

The clock at the Consulate's apartment tells me that I need to be at work in four hours. I've had it with being cooped up in this place. Maybe it's careless, but I can't bring myself to stay in hiding any longer. Maybe it's wishful thinking, but it is harder for Russian gangsters to operate in Hong Kong than in Macau.

It would be almost impossible for The Roman to get into the territory, at least legally. He'd have to hire someone local to kill me. Maybe he could do that, but the local gangsters usually leave us expats alone. Messing with us is almost always more trouble than it's worth. The local gangsters also almost never cooperate with the Russians, it's territorial. It's a risk, but I figure I'm safe so long as I take a few precautions and stay away from Macau.

I set the alarm to wake me an hour before I go into the office and crawl into bed.

| | CHAPTER **THIRTY** | |

Jane brings me a cup of coffee not long after I reach my desk. "Thought you might need this."

"Thanks. Why?"

"You were at the F.C.C. pretty late. Drank a bit too, from what I hear. That Susan is a real looker. Bit young for an old guy like you though."

"That was quick. Word sure gets around."

"It's a small town mate."

"It's seven million people."

"Yeah, but ninety-eight percent of 'em are Chinese. You're not."

"Who'd you hear it from?"

"Sources mate, unnamed sources. Anything I oughta know about you and Susan?"

"Nothing worth talking about, strictly platonic. Just a couple of lonely souls caught in a storm, talking, nothing more."

"Don't go gettin' poetic on me."

"All right already. Thanks for the coffee. I've got work to do." I shoo her away from my desk and bend my head over the stack of Monday morning faxes and emails from our correspondents.

The best thing about this job is the friends I've made all over the region. The updates from Tokyo, Seoul, Taipei, Manila, Bangkok, Singapore and Jakarta are as much entertaining personal letters from pals, as they are business. I still haven't figured out what to do about the story of Black Island, but reading through the reports gives me an idea. I'll take a poll.

I send out an email, thinly disguising it as a hypothetical ethical dilemma. Responses trickle in throughout the day. Everyone thinks I ought to write the story, even if I have to write it for some other publication.

It's a great story. If my magazine doesn't want it, someone else will. They've got to. I'm a journalist and that's what we do; write the story, stir things up, let the chips fall where they may. It's too late for Sasha, too late for those women on the island, fuck it, it's probably too late for Irina and me, but it's not too late to cause some trouble, to fuck somebody up. That's all I can do, all I've got left. If the story makes somebody important mad, even half as mad as me, maybe that's a good thing.

Walking helps clear my brain, helps me think, even if I'm not thinking while doing it. I make a lame excuse and leave the office early by a circuitous route. I think it'd be almost impossible for anyone to have followed me. The streets have already been swept clean, the bamboo scaffolding on the buildings already tightly bound back into place. There's only a light breeze blowing and the water in the harbor just ripples, there aren't even any small whitecaps. I take in everything around me and let it pass through untroubled by thought.

I walk all the way to the Star Ferry and take it across to Kowloon. The streets are full of tourists who seem to feel an obligation to shop, even though Hong Kong is no longer cheap. But isn't shopping what it's known for?

Passing a bookstore I dodge inside and buy a new paperback of *Moby Dick*. I'd thought of it on the shrimp boat and now seems like a good time to reread it. There's good and evil and things that are neither, that are just the way they are. There's man versus nature and the inevitable consequences of battling too hard against things, even when one of those things is yourself.

As Ishmael takes to the sea to escape the demons and doldrums inside him, I take to the crowds. I walk north along Nathan Road, in the direction of China, to Mongkok, the world's most densely populated neighborhood.

It's dusk and the neon is crackling and sputtering to life. Gas generators are coughing before catching into the low chug that powers the fluorescent tubes that light the stalls lining the streets. Waves of black-haired heads emerge from the subway exits and break into individuals who jostle for space on the sidewalks.

Before long I'm caught up in it all, swept along, able to change course or direction only with strategy. I decide to turn left at the next corner for no particular reason. I look ahead and see that the herd is turning on the inside, so I start to edge toward the buildings about a half block away. I make the turn, then continue to drift with the current, just another bit of flotsam.

The torrent that carries me to and then down Portland Street is increasingly male. The yellow sign girls on the western edge of Mongkok do brisk after-work business. A Chinese friend took me here once.

The yellow signs advertise prostitutes, working singly or in pairs. They all have three or four characters that can be read as a name, or with a slight change in intonation a sexual pun or offer. My favorite was one that my friend translated as "big breasted

Korean housewife." I asked him what was sexy about that. He wasn't sure.

The crowds thin as I move down the street. Men are disappearing into the narrow doorways and staircases that lead off to the side. It doesn't take a lot of planning for me to turn and walk a block to Shanghai Street where I enter a wide-open door at the corner. I trudge up the greasy, marble staircase to the third floor, staying to the side to give wide berth to the waiters who somehow don't slip while they scurry up and down.

I find a small booth by the front window. This time of the evening the teahouse isn't very crowded. It's not shrill like it is earlier in the day with the chatter of songbirds in ornate cages hung from poles strung between the rafters. The bird market is nearby and men, always men, bring their birds here when they take them on walks from home or having recently bought them around the corner.

There are several knots of old men, slipping brandy or strong rice wine into their teacups while they admire each other's birds. The cages are taken down from the ceiling one at a time and placed in the center of the small stone-topped tables around which the men sit.

Two tables have been shoved together behind the inadequate screen of three oily, potted rubber trees. Six young toughs are sitting there, drinking brandy and cola from bottles on the table. All of them have their hair tied back in short, stiff pony tails. They wear cheap black suits with the jacket sleeves pushed up to show off tattoos. They're probably fresh triad members, or wannabe triad members, or guys wanting to dress like actors playing triad members. It doesn't matter if they're real gangsters or not. In Hong Kong image is nearly everything and they're sporting a popular one.

I order a pot of strong red tea from Yunnan Province in China and let it sit long enough to get bitter. I wash down bites of a couple of fluffy, steamed, sweet roasted pork buns with it, and the contrast of flavors in my mouth wakes me up as much as the caffeine.

On my way out I pause by one of the tables of Chinese men. I try to admire the bird that they're all cooing and clucking over, but it's an ugly mottled brown and black, scraggly looking thing. I've heard somewhere that the plain ones have the most beautiful songs and this one's whistling, but I don't have an ear for it.

From the kiosk by the door to the street I buy a pack of cigarettes. I don't smoke, but at the moment I think the burn in my lungs and lightness in my head will feel good. As I walk further down the sidewalk, away from Mongkok, it does.

I walk along the stinking, polluted waterfront by the Yau Ma Tei typhoon shelter. Dozens of small wooden *sampans* are tied up, bobbing in the water, waiting to ferry people back to the junks that are anchored offshore. It used to be that a lot of the small boats were brothels. The women would stand in their skiffs, lit by lanterns, crying out to the men who would parade by on the dock.

The city government chased them all away about five years ago. I don't know why they were any more offensive to public decency than the yellow sign girls, but now they're gone.

I stand under a streetlamp, looking out over the lantern lit water and sometimes up at the cloud of bugs swarming the light over my head. I've had enough of the cigarette I'm smoking and I walk to the water's edge to toss it in. There's a small flare when it hits a pool of gas. It's horrible, sure, but there's something so strange about it that it's wonderful too. I light a match and flick it as well, wondering what else I can ignite. But it goes out before it hits the surface.

Walking back to the Star Ferry I skirt the periphery of the tourist maelstrom of Tsim Sha Tsui. On the way back across the harbor I enjoy the night view. Hong Kong's most beautiful by night, most attractive from afar. It's like a magnificent nightclub, illuminated in twinkles and glitter, glorious with artifice. You just don't want to look into the corners, under the tables or behind the curtains when they turn on the main lights.

Still, I love this place. I love it as much for what's terrible about it as what's good. I'm alive here. The energy of the place pulsates through me. I'm always alert, ready, I want to be doing something, anything, even if I don't always know what. I know now that I'm going to write the story, and I'm going to write it in a way that will make people mad, as mad as me if I can write it that well.

At the moment though my legs and feet are aching. I'll probably be lousy company but I want company anyway. One of the things I like about the F.C.C. is that nobody expects much of anything from anybody there. It's a good place to be witty and charming and as good a spot in which to be dull and stupid. Most attitudes are welcome. I end up there a lot of nights. Probably too many nights. This is another of them.

Susan's at the far end of the bar. Mike's with her. They wave at me but I don't go over. I don't want her to think I'm stalking her. I don't want him to think I'm trying to move in on his girlfriend.

There's one table left empty and I sit at it. The waiter, I always forget his name, brings me a vodka and a bowl of peanuts without my asking. I say "thanks" in Cantonese and we try having a short conversation in his language. I'm too tired to be any good at it for long.

He's come and gone with two more drinks when Fred comes over and sits down. I'm not sure I have the energy to be civil.

"Raymond. I have been looking for you. I had hoped we could have a word after work but apparently you left the office prematurely."

"Fred, I'm tired. What do you want?"

"In a bit of a snit, I see. Perhaps we ought to speak tomorrow."

"No, really, I'm sorry. I'm just tired and I've spent a lot of time in a bad mood lately. It'll do me good to get my mind off it."

"Yes, well then…"

He doesn't take my mind off it at all. It's his brother Ed of course, and Marta. They're missing. No one knows where they've gone. They checked out of the resort and haven't been seen since. Ed's financial manager called Fred and told him that Ed had taken a whole lot of money in cash out of his account the day before he disappeared. That was last Friday.

"I understand that you have attempted to help in this matter. I hate to bother you further with it as you have said there is nothing left for you to do. But please, you must understand, there is no one else I know to turn to."

"I don't know what I can do Fred. I shouldn't go to Macau for a while. It's dangerous."

"In what manner is it dangerous?"

"I told you about The Roman, the Russian gangster. He wants to kill me. I made him mad. He's not someone you want mad at you."

He asks, but I won't tell him why. I'm tired of telling people about it. I'm tired of thinking about it. I'll write it up soon enough. I'm wishing I'd just gone home and crawled under the covers rather than come here.

"Do you think my brother is in danger?"

"I think he got all that cash to try and buy Marta out of her contract, and I think that's a really stupid, dangerous thing to do."

"Perhaps he is offering enough money."

"There isn't enough money. I told you that. Especially not now. Now that The Roman's royally pissed off and Marta and Ed are part of what's made him that way."

"Why would he have that impression?"

"What do you think? He's a monster, not a moron. The first he ever heard of me was because I was poking around trying to find out about the love of your brother's life. People are dead. At least four that I know of, there's probably going to be more before this thing's through. You might have to start preparing yourself for your brother being one of 'em.'"

"Isn't there anything we can do? Anyone we can call? I cannot idly sit by and permit my brother to be murdered."

"Oh fuck, look, I doubt it'll do any good but I've got some friends who are bankers in Macau. I've never asked them for any favors and I don't want to, but I'll talk to them. See if they can put me in touch with anyone who might know or can do anything. Just don't get your hopes up. I'd bet dollars to donuts this isn't gonna get us anywhere."

| |CHAPTER **THIRTY-ONE**| |

"**T**ell me you're not really doing this."

"Sorry, I'm doing this."

"Have you lost your fucking mind?"

It's hard arguing with yourself in a mirror.

I'd gone home from the F.C.C. after talking with Fred, figuring I'd call Francisco, my banker friend, in the morning and do what I could over the phone. Maybe he'd put me in touch with his brother-in-law the cop. No harm in that. No danger either. I was tired, but playing it smart.

Then I got stupid. That happens sometimes. Especially when I'm pissed off about something and it seems like unfinished business. I sat down on the edge of the bed and started thinking about Sasha, and Irina, and Hiroko, and the two men I'd killed, and the woman who I watched die, and the woman in the cage and the other women who are probably already dead, and The Roman, and Storm, and Yana, and Gary, and Ed and Marta who just wanted to be left alone to love each other. And I started thinking about myself. And what I might need to do to live with myself. And what am I doing with myself in the meantime anyway? Maybe just writing the story isn't enough.

And now I'm standing in front of the bathroom mirror in the Consulate's apartment with all these thoughts careening around the track inside my skull; getting into crashes, taking turns too fast and skidding into the wall, spinning out, flipping over and somehow always gunning ahead, foot to the floor, wheels to the macadam. And I just can't seem to shut myself up even though I know where this is all heading and it's not somewhere I ought to be going. And there I am in the mirror, talking to myself.

"What the hell do you need to go back to Macau for? Can't you do all this over the phone?"

"It's better in person, people talk to you better, you can read their body language. I'll find out more. Maybe I can find Ed and Marta before they do something really stupid or before The Roman gets them. I don't know what I can do there. I can try and do something. I've got to try. It's because of me that a lot of this has got so fucked up, it's up to me to try and fix it."

"This is because of Sasha, isn't it? You feel guilty."

"That's part of it, maybe a big part, but it's not all of it."

"You're a journalist, why don't you just do what you do and write about it?"

"I'm going to, but that might even make it worse. This is more, more what, definitive I guess. Even if it's on a smaller scale."

I get up off the bed and send an email to Norman, the editor, telling him I won't be in the office for at least the rest of the week. I'm taking a sudden holiday and if he doesn't like it we can deal with it when I get back. I call the ferry terminal and get a seat on the nine in the morning ferry to Macau. I pack a small bag, and then go back to bed, to sleep, hopefully not to dream.

I do dream of course. And whatever it is, it makes for a lousy night's sleep. Most nights are lousy that way these days. Maybe it's just that I'm getting older. If I'm this way at forty-four, how'm I gonna be at sixty? I guess I won't sleep at all by then. Will I be awake enough to take advantage of all that extra time?

It takes a couple of cups of coffee to cheat me into feeling like I've slept enough. I'd like to call Francisco, have him call his brother-in-law and have the police meet me at the dock in Macau with a security escort, but it's too early. Portuguese banker's hours mean I'll be lucky if he's in his office when I get there at ten-thirty or so.

The water's dead calm and the jetfoil skids over it like a Dutch speed skater on a frozen river. On a weekday morning the ferry is only ninety or so percent full. It's too early for anyone other than the most serious gamblers and the surprisingly large number of people who make the commute to work on a regular basis.

I hope it's also too early for any of The Roman's pals to be keeping an eye on the docks. But I wouldn't be surprised if he's got someone on the inside with immigration. I don't think it'll be long before he and Storm know I'm back in town. Maybe if I'm quick I can come and go before they get around to killing me.

I breeze out of the terminal, into a taxi and in a few minutes I'm dropped off in front of the heavy, polished stone columns of the *Banco do Maritimo Asia*. The enormous iron doors are surprisingly gruesome for a bank. In metalwork so fresh it looks like it might have been cast yesterday, ships toss on riled seas, people are impaled on swords and spears, a dozen or so screaming people are boiling in a large vat with skeletons piled by its side, armies clash with angels above and devils below. I'm not sure what it's about. I hope it isn't the history of the bank.

The door pushes open easily, swinging in on massive, well-oiled hinges. It's cool and quiet inside, breezy with air-conditioning and overhead fans. There's the soft clicking of computer keyboards and the ambient mutter of low voices. No one's being cooked alive or skewered on sharp objects. At least not that I can see.

The young Chinese woman at the information booth is dressed in something resembling a sailor suit from about the era when the Portuguese fought off the Dutch invaders to keep control of Macau. She's very short, barely poking her head above the counter. She doesn't look up at me when I speak, so I ask the top of her head for directions to Francisco's office.

He and Tomas share a secretary who remembers me. "Mr. Sharp, how nice to see you. Do you have an appointment?"

"No, sorry, this is a last minute trip. Does Francisco have some time to see me?"

"He is very busy this morning. We have a delegation from Brazil arriving this afternoon."

She picks up the phone and calls into his office. He'll see me. He can spare a few minutes.

He's getting up from his desk when I walk in. "Ray, you have not come to attempt another interview have you? Lunch certainly, but perhaps another day."

I look down at his desk and it's littered with brochures for local massage parlors and saunas. He notices me looking, laughs, picks up the glossiest of them and waves it at me. "The Brazilians are coming, Tomas and I must keep them entertained. This one is new. I think it is maybe very good."

"Glad to see it's business as usual."

"Why should it not be? Coffee?"

They have excellent espresso at his office, and little pastries. I'm not surprised. We're settled on facing armchairs around a low table, as if at a club. Francisco slowly stirs a cube of sugar into his small cup. "Ray, what is it you have come to see me about?"

"I need to talk with your brother-in-law, the cop."

"This is regarding the matter we spoke about previously?"

"Yes, the brother of my colleague has disappeared. I'm trying to find him. I'd like to stop him before he does something really stupid."

"It seems that he has already done something stupid."

"You're telling me. I hate to ask, but do you mind calling your brother-in-law for me? I just want to meet with him, see if there's anything I can do to help the police or to make them take this more seriously."

He does. Ferdinand, who it turns out is the deputy chief, agrees to see me as soon as I can get to his office. Francisco sends me in a company car with a driver and a bank guard and tells them to wait for me, to take me wherever I want to go after that.

The brother-in-law is a tall, portly man with a florid face and a waxed handlebar mustache. His handshake is sweaty but firm. He's got a corner office in a new building that overlooks the ferry terminal and the casino building across from it that is also the location of the Starlight nightclub. There's a lurid oil painting behind his desk of a Portuguese conquistador being set upon by natives on a beach. He sees me looking at it.

"It is Magellan, the great navigator, the conqueror. The natives are about to kill him, then they will feast on him. I was named after Magellan. It is inspirational, no?"

"Is it?"

"Perhaps it is a warning. The natives here, they will kill me and eat me if they can. But I won't let them."

"What about the non-natives? The Russians, for instance?"

"You refer, I think, to the man called The Roman?"

"Yes."

"He is very powerful, very strong. I do not make problems for him and he does not make problems for me."

"Friends in high places?"

"The Roman, he has no friends. But it is profitable to be his associate and it is *fatale* to be his enemy."

"I'm just trying to find out what happened to a couple of people who've disappeared, a guy in love and the woman he's in love with."

"Love is a beautiful thing. Sometimes it is also foolish. It is not smart to love The Roman's woman. It is better to find another woman to love."

"Too late for that. Now they're missing and I just want to find out what's happened. Maybe it's not too late to do something about it."

"Francisco is a romantic. There is nothing I can do."

"I just need to find out where they've gone. If they've left Macau, immigration should have a record of it. Maybe you know someone there you can ask. I just want to know if they've left, when and what direction they were going. That's all, I'm not asking for anything else."

He looks away from me, out the window, pretzeling his fingers together under his chin; thinking, I guess. I look more carefully at the painting behind him. Magellan's got a strong resemblance to Francisco's brother-in-law; enough like him that he probably had it commissioned. He looks arrogant, ready to go down fighting, not believing that these loin-clothed little people could possibly bring him down. It isn't the sort of thing I'd want to be associated with. The mighty navigator looks like he's getting what's coming to him.

Ferdinand "ahems" for my attention. "My wife hired the artist to paint this for me on my thirtieth birthday. We are now divorced. Once, I too was in love. I can do no more for you than to find out the information you have requested. It will only take a minute, the police computer has also the records of immigration."

I give him Ed's name. I don't know Marta's family name so I won't be able to track her. I can only assume that if they've left Macau, they've gone together. He picks up his phone and gives the information to his secretary. We sit silently until she calls him back. He picks up a pen and scribbles on a notepad, then hangs up.

"The man you are looking for departed Macau last Friday afternoon at three. He walked across the border at Zhuhai. His destination was listed as Guangzhou, Canton. That is all I can tell you. I know no more."

"Thank you. I'm not sure what it means, but it's a start. Can I ask just one more question, about The Roman?"

"I will answer if I am able."

"He's from Vladivostok, right? Is he the big boss, or does he work for someone else?"

"He has a superior in Russia. No one knows his name."

I've got a pretty good idea where Ed and Marta have gone and I don't like it. I've got to be sure though. I have the bank's car take me to the Hac Sa resort.

Marta must be with Ed; otherwise he'd've gone to Hong Kong. Even if she could somehow have gotten back her passport, Hong Kong immigration wouldn't let her in; they'd have just shipped her back to Macau on the next ferry. A bribe would probably get her into Zhuhai, even without a passport. There's a big international airport in Guangzhou, which isn't that far away. From there, the only other country she could possibly fly to, and have a hope of being let in, would be Russia.

There were sure to be some complicated travel arrangements. Ed grew up privileged; other people usually do that sort of thing for him. What else is a hotel concierge for?

But they don't do much of anything for free. It costs me a hundred Hong Kong for William to simply nod his head from behind the desk and confirm that yes, he did make travel arrangements for Mr. Lyons and his fiancé. Five hundred more gets me their itinerary.

A car and driver picked them up in Zhuhai and took them to Guangzhou where they'd spent the night at the Garden Hotel. Saturday morning they flew to Seoul where they connected with a flight to Vladivostok. They're booked into the Hotel Versailles, the only swank place in that town.

| |CHAPTER **THIRTY-TWO** | |

Lev, the vulpine-faced business editor sitting across the table from me, is banging a whole fish on the edge of the table. He isn't the only one. I have a fish of my own in front of me, and at least a half-gallon of beer that reeks of formaldehyde. I'm taking in the scene, stupefied and exhausted, wondering how the hell I ever got dumb enough to be here.

I'd left Macau after I found out Ed and Marta had gone to Vladivostok. Sticking around for fun wasn't likely to be good for my health. On the jetfoil back to Hong Kong I figured I'd done all I could. It was out of my hands.

I got back to my office late in the afternoon, told Norman my vacation was over, told Fred his brother had gone to Vladivostok and settled into a giant pile of proof-reading. It was boring, but I kept saying to myself that I was glad to be doing something dull for a change.

But Fred wouldn't leave it alone. I could see him eyeing me from his desk. A couple of times he started to get up, like he was going to come over to talk with me, but then he must've thought better of it. The one time he actually got out of his chair I shot him a dirty look that sat him back down.

He finally got to me when I went into the little kitchen to pour myself a cup of the burnt coffee that had been sitting on the hot-plate all day.

"Raymond, what more can we possibly do?"

"Nothing. We can do nothing. We can leave it alone. Ed's an adult, we can't save him from himself if he doesn't want saving."

"But there must be something. There must be people in Russia who, there must be police or someone."

"I'm sure there are. I don't know them. All we can do is wait and see what happens."

"Did he take the money with him?"

"I don't know, probably. How much was it anyway?"

"His financial advisor would not disclose an exact figure. More than one hundred thousand U.S. dollars."

"In cash?"

"Yes. Do you think that will be enough for his purpose?"

"It's more than enough to get him killed."

"Please, isn't there anything you can think of to do? You know these people; you have met them, isn't there anything? It is simply intolerable that they might harm Edward."

Unfortunately, he wasn't the only one who couldn't leave it alone. I'd been trying to ignore it because that'd be the smart thing to do. But the chorus of nags on one side of my brain shouted down the one little voice on the other side that was sensibly trying to tell me to forget about it, not to be a hero, sit tight, write about it but otherwise let it drop.

Damn Fred anyhow. I'm not doing this for him. It's probably too late to be doing it for Ed. But I had to do it for myself, for Sasha, for Irina, for that woman in the cage and the woman on the cross and a whole lot of other people I don't even know. As much as I knew it was the smart move to let it go, as much as I knew it was probably hopeless and I'd be an idiot for even trying, I couldn't let it end there.

"I'll make some calls, see what I can do. Once again though, I gotta tell you, don't get your hopes up. It might already be too late to do anything."

I walked away before he got too obsequious with his thanks. I called Theresa, our correspondent in Seoul. She wrote a story on Russia's far east about a year ago, I thought she might know someone I could talk to. She did. She went to school in London with a Russian guy who, at least when she did her story, was the business editor of the *Primorye Times*, an English-language weekly based in Vladivostok.

I called Theresa's friend Lev. I caught him as he was leaving his office. It was a stroke of luck for the both of us. At lunch that day he'd been talking with the paper's crime reporter about trying to put together a story on the Vladivostok mafia's activities in Asia. He asked if I wanted to collaborate with them on it. I couldn't say no.

Over the next two days I sold Norman, my editor, on the idea. It helped that Lev set up an interview for me with Alexi Nechaev, President of Far East Oceanic and Touristic Enterprises. He's one of the richest men in Vladivostok, and he's trying to promote trade and tourism in the region. It wasn't hard to arrange, guys like that practically start drooling at the prospect of a friendly article in a major magazine. Lev hinted that there's something else I need to know about him, but he wouldn't talk about it until I got there.

On his end Gregor, the crime reporter, confirmed that Ed and Marta had checked into the Versailles on Sunday. No one's seen them since they had breakfast in the hotel dining room Tuesday morning.

Korean Air leaves Hong Kong for Seoul at around midnight, connecting to Vladivostok late the next afternoon. I was on the flight Wednesday night, choking on tobacco fumes in the one row of business class that was called the "no smoking section." Smoking was okay in all the rows in front of and behind me. I decided to give up and have a cigarette myself. I bummed a Marlboro regular off the guy in the seat in front of me. I lit up and a stewardess was promptly by my side insisting that I put it out. I was, after all, in the no smoking section. A lot of rules are for fucking idiots.

I may have slept a little during the long, dull layover in the lounge at Kimpo Airport. Or maybe not. It didn't do me any good if I did. I was in a snarling bad mood by the time I got to the immigration counter at Vladivostok. Between the officer's heavily accented lousy English and the clamor of construction noise, I couldn't hear a word that the officious, smug bastard in the fraying uniform said. But I gathered that he was in an even worse mood than I was. That brought a smile to my face.

It didn't speed things up though. It probably made them worse. I was subjected to everything they had short of a body cavity search, and my papers were examined and questioned at least a dozen times. I lost count before I got out of there.

At the curb I somehow managed to figure out that the scribbled sign in Cyrillic letters being waved by the enormous swarthy man in torn blue jeans, a bright purple sweater and with two large gun butts sticking up out of his waistband was meant for me. Lev had said he'd be there or I would've turned tail and ran. The newspaper keeps him on retainer. His usual job is to sit in the lobby of the building looking menacing enough to scare off angry readers. He drove me in a smoking wreck of a car with a disturbing head-sized hole in the windshield in front of my seat to meet Lev and Gregor at their favorite beer hall.

I didn't get much of a look at the city on the way into town. What I did see was an industrial suburb designed and built by a government without a lot of money to spend in the nineteen sixties, then left to decay. Some of the buildings I passed were factories, some were apartment blocks, it was almost impossible to tell the difference. There were low, rounded hills and from the tops of them I caught a couple glimpses of what looked like it might be a pretty harbor.

Lev and Gregor's beer hall is in the basement of what I think is an office building. It looks pretty much like everything else; a gray, cheerless concrete exterior with deep set window wells and some sort of tarnished metal plaques screwed into the walls next to the doors.

The big guy walked me down the stairs, pointed out Lev and Gregor, then stayed at the entry when I walked over to meet them.

Gregor, the crime reporter, is sitting on my left. He picks up his fish and is now also slamming it on the table. He and Lev are making a racket like a duo of rhythm-challenged rock drummers. They're beating their fish hard enough that the beer is sloshing out of the tops of our tankards.

Lev stops pounding his fish first, puts it to his mouth and takes a large bite out of its side. He washes that down with a mighty swill of beer, then looks up and lets out a loud, satisfied belch.

I'm too tired and cranky to bother being polite. "What the hell are you guys doing?"

Lev looks at me with a broad smile and points to my fish. "This is *vobla*, salt fish, you bang on table to make soft for eating. It is very good, you try."

I figure it's gotta be some sort of joke but I'll be a sport and go along with it. So I thwack mine on the edge of the table. I look around and no one's laughing. Gregor, who's had his own bite and gulp, motions for me to hit it harder. I do. I work it up and down the edge, putting a lot of strength into it. Salt, scales and flecks of flesh fly off, spattering my shirt. Finally Lev points a finger at my mouth.

For all the beating it's gone through, the fish is still tough and chewy. And salty, really salty; my mouth shrivels and puckers as every last molecule of moisture is vacuumed out of it. I can't get to my beer fast enough or open my mouth wide enough to get as much of it down as I need. When I lower the tankard it's half-drained but my thirst is just revving up.

They both laugh. Gregor slaps me on the back with one hand while taking his next bite of fish with the other. As the beer hall fills up for the evening it gets harder to hear each other over the drumming of fish on wood tables and the bellicose laughter and conversation around us.

The noise is good though. It masks what we're talking about. In a quieter room someone might overhear us.

I tell Lev and Gregor my story in greater detail than before and it doesn't seem to shock them in the slightest. That gets me worried. When I'm done, they look at each other and shrug their shoulders.

"You guys don't seem shocked, or horrified or anything. What's the deal?"

Lev speaks better English. "No, it is a terrible story, of course, but it is business as usual, it is no surprise. The mafia here are very bad, they are stealing the whole country."

Gregor raises his glass and an eyebrow. "Before, communists steal Russia, now mafia steal Russia, for Russia people only *terlyohzka.*"

I look at Lev for an explanation. He's laughing, lightly, his mouth turned up at the edges and his shoulders jiggling. He quickly shuts it down and looks serious. "*Terlyohzka* is the greatest strength and also the greatest problem for Russia. It means be patient. If things are bad? Be patient, maybe they will get better. If things are good? Be patient, they will get bad. All there is to do is to be patient."

Maybe it's because I'm an American; I don't have that sort of patience. "Writing this article isn't going to be just waiting around. Aren't you guys trying to do something?"

The Russian journalists exchange two of the saddest, most resigned looks I've ever seen. Lev turns to me but doesn't quite look at me. "Ray, we hope you will be our friend. We want to help you, we want to work with you. But we cannot write this story for our newspaper. It is too dangerous. Maybe your magazine can print the story, maybe some other newspaper. Maybe it will be better for Russia if you have no *terlyohzka*."

I need more beer. If I had to drink it by itself I couldn't. It's terrible. That's gotta be what the salt fish is for. It makes you thirsty enough that you have to drink the stuff. You'd swallow the local, polluted, poisonous water if it was in front of you. I take another bite, drain the tankard and wave it upside down in the air like I've seen other people doing.

Soon we have new beers, but the same old fish. I ask Lev what it is that he needs to tell me about Nechaev. "Has he got something to do with the mafia?"

Gregor and Lev nod their heads together to talk, then Lev leans close to talk to me. "This man that you have problem with, The Roman, he is only one of bosses. There are three or four bosses in Vladivostok, but only one *krysha*. We think *krysha* is Nechaev."

"What's *krysha*? Is that like the godfather or something, the big boss."

"Yes and no. He is a very powerful, very rich businessman. He does not tell other bosses what do, but he gives them protection. Maybe he gives them money like an investor, maybe they give him money so that he will stop any trouble for them. If they need to agree on a problem between them, they go to him."

"So does Nechaev know what they do? Is he in on it?'

"We don't know. Maybe a little. Maybe he does not want to know what the bosses are doing."

"Why's he going to talk to me?"

"He is also a very big businessman. He owns hotels, ships, trucks, he controls much of the harbor. He wants investors to come here. He will not give interviews to Russian newspapers, but a business magazine from Hong Kong, that is different."

It seems worth a shot. If he thinks I can help him get the sort of publicity he wants, maybe he can help me find Ed and Marta and get The Roman off all our backs. It's not a lot to trade, but it's something.

Is it ethical? Aren't I supposed to write the truth no matter where it leads or what it does? Does that include getting people killed, especially me? Maybe I'm giving up my shot at journalistic glory but at the moment horse-trading with the big cheese seems like the smartest move.

I manage to choke down the rest of my fish with one more tankard of beer, after which I want to go to my hotel.

The hotel isn't far but they insist on driving me. The streets are dangerous at night, they say. Especially for foreigners. Especially for foreigners who've been drinking.

Near as I can tell the most dangerous thing about the streets of Vladivostok is guys like Gregor driving on them. I don't know how he can see past the spider web of cracks on his windshield. Both the passenger and driver's side have been hit, hard, by something from the inside. I'm squeezed into the back seat next to the big guy. One of his gun butts is poking my chest as I slump as far down in the seat as I can without being too obvious about it.

The ride lasts only a screeching, careening, bone-jarring five minutes or so. It's the sort of thing that people would pay good money for at an amusement park. Not me. It seems like an eternity before we skid to a stop half on the sidewalk in front of the Hotel Vladivostok.

I convince them that I'll walk to their office in the morning. It doesn't take a lot of convincing on their part for me to agree that the big guy will show up to escort me there. They make certain I don't want to go out for another drink, then tear off into the yellow, mercury vapor lit night leaving me and the big guy on the sidewalk. I ask him his name and he just looks at me blankly.

There's no doorman in front of the hotel, just a taxi idling on the sidewalk to the side of the front door. The driver's smoking what looks like a homemade cigar and nipping from a small bottle of vodka.

I look up at the building. Some functionary in a dreary, windowless office in Moscow in the late 1950s must have thought it was an impressive plan. It's big, it's yellowish-brown in the streetlight, it has row after row of same-sized windows. Almost the only distinctive feature is a large, rounded concrete awning that hangs over the front door. It's outlined with burnt-out light bulbs.

The building could be an administrative office for one of the less glamorous ministries, mining, or forestry, or the postal service. If it doesn't fall down before then, historians may eventually preserve it as a prime example of a particularly hideous type of socialist bureaucratic architecture.

There must be forty women in the lobby. They're all in stylish clothes and high heels. They're lounging on tatty sofas, sprawled in ratty armchairs and slumped against the walls. I can almost hear their heads snapping alert when we walk in. Most of them are blonde and a blur of golden hair swishes across my eyes.

There's no one else there, at least that I can see. There's a high arched doorway leading off the lobby with a small red neon sign over it saying "casino." I can hear a modest hubbub coming from there, the clicking of chips, soft voices, but otherwise it's only all the women, me and the silent big guy.

Eighty eyes follow us to the front desk. There's no one there and no bell to ring. I turn around, lean against the counter and watch the women watching me. One of them separates herself from a trio arrayed around a chipped and bruised classical looking column and approaches fast on very high stiletto heels that click on the cracked, polished stone floor.

She looks like she'd be about my height in bare feet and if I buy what she's selling I'll be able to confirm that later. Lev booked me into the hotel, then cracked wise about how a guy would never be lonely staying in it.

She walks up very close to me, so close I can feel her breath on my lips when she speaks. "*Zdrastvuyte.*"

She's got a deep, melodious voice that comes out of bright red lips playing peek-a-boo with a shock of honey blonde hair. Most of the rest of her is playing the same game; her hair hangs down to the bottom of her well-formed ass. I think the hair's real. I've never seen anything like it. She's got gray-green eyes, so shiny and saturated that if it wasn't obvious she can see I'd think they were made of the finest glazed crystal. When she speaks to me it's like everything comes loose inside my skin. I'm surprised I don't melt into a puddle, right here at her feet. I'm sure I've got a really stupid expression on my face.

"Uh, um hi. Sorry, I don't speak Russian."

"*Amerika?*"

"Yes. Do you speak English?"

"Little. What you want?"

What do I want? What more could I possibly want than to just hear her say that to me and to know that for something as comparatively worthless as money I can have what I want. At least what I want now. What any straight man would want. I've only been here for an evening, but already Russia is proving hard on the conscience.

I choke out a smile and something other than what I'm thinking. "At the moment I want to check in. Does anybody work here?"

That's sort of funny, the lobby is full of women who work here. They just can't register me into a room.

Her hair brushes against me and a scent like dewy flowers in freshly turned black soil moisturizes me as she leans over the counter and pushes a button hidden away underneath it. I stumble at her proximity. A couple of other women who are nearby notice it and laugh. I can hear a buzzer somewhere past a door behind the counter. She steps back, then moves in close to me again. She holds the shock of hair off her lips and lightly lashes me on the cheek with it.

"My name Nina. What name you?"

"Ray."

"You want me come room Ray?"

Sure I do, and I'm about to say so when the big guy steps in between us and growls something at her. She looks very unhappy, begins to say something back but then thinks better of it. Watching her walk away I'm thinking maybe I don't want a bodyguard after all. But I guess he knows what he's doing. I hope so. He turns back to look at me, fishes in his pocket and pulls out a piece of paper.

It's a note from Lev. "If you want a girl, don't go with any in the hotel. Maybe dangerous. Call this number, tell them my name." I don't know why he didn't just tell me this in person. Maybe he wanted to save himself the embarrassment if I was shocked or something. I smile at the big guy, fold the paper and put it in my pocket.

Someone clears their throat behind me. A bulldozer of a middle-aged woman is standing behind the desk. She pokes a finger the size and color of a large veal sausage at me then points to a stack of papers on the counter. She has a lot of forms to fill out and seems to want to copy just about everything from my passport. I sign in five different places and finally fork over a thick wad of cash. The hotel doesn't take credit cards. The room's cheap, but the ruble bills are small.

As I take the key and turn away to go up to the room, she "ahems" at me. I turn back to her and she's holding out a large towel, a face cloth, a gray roll of toilet paper and a bar of soap. I wedge them under one arm, pick up my suitcase with the other hand and begin to turn away again.

"Mister, you want more towel? You want vodka?" She looks from me to the girls then back at me. Nina, displayed artfully against a pillar, smiles at me and slowly slides one leg against another. That reminds me of the note in my pocket. Maybe an extra towel and vodka are a good idea. I'm not sure I'm going to want them, but it can't hurt to be prepared. The bulldozer wants dollars for them, U.S. dollars. Luckily I've got some. I hand her a twenty and she holds it up to examine in the light.

I guess the bill passes muster because she turns and heads back out the door behind the counter. In a little while the woman returns with a dented metal bucket filled with ice, a bottle of vodka and two thick, chipped water tumblers. She drapes a towel from behind the counter over it and hands it to the big guy, then grunts as she motions us away.

As we walk in the direction of the elevator together, the other women slump back into their at-ease postures, waiting for another customer to arrive.

I'm about to push the button for the elevator, but Nina yells at me, "Elevator broken. Everything Russia broken. Go stairs."

The big guy follows me all the way up. He goes into the room first and looks around. He hands me the key when he leaves and points at the lock. He points to nine on his wristwatch, then himself, then makes a gesture like he's knocking on the door. I get it. I smile and watch him walk down the hall before I close and lock the door.

It's a surprisingly nice room. There are three windows that look out over the city to the open waters of the Amursky Gulf. Lights from boats bob and twinkle at sea and the moon is coming up over the small thickly forested hill outside the left window. The room has a high ceiling, a fairly plush carpet, has been painted within the last year or so and is dominated by an enormous, high, four-poster bed.

I put my suitcase down and walk to the bathroom. It's big, with an extra large tub set on legs. I want to splash water on my face but the tap in the sink is dry. I try the bathtub faucet and all it does is cough and produce a small, brief trickle of brownish muck. Luckily there's a phone in the room, I can call downstairs rather than walk.

Sitting next to the phone I take out Lev's note and think about it. I think maybe I've had enough trouble with Russian prostitutes for a while. What I really want anyway is for Irina to be here, or Sasha. But neither of them are at the number on the note. I open the vodka instead and pour a slug of it into a glass.

I'm in Russia, so I'll drink it the way I've seen Russians drink. I tilt my head back and pour it straight down. As soon as the booze hits the back of my mouth I know I've made a mistake. My throat catches fire, my chest swells like a volcano moments before an eruption, I double over coughing, seeing red.

Friends've warned me about vodka in Russia. Apparently there's a lot of it that's bad, really bad, deadly even. Some of the name brand stuff is counterfeit, made from ingredients that if you're lucky will only make you go blind. I've got my eyes squeezed shut and so I don't know if I can see anything or not. Does it happen this fast?

I'm doubled over like I've been sucker punched. I reach around blindly for the bucket of ice, find it, scoop up a handful and bring it to my mouth. As it begins to melt it helps a little. The burning and hacking are subsiding. Maybe I'll live. But I probably ought to wait before having another drink in case this one does kill me.

I lay down on the bed and open my eyes. I haven't gone blind. That's a relief. I'm feeling better. I'm actually feeling pretty good. I sit up, but then, just as the rest of my body is calming down, a tidal wave of drunkenness and exhaustion slams into my brain. It knocks me back onto the mattress, my legs dangling off the edge from the knees. I wish the ceiling would stop spinning like that. Or at least slow down.

| |CHAPTER **THIRTY-THREE** | |

wake up on the floor. I must've fallen there during the night. I feel stiff but okay. My head doesn't even hurt. That's a surprise.

I go into the bathroom, where the water works in the morning. Standing in the tub, taking a shower with a short hose attached to the faucet, the view out over the gently sloping hills of the city to the bay is beautiful. The buildings aren't distinctive; mostly low-rise concrete and stucco from the 1960s, but the sun sparkles off the water, there are a couple of small wooded islands in the distance, a lot of boats chugging out to sea and puffs of downy clouds. It's early fall and there aren't many trees in the city, but the ones that cling to life on the built-up slopes are awash in lively colors with dying leaves.

A little after nine the big guy's at the door as promised. He even smiles at me when I say good morning. It's a nice day for walking. I don't know how he feels about it, but the newspaper office is about a mile away and I don't need to be there until ten. I follow the route on my barely adequate map as I'm led down Svetlanskaya Street to the main square.

About a half block past an enormous bronze soldier heroically holding up a gigantic bronze flag to commemorate "the Fighters for Soviet Power in the Far East," I come across Special Burger. It has a greasy, slightly sour, familiar smell that I'd steer clear of almost anyplace else. But I don't know Vladivostok at all and there's an under layer of burning coffee that also oozes from the place, so I stop the big guy and motion us inside.

It's a riot of Russians eating ugly little, ketchup drenched burgers and paper-thin slices of what passes for pizza around here. None of it looks like breakfast to me. I push my way to the counter and order a large coffee. Luckily "coffee" seems to be one of those universal words, like "okay" or "fuck." I look at the big guy and gesture that I'm buying, but he doesn't want anything.

The thin Styrofoam cup that the bitter brew comes in provides scant insulation. Holding onto it burns my hand until I find a small counter to set it on. I notice that everyone else drinking coffee is wearing gloves. I stand, as much out of the way of the throng as I can, blowing on my cup, hoping it will cool down enough to drink.

Everyone's furtively looking at us. I suppose I must seem like someone important if I've got a bodyguard. I don't know. When I catch anyone looking I smile at them, most look away, some of the younger ones smile back.

It takes a few minutes before my lips are only slightly singed by the first sip and my fingers are warmed almost, but not quite, to the point of pain. I take the coffee and we cross the street to the newspaper office, dodging cars that have no apparent concern for the fact that we're in their way.

The entry to the building is dark and I can't figure out, or much see, the directory. It's only a five-story building and none of the lights on the elevator panel are lit. The big guy points to the stairs and holds up three fingers. I leave him below.

I poke my head through the door on the third floor. Lev waves me over to his desk. It's in a corner at the front of the building, with a view out a window that probably hasn't been cleaned since before Brezhnev. Through it I can just make out the harbor. It's crammed with the gray and rust colored peeling hulks of navy ships, the old Soviet Far Eastern Fleet. It doesn't look like a threat to anyone.

I sit down on the edge of his desk and toast him with my coffee cup. "Morning, you fellas get home allright?"

"And you Ray?"

"Slept like a baby, a drunk one."

"Where did you buy coffee?"

"Across the street. Special Burger."

He makes a face and points to his metal wastepaper basket. "It is terrible coffee. The coffee here in the office is only bad, it is not terrible."

That sounds like a recommendation. I set my cup down and he leads me to a small kitchen where a teakettle is whistling on an electric hotplate. He unlocks a cupboard and pulls out an obviously precious jar of instant coffee. He puts a carefully measured, rounded teaspoonful into a delicate china cup and gently stirs hot water into it.

I take it back to his desk and he's right. It's bad, just not as terrible as what I'd been drinking.

"When am I meeting Nechaev?"

"He will see you at four this afternoon."

Gregor brings over his file on Nechaev. It's a nice gesture; it would be useful if I could read Russian. No one in the office has any time to sit with me and translate. I ask Lev if he has any ideas where I can find a translator.

He looks a little embarrassed, but then smiles. "Did Mikhail give you my note last night?"

So that's the big guy's name. "Yeah, thanks but I need a translator."

"You can go to the university. If you find a translator there, maybe they can work for you today, maybe they cannot. Some of the girls who work at the phone number I give you are also students at university. Some of them speak very good English. It will be more fast and maybe not so much money as official translator."

He's got a point. I use his phone. The woman on the other end doesn't speak English so Lev takes over and tells her what I want. It involves a lot of laughing and some winking in my direction. Finally he hangs up.

"A girl who has good English will be at your hotel room in half hour. You pay for her time, so it does not matter what you do in that time. Maybe if she is a fast translator you will have time for something else." He hands me a set of car keys and tells me to give them to Mikhail who will drive me to the hotel.

About ten minutes after I get to my room there's a knock at the door. Marina looks like a fresh-faced college student. She's carrying a book bag slung over one shoulder. She's wearing blue jeans and a simple black pullover sweater. She's the first Russian woman I've seen who isn't wearing makeup, or at least not much of it if she is. She doesn't need it. She's got lush, dark short hair, satiny pale skin and bright blue eyes. She takes in the room from the door and smiles at me a little nervously. I smile and step back to let her in.

She walks to the desk and puts her bag down, turns to face me and starts to pull off her sweater.

I can hardly believe what I'm saying. "No, wait, please, didn't they tell you what I want?"

She finishes pulling off her sweater, tosses it on the bed and is standing looking at me with her hands on her hips. She's wearing a bright red, lacy bra that is just barely clinging to firm, young, pillowy breasts. In a moment I'm going to forget all about work, but I can't do that.

"Really, please, put your sweater back on. We can talk about other stuff later, right now I just need you to translate some papers for me."

"That is what they tell me at the agency. It is true?"

"Yeah, really, it's true. It's important. I have to get this work done. If you don't put your sweater back on I'll never get it done and that'll be bad."

"I like to be bad."

"So do I, but not now, later. Okay?"

Marina shrugs her shoulders and puts her sweater back on. I ask if she wants anything to eat or drink while we work. I order coffee and toast from room service.

Her English is good. She really is a student, at the geological institute. She reads the whole file out loud to me while I take notes. She only stumbles over a few words but has a dictionary in her bag that bridges the gaps. She has a nice, soft, steady voice and where there are local references that I might not understand she explains them.

I get more than enough information to pretend I'm interviewing Nechaev about his legitimate business. If you can call it that. Vladivostok was a closed, military city for many years. He showed up in town with bundles of cash just after the travel restrictions were lifted and the government began selling off its assets. No one has any idea where all the money came from. There are the usual rumors about drugs, guns, gambling, loan-sharking and all that. Some people say he came from Chechnya, some from Belarus, some St. Petersburg. No one really knows anything about him.

The first thing he bought was an old rundown hotel. He found Japanese investors and classed it up. He bought a lot of navy ships and began converting them to civilian freight use. He bought up trucks, and now pretty much controls the roads in this part of the world. He owns other hotels, nightclubs, he even owns Special Burger. I'll have to complain about the coffee.

There's nothing solid linking him with the mafia. The Roman and the three other mob bosses in town hang out in his nightclubs and seem to pay him a great deal of respect. They were all fighting each other over territory before he showed up. Since then there's been peace between them and the spoils have been pretty evenly divided. Maybe that's just a coincidence, but no one really thinks so.

That's about all there is. He gives a lot to local charities. Sometimes he's seen in public with a former Miss Japan on his arm, sometimes it's a set of identical twins. He's always polite to the press but never gives interviews. I guess I got lucky.

It takes us a couple of hours to go through the file. By one we're finished and I order lunch from room service. Marina just wants a bowl of soup and some bread. I tease her. "What, no caviar, no champagne?"

She has a nice, sincere looking smile. "I am a prostitute, but I am a simple girl, not greedy."

Marina came to Vladivostok about three years ago from St. Petersburg. She'd heard it was a wild, corrupt, dangerous place, but also a newly opened one, ripe with opportunities. It took her three months to find work, crappy work at Special Burger. Even to get that job she had to fuck the manager. Three months later she'd had more than enough of flipping burgers, looked around for another job then gave up and joined the crowd of women in the lobby of this hotel.

"I work here for one year. I am paying my manager and saving money, always saving. My manager wants to make loan to me, to buy expensive things, but I do not. I live a simple existence.

"At the end of one year I am accepted into university, to study geologic. Since I was a little girl I have always wanted to go to Kamchatka, now I go there with my school."

The Kamchatka Peninsula is about fifteen hundred miles to the northeast. It's a prehistoric region filled with massive volcanoes spewing smoke and fire, steam shooting out of the ground, huge brown bears swatting salmon out of the rivers. She'd got back a month ago from a three-month study tour.

"Still, I live simple, in student housing. But school is expensive. I need money. I make more money and also have more time for study when I work as prostitute. But now I work with the agency. I do not work so much. It takes smaller money from me than the managers."

After lunch she's sitting on the edge of the bed and wants to know what else I want.

She's attractive, smart, and easy to be with. I like her. I want her to like me. I'm tired of paying for sex. The fantasy it buys isn't working as well as it used to. Maybe I think too much, but I'm sick of wondering if that's why a woman likes me or not.

"Marina, be honest with me. If it wasn't for the money, if it was just us, just a couple of regular people who met through work, or in a bar or something, would you want to have sex with me?"

She begins to answer quickly but then stops herself and twists up her lips. "Okay, you want me to be honest, I will be honest. I do not know. Not now. Not so soon after I meet you. You are an older man, maybe that is no problem for me. Many Russian men who are same age that I am are boring. They are not sophisticated like western men. They are not good to women. But if we meet in a normal way, I will want to know you better before we have sex." She seems a little embarrassed about having said that, and maybe a little relieved.

I smile at her and take her hand. "Okay then, let's just be friends. I like you, we can talk, maybe have dinner or drinks. When I need someone to translate for me or if I need some help here in Russia,

I'll pay you for that. Maybe sometime we'll have sex, maybe we won't, it's not important. Okay?"

It's okay with her, although probably a little inconvenient. Now she's got to find another customer. I need to make some notes for my interview, and then get Gregor's file back to him.

I'm sitting at the desk and she walks over to me. I pay her for her translation help, more than what's probably the going rate but a lot less than she probably would've made if we had sex. She gives me her phone number, pecks me quickly on the lips and walks out.

When I go back to the newspaper office to return the file, Gregor hasn't got anything new from the Versailles. Ed and Marta are still missing, their luggage is still in their room and since they're paid up through the end of the week, it's staying there. He got the concierge to let him into the room and he snooped around. Nothing came of that. It's a dead end.

Lev calls Nechaev's secretary to make sure I'm still on at four and to check if I need to bring a translator. I am and I don't.

I've got an hour before the interview. Nechaev's office is at the Marine Terminal. It's across the road from the central railroad station, which is one of the city's few tourist sites. Mikhail sticks close by my side as I walk down there early to take a look.

It's a quiet sort of town, not too many people on the streets, traffic eases past at a steady clip. Most of the city's built onto a peninsula. Walking in the direction of its tip the harbor is on the left, a beach and open sea on the right. There are a few old buildings, from the turn of the century, that look like they might have come from France. For the most part they've been well maintained. Much of the architecture though is more recent. It's drab and colorless like the communist government that built it.

While the surrounding islands and mainland at the back of the city are heavily forested, and a large verdant park greens the ridge that runs halfway across the peninsula, there aren't many trees or even bushes in town. It's pretty much all concrete.

It's a good natural setting for a port city. All it would take to make the place beautiful would be the demolition of about ninety percent of the existing structures followed by an ambitious, well-thought-out and well-funded program of planting and building.

The railway station is one of the buildings you'd want to keep. It's impressive, built a few years before the 1917 revolution and recently restored. It looks classically French, with a high sloping A-frame roof made of some sort of slate or slate-colored metal and a white façade with a great, colonnaded curved arch over the entry. Inside there's a dome festooned with cartoon-colored socialist realism paintings showing off muscular, grinning farmers, factory workers and soldiers staring out at a bright future that hasn't got here yet.

Lenin Square is at the north end of the station. A tall, grandiose statue of the leader of the revolution flutters a hand in the direction of Japan. Drunks and empty vodka bottles litter the base of its pedestal.

The Marine Terminal is large, long and dull; utilitarian, nothing more. Nechaev's secretary is a stout, elderly woman who looks like she used to work on the docks. She looks suspiciously at Mikhail and points at him, then back out the door. Before I can get my name out she jerks a thumb at a door behind her. "Go."

I walk in without knocking. The office is on the top floor and looks out over a tangle of cranes and a puzzle of stacked containers. Nechaev doesn't own all of it, but there isn't much that he can see that he doesn't have at least some piece of. He's standing behind his desk when I walk in.

He's a large man, beefy, with close-cropped blond hair and light gray eyes. He looks fat, but when he steps forward to greet me he moves confidently, like someone who's almost all muscle. His handshake lets me know he's strong, but he's not about to bother pressing the point.

His English is heavily accented, but very good. "Mr. Sharp, welcome. I read with interest *Asian Industry* magazine. I hope my little business can be of interest to you." He pumps my hand enthusiastically up and down, then holds onto it while he gestures at the view with his other one.

"Please, admire my harbor. The new Russia is alive with commerce and opportunity. Perhaps there will be investors who read your publication and will see the opportunities here."

I butter him up, assuring him that there are, as well as fund managers and manufacturers and nearly a hundred thousand other people he might want his story told to.

He walks me to a side table where there's a large, bubble shaped *samovar*. Its polished curves reflect clearer than the mirror in my hotel room. I wonder if he'd mind if I come back with my shaving kit. A thin jet of steam whistles out of the top.

"I have prepared tea Mr. Sharp. Or perhaps, if you would care for something stronger, I have a very fine cognac."

"Tea's fine, thanks."

He moves to make me a cup. "How many sugars please?"

"I'll just take it black, thanks."

He drops a lump of sugar into the cup anyhow and stirs it briskly as he walks it over to me. "In Russia Mr. Sharp, tea must always have a little sugar. For so long, life was bitter." He hands me the cup then turns to fix himself one with three lumps. "In the new Russia, if a man is smart, life can be very sweet."

We sit in plush leather chairs facing each other. He insists that I take the chair with the view; it makes him a little hard to see with the sun sinking behind him.

"President Nechaev, perhaps we can start with some questions about your background, how you came to Vladivostok and how you started in business?"

"Please Mr. Sharp, you come from a Hong Kong publication, but you are American, no?"

I nod my head "yes."

"One of the many things that I admire about your country is that your people are not so formal. So please to call me Alexi. If you do not object, I will call you Raymond."

"Ray."

"Okay Ray. My history? It is not important. It is the typical history of my country. My father was a factory worker. I went to university to become an engineer. It is a good job in the old Russia. I traveled, I learned much about the world, I see for myself how life can be. But it is also a torture. Always I come home to Russia where life is bitter and only the tea is sweet." He takes a loud, long slurp from his cup.

"Then comes Gorbachev and then Yeltsin and the communists fall. All Russia is in chaos, in confusion. But the Chinese, they say that in chaos there is opportunity. They are smart, the Chinese. More smart than us Russians maybe. I have good luck. I work hard, but in Moscow, in St. Petersburg there is much competition. Here, in the east, there is more chaos and also I think more opportunity."

I lull him, and myself, into a drowsy, comfortable state with softball questions. For the next hour he tells me about his different businesses, his companies, his plans to expand into Asia and his plans to make Vladivostok a major financial and trade center. What I haven't heard before, I could have guessed.

When he winds down he's happy. He's told me what he wants me to hear, he figures he'll get the story he wants. Maybe he will. But I've got some other questions.

"Alexi, your business is very impressive and I think it's got a lot of potential for bigger things. My readers will be very interested. But I have some other questions. Maybe some questions you won't like."

He smiles. He's subtle about the effort it takes, but I catch it. "Ray, please, ask your questions. If I do not want to answer them, I will not answer them."

I decide to just come out with it, see what he does. "There's a lot of mafia activity in Vladivostok and a lot of the Russian mafia who are active in Asia come from here. There are four major bosses. Before you came to Vladivostok they fought with each other. Since you've come, they don't. I've heard that you are the boss of the other bosses."

He puts his teacup down, puts his hands on his knees and stares at me. Then he starts laughing, loud and honest. It's not forced in any way. It goes on for at least a full minute. When he stops he wipes his eyes with his sleeve, shakes his head slowly back and forth and looks up at the ceiling.

Finally he looks right at me, a big tight smile on his lips as if he's holding back more laughter. "You have been so polite. It must be difficult for an American journalist. I have waited for you to ask me this. I have seen many of your movies. Am I the godfather? Yes, and no. It is different in Russia. Please, allow me to pour us each a cognac and I will explain."

| |CHAPTER **THIRTY-FOUR** | |

don't usually like cognac. I like this. It's complicated and powerful, relaxing and stimulating at the same time. We're back in our chairs, eyeing each other over our glasses.

"I do not know why, but I want to tell you these things. Ray, can I trust you? It should be obvious, that which I wish to remain discreet."

"I can't make any promises. If you don't want me to write something, either don't tell it to me or tell me it's off the record. That's the best I can do. I will write a story about your legitimate businesses, about the economy of Vladivostok. Anything else, I don't know yet."

He shrugs. "This is Russia, no one believes what journalists write, and if they do, a powerful man is admired, he is not despised."

He puts his head down, his chin in a hand as if imitating Rodin's Thinker. I take another sip of my drink and wait for him to talk.

"I do not tell the four, bosses you call them, what to do. They have their own business and it is not my business. I know about some of what they do. I do not know everything. I do not want to know everything. But before, when they fight with each other, that is bad for my business, bad for Vladivostok, bad for everybody. I come here with very much money. I will not tell you where I get so much money. When I come there are shootings, bombings, buildings burning down; it is a bad place for me to do business.

"I ask questions and find four very bad men. They are the ones who are fighting with each other, who are causing so much trouble. I invite them to a dinner party. We drink much vodka, eat much caviar, they are drunk and they are still fighting, always fighting. I tell them to be quiet, to listen to me. I have a good idea that will make them rich, and it will make me rich also, so it is a good idea for everybody.

"I tell them Vladivostok is a very small poor city, but Asia is a very big rich place. I will be their investor, give them money for them to do business in Asia, in China, Thailand, Macau, Korea. I only want a small percent of their business in Asia, maybe ten percent, maybe fifteen percent. But, if I give them this money, then there will be no more fighting in Vladivostok. No more trouble here. That is three years ago. It is working very good."

"So far."

"Why do you say 'so far?' Is there maybe a problem I do not know?"

I get the impression he's being honest with me. Maybe I'm wrong, maybe it's the cognac dulling my senses, but I feel like I can trust him, like I can tell him everything. So I do.

"You might be having problems in Macau. Because of them it will be hard to convince people in Hong Kong, and other parts of Asia that businessmen from Vladivostok aren't all gangsters."

"Why do you say this?"

"It's a long story. If you have time, I think it will be clearer if I can tell it to you from the beginning."

He doesn't say anything, just nods his head at me and gives me his attention. I tell him the whole thing, about Ed and Marta and Sasha and the women on the island and The Roman and Storm.

Halfway through I start getting scared, real scared. Maybe I've miscalculated. Maybe he's behind all this and I'm just getting in his way. Maybe he doesn't care if people think he's a gangster, if they're afraid to do business in Vladivostok, because maybe he makes enough money from his gangster pals that everything else doesn't matter. If anything I've done is going to get me killed this is probably it.

But I've started and there's no going back. I just tell him the facts, the ones I know. I don't tell him about my nightmares, about the pain that crackles through my whole body, that echoes in my skull. I don't tell him about how much I miss Sasha, how I don't want to lose Irina, about how the face of the woman in the cage and the woman on the cross haunt me, how I think sometimes I see them, like ghosts in my peripheral vision. I just tell him the facts and it doesn't take as long to tell the story as I thought it would

He listens all the way through, not asking any questions, not saying anything. His chin held up in a weave of fingers. When I finish he stands, walks to the sideboard and pours himself another cognac. He waves the bottle at me then goes and faces the window, surveying his domain.

It's gone dark outside, the lights have come on in the buildings surrounding the harbor, red and green warning lights twinkle at the top of the cranes. There are a few bobbing sparkles out on the water and a scattering of pinpoints in the sparsely populated hills that slope down to the sea in the east.

I pour myself another cognac, sit and sip it slowly, waiting for him to lower the boom. If this is gonna be my last drink, at least it's a good one.

Sometimes five minutes is a very long time. That's about how long it is before he turns around to look at me. "Ray, thank you for to tell me this. When you tell me this, you give me trust, respect. You are honest to me. I believe what you say. I do not like to hear this. But it is good I hear this."

I slump in my chair in relief. I don't think he's going to kill me after all.

"When I hear you want interview I call business associate in Hong Kong and ask him about you. He knows nothing, only that other business associate in Macau is very angry, he wants to kill you.

"Already I tell you that I know little of the business of the men you call the bosses. That is true. But I am curious. What do you do to make this one man so angry? I want to know. If he does kill you and in the newspapers there is much writing about Vladivostok and mafia, then maybe that is not so good for me. I want to know.

"This man you call 'The Roman', he is very good business-man, he make much money. But now, maybe he also make trouble for me. For his business, publicity is no good. Newspaper articles are very bad. If he is stupid and his business no longer is secret, it is very bad for everybody. He is in city now. You be careful. I will talk with him. You will be safe here."

I guess honesty can be the best policy sometimes, even for a journalist. We finish our drinks and make small talk. He has a lot of questions about the U.S. and I do my best to answer them but I haven't lived there in nearly seven years.

When I leave, Nechaev takes my right hand in both of his. He tells me to write whatever I want, just make sure it's the truth. I don't bother telling him I'd do that anyway. He tells me that if I ever need a job, he'll be happy to find something for me in his organiza-tion. I'm not really tempted. He tells me that if he finds out anything about Ed and Marta, he will let me know. That, I can use.

Mikhail and I walk back to the hotel where he leaves me in the lobby. No one's tried anything so far, so I guess he figures I'll be safe, at least here. Word must've got out to the women in the lobby that I'm not interested, because while their eyes all follow me closely on my way to the stairs, no one approaches me. I make the trudge up to the seventh floor and into my room.

There's a woman's clothes tossed on the bed. The door to the bathroom is cracked open and through it I catch a glimpse of red toenails poking up out of crystalline bubbles at the edge of the tub. I hear feminine humming, a tune I don't know. I have no idea who it is and I'm not sure if I should be worried or excited.

I quietly put my notepad and pen on the desk and pick up the heavy metal ashtray that's the only thing I can see that might make a weapon. I pad softly to the bathroom door and push it open. There's barely a moment to admire the view of Nina, only partly covered with bubbles, when a hand reaches out from the side and grabs me hard in the crotch. A fist arcs in from the same side, fast enough and blurry enough that all I can remember is something like a comet, and buries itself in my stomach.

Air and cognac erupt out of me and I fall back on the floor, doubled over. Everything's gone white, shot through with red streaks in front of my eyes. There's a weight on my back, pressing me down, my face between my knees.

I'm pretzeled, trying to find a way to work air back into my lungs that doesn't hurt so much, when I'm lifted off the floor. At least it isn't easy for whoever's doing it. I can hear them grunting with the effort. They walk me a few steps then throw me on the bed. I lie there for a moment, sucking in oxygen, trying to will some blood back into my muscles. If I'm going to fight back, now's the time to do it.

I tense my legs for a push off the bed. I'm not really ready for this but the longer you go without fighting, the harder it is to do. My eyes are still squeezed shut and I'll have to open them.

When I do, I give up on the idea of resisting. There's a round, black hole about six inches away, with a little gunmetal blue sight that's shaped like a shark's fin on top of it. I blink a few times and relax my muscles. I switch my focus back a couple of feet to see who's holding the gun.

It's The Roman, and he doesn't look happy. He's red in the face, the new scar from the cut I gave him standing out in relief on his forehead. He's snarling through gritted teeth. "*Mandavoshka*. You little bug, tickle hair my cock. I pick you out and cut you two pieces with fingernail." He leans in close behind the gun. "I shoot you is too easy. You die slow, too much hurting. Maybe I no kill you. Maybe make you *kastrat* and sell you China man, Arab man."

He's grinning. He looks happier now. I'm not. I hear someone else and swivel my eyes to look. It's Storm, of course, and she's sporting a broad smile under her very crooked nose. She looks downright jolly. It's not infectious.

The Roman barks at her in Russian. She comes around to the side of the mattress and while he holds the gun she pulls my clothes off. I've never felt so naked. When that's done she yanks one of my hands up to one of the bedposts. She ties it tightly with a piece of rough rope. It quickly starts going numb. She does the same with the other hand, then my feet. I'm spread-eagled on the bed and there is nothing at all I like about it.

The gun barrel shoves up hard against the bottom of my balls. I squeeze my eyes shut again, try to make my mind a blank but it doesn't work. The whole world is clearer than it's ever been; my body's alert, alive, awake. Everything slows down and sharpens. I feel like Superman, with super hearing, smell, taste, touch and x-ray vision. If I only had super strength I could break the ropes, stop the bullet and put away the bad guys. I can't though. I can just lie here, not moving. Why can't my senses be as paralyzed?

The gun moves away. I sense movement. I feel warm breath. I smell a faint odor of sweet booze and garlic. There's a sharp slap on the side of my face. That doesn't hurt. Now my face doesn't feel anything. But I open my eyes and The Roman is inches away.

"I no hurt you now. Have important meeting. Want take long time, have fun with hurt you. You staying here with Storm. She have fun first. I come back, is my turn." He slaps me again and moves away to stand by the side of the bed. He snaps his fingers.

Nina comes into view. She stands next to him, toweling off her beautiful long hair. He puts an arm around her. "Ninotchka, she is very beautiful, no? She belong to me, same my car, my dog. She say to me everything. She say to me you here. You stupid man. If you smart man you no say no to Nina. Then you lucky, you last time fucking is such beautiful woman. But no so lucky."

He pulls her face to his and kisses her, long, sloppy with lots of tongue. I can't tell if she likes it or not, but she doesn't struggle and doesn't try to turn a cheek to him. When he stops she looks down at me. Her eyes are impassive, empty, like I'm not really here or she's gone blind.

She pulls her clothes off the bed and gets dressed. When she's finished they kiss again. When that's done they walk away together. I hear the door close behind them.

That leaves me alone with Storm, tied up on a bed, shivering, and it's not from the cold, not because I'm naked in a drafty hotel room.

I'm surprised when she pulls the desk chair up alongside the bed by my head. She sits in it and looks at me. I can't read her expression.

"Why you stupid man? Why you have feeling for whore? So many girl, is easy, no feeling, only money, only fucking, no problem. But you, problem. Why you so stupid man?"

She looks like she actually wants to know. Maybe if I can get her talking I can talk her into helping me. Fat chance, but it's my only chance. It takes me a couple of false starts before I can get anything out. It takes everything I've got to try and sound calm.

"They're women aren't they? Just because they're whores doesn't mean they aren't women. They're like anybody else; some of them I like, some of them I don't like. Depends on the person. Sasha was my friend, I liked her. You killed her."

"Friend? Hah, she only whore. Why always go with whore? Why no meet good girl?"

I can't believe she's asking me this. She looks like she means it, like she really wants to know. It's so bizarre that it distracts me for a moment. My brain reels away into fantasy. Is she her idea of a "good girl?" Maybe I should ask her out. We can go share a soda, get to know each other better. Fuck this is weird. Why doesn't she just start beating me up and get on with the business we're really here for.

Why the hell do I want to explain myself to someone who wants to kill me, or hurt me really bad? I just know I've got to keep her talking. As long as we're talking, she isn't hurting me.

"What about you? What's your story? How'd you get into this?"

What the hell did I just say? I'm hurt, I'm scared shitless, I must've lost my mind. I might as well have just come out and asked her, 'what's a nice girl like you doing in a place like this?' I think about it and chuckle, but it's nervous laughter, it just burbles up and out of me. Acrid, rank sweat is also pouring out of me, filling the room with the sort of stench that attracts predators. Any minute I'm going to start babbling. Maybe if I go crazy enough she'll leave me alone.

She doesn't though. She scowls at me and gets up. "No more talking." She reaches up under her short skirt and pulls down her panties. She steps out of them, picks them up, moves closer to me, pries open my mouth and crams them deep into it. I'm choking on them, panicking, my eyes feel like they're bulging out of their sockets.I try spitting the slightly damp, lacey cotton out but she clamps a hand across my lips. With her other hand she shakes a pillow out of its case, and then ties the pillowcase tight over my mouth and around my head. She moves out of sight. I hear a match struck. I smell a cigar, one of those really foul small fat ones.

I'm wiggling as much as I can, trying to worm my hands or feet out of the knots or yank off a bedpost. I'm rubbing the back of my head against the bed hoping to loosen the fabric holding the gag in place.

She comes back into view, standing, looking down at me and grinning. I don't know what she's planning and I don't want to find out. Storm steps up onto the bed, her legs spread out on either side of my chest. I've got a good view up her skirt but I don't care. I've seen it before. And everytime I have, something bad happened. She moves back and sits down, pinning my legs under her. My hands are still pulling at the ropes, trying to break free, but it isn't getting me anywhere.

She's sitting on top of me, looking comfortable and calm, taking deep hits off her smoke, sucking it into her lungs so that her chest expands, then letting it ease out her nose.

The she does something else with her hands. The same thing she did the last time we were in this position. She's got good hands, surprisingly soft and feminine. I don't want to respond. How can I? I've never been so terrified in my life. But there it is, somehow I grow hard in her hands as she moves them in a nice steady rhythm, firm, with a slight twisting motion. She finally takes the cigar out of her mouth with one hand, works up a good load of spit and lets it ooze down onto me for lubrication.

She picks up speed, staring straight into my eyes and smiling. I can't help it but I'm thrusting upwards, my butt lifting off the mattress. I'm swelling, beginning to throb against her saliva-wet hand. I'm fighting it. It's stupid. I hate myself for feeling this way. I'm so close.

Then it all stops and there's a searing flashpoint of red hot pain that tears into my inner thigh and explodes outward, radiating in waves of agony down my legs and up my torso. If it wasn't for her panties I'd surely bust my teeth against each other as I clamp my jaw shut. My whole body goes rigid, then begins to quiver, then spasms and writhes trying to escape itself. Tears stream from my eyes and sweat jets from my pores. I'm swallowing as fast as I can to keep up with the streams of fluid that the cloth in my mouth can't absorb. The burning goes on and on. It feels like she's trying to burn a hole all the way through to the other side of my thigh.

Why am I still conscious? Why can't I just pass out? I try to will myself away and I can't. I'm too focused on the pain.

Finally it eases, just slightly, just enough. My muscles are limp with suffering, puddled into the sweat-drenched sheets. I open my eyes and look at her. She's looking back, curious, like she wants to see what I might do next. Maybe she's wondering how it feels. I'd like to show her.

She smiles, lifts the cigar to her lips, takes a big drag then leans over to put her face just in front of mine. She presses her lips against mine and lets the smoke ease out of her mouth. It wraps around our heads. Some of it gets in around the edges of the pillowcase and her panties, and up my nose. I start hacking. The cough can't get out so it echoes around the back of my throat, bounces down into my chest and burns.

She sits back up and starts in on me with her hands again. It can't work this time. It can't possibly. Hard-ons aren't completely involuntary, are they?

Maybe they are. It takes a while longer, but not much. My head is swollen with the memory of the pain, frantic with thoughts of escape. There's nothing even slightly sexy about any of this, I'm struggling to pull away from her but my dick doesn't seem to get it.

Of course she burns me again. And again. The fourth time she has to use her mouth to get me up. It takes a long time and almost doesn't work. But it does finally, and again she burns me before I can come and I almost pass out from the agony. I come so close to passing out. That's what I want. I barely cling to consciousness and I don't know why. I just hope The Roman will show back up and kill me sometime soon.

She's just about to start again when the phone rings. She gets off me and answers it. She speaks rapidly in Russian. It sounds like an argument. She hangs up hard and comes to stand by my head. She leans down to look at me. She's got the cigar in her fingers and it's close enough to my eyes that I can feel them drying out from the heat of it.

She moves her lips up and flattens them almost tenderly against my forehead. She strokes my hair with a hand. Then the pain explodes on my cheek. It feels like a laser is burning through to my mouth. Everything goes out of focus as all my attention is concentrated on that one spot. When it settles into a long, slow burn and I can see again, I look at her.

Storm's smiling down at me, that disturbing look of curiosity and something almost tender in her expression. She bends over, reaches out a hand and softly strokes my penis. She puts her lips up close to the cloth covering mine. "Don't worry, I come back, we have more fun." A few moments later I hear the door open, then close.

I struggle to get loose. I go back to rubbing the back of my head against the mattress; maybe I can loosen the knot on the pillowcase. I can't. I try to will feeling back into my hands and feet. If my brain can make them move, maybe they can wriggle free of the ropes. I don't know if it's working or not, I still can't feel anything. The phone rings and there's nothing I can do other than let it. I'm helpless. Storm and The Roman will come back and if I'm lucky they'll be in a hurry and just kill me quick.

I'm lying there, trying to figure out if there's anything at all I can do. I try to relax. I can think better when I'm relaxed. But it doesn't do me any good. I can't relax and I can't think of any way out of this either. If I could move enough to make some noise maybe I could attract someone's attention, but I can't.

I can just lie here and wait. What'd Lev call it? *Terlyohzka*, that's it. But I'm still not that kind of patient. I wish they'd hurry up and come back and get it over with. My brain twirls off into tangents. There's nothing else it can do.

I don't believe in God or heaven or hell or ghosts or any of that sort of crap. But if somehow or another I did see Sasha again, what would I say to her? "I'm so sorry I got you killed, tortured to death even. But me too. See, look at these burns. Does that make it okay? No, I guess not. You didn't know what I was getting you into. I made my own choices. Stupid ones, but my own.

"If I could do it over again, what would I do? Damned if I know. If I can get out of this what'll I do? How can I make any of this right?"

I'm thinking there might be some other dead people I'd like to make amends to when there's a knock on the door. I try to struggle, to shout through the gag, anything to make noise. The doorknob's rattling and someone is shouting something I don't understand. Then I hear a key in the lock and the door opens.

It's the bulldozer lady from the front desk and she looks mightily pissed off. Her eyes sweep the room and she's making a huffy tsk-tsking sound as she approaches the bed. She looks me up and down, disapproval sprayed large across her features. She yanks out the sheet from underneath me and throws it over my crotch. Then she reaches behind me and tries to untie the pillowcase. She can't get it undone so finally she just tugs it off, roughly over my ears and head. I manage to spit out Storm's panties.

I'm twisting up my mouth, trying to unlock it, to make it talk. She works her stubby fingers into the knot around my left wrist and unties it. I flex the hand and bend the elbow. Pins and needles knife all the way up and down my arm. She's moved away from the bed. I guess I'll have to finish untying myself when the blood settles down to its normal pace in my veins.

Bulldozer lady picks a pillow up off the floor and grunts. She points to a burn in it. "You pay damage." I nod yes. She looks at me sternly, looks around the room again and looks back at me frowning. "Tomorrow, you go other hotel." I nod yes again. She scowls some more then fishes in a pocket in her long, thick skirt and comes out with a piece of paper. She drops it on top of my chest. "Telephone." She turns and walks out of the room, slamming the door behind her.

When my fingers stop tingling enough to hold it, I look at the piece of paper. It's Lev's phone number.

It takes five or so long minutes to get myself untied and another ten working feeling back into my hands and feet before I can raise myself off the bed. I need something to drink, something to wash out my mouth. It's hard to move while keeping my thighs far enough apart that the burns don't rub against anything. I'm slow and awkward.

The water in the bathroom's turned off for the night. Yesterday's ice bucket is still in the room, on the desk. The ice is melted and the water looks suspiciously gray, with little black and brown specks floating in it. I don't care. I've never tasted water so good.

I've got to get out of the room in case The Roman and Storm come back, but I might need help. I need protection. I call Lev.

"Lev, it's Ray."

"Where did you go? Gregor and me try to find you. Secretary of President Nechaev telephone office, say for you not to worry, people from Macau are no problem for you now. Also say go *ulitsa Sukhanova* number one four three eight, apartment number six-two. She say it is very important. We going now, you want to come with?"

If Nechaev says I'm not supposed to worry about The Roman and Storm, I guess I believe him. I'd like to believe him. That must have something to do with the call that sent Storm out of the room. So now I don't want to go anywhere. I want to send downstairs for a bottle of vodka and drink myself into near death.

I tell Lev I'll meet him downstairs in fifteen minutes.

| |CHAPTER **THIRTY-FIVE**| |

Putting on pants, even my baggiest, then getting downstairs hurts so much I almost don't make it. I walk bow-legged and lean heavily on the bannister the whole way down. By the fourth floor I have to take out my wallet and put it in my mouth because I'm gritting my teeth too hard against the pain. I almost bite through it. I'm developing a terrible headache. My cheek is also in agony, but it's tolerable if I keep my face still. I couldn't bring myself to look in the mirror before I left the room.

It takes twenty minutes to get downstairs. The guys are there, waiting in the sputtering car out front. I put the wallet back in my pocket before they can see it, then carefully lower myself into my spot in the back seat. I slump low, spread my legs and pinch the fabric to hold it away from my thighs.

Gregor's driving, Lev turns around in his seat to ask what I've been doing since I left Nechaev's office.

I'm punchy with it. Happy to see them, almost silly with exhaustion and relief. "I was all tied up with something." I start laughing and have a hard time stopping even though it sends searing pains through my cheeks and jaw.

Gregor stops the car and pulls over. They both look at me. Lev reaches out and takes my chin; he turns my cheek toward them. The looks on their faces tell me more than I want to know about how I look.

"What is it? What is this 'tied up'?"

"Nothing. I had some trouble. I'll tell you later. I don't want to talk about it now, okay?"

It's not okay, obviously. But something in my expression tells them to back off, at least for now. I appreciate it and I've got to give them something in return.

"The interview with Nechaev went well. I've got everything I need about his business. He also told me he is the big boss. He told me how it all works."

Lev and Gregor look dubious. Gregor says something harsh sounding in Russian. Lev leans over his seat to get closer to me. "Why would he tell you this?"

"I asked. I don't know. He just wanted to talk. Maybe it feeds his ego. He liked it that I didn't try to trick him into it. He figures even if I write something, nothing's gonna change anyway. No one's going to give a shit."

"Why did his secretary telephone?"

"That, I don't know. I don't think it's a trap. I believe him when he says I'm safe. Let's just get there and find out."

It takes about fifteen minutes. The clunker slows to a crawl as it tries to head up one of the steeper streets in the city. Trolleys going both ways pass us and I take some mild comfort in that. We approach a fairly new, but still utilitarian and ugly, huge apartment block. There's not a tree anywhere in sight. No grass, no bushes, just bare concrete bathed in the yellowish streetlight. The only signs of life are three police cars parked in front, their red, white and blue roof-lights lazily rotating.

We pull up behind the last of the cop cars. As we get out a young patrolman walks up to us and calls out in Russian. He's probably telling us to get out of there. Lev walks up to him and flashes his press pass. I notice he also slips him something when they shake hands. The young officer waves us into the building.

It's a new building. A plaque in the lobby claims it was built in 1993, two years ago. That doesn't mean the elevator's working. It isn't. We're going to the sixth floor. Lev and Gregor slow down so I can keep up with them. I'm trying to walk upstairs and hold my pants legs out at the same time. They can't help but notice. They exchange looks and after the first floor they stop and turn to me.

Lev looks annoyed, or worried, or both. "You are hurt. What happened? You must tell us."

"I've got burns, bad burns, on the inside of my legs. When my pants touch them it hurts. I'll tell you about it later."

They try to convince me to stop, go back, wait for them, then they can take me to a doctor. I refuse and they give up. I do have an idea though. I take off my pants. My boxer shorts don't brush against the burns as much and it speeds up the horrible trudge up-stairs. I don't know if the fresh air on the burns is good for them or not, but it feels better for now.

It's cold in the stairwell. A wind whips through it from the open roof to some sort of wide-open vent at the bottom. Gusts burst against us as we slog upwards. Even if I was in better shape for it, it'd be slow going.

On the sixth floor I put my pants back on before we open the door to the hall. There's a patrolman guarding the entry. Lev's press pass doesn't impress him, neither does a handshake. They start arguing and I'm thinking we've come all the way up here for nothing. Gregor steps up, whispers something in the cop's ear that snaps him to attention. He holds up a finger in warning and scurries down the hall. The three of us stand there waiting.

The officer's back soon and he motions us ahead. The hall's narrow, with a poured concrete floor and buzzing, sickly green fluorescents running along the middle of its low ceiling. We move down it to the knot of policeman standing in front of an open door at the far end. As we get closer there's a terrible stench. It's shit and piss and the worst sour body odor I've ever smelled. I've read descriptions in books, none that've come close.

At the door a big cop, a high-ranking one to judge by the polished gold badge and the frills and medals on his uniform, stops us. He greets Gregor by name and shakes his hand. The crime reporter introduces us. He's the chief of detectives. He takes Gregor to the side for a whispered conversation.

I can see through the door to a large picture window with the best view yet over the city and the harbor. It's beautiful from up here; the hills festooned with strings of lit houses and the hulks of glowing buildings in downtown; radio and radar towers, shore beacons and buoys all blinking red and green as if punctuating the night scene. The moon is setting over an island out to the west, sending a thick tendril of blue light out across the water. A large ferry, shimmering like a phosphorescent sea creature creeps toward the moonlight from the east. Other faint lights, fishing boats, bob on the swells looking like fireflies in a dark forest.

I could just stay out here in the hall. I don't have to go into the apartment. I don't have to see what I think I'm going to see. I can breathe through my mouth to avoid the smell and I can stay put, admiring the view.

The captain and Gregor edge back into the doorway. Gregor leans over to whisper to Lev. Lev turns to me. "It is very bad inside. I do not know why secretary of Nechaev telephone to us to come here. It is the job of Gregor. Gregor will go inside and look. Maybe you do not want to look."

I nod, but then follow Gregor into the apartment. The front door opens into the living room. I see which way the people in the room are looking and I follow their gaze to the wall that backs up against the hallway.

There's a dead man tied to a heavy wooden chair. Ropes wind around his legs from ankle to knee, holding them tight against the chair legs. Another rope starts at his waist and coils around his torso to just under his armpits, strapping him to the chair back, his arms pinned to his sides. His head has fallen forward at an unnatural angle. I can see a large, ragged exit wound at the back of his head. There's a tidy red and gray splatter pattern on the wall directly behind him. I have to stoop to see the face. Even with the black, crusty hole where his right eye used to be, I recognize Ed.

Even though I'm expecting it, it hits me like a solid fist in the stomach. I close my eyes tight and bend over, my hands on my knees. I try to picture him alive. I never knew him well but I liked him. I try to picture him the way I want to remember him; alive, in love, maybe stupidly in love but bursting with life because of it. I can't see him that way. Behind my eyelids all I can see is that black hole.

I feel Gregor's hand on my shoulder and I straighten up. I open my eyes and follow his finger to a tarp-covered lump on the floor at the foot of Ed's chair. Two policemen pick up the covering by its ends and move it slowly away. It's Marta. What used to be Marta. What's left of Marta.

Her face is turned toward Ed. It's unmarred, but it's marked with a frozen look of agony and despair greater than any I've ever thought I could even imagine. It's a look that makes me want the world to end, just so long as it comes quickly. I don't know if I'm really seeing it, or if it's the worst hallucination anyone's ever had.

She's been tortured. It won't take the coroner to figure that out. She's been sliced and stabbed and parts of her have been severed. The ends of two monstrous phallic objects protrude from where they've been shoved deep into her. I take it all in at a glance and I know I'll never remember her any other way.

I turn and walk to the window. I open it and lean out. I look down at the pavement, six floors below, and think about it. Two, maybe three more seconds of horror and it'll all be over. I'll never have to be a part of any of this again.

But the moment passes. I take a deep breath as an ocean breeze wafts by and it smells fresh and good, even with the faint note of diesel fumes mixed in. And it is a beautiful view. The ferry is still in sight, it's passed to the other side of the moonbeam and it's chugging west to somewhere. I don't know where. And damn it all, that's the hell of it, I want to know. I've always got to find out what happens next. No matter what it is.

| |EPILOGUE| |

At least they had a medic in the police station. He put some kind of salve over my burns that numbed the area, then loosely bandaged them. They also had good coffee. The best I had in Russia. It kept me awake all night after I identified the bodies. I wasn't a suspect, but I knew a lot about how they'd got there that the police didn't. They especially wanted to know about the money. It was missing. They'd have liked to have found it.

I went over the story several times and each time it took longer as I remembered more details and got sleepier and my patience with their translator wore thin. When I was done they offered me protection and a ride back to my hotel. Outside on the street the sun was up and bright and it hurt my eyes.

When I got to the Vladivostok, bulldozer lady stopped me before I got to the stairs and handed me a folded piece of paper.

It was a message from Nechaev's secretary. My bags had been packed and moved to the Hotel Versailles. I shouldn't worry about anything, I was safe now.

I walked out of the Vladivostok's dingy lobby, got back into the police car and had them drive me to the Versailles. They left me at the entrance to the hotel's grandiose, vaulted reception hall. The concierge came out from behind his desk and ushered me into a working elevator to a suite on the top floor. He handed me a menu and told me to call him personally with my order when I felt like breakfast.

What I felt like was sleeping. The room seemed safe enough. The door was heavy and armed with three reasonably secure locks. I'd just about gone under when the phone rang.

It was Nechaev. He didn't want me to worry. The Roman and his bodyguard would never bother me again. He guaranteed it. This was the third time I'd heard it, and I believed it. He was sorry for what had happened, the room was mine for as long as I wanted and please let him know if I needed anything else. He was looking forward to reading my article about Vladivostok.

Since I was awake anyhow, I called Lev, told him about the rest of my night and asked him and Gregor to meet me for dinner. I called Marina and asked her to meet me for lunch. Then I managed to sleep.

I think I dreamt about Sasha. It's not clear. Just as I was waking up I have a foggy recollection of her being there, but far away, waving at me, mouthing something I couldn't understand. It didn't seem important by the time I was fully awake.

A knock at the door got me out of bed. I went to the peephole. It was Marina. She waited in the room for me while I took a long, careful shower. I considered asking her to help but I didn't.

We had lunch in the hotel dining room. I ate more than I think I ever have before at one sitting. Marina had a thick soup and a thin salad. We talked about what we wanted to do with ourselves. She wanted some sort of work in Kamchatka, but she wasn't sure what she could do there. I wasn't sure what I wanted to do with myself. My heart wasn't in journalism anymore. I liked the research, the investigating, but something was lacking. I wasn't sure what it was.

When we parted company we kissed and our lips lingered just long enough that I almost asked her back up to my room. But I didn't.

Dinner with Lev and Gregor was another drunken fish fest. They weren't going to be able to print much more than a standard crime story and they weren't happy about that. I told them I'd see what I could do in my magazine, but I didn't think I could do much.

They drove me to the airport the next morning and left me at the gate with a bottle of vodka and two salted fish. I brought the vodka home; the fish went into a trashcan after they left.

No one ever saw The Roman again. A new thug, a kinder, gentler one named Vlad, took his place in Macau. He sent me a note when he got to town saying I was welcome at any of his clubs and promising to introduce me to his most beautiful girls. I haven't taken him up on his offer yet. I doubt that I will.

Storm disappeared too. Although a couple months after I got back from Russia I got a call from Francisco in Macau. After a business meeting with a Chinese banker in Zhuhai, he was taken to the swimming pool nightclub at the Imperial. There was a new, very tall Russian woman there. She had lurid tattoos of women on her arms. He'd been intrigued at first, but she was so stoned and out of it that he'd lost interest. I was tempted to go see for myself. I haven't gotten there yet.

Fred went to Vladivostok to claim his brother's body, and then flew it home to England to be buried in the family plot. No one claimed Marta's corpse. It was cremated, the ashes dumped into the sea.

Gregor wrote the story, putting just enough in it that if you read between the lines you'd have some idea of what really happened. It caused a small ruckus for a month or two. There were calls for an investigation of mafia activities in Vladivostok, but nothing ever came of it.

Norman, my editor hacked all the crime references out of the story I wrote for *Asian Industry*. It ended up reading like a puff piece for Nechaev, an investment brochure for Vladivostok. I guess that was okay. I owed the Russian mogul for saving me. I suppose the article that did come out was payback, but Nechaev's thank you letter made me feel like crap.

When I got over it, I decided someone ought to benefit from the bigshot's happiness so I called Marina and asked her if she was interested in a job in Kamchatka. Of course she was. One of Nechaev's lesser plans was to promote eco-tourism. I put the two of them together. She now leads tour groups through the volcanic peninsula. I'm planning to take one sometime.

I never could get any of the English language publications to take a story on the brothels in Zhuhai and on Black Island. I finally called a friend who writes for one of the Chinese language tabloids and told him all about it over lunch. He wrote a story that no one believed. Or if they did they weren't saying so.

I sent a report to the UN's commission on slavery and also to an international human rights organization that monitors and tries to fight the trafficking in women. I got nice thank you letters from each and now I get regular solicitations for money from the human rights group. I send them a little in Sasha's name from time to time. I never could find out if they followed up on my report.

Hiroko went back to making bondage movies. The story of what'd happened to her was leaked to the press. It was great publicity and she was a bigger star than ever. We had dinner once when she was in Hong Kong on tour. She took me out and spent more money than I thought it was possible to spend on sushi. She gave me ten of her videos. I've still got them but I haven't watched them. It's nothing I want to see.

I don't know what happened to the other women on the island. I'd like to believe they're okay, that they got away and are living happily ever after somewhere, somehow. I'd like to believe that the place got closed down and didn't reopen someplace else.

There are a lot of fairy tales I want to believe. But I don't. The woman in the cage, the woman on the cross, all those women in the cells, Sasha; the only place they're still alive is in my nightmares. I don't sleep as well as I used to. I doubt I ever will.

Irina finally blamed me for getting Sasha killed. We had two very long, very painful phone conversations. I told her I wanted to come down to Jakarta to talk in person. She didn't want to see me. She didn't want me to call her for a while. I don't know how things stand between us now.

Susan and Mike broke up. I remembered what she'd said that night at the F.C.C. and I asked her out. We've become pretty good friends. Once in a while if we're drunk and lonely we're more than that, but it's no big deal for either of us.

Bill Warner called me about three months after I got back from Vladivostok. He wanted to take me out to lunch. He suggested the Grill at the Mandarin Hotel, his treat. I told him he didn't need to impress me and countered with my favorite Chiu Chau noodle shop. We settled on *dim sum* at the City Hall Restaurant, an enormous, deafening, blindingly lit hangar of a place where all the noise and commotion help keep conversations private.

We sat next to a table of eight businessmen or bureaucrats from China. They're pretty much the same thing. Their accented Mandarin was an easy giveaway. But even without it you could tell by their cheap dark suits, bad haircuts and clunky shoes.

"You know Bill, this place makes me think of that movie, *Cabaret*. You ever see it?"

"Yeah. Why?"

"Remember how in the first scene, they're in the cabaret and there's a table with a Nazi or two? The bouncers chase 'em out and then beat 'em up in the alley. A little later in the movie there's a couple of tables of Nazis and they're left alone. A little later the place is about half-full of Nazis. By the end of the movie they've overrun the place and that perfect Aryan specimen kid is singing."

"Yeah, what's that got to do with this?"

"First time I came here was in 1978 and you never saw anyone from the Mainland. Then in the late 1980s there was a table or two of 'em. Now look around, there's what, nine or ten tables of guys from China and you hear a lot more Mandarin being spoken. In a couple of years the place is their's."

"Mainland Chinese aren't Nazis you know."

"Yeah, I know, just makes me think. Everything changes. I like it, mostly."

"That was a mess up in Vladivostok."

"Changing the subject?"

"I thought we'd exhausted the last one."

"Yeah. I guess. It was a mess. I didn't manage to save anyone."

"Nothing you could've done. Nechaev saved your ass though."

"How'd you know about that?"

"Trade secret. At least The Roman's gone. World's a better place without him."

"You sure he's gone?"

"Yeah, we're sure. Another trade secret."

"You get off on holding all the cards?"

"Not really. I'm getting out."

"What're you gonna do?"

"Private sector. I'm starting up a corporate investigations firm, due diligence, different sorts of trade secrets, security. It's why I asked you to lunch."

"You offering me a job?"

"You want one?"

"I'll think about it." I thought about it.

| |AUTHOR'S NOTE| |

This story is loosely based on real events. The basic details of the ill-fated love affair between Ed and Marta are true, as are the descriptions of many of the places where the story unfolds. The names and descriptions of people and companies are fictitious and any identifiable similarity to real people and companies, living or dead, solvent or defunct is strictly coincidental.

Slavery, of all sorts, is a real, terrible and ongoing problem all over the world. The situation has not improved since 1994 when the story on which this book is based took place. There are a number of organizations working to fight this scourge. Two that I think are doing particularly good work are The Anti-Slavery Society www.anti-slavery.addr.com and Human Rights Watch www.hrw.org. For further information on the grim realities on which this book is based, and for information on what you can do to help the fight against slavery of all kinds, their Web sites are good places to start.

| |ACKNOWLEDGEMENTS| |

I would like to acknowledge the invaluable support, advice and friendship of the following people:

My mother, Elaine Stone, who instilled in me the love of travel, literature and the other arts, and who once gave me the very sage advice: "the most important ingredient is the wine that goes into the chef."

My father, Martin Stone, who inspired in me, among many other things, my interest in economics and politics, something that I hope informs and improves all my writing.

My fabulous agent, Janet Reid, who I met through her love of this book and who has worked like a crazy woman to find a good home for the paperback you're holding in your hands and for the next books in the Ray Sharp series. (Don't worry Janet, one of these days there might be more than a good dinner's money in this for you.)

Ben and Alison at Bleak House Books who have made me feel right at home.

Win Blevins. It's hard to imagine a better friend and more conscientious manuscript editor.

Meredith Blevins. She's given me encouragement, friendship and more fun than I can fully recall through the fog of the nearly 40 years we've known each other.

Amitabha Chowdhury. He lured me to Asia with the promise of an underpaid job and lit a fire under my curiosity about the place once I got there.

Topol, Edward, *Dermo! The <u>Real</u> Russian Tolstoy Never Used*, Translated by Laura E. Wolfson, Illustrations by Kim Wilson Brandt, Plume Books, New York 1997. A truly, wonderful, witty, informative and undoubtedly useful for getting myself into trouble should I ever travel to Russia, book on Russian slang.